Rival
Sisters

OTHER TITLES BY LOUISE GUY:

Rival Sisters

LOUISE GUY

LAKE UNION
PUBLISHING

This is a work of fiction. Names, characters, organizations, places, events, and incidents are either products of the author's imagination or are used fictitiously. Any resemblance to actual persons, living or dead, or actual events is purely coincidental.

Text copyright © 2020 by Louise Guy
All rights reserved.

No part of this book may be reproduced, or stored in a retrieval system, or transmitted in any form or by any means, electronic, mechanical, photocopying, recording, or otherwise, without express written permission of the publisher.

Published by Lake Union Publishing, Seattle

www.apub.com

Amazon, the Amazon logo, and Lake Union Publishing are trademarks of Amazon.com, Inc., or its affiliates.

ISBN-13: 9781542015974
ISBN-10: 1542015979

Cover design by Sarah Whittaker

Printed in the United States of America

*In loving memory of my kind and generous
grandmother
Phyllis Budd 1905–1995*

Prologue

Eighteen Years Earlier

Nat braced herself, inched the front door open and slipped inside. Her father was going to kill her. She'd promised to be home by five for her mother's birthday celebration and it was now just after seven. Hopefully they wouldn't have done the cake yet and she could redeem herself with a few nice words. Relief settled over her as she saw that the hallway was clear, allowing her another minute or two before she felt the full force of her parents' disappointment. She sighed as she shook off her winter coat and opened the hall closet. If only they could remember being fifteen and in love for the first time. *In love?* Did she love Callum? She smiled at the memory of being wrapped in his strong arms, the tingle of his lips on hers.

Footsteps clattered in the hallway, causing Nat to freeze. She was just able to make out her older sister's lean frame through the join in the closet door. She let out a breath and took a hanger from the rack. 'Thank God, it's you. Dad's going to go mental that I'm so late. Can you back me up when I tell him Perry asked me to do a few extra hours at the newsagent?'

Nat finished hanging her coat, closed the closet door and grinned as she turned to Hannah. 'Sorry to ask you to lie again but he's way too overprotective when it comes to me and boys.' Her grin slipped as she took in her sister's pale, tear-stained face. She hurried over to her. 'Han, what's happened? You look awful.'

The vein in Hannah's forehead twitched, a sign that usually meant she was upset or angry. Nat was sure she hadn't done anything to cause this kind of reaction in her sister. In fact, she couldn't remember the last time they'd even argued; they were usually extremely close. Only that morning they'd been talking about their annual Christmas in July party that was just over a week away, and Hannah had laughed at how it surprised her friend Abbie that she and Nat threw a joint party. 'Abbie can't stand her sister and has never understood how you and I choose to spend time together,' she'd said. 'It makes me realise how lucky we are.' Looking at Hannah's face now, Nat wasn't sure her sister was feeling the same as she had been earlier in the day.

'Where have you been? You've been missing for hours. You can't just go off anywhere you like without keeping in touch.' Hannah's voice shook as she forced the words out.

But it wasn't anger that tinged her words, it was something else. Something Nat couldn't put her finger on. A sudden and overwhelming sense of dread settled over her. Her throat constricted with panic as confused thoughts swirled in her mind. She'd lied to her parents but she'd told Hannah of her real plans. Hannah had been happy to cover for her, as she always was. It was one of the things she loved most about her sister – she could always count on her. So why was she making Nat feel like she'd done something wrong? Maybe she just needed a gentle reminder, then everything would be okay. 'Han, I told you I'd be with Callum. Did you forget?'

'I called Callum's mum but she had no idea where you were. You're not to disappear like that again.'

Nat's stomach churned. Not only was Hannah upset with her, she'd called Callum's mum? Her parents would freak if they knew she'd been with him. 'Do Mum and Dad know where I was?'

Hannah shook her head before closing her eyes momentarily. She looked completely distraught.

Nat continued to stare at her sister. She should feel relieved that Hannah had covered for her, but she felt anything but relief. Pain was etched deep in Hannah's face. 'Han, what's wrong? What's happened?'

Hannah wrapped her arms around her body, her bottom lip trembling as she opened her eyes.

'You're scaring me. Where are Mum and Dad?'

Phyllie appeared in the hallway behind Hannah, wringing her hands together, her lips forced into a tight smile. 'Come and sit down, love. We've some bad news, I'm afraid.'

Hannah stifled a sob as the words left their grandmother's lips, causing the skin to prickle on Nat's arms. She reluctantly followed Phyllie into the living room and sat on the couch next to her.

Phyllie took a deep breath, wiping her eyes on the back of her sleeve before meeting Nat's gaze. 'There's been an accident, love.'

Nausea swirled with the nerves in the pit of Nat's stomach. Hannah was now sobbing quietly, her face buried in her hands.

'It's your mum. She had an accident on the horse. A bad one, I'm afraid.'

'How bad? She'll be okay, won't she?'

Phyllie shook her head. 'We had to say our goodbyes. The doctors did their best, but her injuries were too extensive.'

Nat stared at her grandmother and then back at Hannah, numbness settling over her.

Hannah spoke, her face softer, her words gentle. 'She was so upset she couldn't speak to you. She wanted me to give you this.' Hannah moved on to the couch and took Nat in her arms and hugged her. 'She wanted you to know how much she loved you and said she hopes you'll forgive her that she couldn't hold on long enough to say goodbye.'

A single tear rolled down Nat's cheek as she hung limply in Hannah's embrace. Her mother. Her gorgeous, adventurous mother. Gone. It was unthinkable. She closed her eyes, memories of the morning rushing back to her. Of lying about her plans; of promising to be back in time for the small party her father had organised. Of seeing the flicker of disappointment in her mother's eyes when she shook her head at the invitation to join her for the birthday horse ride. She couldn't wait to try out the new saddle Hannah had insisted they give her.

She pulled out of Hannah's arms and put her head in her hands, tears flowing down both cheeks. A sob caught in her throat. Her lies and selfish behaviour had cost her the chance to be with her mum, to tell her she loved her; to say goodbye. It wasn't a matter of forgiving her mother, it was whether she could ever forgive herself.

Chapter One

Present Day

A celebratory smile spread across Hannah's face as she dropped her briefcase and bag on the kitchen counter before trotting up the stairs to the second floor. She needed to get ready for the family dinner before picking Amy up from after-school care on the way to her father's house. Warmth infused her body as she entered the bedroom. She'd describe a normal workday at No Risk as predictable, but today had been anything but. News of an unexpected promotion had left her mind whirling. How had she missed the whispers and gossip that she'd now learned had been going on for weeks?

She stopped, took her phone from her pocket and put it on the mahogany dresser, before picking up a silver photo frame. Her mother, on the morning of her fortieth birthday, looked back at her. Only four years older than Hannah was now. It was the last photo taken of her. She was smiling at the camera, tawny-brown ringlets framing her face. Cherry lipstick, her trademark, glowing from her heart-shaped lips. She wore a white peasant shirt, with a silver necklace around her neck, which she didn't think she'd ever seen her mother without. Hannah's hand instinctively reached for her neck and she fingered the heart pendant; a wedding present from her father to her mother. Having inherited it, she rarely took it off.

Her mother's eyes sparkled with delight as she smiled into the camera. As she'd grown older it had comforted Hannah to know that on the day she'd died her mother had looked so happy. Her throat thickened as she replaced the photo, remembering how their own lives had been upended on the day of the accident. It was always a strange day, celebrating her mother's birthday, but marking the anniversary of her death at the same time.

She took off her suit jacket and hung it in the walk-in-robe, her heart leaping as her mobile phone rang. Hannah hurried back to the dresser, hoping it would be Damien; she couldn't wait to share her news. Her breath caught as she saw that the caller was not her husband; it was *him*. She stared at the screen, her hand frozen around her phone. Her stomach churned, raking up the feelings of guilt she'd done her best to suppress over the last twelve years. Why was he calling now? She'd made it clear he was never to contact her again. The phone stopped ringing as it clicked over to voicemail. She held her breath, hoping he'd dialled the wrong number and there would be no message. Within seconds her hopes were crushed as the phone pinged.

Why had she ever put herself in this position? Lying to her husband, betraying his trust. The guilt she'd suffered had taken years to push into the past, and now here he was again.

With trembling hands she pressed the button to listen to her voicemail. As his voice erupted from the phone she could picture him, his expensive suits, his knowing smirk. She should have known better than to get involved with someone she knew deep down couldn't be trusted. The irony of this thought wasn't lost on her. She was hardly in a position to judge.

'Hey, Hannah. A blast from your past. It's Zane. Zane Fox, in the unlikely event you've forgotten who I am.' He chuckled. 'I highly doubt that after what we got up to. Anyway, there's been a development and I need to talk to you. Please give me a call. It's quite urgent.'

A development. She closed her eyes. She didn't want to know about a development. She just wanted him gone. He had the potential to destroy her marriage and everything she held dear.

Hannah placed the phone down next to her mother's photo. The euphoria she'd felt only moments before had been short-lived. If she ignored him, hopefully he'd take the hint and disappear.

She took a deep breath. Today was not the day for extra problems. Adding Zane Fox into the mix brought a whole other level of stress. The promotion had helped distract her for a short time, but 17 July, the anniversary of her mother's death, was the one day of the year that no matter how hard she might try to suppress her feelings, they always exploded to the surface. Guilt rushed through her in waves as she thought back to that day eighteen years ago. Why hadn't she listened to her father? Gone along with his idea of seeing a matinee performance of *West Side Story* before going out to dinner, rather than insisting they buy a new saddle for her mother and go riding? If she hadn't been so insistent her mother wouldn't have been on a horse that day. She did her best to suppress her guilt for most of the year but on the anniversary it rose to the surface very quickly. She'd never told anyone how she felt. She couldn't bear having to listen to her father or Phyllie as they did their best to convince her it wasn't her fault. Burdening them with her guilt was hardly going to be helpful for anyone. She'd certainly never told Nat.

Her thoughts shifted to her sister. She wondered, as she did most years, if their mother hadn't died what her relationship with Nat would be like now. Before the accident they had been so close. Best friends as well as sisters. Even with the three-year age gap, Hannah loved spending time with her little sister. She'd loved watching and supporting Nat's achievements. It had been a special relationship – until the accident. After that, instead of seeking out Hannah's advice Nat had started to push back. Accusing Hannah of being overprotective, of smothering her and trying to control her. Of course Hannah became more protective of her family after the accident. She still couldn't understand why Nat saw her risk assessing and cautious outlook as a negative.

Hannah sighed. She didn't have the headspace to deal with anything more than getting through the evening. She hadn't heard from Nat since her sister's birthday the month before, which was probably a good thing. Her lack of gratitude over the gift she'd given her had been incredibly disappointing. Why was it that Nat couldn't see Hannah's only motive was to help her? That she worried about her and wanted to make her life easier? If only Nat listened occasionally. Instead she managed to create drama after drama, sending Hannah's stress levels through the roof. However, if she wouldn't accept help when it was offered, then there wasn't a lot more Hannah could do. She just hoped that whatever Nat's latest dramas were they wouldn't spoil the evening. But if her sister's track record was anything to go by, it was almost guaranteed she'd be dealing with the fallout from one screw-up or another.

Nat stared at her reflection in the bathroom mirror. Her golden-brown hair looked lacklustre and was void of its usual waves, while her unusually pale face highlighted the dark circles under her eyes. She pulled out her make-up bag from the vanity and rummaged through it. She was going to need a miracle to make herself even half presentable. She wished she could curl up in a ball and sleep off the rest of this day. How she hated 17 July. It was the one day she dreaded every year, but this year it was so much worse. This year it wasn't just about her mother and getting through another family dinner, this year she had other problems to deal with. Problems that were magnified by the very fact she didn't have her mother to turn to for support. Yes, she had her father and she had Phyllie, but it wasn't the same; it never had been.

She sighed as she curled her lashes before applying mascara. How had she arrived back at this point? Not only would she have to listen to her *brilliant* sister's achievements, but when Hannah found out Nat was once again unemployed and about to be homeless, she'd have a field day with it. It was a ridiculous situation to find herself in at her age, she knew that, but Hannah's reaction would make it ten times worse; she could just picture the look of disgust she'd give her. Not everyone was a corporate success; and the home situation, well, that was hardly her fault either. But Hannah wouldn't see that. She'd remind her of how often Nat had been fired, how often she'd needed to find a new place to live. That it was 'completely avoidable if you just thought for one moment'. No doubt the life coach would be brought up again. Nat still couldn't believe that Hannah had thought she'd actually appreciate this as a birthday present when she'd given it to her the previous month.

'Six sessions with a life coach,' Hannah had proudly announced, handing Nat a gift certificate. 'After these six sessions your life will be turned around. You'll have goals set, a plan to start achieving. I'm so excited for you, Nat.'

Nat had just stared at her sister. Hannah genuinely thought she was going to want this. 'I'm happy with my life how it is.'

Hannah had laughed. 'Nat, you've just turned thirty-three. You have no assets, a low income and the longest relationship you've ever had lasted about six months. You need help. The life coach will help you make changes to every part of your life. You won't recognise yourself.'

With her eleven-year-old niece in the room observing the interaction, Nat chose her words carefully. 'When will you realise that I am doing what I want to, how I want to?' She handed the gift certificate back to Hannah. 'I don't need a life coach, I know exactly what my goals are.'

Hannah rolled her eyes. 'Really? Then how come we never hear of you achieving any of them?'

Nat took a deep breath and stood. 'You put me down at every opportunity, but I'm not listening to it on my birthday.' She turned to her father and stepmother. 'Thanks for lunch and the cake. I'm meeting Pip for drinks, so I need to get going.' She didn't bother to say farewell to Hannah, whose mouth was hanging open in disbelief, and she hadn't spoken to her since.

One thing she knew for sure, if her mother was still alive she'd be Nat's biggest cheerleader. She wouldn't be suggesting life coaches or anything else as ridiculous. She'd understand why Nat got herself into these situations and she'd support her decisions and actions. She always had.

Nat swallowed, doing her best to blink back tears as she put the lid back on the mascara and slipped it into her make-up bag. Eighteen years later and she was still wracked with guilt when she allowed herself to think back to that day. For most of the year she did her best not to. She thought of her mother but didn't allow herself to dwell on the day she died. If she did, she'd be a basket case. But on the anniversary, with dinner looming, it was impossible not to. She'd never been able to forgive herself for letting her mother down, and while she'd never actually said it, Nat was pretty sure Hannah hadn't forgiven her either. She'd been by their mother's side when she died and had seen first-hand how upset she was by not being able to say goodbye to Nat. If only she'd put her mother first that day and spent her birthday with her, or at least been contactable. They would have had the chance to say their goodbyes and Hannah would have no reason to resent her.

Chapter Two

Nat glanced at her phone before turning the key in the ignition and pulling out into the street. Still no contact from the owner of the house in East Melbourne she'd looked at that morning. He'd promised to check her references and get back to her by the end of the day. Not that she was really holding out hope. Her references were hardly glowing with her housemates evicting her and her employment being unexpectedly terminated. A sick feeling had planted itself in the pit of her stomach ever since.

Her thoughts drifted to the previous day, to Todd's smirking face when Lydia, head of human resources, entered the open-plan office area carrying an empty archive box. He'd never liked Nat, making it difficult for her to fit in with the staff of the not-for-profit. Everyone knew what that box represented: instant dismissal – *pack your stuff and go*. Nat's heart had caught in her throat as Lydia inched closer to her desk with every footstep. Minutes later she'd found herself sitting in Lydia's office, the archive box with her belongings on her lap.

'I'm sorry,' Lydia said, 'but the company is unable to overlook what happened last week with Frank Barton. No warning is required in the circumstances. Your actions breach company policy and termination is the consequence.'

Nat gripped the archive box, doing her best to remain calm. It was ridiculous that this is how it ended up when she was only trying to help people. 'What would you have done, Lydia? There were no vacancies in any of the support houses for him, and all emergency accommodation was full. It was three degrees outside.' Her actions had been in the best interest of their client. Surely she could understand that?

'We don't take clients home with us. That's drilled into every employee of Benedict's. No matter what the circumstances. It's unacceptable and potentially dangerous.'

'It was only for one night.'

'Not the point.' She raised an eyebrow. 'And not the only breach of company policy.'

'What do you mean?'

Lydia sighed. 'You've crossed the line before, Nat. Given clients money, taken them out for meals and driven them to appointments after hours and on weekends.'

Now, Nat shook her head as she pulled to a stop at a red light. How could putting others first be a bad thing? They worked for a not-for-profit, for God's sake. They were supposed to be helping people, that's why they were there. But then her housemates had reacted similarly. They'd been disgusted when she'd brought Frank home with her. Their lack of compassion had floored her. Couldn't they imagine themselves or someone they cared about in the same situation? Needing a hot meal, a shower and their clothes laundered. Wouldn't they want to help them? Apparently not. She'd be glad to get out of there, she just wished the timing was better. Finding a new home without a job was going to be difficult.

The traffic started up and Nat continued along Dandenong Road towards her father's home in East Malvern. Her stomach grumbled, reminding her that she'd hardly eaten. After looking at the house that morning she'd spent a number of hours at Shared, the community garden and soup kitchen she volunteered at. Digging had been cathartic, and when she'd finished preparing the trench for the leeks to be planted, she'd at least felt a sense of achievement. That feeling had been boosted by Robyn, the centre manager, when she'd flung an arm around Nat's shoulder and squeezed it. 'The number of hours you dedicate to Shared each month is simply incredible. It's people like you that make a difference in this world. Don't you ever forget that.'

A lump lodged in Nat's throat as she thought about those words. The difference she was making was about to be reduced significantly. Without an income she'd have to immediately cancel her charitable contributions. She sighed, feeling very much alone. She'd thought about ringing her best friend, but Pip would be at work and she was so caught up in her wedding planning that having to listen to Nat's problems, again, was probably the last thing she needed.

A weight settled on her shoulders as she turned off the main road and into the quiet tree-lined streets of East Malvern. Dealing with these issues alone was hard enough, but now she had to face her family and admit that she'd failed once again. Hannah would no doubt lecture her on the way she should have done things. She really wasn't sure that she had the capacity to deal with any of this tonight.

Chapter Three

Hannah's grip tightened on the steering wheel as her phone rang and she pulled off the main road and into the side street that led to her father's East Malvern home. Zane Fox's name briefly flashed up on the car's dashboard display before she had the chance to cancel the call. Her heart raced as she glanced in the rear-view mirror. Had Amy seen his name? Her daughter's eyes met hers before returning to the book she'd been engrossed in when Hannah arrived to collect her from after-school care. Her phone pinged. Another message. For once she wished her car didn't have Bluetooth and her phone didn't automatically connect.

'Aren't you going to listen to your message?'

Amy's question sent a shiver down Hannah's spine. She shook her head and did her best to make her voice sound normal. 'No, it'll be work-related. I'll deal with it later.'

Amy raised an eyebrow. 'Really? But you hate missing a call. You never cancel them. And you just told me you got a promotion today, it might be about that.'

Hannah shrugged, glad Amy couldn't hear her heartbeat, which was thumping out of control. 'Tonight's not about work or anything else. I just want to keep my thoughts on my mum, your grandma. She's what we should be focused on.' Hannah averted her eyes from the mirror when she saw sympathy flood Amy's face.

If it wasn't bad enough that she'd been lying to Damien for twelve years, now she was lying to her daughter too.

Another text pinged on her phone, causing her to brake inadvertently. She let out a long breath as she saw it was Damien. The text appeared on the display.

Running a bit late. Will meet you at your dad's. Xx

'Dad's acting so weird lately,' Amy said. 'Is he sad about something?'

Thoughts of Zane Fox momentarily left Hannah's mind as she considered Amy's question. Her daughter was very perceptive; Damien had been distant and distracted lately. She could pinpoint exactly when it started – the second Sunday in June. The morning after his monthly poker game he'd not been himself. He'd dropped in to see his parents that morning and judging by his mood when he'd returned, she'd worried that something was wrong with them. He'd assured her they were fine, that he was tired and had a few things on his mind. 'I think he's just stressed with work,' she told Amy.

'Well, I need him not to be. I have to talk to both of you about something important and if he's stressed he's just going to say no.'

'Oh? What's that?'

'I'm too old for after-school care and . . .'

'We've discussed this before and the answer's still no,' Hannah snapped, cutting Amy off. 'It's not a matter that's up for discussion. When Dad and I are working, that's what you have to do. End of topic.'

'Fine, I'll speak to Dad. Even when he's stressed he lets me finish my sentences.'

It was impossible not to miss Amy's scowl in the rear-view mirror as Hannah opened her mouth, ready to respond. She closed it again. What she really needed was to take a deep breath and do her best not to let Zane Fox's sudden reappearance rattle her. She didn't deal well with stress, and unfortunately those closest to her usually felt the fallout.

'Nat's here,' Amy announced as they slowed in front of the magnificent Edwardian brick house.

Nat's presence was hardly going to lift Hannah's spirits. They hadn't spoken since the disastrous life coach birthday gift. She still didn't understand her sister's reaction. Life coaches were amazing. She'd seen one five years earlier and now made appointments every six months to make sure she was on track to meet her goals. She couldn't comprehend how Nat interpreted the present as anything but an opportunity. She wasn't planning to bring it up tonight though. She would do her best to be friendly and hope Nat reciprocated.

Hannah took Amy's hand, surprised that her daughter let her, as they made their way along the pebbled path to the front door. She drew in a breath and managed to smile, noting the lavender-blue hydrangeas were still in flower in the garden bed that ran along the front of the house. To have flowers in mid-July was a sign, according to her father, that 'all was well in heaven'. Her mother had adored hydrangeas, and when they were still in flower on her birthday she'd said the gods were looking down on her and preparing her for a wonderful year ahead. Following her death, it had always seemed extra special when they were in flower on her birthday.

The garden was well looked after. The lawns were neatly mown and the two bushes either side of the path had been recently trimmed. She'd never considered it anything special when they were growing up, but now East Malvern was a sought-after area in Melbourne's south-east and her father's house retained its character and charm. Newly built townhouses surrounded it, but the leafy garden kept it private and tranquil.

Amy dropped her hand and broke into a run to reach the door first. She knocked and it opened instantly. Hannah's father, his thinning hair now almost totally grey, was waiting on the other side. He scooped Amy into a tight embrace, eliciting a muffled cry of objection from his granddaughter.

'Hi, Dad.' Hannah leaned towards her father and planted a kiss on his cheek as Amy squirmed out of his arms and went inside, no doubt in search of his beloved dog, Toby. 'How are you?'

Her father linked his arm through hers. 'Good, love. Now come in, it's freezing out there. We've got the fire on and the wine open.'

'Damien will be here any minute,' Hannah said as he led her along the wide hallway to the back of the house. 'He's running a bit late from work.'

'That's fine, Han.' Sue looked up from the kitchen bench as they entered the open-plan kitchen and living area. Her father let go of her arm and went in search of more glasses.

'Sorry, I'd come and hug you but my hands are covered in flour.'

Sue was the one woman Hannah knew for sure her mother would have approved for her father. Her best friend for twenty-eight years, Sue had been part of the family well before she officially joined it when she married Hannah's father ten years earlier. Connected in their grief and mutual love of a wife and best friend, they were perfectly suited. She smiled at her stepmother. 'Where are the others?'

'In your dad's study. Just Phyllie and Nat.'

'Go and say hello, love,' her father suggested. 'I'll bring you a glass of champagne in a minute. I've got some sparkling grape juice for Amy. Is that okay?'

Hannah bit the inside of her lip. He already knew the answer to that question.

'I just thought, it being a special day and all, that she might like a change from water. And it's organic.'

She took a deep breath, deciding tonight wasn't the night for an argument. 'If you put it in a champagne flute, I'm sure she'd be over the moon.'

Her father beamed. He was so used to her saying no to treats and sugary drinks he'd be thinking something was wrong with her. It didn't make sense to Hannah to drink anything loaded with sugar, and she certainly wasn't going to poison her daughter and risk tooth decay, type 2 diabetes or heart disease. But it was a special day and she didn't want to spoil it. One glass wasn't going to hurt any more than a glass of champagne would hurt Hannah. She was looking forward to a drink. She wanted to celebrate her promotion, even if her mood had been soured by Zane's phone calls. She planned to sip the champagne and privately dedicate it to both her mum and her own achievement.

'Go and join Phyllie and Nat,' her father encouraged again. 'They can't wait to see you.'

Hannah gave a wry smile. They both knew that was very unlikely. Phyllie might be happy to see her, but Nat certainly wouldn't be. And after her last conversation with Phyllie, she expected a chilly reception from her grandmother too.

Chapter Four

A familiar uncomfortable feeling settled over Nat as she heard her sister's voice in the hallway. She took a large sip of her wine.

'What is it with you two?' Phyllie asked. 'Your face changes the moment Hannah's mentioned, or like now when you can hear her. The two of you used to be so close. Is she that terrible?'

Nat considered the question. Hannah wasn't terrible, but she was no longer the Hannah Nat had adored as a young girl and teenager. Hannah's change in attitude towards her immediately after the accident had been the equivalent of a slap in the face, reinforcing that Nat should feel guilty for letting their mother down. There was never any question of Hannah covering for her following the accident. Instead, she went from being an ally to constantly telling Nat what she could and couldn't do. Not only did she find this unbearable, it shook her confidence. She no longer had the support of the sister she looked up to. Encouragement was replaced with constant worry, of evaluating the possible negative outcome of every situation. Hannah developed the knack for sucking the fun out of everything. And then of course there was Hannah's continued success, which contrasted with Nat's spectacular ability to fail. She knew Hannah considered her a failure, she saw it in her eyes and heard it in her words. It was hard not to get defensive when someone always made you feel inferior. However, telling Phyllie any of this would just have their grandmother defending Hannah, and Nat didn't need that right now.

'Just a clash of personalities.'

'That's an understatement if ever I heard one,' Phyllie muttered as Hannah walked into the room.

At least she'd changed, was Nat's first thought. It was unlikely her sister had worn the skinny black jeans and beige, curved-hem jumper to work. She usually had her chestnut-brown hair tied back or up in a messy bun for work, not hanging loosely around her shoulders as she did now. She looked quite relaxed compared to the usual uptight way she presented herself. Nat's eyes travelled to her sister's feet. She couldn't help it. Which boots would she be wearing today? It had become a joke, Hannah's obsession with boots.

A red wedge heel. That was a surprise, although she did vaguely recall Hannah boring them all about the need to rotate footwear so as not to overuse one particular set of muscle groups or joints.

Phyllie stood when Hannah entered the room so that her granddaughter could hug her. 'How are you, love?'

'Good thanks, Phyllie. You?'

'Very sprightly, thank you. Full of beans, in fact, and ready to run a few miles after I leave here.'

Nat raised an eyebrow, which she ignored. Phyllie had shirked the title of grandmother when, at age two, Nat had sat on her lap stroking her hair, saying, 'What a pretty young filly.' She was parroting her mother's words after Nat had watched her grooming her favourite horse, not realising that the name Phyllie had come from her grandmother's real name of Phyllis. Nat had refused to believe this was the case. 'It's the name you call the things you love,' she'd insisted. Knowing the sentiment behind it, Phyllie insisted they all refer to her by her first name from that day forward.

Hannah turned to Nat. 'How's work?'

Nat gritted her teeth. Not how are you, Nat? What's new in your life? Have you seen any good movies? Always straight to work. Today was not the day to ask.

'Fine.' She took another sip of her drink, her eyes moving to her father's bookcase, which ran the length of an entire wall. It was full of thrillers and had a shelf dedicated to new releases he had yet to read. It looked like he'd added at least five new titles since she'd last been here.

The silence in the room was broken when her father walked in with a glass of champagne. He handed it to Hannah just as her phone rang. She set the glass down and somewhat reluctantly took the phone from her pocket. Her face paled as she glanced at the screen before cancelling the call.

'Everything alright, love?' Phyllie asked.

Hannah nodded before slipping the phone back into her pocket. Nat frowned. How very un-Hannah-like to not answer a call. Usually she'd make a huge performance about everyone being quiet while she took it, or would leave the room.

Her father cleared his throat. 'Sue will be in in a minute, and then I'll go and find Amy, who I'm guessing has headed out the back to play with Toby. We should have a toast for your mother before the night gets underway.' He looked from Hannah to Nat. 'I hope everyone has remembered exactly why we're here tonight.'

'Of course.' Hannah looked pointedly at Nat. 'Think you can manage to keep tonight drama-free?'

Hannah's words, implying she was the one that caused their dramas, sliced into Nat like a knife. Five minutes. It had taken less than five minutes for Hannah to get her first dig in.

Phyllie clapped her hands together. 'Enough.' She held up her empty champagne flute. 'One of you top this up, please. If I have to put up with this kind of nonsense, I'll need plenty of bubbles.'

Following Damien's arrival and numerous toasts for their mother's birthday, Sue placed a platter of nibbles on the coffee table and suggested they all relax before dinner.

Phyllie remained standing and moved in front of the crackling fire, warming her hands while the others sank on to the comfortable couches.

Nat noticed Sue frowning as she studied Phyllie's back.

'You're unusually quiet today, Phyllie,' Sue said. 'Everything alright?'

All eyes went to the matriarch.

Phyllie nodded and turned to face them, her lips pursed. 'Just observing my lovely family. Missing my daughter-in-law and reflecting on what a wonderful mother and wife she was.'

'I don't know, Mum,' Nat's father said. 'As much as I'd like to believe you're standing there thinking lovely thoughts about Carmel, I can almost hear your mind ticking over. What's going on? Is something worrying you?'

Phyllie sighed and moved to the rustic wingback armchair closest to the fire. 'I guess I'm sick of the fact that the world considers me to be an old woman.'

'But you are, Phyllie.' Amy stretched her legs out towards the fire. 'You're eighty-nine. That's ancient.'

'Thanks, love.' Phyllie gave a wry smile. 'What you'll realise when you get to my age is that your body feels old and has aches, but your mind's as sharp as it was fifty years ago.'

'I don't think of you as old,' Nat said. 'You're amazing. I think you'll be ticking along for years after we're all dead and buried.'

Phyllie smiled. 'Thank you, Nat. But I think you'll find some people here disagree with you. Some people think I should be put away – taken from my home and locked up.'

Silence descended on the room.

'What on earth are you talking about?' her son eventually asked. 'Who said that?'

Phyllie looked pointedly at Hannah, whose cheeks reddened.

Amy gasped. 'You said Phyllie should be locked up?'

Hannah shook her head. 'Of course I didn't. I suggested we look into some assisted living centres, that's all. There are some amazing places around, and if Phyllie was in one of those she'd have help available twenty-four hours a day. They're also very social places, with lots of people her age to chat with.'

Phyllie rolled her eyes. 'Social? Yes, if you enjoy eating little sandwiches three times a week at all the funerals you attend. That's why those places exist, don't you realise that? It's to put all the old people in one place, so it's convenient to ship them off to the funeral home when their time's up. They have a car on standby at all times for that very purpose. You know, like Uber, but for the dead.'

Nat snorted. 'They do not. You made that up.'

'How do you know? Have you ever been forced to spend time in one of those institutions?'

'They're hardly institutions,' Hannah said. 'It's assisted living, that's all. They have very nice grounds and plenty of activities. You can join in with meals or cook your own. It's flexible, and people rave about them.' Hannah's phone rang again. She took it from her pocket and declined the call.

'Why aren't you answering your phone?' Damien asked.

'She's been ignoring calls and messages ever since she picked me up,' Amy piped up. 'She's acting really weird.'

Hannah's cheeks flushed. 'I'm not acting weird, it's just work and I don't want it interrupting our night.'

Nat looked from Hannah to Damien, noting his frown. Hannah ignoring her phone *was* weird. She usually put work before everything else, to the point that it irritated Nat. She imagined Damien was wondering the same.

'Back to the assisted living.' Her father's gaze was fixed firmly on Hannah. 'How do you know so much about this?'

Phyllie's eyes blazed. 'How do you think? She's done a full risk assessment of me living at home compared to going into one of these places.'

'Have you?' Nat gasped. She knew Hannah was obsessed with making charts and analysing outcomes, but Phyllie wouldn't tolerate being the subject matter.

Hannah nodded. 'I have, and if you'd like me to show it to you, you'll see unequivocally why Phyllie needs care. Did you know that the likelihood of falling once you're over the age of eighty-five increases by fifty percent? That's a huge risk. And a fracture in an elderly woman increases their risk of death by twenty percent.'

Phyllie rolled her eyes. 'This is what I have to put up with.'

Hannah shook her head. 'I wish you'd take this seriously. Your house is too big for you to manage and the stairs pose a real danger.'

'I want to make it very clear to all of you right now that I intend to stay in my home as long as possible. Ideally, I'd like to be carried out in a body bag upon my death, and preferably not before. You're not to do anything behind my back, like sell my house or have me put in one of those places. Betty Mason's children did that to her, you know. She died three weeks later of heartbreak. Missing her house and her little dog; it was a criminal thing to do and they ought to be ashamed of themselves.'

Her father glared at Hannah before turning to Phyllie. 'Don't worry, Mum, no one's planning to do anything like that to you.'

'And,' Sue added, 'you'd come and live with us before we ever put you in a home. Your grandchildren' – she stared directly at Hannah – 'would be much better off working out how they can help you stay in your home. How they can come and do your garden, clean your windows, cook your meals and take you shopping, rather than spending their time putting spreadsheets together showing you the risks of staying there.' Sue stood. 'Now, on a more cheerful note, I'll go and check on dinner. It should be ready in a few minutes.'

Sue always served a favourite recipe of their mother's at this dinner, and Nat had just put her cutlery down, savouring the last mouthful of the much-loved chicken cacciatore dish, when Amy turned to Hannah.

'Aren't you going to tell them your *big* news?' The sarcasm inflected by Amy on the word 'big' confirmed to Hannah that she hadn't been forgiven for being so short with her during the car ride.

'She got a promotion,' Amy continued before Hannah had a chance to speak. 'She's *really* important now.'

Hannah's face turned a deeper shade of red. 'Not exactly how I would have told you all, but yes, Amy's right, I was unexpectedly promoted today.'

'That's wonderful!' Their father's eyes were bright.

'Tell us about it,' Sue prompted. 'Will it be a big change for you?'

Nat noticed Hannah stealing glances at her husband as she gave them a brief overview of her new responsibilities. His smile didn't reach his cloud-grey eyes. Something was off about Damien tonight.

Her father raised his glass to toast Hannah, glancing at Damien as he did. 'You must be proud of your wife, Damien.'

Alarm crossed Damien's face as he looked around to see all eyes were on him. 'Sorry, I'm a little distracted.' He turned to Hannah and took her hand. 'I'm incredibly proud. You deserve everything you've worked for.'

25

Hannah's smile was full of uncertainty as she accepted his praise. Nat's interest was piqued. Something was going on with her *perfect* sister and her *perfect* marriage. It had always amazed Nat that a man like Damien, blessed with natural good looks, kind, intelligent and with a smile that lit up the room, had fallen for her neurotic, control-freak sister.

'When does the new role start?' Phyllie's words broke into Nat's thoughts.

'Not until mid-September. I have eight weeks to hand over some of my existing work and be brought up to speed with the new responsibilities.'

'Let's raise our glasses to Hannah.' Sue held up her champagne flute. 'A perfect day to celebrate some good news. Your mother would be proud of you.' She looked across to Nat. 'She'd be incredibly proud of both of you and what you've achieved.'

They clinked glasses.

'How about you, Nat?' Sue asked. 'Should we be toasting something that's happening in your life? An opportunity at work, or a new man? A new interest?'

Nat choked on her champagne and shook her head. Definitely nothing to celebrate in her life right now.

'Really?' Hannah narrowed her eyes. 'There must be something good happening.'

Nat stared at her sister. 'Why?'

Hannah frowned. 'What do you mean why?'

'I mean why *must* there be something good happening?'

'I don't know. I guess I just hoped for your sake there was.' She gave a little laugh. 'Something less dramatic perhaps than you got fired or dumped or are homeless again. Pick one good thing from the last week.'

Nat continued staring at Hannah. She really was a piece of work. Just because she was constantly achieving greatness didn't mean they all had to be. She took a large gulp of her drink before speaking. 'Let's just say I like to keep things dramatic. In fact, you got two out of three right for my week so far.'

Nat could have kicked herself as mouths fell open around the table. She hadn't planned on talking about her current failures with everyone.

'Oh Nat.' The weary sound of disappointment in her father's words reinforced exactly why she shouldn't have said anything. If only the ground would swallow her up and she could avoid the humiliation to come.

Phyllie, who was on her right, immediately placed a hand over Nat's. 'You poor love. What can I do to help?'

Tears welled in Nat's eyes. She shook her head. 'Nothing. I was stupid and now I'm paying the price.'

'Please don't tell us you took another homeless person home?' Hannah said. 'We all know what the outcome of that would be.'

Nat clenched her jaw, refusing to meet her sister's accusing gaze.

'You know,' Sue said, 'your mum would be incredibly proud of you for caring so much about people. If you took someone home, then all I can say is good for you. I'm sorry if that ended your job but your selflessness is inspiring.'

Nat sighed, deciding to ignore Hannah. 'Yes, I took a client home for the night as all the shelters and emergency accommodations were full. It's against company policy, so I was fired this morning.'

'When are you going to learn?' Hannah said. 'You were fired from St Josephine's for doing the same thing and warned when you worked at J&J's Support. Why would you risk it again? It's almost guaranteed to get you fired.'

'Because, as Sue has just pointed out,' Phyllie said, 'Nat puts others before herself, that's why. Something we should all be doing.'

'Not if it gets you fired; that's just ridiculous,' Hannah said. 'You said I got two out of three right, what was the other one?'

'I was given notice last weekend at my house. I've got just over a week to find somewhere new to live.'

'Oh Nat,' Sue said. 'You poor thing. Have you looked for something else yet?'

Nat nodded. 'Unfortunately my references aren't exactly glowing.'

'Finding somewhere to live without a job isn't going to be easy,' Hannah said.

Nat stared at her sister. 'Do you think that any of your comments are helpful? I know I messed up, but I'd do it again in a heartbeat, and I know getting another job will be tricky, as will finding a place to live. I don't need you being so condescending about it all.'

Hannah's cheeks flamed red. 'I wasn't being condescending, I was just stating a fact. I'm sorry if you took it any other way.'

'You should move in with us,' Amy said. 'That would be so much fun.'

'And listen to your mother telling me how stupid I've been, how I take too many risks and now have to live with the consequences . . . no thanks.'

'I don't think you're stupid,' Hannah said. 'I just think there are better ways to do things. There's that saying that banging your head against the same wall and expecting a different result is madness. That's what I see you doing. Yes, it's admirable to be helping people but not when it's at a massive cost to you. There are other ways to go about helping without having to suffer yourself. I know you said no to the life coaching sessions but I wish you'd give them a go. The sessions force me to set goals and stay focused. I wouldn't have been offered this promotion if I hadn't made a plan and worked towards my goals.'

Nat rolled her eyes. She knew when she'd handed Hannah the present back that it was unlikely to be the end of it. 'Like I said on my birthday, I'm happy with my life. I don't need a stranger giving me advice. God, I get enough of it from you for free, which I ignore.'

Hannah folded her arms across her chest. 'Maybe if you didn't ignore it you wouldn't be back in a difficult situation once again.'

'Maybe if you stopped dishing out unsolicited advice I would relax and not feel like I was being judged the whole time. And don't worry, there's no way on this earth I'd ever want to move in with you, so you won't be put out.'

Phyllie clapped her hands together. 'Enough. We're here to celebrate my gorgeous daughter-in-law's birthday and the anniversary of her passing. You two will stop your bickering and, Nat, you will move in with me. End of discussion. We'll sort out the details later.'

'But . . .' Nat started to object.

'No buts. It will help you out temporarily and' – she turned and glared at Hannah – 'hopefully get your interfering sister off my back about assisted living.'

Nat couldn't help but smile as Hannah's cheeks blushed an even deeper shade of red.

'There will be no more arguing tonight,' Phyllie continued, looking from Nat to Hannah. 'We are not here to act like children.' She glanced at Amy. 'No offence, honey, you behave a lot more maturely than these two at times.'

Amy grinned. 'And I have news too. Exciting news.'

All eyes turned to her.

'I was one of ten students to win something today!'

'That's marvellous,' Phyllie said. 'What did you win?'

'A place in Equestrian. Studying the behaviour of the horses and learning to ride. We can also volunteer to work at the stables after school or on the weekend.'

'No,' Hannah spoke with authority.

All eyes shifted from Amy to Hannah.

'It's too dangerous. We've had this conversation before and you know my feelings on it. This is not something to discuss now. We'll talk about it when we get home.'

'Sounds like you've already made your mind up,' Nat said. 'Not much of a discussion.'

'Stay out of it.' Hannah was biting her lip, a sign her anger was escalating.

Damien held up his hands. 'Okay, this is a discussion for us to have at home. Not during Carmel's celebration.' His eyes drilled into Amy's. 'Not the best night to ask, Ames.'

'Why not? Grandma would have wanted me to join the pony club. And the lessons through school are free. There were only ten places in Equestrian for this term, and I got one of them. You can't say no.'

Hannah took a large sip of her champagne, looking as if she was trying to contain her irritation. 'Even though you never met her, you believe your grandma would have wanted you to put yourself in danger unnecessarily?'

Amy nodded. 'I don't need to have known her. You've all spoken about how adventurous she was, how she loved horses and how if she'd survived the accident she would have got back on and kept riding. Now I can get back on for her. And anyway, in Australia only twenty people a year die from horse-related accidents, you said so yourself.'

Hannah shook her head. '*Only twenty*. That's twenty people too many. The figures of how dangerous horse riding is were supposed to put you off, not make you think *only twenty*.'

'Twenty out of millions is nothing,' Amy said. 'You're overreacting.'

Nat stifled a laugh. Overreacting was an understatement when it came to Hannah. She grinned at her niece. 'Twenty out of millions isn't many, is it. I guess that means it's safe for you to go.'

Amy looked to her mother, her hazel eyes full of hope. 'Does it?'

Hannah shot daggers at her sister. 'Of course not. Twenty deaths a year confirms it's dangerous. People worry about dying from spider and snake bites and shark attacks, yet they don't seem to realise that the deadliest animal of all is the horse. There are more horse-related deaths per year in Australia than any other animal. Now, let's change the subject.'

'We'll talk about it at home,' Damien repeated. 'Tonight is about celebrating your grandmother's life, not arguing about things that don't need to be resolved right now.'

Amy's glare was lost on Hannah as her phone rang, again. The colour, which had become quite red as she got more and more worked up, drained from her face as she took it from her pocket and glanced at the screen.

'For goodness' sake,' Phyllie said. 'Someone's obviously needing to speak to you. Go and answer it.'

Hannah nodded before standing and pushing her chair back. She put the phone to her ear as she retreated from the room. 'Hold on a minute, Martin, I'm at a dinner so I need to leave the room.'

'Martin's her boss,' Damien said, in what appeared to be an apology on Hannah's behalf. 'I'm sure she won't be long. She knows how important tonight is. It's probably why she was ignoring his calls, she wouldn't want Carmel's night interrupted.'

Hannah walked to the far end of the house, ensuring she was well out of hearing distance before clearing her throat. 'I'm at a family dinner, Zane. It's the anniversary of my mother's death, which takes

31

priority over anything you could have to say to me right now. I told you twelve years ago I wanted you gone from my life. You agreed I'd never hear from you again.'

Zane laughed. 'Should I even ask who Martin is? While you lying to your husband obviously hasn't changed, other things have, which is what I need to discuss with you.'

'Not tonight.' Hannah ended the call and slipped the phone back into her pocket. She leaned against the wall, her legs trembling. She closed her eyes, the wretched feelings of twelve years earlier resurfacing as she thought back to what she'd done.

Nat's laughter infiltrated her thoughts. Bloody Nat. On top of everything else that was going on tonight, there was Nat undermining her when it came to Amy and the horse-riding opportunity. Her eyes jolted open. She might not be able to control the Zane Fox situation, but she could definitely make her feelings on this issue very clear.

Phyllie rose as Hannah re-entered the room. 'Amy, why don't you come out the back with me? Toby needs to be fed, and I think you and I could manage that between us.' She glanced across to Sue. 'Perhaps we could do the cake a little later?'

Sue nodded, and Nat watched as Amy followed Phyllie through to the kitchen to prepare the cocker spaniel's dinner. Cold, angry eyes met hers when she glanced at Hannah. It appeared her phone call had done nothing to cool her anger over the horse-riding discussion. Nat silently counted how many seconds it would take before Hannah exploded.

Exactly four.

'Why did you do that? You know why I don't want her on a horse. Jesus, I hardly have to spell it out.'

Nat rolled her eyes. 'Oh, come on. The likelihood of her having an accident is slim. She'll be under supervision and wearing a helmet. It's not a big deal. You worry too much.'

Hannah closed her eyes, rubbing her hand against her forehead. 'How can you be so flippant about it after what happened?'

'Mum was unlucky,' Nat said. 'In all your facts and figures, how many of the twenty who die each year are thrown from their horse because a snake bites it?'

'You don't have to be thrown, just falling off and hitting your head can be enough to kill you.'

'You're being ridiculous. You let her go in the car every day, yet according to you, one thousand one hundred and forty-six people died last year in car accidents in Australia. Does that mean you're irresponsible for allowing her in the car? And you let her eat. Didn't you say death by choking was up seventeen percent? Perhaps we should start pureeing her food?'

Hannah opened her mouth and closed it again. She turned away momentarily and shook her head before turning back to Nat. 'You're not a parent. You sail along in life only having to look after yourself, and from what you've told us tonight about being fired *again*, you can't even do that successfully. Don't tell me how to parent my child and don't undermine me like that in front of her.'

Nat pushed her chair back. There was no point trying to have a discussion with Hannah. She managed to get in as many digs at Nat as possible. 'You know, Phyllie's right. She said we are here for a celebration of Mum's life, not an argument. How about you respect that?'

'Me? This is a discussion and, if anything, I'm voicing exactly what Mum would say.'

Damien cleared his throat. 'David and Sue didn't invite us here tonight to listen to you two arguing. Hannah and I will clear the table and do the dishes while you all relax by the fire.'

Nat didn't look at Hannah as she made her way out of the room. It was on nights like this she wished her mother was still alive. She would love confirmation that Hannah was in fact her sister. If she'd been told she was adopted, or they had different fathers, life would make a lot more sense.

Nat didn't retreat to the family room as Damien had suggested, instead she checked that Phyllie and Amy had returned from feeding Toby before letting herself out of the back door and into the large courtyard that led to her father's lush green lawn. Toby was at her side immediately as she shivered, wishing she'd put her coat on first. She picked up the ball Toby dropped at her feet and threw it across the dark lawn, watching as the cocker spaniel rushed after it. She let out a deep breath, tears pricking her eyes. She had enough to deal with today without Hannah adding to it.

She froze as the back door opened and footsteps followed after her. She needed time by herself right now. She turned, fury rising within her as Hannah approached her. She wasn't going to put up with any more of her attitude and criticisms tonight. 'Leave me alone. I've got a lot on my mind and I'm really not interested in arguing with you again.'

Hannah put her hands up. 'This isn't the night to be arguing about anything. We've all got a lot going on and need to set it aside as best we can for Dad's sake, if nothing else.'

How about for my sake? Nat thought as she stared at her sister. *How about an apology?*

'It's freezing out here.' Hannah wrapped her arms around herself. 'Why don't you come back in by the fire?'

'And wait for you to remind me again that I'm not a parent so I can't have an opinion or to take your next dig at me?'

'Dig?'

'Yes, that I should have known better than to take a client home. That I'm constantly disappointing everyone. Have you got any idea how belittling it is? How embarrassed I am to have to tell you all?' Nat's cheeks flamed with heat as she spat the words at Hannah.

Hannah shook her head. 'I worry about you, that's all. I guess I want to make you see things my way sometimes. That some of the situations you put yourself in are avoidable.'

'I know they are, Hannah. It's not like I go out deliberately looking to sabotage my job or my life. But when someone's in need I'm not going to turn them away. I'll deal with the consequences.'

'But surely . . .'

This time Nat held up her hand. 'No, you listen for once. I don't need your suggestions or your risk assessment of my actions. I just need you to let me live my life. My stuff-ups have no impact on you at all. I'm not asking you for somewhere to live or for money to get by on. I'm actually not asking you for anything, particularly not your opinion. I know what that is before you even open your mouth.'

Hannah's phone rang, distracting her. Her face paled as she looked at the screen, switched it off and slipped it back into her pocket. Something was definitely going on, Nat thought. Hannah was unusually flustered.

She cleared her throat and returned her gaze to Nat. 'You're wrong.'

'Of course I am.' Nat marched past Hannah towards the back door. 'I'm always wrong, according to you.'

Hannah grabbed her arm, stopping her before she could disappear inside. Her voice was gentle. 'I meant you're wrong that your problems don't have any impact on me. Of course they do. I just want what's best for you.'

Nat shook Hannah's hand off her arm. 'No, you want to control me, just like you do with Amy and Damien. You want us all to conform to how life should be lived according to Hannah. That's never going to happen with me, you should have worked that out by now. However, the one thing I will agree with you on is tonight. We both need to put on our best behaviour for Dad's sake. Tonight is supposed to be about Mum, about celebrating her life.' She didn't wait for Hannah's reaction, but opened the door and let herself back inside.

When Hannah returned to the family room she gave Nat a nod and a tight smile. Her signal that she agreed to behave for their father's sake.

At Sue's insistence they always played Carmel's favourite game before the cake was cut. The mood shifted to a much lighter one and laughter increased in volume as each round of charades passed.

When it was her turn, Nat took a deep breath and put her hand into the small bag. She was partnered with Damien and Amy and was the last in her team to act out a title. With the two teams tied it would be down to her attempt.

She glanced at the paper and shot Sue, who'd compiled the titles, a dirty look. *Fifty Shades of Grey*? How was she supposed to act that out when there was an eleven-year-old in the room?

Sue's eyes twinkled. Nat could only imagine what other book and film titles were in the selection.

She went through the motions of acting out that it was a film and book, and was able to convey the word grey by pointing at the chair her father was sitting in.

'*Fifty Shades of Grey*,' Amy piped up, silencing the room.

Nat clapped a hand over her mouth, unable to contain her laughter. She hardly dared look at Hannah. When she did, her sister's face was exactly as she'd expected. Her mouth open, her cheeks flushed.

'Where did you hear about that book?' Hannah asked.

Amy looked confused. 'Book? I thought it was a movie.'

'It's both,' Phyllie volunteered. 'And I can say I thoroughly enjoyed each version. I've just read that lovely author's new book too and loved it. It's exactly the type of literature a woman of my age should be reading.' She winked. 'Takes me back down memory lane it does.'

Nat's laughter escaped, and she bent double trying to get her breath back. 'Sorry,' she managed once she was upright again. 'Just a bit unexpected.'

'I'll say,' Damien murmured.

'So, the movie then,' Hannah prompted Amy. 'How did you hear about it?'

'It's on Amazon Prime. Let's watch it on Saturday night when Dad's at his poker game. A lot of the girls at school talk about it. I think I'm the only one who hasn't seen it.'

Phyllie clapped her hands together. 'And I think those girls might be pulling your leg, Ames. Now, we might declare Amy's team the winners and cut the cake and make some tea. Something sweet would go down very nicely right now.'

They followed her through to the kitchen.

'Poker's this Saturday?' Nat asked Damien as Sue took the cover off the decadent white chocolate mud cake she'd ordered specially for the celebration.

He placed his empty beer bottle on the kitchen bench and nodded. 'We've got a spare seat, if you're interested. It's Texas Hold 'Em. You remember how to play, don't you?'

Nat nodded. Damien had invited her once before to his poker night. She'd lost the fifty dollars she'd taken with her, but it was a fun night with great company.

Hannah interrupted. 'Nat probably shouldn't be wasting money on something like that right now.'

Nat opened her mouth, about to tell her that she'd make her own decisions and didn't need Hannah's opinion, but shut it again. She thought for a moment. As much as she hated to admit it, Hannah was right, she'd just lost her job and couldn't afford to lose any of her money playing poker.

Phyllie appeared to sense her hesitation. 'Do you know how to play, love?'

'I do, but just the basics. I don't know the strategy, assuming there is one.'

'If you spend some time with me beforehand, you won't lose.' Phyllie winked. 'Been playing Hold 'Em, as it used to be called, since the sixties. I've a few tricks up my sleeve. Come over on Friday and take a look at the spare room. We can work out the new living arrangement and I'll give you some pointers. I'm also happy to invest in your night out on Saturday so you can enjoy it without worrying about what you lose. No arguments to any of that.'

Nat smiled. There didn't seem to be anything Phyllie hadn't experienced. 'I appreciate the offer, but I wouldn't want to lose your money.'

'You won't lose if you follow my instructions. If it makes you feel better you can pay me back my investment from your winnings. Now, I'll be working in the charity shop until two on Friday, but you're welcome after that. We can have an early dinner together and get used to being housemates.'

'Sounds perfect.' And it would be. Regardless of the poker, Saturday night hanging out with a group of hot paramedics wasn't something she was going to turn down in a hurry. She grinned and turned to Damien. 'I'd love to come. Thank you.'

Sue lit the two candles on the cake, a five and an eight.

'I can't believe she would have been fifty-eight.' Unshed tears glistened in Hannah's eyes, bringing a lump to Nat's throat.

It was the same every year. No matter how the evening unfolded, the mood always shifted when the cake was cut. The number on it each year seemed to jolt something in all of them. A melancholy settled over the room as they went through the motions of singing 'Happy Birthday'.

It was also the moment when Nat wondered how life might have been if things had been different; if her mother hadn't celebrated her fortieth birthday on the back of a horse; if she hadn't died and had been there to guide them into adulthood. Would she be such a disaster if she'd had her mother to confide in and accept advice from? Unfortunately, it was something she would wonder about each year as they cut the cake but knew she'd never receive an answer.

Chapter Five

Hannah lapsed into thought as she and Amy drove home from her father's. Another year had passed, and another celebration of her mother's life was over. She was glad it was over too. On top of Phyllie's annoyance with her, being in the same room as her sister often felt suffocating. While on the one hand she felt sorry for Nat having lost her job and needing to find a new place to live, it didn't excuse Nat always trying to show her up in front of her entire family. She was sick of it. She spoke of Hannah taking digs at her, yet she was happy to dish out as many as she could muster. Zane Fox's constant ringing and texting hadn't helped either. She'd ended up turning her phone off. She'd message him and try and get rid of him once she was on her own later.

Hannah turned into the driveway and pulled up alongside Damien's blue SUV in their double garage.

She switched off the engine and turned to Amy. 'Grab your bag and let's head inside. It's late. I'd like you to go straight in and have a shower and get ready for bed, okay?'

'But we have to talk about the horse riding. Dad said we'd do that as soon as we got home.'

'No, he said we would talk about it at home, not as soon as we got home.'

Amy kicked the back of the front car seat. 'That's not fair.'

Hannah held up her hand. 'Dad and I will discuss it, but if you're going to act like that, I can tell you what the answer is straightaway. You're eleven, as you keep reminding me, and kicking things and having tantrums to get your own way isn't going to work.'

Amy opened her mouth, appeared to think better of it, and closed it again. She pushed open the car door and disappeared through the internal access and into the house.

Damien appeared in the garage. 'You okay?'

Hannah loved her husband for those two little words. He knew her better than anyone, and could probably tell from her face that she was tired and not in the mood for anything else tonight.

She mustered a smile. 'Big day, and Amy's not too happy with me.'

They walked through to the warm wood tones of the country-style kitchen, and after putting her bag in the nook she'd had specially designed to ensure clutter was contained, Hannah pulled out a stool from the island bench and sank on to it.

Damien picked up Amy's school bag from the kitchen table where she'd left it. He unzipped the bag and removed her lunchbox and drink bottle. 'What was with your phone tonight? Martin doesn't normally contact you after hours.'

'Problem with a client.' Hannah avoided her husband's gaze.

'Really? It's unusual that they'd expect so much after-hours attention.'

Nausea swirled in her belly. 'They're worth a lot, and if we want to keep them then Martin needs to be available. He's been keeping me up to date, that's all. I'll sort it out tomorrow.'

Damien raised an eyebrow. 'Martin's your boss, can't he deal with a problem client himself?'

Hannah hesitated; she hated lying to her husband. 'Usually, but as it's one of my clients he's keeping me in the loop. I'd prefer not to talk about it, if that's okay. It's been a hard day and I'm done in.'

'I assume Amy added to that on the way home by badgering you about the horse riding?'

'That and after-school care. She wants to be allowed to come home by herself.'

'Fair enough.'

'What?'

Damien looked up from the lunchbox he was removing empty packaging from. 'It's pretty normal for kids to walk home and look after themselves in the afternoon.'

'But things are different now. There are so many more dangers and predators. Kids aren't safe like they used to be.'

He smiled.

'What? Are you saying I'm wrong?'

He put Amy's lunchbox in the drying rack and came around and sat on a stool next to Hannah. He took her hands in his. 'Yes, I am.'

She pulled her hands away from him. 'And what do you base your finding on?'

Damien pushed his fingers through his thick black hair. 'I don't think much has changed at all. Predators were around when we were kids and accidents happened. Social media is the difference. Back then, you only heard about those things if it was your school or near your home. Now you hear about everything from every part of the world. It's surprising anyone goes out at all with the dangers we're supposedly all facing.'

'Not supposedly, Damien – they're real dangers.'

'With very low percentages actually affecting you. You need to live life, not be scared to venture out of your comfort zone. That's what we should be teaching Amy, not that she needs to be scared of everything.'

'So, you want her to come home to an empty house?'

'I didn't say I *want* her to; I'm saying I don't have an issue with it.'

Hannah shook her head. 'I imagine you're also going to say she should go horse riding too?'

Damien smiled. 'Yes, that's exactly what I'm going to say.'

'But my mother died from riding. That proves it's dangerous.'

'That proves she was unlucky and, to be honest, irresponsible. If she'd been wearing a helmet, things could have ended up very different. She hit her unprotected head on a rock. That's the lesson we need to drill into Amy. To wear protective clothing and helmets when riding horses or bikes. To think about risk and minimise it.'

'Not doing it eliminates it.'

'You can't continue to wrap her in cotton wool. I know you're doing it because you love her, but you'll end up pushing her away and causing her to rebel. What are you going to do when she's old enough to drive? Refuse to let her get her learner's permit? Ban her from getting her licence? And what about when her friends have their licences, are you going to stop her going in their cars?'

Hannah didn't respond. *Yes, yes and yes* was what she wanted to say but she also knew he had a point. She might only be eleven now, but she was growing up and was going to push beyond Hannah's comfort level.

'You can't control everything, Han. It's just not possible. Sometimes you need to relax and allow situations to unfold as they're supposed to. Without interference.' He hesitated for a moment.

'What? You were about to say something else.'

'Just that I think you need to be a bit careful with Nat too. The way you spoke to her tonight wasn't very kind, under the circumstances.'

Hannah felt like she'd been slapped. Damien rarely criticised her, he usually had her back. She folded her arms across her chest.

'Did you happen to notice the way she spoke to me? Deliberately undermining me at every possible chance with Amy?'

He nodded. 'I did, but I think it was retaliation. She needed comfort and support tonight, not a reminder that she's been in these circumstances many times before due to her reckless decision-making. She has to live with the consequences, not us.'

Hannah sighed. Damien was saying exactly what Nat herself had said. 'I didn't mean for it to come out like that.' And she hadn't. When she was stressed Hannah was at her worst. She knew that but found it hard to control. Zane Fox's reappearance coupled with the anniversary dinner had been a lethal combination. It was no wonder she'd been on edge. On a normal night she'd have a longer fuse with both Amy and Nat, but tonight had been anything but normal. Usually she could tell Damien this, and enjoy his comfort, but with Zane back in the picture it just wasn't possible. She took a deep breath, realising he was waiting for her to explain.

'I just worry about her. She's thirty-three, about to be homeless and unable to hold down a job for more than a few months. It's not a good position to be in at her age.'

'No, but again, it's not our life to live. She'll move in with Phyllie next week, so that's one problem sorted already. She does so much volunteer work that I'm sure something will lead from that. She puts everyone else first, babe, and karma has to repay that at some stage.'

Hannah nodded. *Karma.* Her gut twisted at the word. She had a nasty feeling karma, in the form of Zane Fox, was about to come back to bite her.

Hannah waited until Damien headed upstairs to have a shower before switching her phone back on. Twelve text messages and two missed calls. The last three text messages said the same thing.

> Don't ever hang up on me again. Call me immediately or there will be consequences.

A shiver ran down Hannah's spine. She wasn't going to ring him. Instead, she started keying a message into her phone.

> What do you want? Our business was finalised twelve years ago.

The response was almost immediate.

> Like I said, a development has occurred. Meet me tomorrow at that cafe near your work.

> No. I want nothing more to do with you. Don't contact me again.

Hannah's fingers trembled as she hit the send button on her phone.

> Not your call. Meet me at the cafe at eight a.m. tomorrow. I only need a few minutes of your time. If you're a no show I'll pay a visit to Damien instead. I'm not sure if he'd find meeting me devastating or enlightening. See you at eight and don't be stupid. I have the potential to ruin you.

Hannah stared at the message before turning off her phone and closing her eyes. He was right. One conversation with Damien and he could ruin her completely.

Hannah tossed and turned most of the night, waking in a pool of sweat. Amy had been the focus of her dreams; riding a horse at breakneck speed, bareback and at times standing up. Her mother was on the sidelines cheering her on. It was a relief to wake up, but then the thought of the day ahead, particularly the meeting with Zane Fox, rattled her. She'd elected to wear a grey pencil skirt and jacket with her heeled ankle boots. Today she needed the extra boost a favourite pair of boots would give her. Her hair was secured in a high bun, and she hoped that she exuded a *don't mess with me* air. There was only one scenario she could imagine would bring Zane Fox back into their lives and, no, she wasn't going to allow herself even to think it.

Hannah pulled into her parking space underneath No Risk's offices and switched off the engine. She got out, took a deep breath and walked swiftly to the lifts. There was nothing to worry about. She said this over and over in her head, trying to convince herself the words were true as she caught the lift to the ground floor and walked out of the building toward Cafe Reiki.

Zane, balding and at least ten kilos heavier since she'd last seen him twelve years ago, was sipping his coffee at a table at the back of the cafe, partially hidden by a large plant. That was good at least; no one was likely to see them together.

He stood and held out his hand when she approached the table. Was he kidding? She was not going to enter into any pleasantries. Her only objective was to get rid of him. She ignored his hand and sat in the seat across from him.

'Coffee?' He nodded toward the menu.

'I'm not interested in anything other than having you confirm you'll never contact me again. Why am I here and what do you want?' Hannah was relieved that her voice sounded strong and steady. Luckily he couldn't see her knees trembling beneath the table.

He raised an eyebrow as if to suggest her rudeness was uncalled for. 'There's been an unexpected development.'

She felt her heart rate increase as he took a notepad from his briefcase and laid it on the table. It was open on a page full of writing.

'I had a phone call from Family Information Networks and Discovery last week. As you may recall, FIND was the agency that helped us find out what happened to Damien's parents.'

Hannah nodded. She remembered the name.

'Damien's biological mother, Janine Markinson, contacted them and was subsequently put in touch with me. She would like to meet her son.'

A cold chill ran through Hannah. 'Why?'

'What do you mean why?'

'I mean, why after all these years does she suddenly want to find Damien, and why did they refer her to you?'

'She wants to find her son as his biological father died recently and she feels she now has closure with what he did to her. As for why they referred her to me, when we did our investigations years ago to provide Damien with information about his family, we had him sign a document that said he was preventing any future contact from anyone related to his biological family. I was listed on that form as his legal representative.'

Hannah thought back to the original findings. It had been a devastating shock to learn the truth about Damien's biological parents; that his mother, at seventeen, was the victim of a brutal rape from which Damien resulted. Hannah had made the excruciating decision to keep this information from him. She'd explained to Zane at the time her reasoning for this decision, and for an additional fee he'd agreed to help her. At the last minute he'd increased his fee by five thousand dollars, threatening to tell Damien everything, including Hannah's request to keep the information from him if she didn't pay. What had started as an honest business trans-action turned sour very quickly.

'What happened to his father?' Hannah asked. 'You said he died. Did you find out how?'

Zane nodded. 'Of course. I found out everything I thought you'd want to know.' He consulted his notebook. 'He was stabbed in a prison riot two months ago. He's been in and out of prison over the past twelve years for a range of offences. The last one was a hit-and-run involving a three-year-old child.'

Hannah swallowed. A three-year-old. How could anyone live with themselves after doing that? 'Nothing's changed,' she said to Zane, 'I don't want Damien learning any of this.'

'His mother hasn't done anything wrong,' Zane said. 'I did a bit of poking around, and she's a schoolteacher. She never married and has no other children. From all reports, she's a good person who suffered terribly as a consequence of what happened to her.'

She certainly had – the poor woman. 'As I said, it doesn't change anything. I feel sorry for her, but I can't even begin to imagine how Damien, or his adoptive mum, would take all of this. Please tell the agency that our position hasn't changed. That we don't want any information released.'

Zane's eyes were on Hannah. He picked up his coffee and sipped it.

'What? You have a problem with my decision?'

'No. To be honest, I don't care what your decision is. But you've put me in a compromising position. I'm the gatekeeper to whether Janine can find information about her son. I'm no longer comfort-able having my name all over the documentation that prevents her from gaining any knowledge about Damien.'

Hannah breathed a sigh of relief. 'If that's all, let's have the documents changed. Get my name put on them, or a lawyer's. I'm sure that's not a big deal.'

'You'd have to get Damien to sign them again.'

Hannah smiled. 'Damien blindly signs anything I put in front of him. That's not a concern.'

'So, he trusts you.'

'Of course he does. He's my husband.'

'But he shouldn't, should he? Not with the lies you're capable of telling him.'

Fear flooded through Hannah. 'What is it you're after, Zane?'

'Compensation. I will have my name removed from the forms and sign a document saying I'll never reveal anything about the case. My fee for this is ten thousand dollars.'

Hannah gasped. 'What? You've already been paid, and you've signed a confidentiality agreement. I have a copy of it. You've had twelve years to blackmail me since then, why now?'

'The agreement from twelve years ago clearly states I won't reveal any information that we discovered about Damien's birth parents. It says nothing about his birth mother making contact twelve years later, requiring me to tell more lies. If you wish me to continue lying for you, I expect compensation. It's as simple as that.'

'Blackmail is hardly simple.'

'It's not blackmail. You are asking me, again, to do something unethical and this is my fee.'

Hannah stood and slung her bag over her shoulder. Her legs were trembling. She wasn't going to listen to any more of this.

Zane wrapped his hands around his coffee cup. 'Like I said in my text – don't be stupid, Hannah. You've got a week to come up with my fee. If I don't hear from you, I'll happily tell Damien's mother what you did twelve years ago. How *you* covered up her story and lied to your husband. She should at least be warned about her daughter-in-law before she becomes part of her son's life.'

Hannah turned and walked out of the cafe, bile rising in her throat with every footstep.

Chapter Six

On Friday afternoon, Nat stopped off at the shops on the way to Phyllie's and bought a bottle of her grandmother's favourite Brown Brothers Prosecco. It was a relief that Phyllie had such inexpensive tastes when it came to wine. Even in her unemployed state, the twelve-dollar bottle was affordable.

A little after three, she brought her blue Hyundai to a stop on the road outside Phyllie's adorable white two-storey home with its burgundy roof and trim. She couldn't remember when she'd last spent time on her own with Phyllie. Obviously, that was going to change if she did move in with her. While she appreciated Phyllie's offer, the idea of having to move in with her eighty-nine-year-old grandmother because she was such a failure was depressing. She should be buying her own house at this stage and settling down, not running back to family every time she stuffed up.

She sighed. The reality was she had no choice right now. Having somewhere to live would at least take one stress off her and allow her to devote her time to job hunting. As she slipped the bottle of wine into her bag and opened the car door she was greeted by a high-pitched squeal coming from the side of Phyllie's house. An explosion of expletives followed it.

'Get the hell out of here, you great bastard,' Phyllie's crystal-clear tone rang out.

Nat slammed her door shut and ran down the driveway and around the side of the house. She stopped as she reached the back garden, her hand flying to her mouth. *What on earth?* Phyllie was standing in front of her flowering camellia hedge with a broom in her hands, swatting it in the direction of a large white goat. Its head was down and short beige horns pointed in her grandmother's direction.

Phyllie looked up, relief flooding her face as she saw Nat. 'Thank God you're here. Turn the hose on this bloody creature, would you? It's already eaten my sweet alyssum and by the look in its eyes right now I'd say it might eat me if it means getting to my camellias.'

Nat looked about, spying the hose attached to the side of the house. She quickly unravelled it and turned it on. She directed it at the goat, causing Phyllie to squeal. 'Just the goat, not me, you silly girl.'

The goat spun round as the water hit it and Phyllie shoved the broom at its bottom. 'Be gone with you,' she yelled.

Nat had to jump out of the way as the goat came galloping past her and out on to the street. It turned right and disappeared.

Nat turned off the hose, dropped it and ran over to Phyllie. 'Are you okay?'

Her smile wobbled. 'Course I am. Bloody Leon and his stupid goat.'

'Who's Leon?'

'Neighbour two doors down. He took it on to help out a sick friend. Stupid beast gets out all the time.'

Nat took the broom and tucked her arm under Phyllie's. She couldn't miss the fact that she was trembling, or that her arm was bleeding. 'You're hurt.' The cut on her arm was deep. 'This is going to need stitching.'

Phyllie tut-tutted. 'We don't have time for that. We've got poker to learn and, looking at that bottle sticking out of your bag, bubbles to drink.'

'Not with your arm bleeding like that.'

'He's got sharp horns that little bugger. Got me before I could get to the broom. I need to be more vigilant and have my goat protection kit in easier reach.'

Nat led Phyllie into the house via the back door, through the sunroom and kitchen and into the living room, where she deposited her into her favourite high-backed armchair. An eighty-nine-year-old woman shouldn't need a goat protection kit, whatever that might entail. 'This has happened before?'

She nodded. 'A few times. He's partial to my roses when they're blooming. I guess I'll have that to look forward to again in a few months.'

'Phyllie, I'm pretty sure you aren't allowed a goat in your garden. Let's ring the council.'

A look of horror crossed Phyllie's face. 'And dob Leon in? Gosh no, he'd never forgive me. I'll be fine, love. You don't need to worry about it.'

Blood was now seeping on to her sleeve.

'I need to take you to the doctor.'

She shook her head.

'It needs stitching and cleaning up. You'll probably need a tetanus injection too.'

Phyllie rolled her eyes. 'You're beginning to sound like that worrywart of a sister of yours.' Her lips curled into a smile. 'Bet she could tell us exactly how many injuries and fatalities there have been from goat-related incidents. You're not to tell her about this, you hear me. She's already worried about me falling; add a goat into the equation, and even with you living here she'll have me shipped out of here immediately.'

Nat nodded. 'I won't tell her, but unless you let me take you to the doctor, I'm calling Damien. If he's in the area, I'm sure he'd drop in and stitch your arm.'

Phyllie thought about this for a moment. 'There's probably a confidentiality aspect to his job, so he wouldn't be allowed to tell Hannah. Okay, call him. Then once we get rid of him, you'll need to find the wine glasses and the cards. We've got some poker to learn.'

Half an hour later Damien knelt in front of Phyllie's armchair, his paramedic bag by his side, and secured a dressing over the wound he'd just finished stitching. 'I really think you should go and see your doctor.'

'Why? You've given me a tetanus injection and stitched it. What more could I possibly want?'

'A complete check-over for a start. You should be monitored at your age.'

Phyllie tutted. 'Not you too! You sound as bad as that overprotective, ridiculous wife of yours.'

The corners of Nat's mouth twitched.

'She just cares about you, Phyllie.'

Phyllie frowned. 'You are not to tell her about this visit today, Damien, do you hear me?'

He nodded.

'And Nat and I have poker training to complete this afternoon, so there's no way I have time for a doctor's visit, so let's just forget about that.'

'That sounds like an unfair advantage.' Damien winked at Nat. 'You'd better not bankrupt me.'

'Very unlikely,' Nat said. 'I don't have all that much to invest tomorrow night anyway.'

'You'll have my hundred-dollar investment,' Phyllie said. 'I'll be trusting Damien to make sure you don't use any of your own money. Not that you'll need to. It only takes a couple of hands to build your bank, and you'll do that easily once I've imparted my wisdom.'

Damien sighed. 'Maybe I'd better stay and have this wisdom rub off on me.'

Phyllie's eyes narrowed, and she pointed to the chair across from her. 'Take a seat.' She turned to Nat. 'Go and fetch the poor man a drink, would you. He looks exhausted.'

Nat had to admit that Phyllie was right; Damien did look exhausted.

'Just water thanks, Nat.'

She left the room, still able to hear the conversation clearly from the small kitchen.

'Are you okay, love?' Phyllie asked. 'You seem to have lost all your spark.'

Nat stopped momentarily. Phyllie was right, Damien did seem very flat. He had at dinner the other night too. She wasn't surprised really, being married to Hannah could hardly be a barrel of laughs, but he'd always seemed upbeat before.

'Just long hours,' he answered. 'Wearing me a bit thin at the moment.'

'You're sure that's all?'

'I'm sure. Now, I'd better get on. Pam's waiting for me in the ambulance, and other jobs have probably come in while we've been here.'

Nat opened the fridge and poured a glass of cold water from a jug into a glass and took it back to the living room. She handed it to Damien.

He accepted it gratefully, chugged it down and then stood. 'Now, you look after yourself, Phyllie. I'll pop back in on Monday and check the wound for you, but if it starts bleeding, oozing pus or smelling, you call me straightaway. It means it's infected and we'll need to organise antibiotics for you. I've left you fresh dressings, so make sure you change them at least once a day. This one will be alright until the morning.'

Phyllie saluted him. 'Yes, sir.'

Damien grinned as he handed Nat the empty glass. 'I'll see you tomorrow night. You've got the address?'

Nat nodded.

'Be prepared to lose all your money,' Phyllie called after Damien as he made his way towards the front door. 'Nat will be ready for Vegas by the time we're finished this afternoon.'

'Looking forward to it.' Damien headed out of the door and along the shrub-lined path to where the ambulance was parked at the start of the driveway.

Phyllie let out a laugh before turning to Nat. 'Now, why don't you go and get the cards, the wine and the platter of food that's in the fridge, and we'll get on with the real reason you came over today. All this interruption from goats and Damien has thrown us way off schedule. Poker first, then we'll look at the room. I was thinking that it would suit me if you moved in on Thursday. That will give us both a few more days to enjoy our freedom.'

Nat nodded. It would give her a few days to organise her belongings, not that she had much to move, and give more thought to her job situation.

As Phyllie explained the tips and tricks that would ensure Nat had an advantage over most Texas Hold 'Em players, the two women enjoyed the Prosecco, and the cheese and antipasto Phyllie had prepared. The conversation soon turned to Nat's unemployed status.

'Have you had any thoughts about where you'd like to work next, love?'

Nat sighed. 'I don't have the energy to even look. I'm pretty sure most employers will look at my résumé and throw it back at me. Five jobs in two years doesn't thrill prospective bosses, especially when I was fired from all of them.'

'Put me down as a reference,' Phyllie said. 'I won't say anything negative at all.'

Nat laughed. She could imagine her grandmother singing her praises to a potential employer. 'Thanks, but I'll sort it out myself. I can continue my volunteer work at Shared while I'm looking. It keeps me busy and at least I'm valued there.'

Phyllie picked the cards up and dealt them each two cards face down, ready for their preflop betting. 'You have a good heart, Nathalia. You remember that. It's much more important than competing for promotions or pats on the back. Stay true to who you are and don't worry about other people. Good things will come to you if you're patient, you mark my words.'

A round table with a green felt Texas Hold 'Em mat covering it, poker chips and dim lighting cleverly transformed Damien's workmate's family room to provide the atmosphere of a real casino. Phyllie's words from the previous day replayed in Nat's head as excitement flittered in her stomach. Was this what her grandmother had meant by *good things will come to you if you're patient*? She couldn't believe the pile of winnings in front of her, which was growing with nearly every hand. Nat turned over her hole cards to reveal an ace and a jack. When added to the five cards already drawn, she had a straight. A collective groan went up around the table, while excitement caught in Nat's throat. She'd won, again!

'Why'd you invite her?' Stu threw his cards down in mock disgust.

Damien laughed. 'I'll be asking for commission at this rate. I should have stuck around at Phyllie's yesterday if her teachings have led to this.'

'Beginner's luck,' Nat said. 'I'm not doing anything special, just getting lucky draws with the cards.'

'Let's take a break,' Pam suggested. 'Refresh the drinks and taste test those amazing-looking sausage rolls you brought with you, Damien.'

'Hannah's sausage rolls?' Nat's eyes lit up. The one area she was quite happy her sister excelled at was cooking. She wasn't a bad cook herself, but Hannah's baking was to die for. The pastry on her sausage rolls melted in your mouth.

The group moved from the dimly lit family room out to the back veranda. It was a chilly night, but Matt had the outdoor heaters going and the area was very cosy.

Nat sipped a glass of mineral water. She wanted to keep a clear head to remember everything Phyllie had instructed her on the previous day.

'Hear you had a run-in with a goat yesterday,' Pam said.

Nat shook her head. 'Not me, my grandmother. I'm still not exactly sure how the neighbour gets away with keeping a goat in his back garden, but my grandmother doesn't want to report him. I hope she doesn't get knocked over by it and badly hurt next time.'

'Did you speak to the neighbour?'

Nat shook her head. 'I went over and banged on his door, but he wasn't home. He probably won't be very appreciative of the note I left him.' Nat had stuck a sheet of paper to Leon's front door that simply said, 'Stop your bloody goat from escaping, or the council will be called.' She knew Phyllie didn't want her threatening him with the council, but as she hadn't signed it, Leon would never know who'd written it.

'So, this grandma of yours is a poker expert?' Matt joined the conversation.

Nat laughed. 'I don't know about that, but some of her tips are certainly helping tonight. Although I've been lucky with the cards I've been dealt.'

'I don't know,' Matt said. 'There's the cards, of course, but there's a lot of skill and strategy involved too. I think you're under-playing how good you are.'

Nat's cheeks burned with a combination of embarrassment and delight. Matt's words were like a validation. Maybe she was actually good at something. Part of her wished Hannah was here to hear him. To know she wasn't a complete loser.

'While I'm scared that Matt's words are probably true,' Pam said, 'we're hoping you're right about beginner's luck. Taking a break might stop your winning streak and we'll get our money back from you.'

'It's nice to see someone other than Matt winning for a change,' Damien said.

Matt laughed. 'Might be part of my strategy. Don't worry, I have weapons of my own I haven't even brought out yet.'

Damien raised his eyebrows. 'That sounds like desperation talking.'

Matt clapped him on the back. 'You won't be saying that in a couple of hours when I have all of Nat's money and yours too.'

Nat laughed, enjoying the friendly ribbing. It was such a con-trast to being around the staff at Benedict's. Todd had done his best to make her feel inferior in her position, and even though her focus was always on her clients and their well-being, it was hard not to be affected by it. She'd felt like an outsider among the cliquey staff, reminding her of her teenage years, of not fitting in at school and of feeling inferior as she watched Hannah excel at everything academic. She tried to explain to her father, when he suggested tutoring, that it wasn't that she didn't understand the subject matter, she just didn't have time to study it. She was too busy reading up on community interests and, as she got older, attending protests and fighting for causes she believed in.

It wasn't until the final year of high school when she met Pip that she found an ally, someone who thought as passionately about causes as she did. But tonight, for the first time in a long time, she was surrounded by a nice group of people who wanted no more than to have a fun night and treated her with the same kindness and friendliness as they treated each other. On top of that, she'd won close to a thousand dollars. Enough to get her through the next couple of weeks while she tried to find another job. She just needed to make sure she didn't fall prey to Matt's strategy and lose it all.

She didn't.

Not only had Nat retained the initial thousand she'd won, but she'd more than doubled it. As she wound her way through the quiet streets of Donvale, she couldn't believe she'd walked away with twenty-six hundred dollars. When Damien had invited her to join his friendly poker game, she hadn't realised that the stakes would rise as high as they had. She wasn't sure if it was the adrenaline of winning a few hands or the buzz of being among such lovely people, but Nat had felt confident with each bet she made. When she won five hands in a row, she'd considered stopping. But a little encouragement from Matt to continue was all she needed. 'Come on,' he'd said. 'You can't take that much from me and then stop. You've got to give me a chance to win it back.' He'd be regretting that encouragement now. She'd cleaned him out.

He'd just laughed and shrugged it off when at the end of the night she'd offered to reimburse him. 'Don't be silly. It's only once a month, and I normally win.' He'd waved his hand in the direction of the others. 'It's this lot that usually walks out with tears streaming down their faces. I'll survive.'

Her chest had expanded with pride as he'd once again told her that she was a natural, that she had a skill she shouldn't ignore. 'You could win a lot on the online tables.' He'd written down the names of two of the poker sites he played regularly and handed them to her. 'Ring me if you need a hand on how to set up accounts, or ask Damo – he does pretty well too.'

That last comment had piqued her interest. Damien played online poker? It was the first she'd heard of this.

'Do they always play for that much?' Nat asked Damien as they made their way home. Hannah and Amy had dropped him at Matt's earlier in the evening so he could have a few drinks, and she'd offered to drive him home.

'Not usually.' He grinned. 'I think he smelled fresh blood and thought you'd be a walkover.'

'He gave me some info about online poker and suggested I try it out. Said that you played it too.'

'Don't tell Hannah.'

Nat laughed before turning to Damien and realising he was serious. Her smile faded. 'She doesn't know?'

He shook his head. 'She knows I play cards and other games online, but she doesn't know I bet money. You know what she's like, she'd have every gambling statistic known to man charted and stuck to the wall. I don't play for much and my account is actually in credit, so I'm not losing money. It's just a bit of fun and something I do to unwind.'

Nat kept her attention on the road ahead, letting Damien's words sink in. She knew Hannah was a pain when it came to just about everything, but she also knew her well enough to know she'd be devastated if she found out her husband was keeping a secret from her. It surprised her to feel a jolt of loyalty towards her sister.

'I think you should tell her. If you haven't lost anything then it isn't a big deal. But if you did start to lose a lot then it's probably good someone else knows about it and can help you put the brakes on it.'

Damien laughed.

'What?'

'You're the last person I'd ever expect to stand up for Hannah. Don't get me wrong, it's lovely to see. Just very unexpected.' He sighed. 'But yes, you're right. I probably should tell her. I'd hate it if she had secrets from me. And I take it you're going to tell her if I don't?'

Nat didn't respond immediately. Would she tell Hannah? She felt like she'd have to. Lying, in her opinion, was a kind of cheating, and whether he'd won or lost money, that was in effect what Damien was doing.

'Don't answer,' he said. 'If nothing else, I'm glad to see you care about your sister enough to be worried. I'll tell her tonight if she's still awake, or tomorrow morning.'

Nat turned to him. 'Really?'

He crossed his arms, a smile playing on his lips. 'I think after your success tonight, you should be shouting us breakfast tomorrow. Come over in the morning with some bakery treats under the guise of being a grateful sister-in-law and you can grill Hannah then.' He laughed. 'Although she might have already filed for divorce once she hits the roof about my non-existent gambling problem.'

Chapter Seven

Hannah's mind ticked over as she wiped down the kitchen benches. She was desperately trying to find a solution to the Zane Fox situation that didn't include paying him more money, and didn't include telling Damien the truth. So far she'd come up with nothing. How had she got herself into this? She'd done her best to convince herself at the time that what she'd done was in everyone's best interest. Damien would be devastated if he learned the truth about his biological parents, and Trish, his adoptive mother, had been under extreme stress with her cancer treatment. She'd confided in Hannah early on in her relationship with Damien that her main fear with adoption was that one day she wouldn't be enough for her son. That he'd decide he wanted a real mother, which would confirm for her that he'd never thought she was.

Now Damien's biological mother wanted to make contact. Why after all these years? He was forty, that was a long time to stay away. She couldn't imagine giving up her baby at birth, no matter what the circumstances. Although she certainly sympathised with Janine. She'd had Amy when she was twenty-four and married, which was a big difference to being a seventeen-year-old schoolgirl and rape victim.

Hannah wondered what Janine was like. She rinsed the cloth under the tap and suddenly dropped it in the sink. She knew her name and the town she lived in. Why hadn't she thought to google her after Zane dropped his bombshell?

She hurried upstairs, poking her head into Amy's room on her way to the bedroom they'd converted into a home office. Amy was sprawled on her bed reading a book. 'You need to get your homework done before we go to Mia's party later this morning.'

Amy groaned. 'Do I have to?'

'Yes, now! Or you can forget about the party. Go downstairs and get your books from your bag. You can do it in the living room or at the kitchen table, if you prefer.'

Amy rolled off the bed, dropping the book on her bedside table. She scowled at Hannah on her way past. 'You don't have to be so mean about it.'

Hannah swallowed. Her tone had been sharp. In fact, her tolerance for anything right now was non-existent. She needed to be more aware of how she acted. It was hardly fair to take her stress out on her daughter, or anyone else.

She continued on to the office, sat down at the desk and keyed in her password, waiting as her computer sprang to life. How would she explain what she was doing if Damien walked in? She hesitated before typing in Janine's name and hometown in the search bar. She looked up people all the time for work, and if he did come into the bedroom, he wouldn't be interested in the specifics of what she was doing. He was out in the garden fixing some loose wooden slats on the decking, so was unlikely to come into the house at all, let alone upstairs to her office.

The search results came up, and Hannah swallowed. *Janine Markinson, Rape. Teenage victim of rape pregnant. Rape Baby Given Up for Adoption.* There were a number of other more recent results. *Teacher Awarded Victorian Education Excellence Award. Tallangetti Primary Honours VEEA Recipient.* She clicked on a recent article and drew in a breath when the smiling face of Janine Markinson filled the screen. The similarity between her and Damien was unmissable. Her thick black hair curtained her face; her smile was full of warmth and humour. She'd been awarded the Excellence Award for her service both within the school and the community. From what she read, Janine Markinson was a much-loved teacher and a highly valued member of the Tallangetti community. Tears filled Hannah's eyes. This was Damien's mother. When, twelve years earlier, she'd decided to lie to him about his biological parents, the image she'd conjured up of his mother had been very different. She'd imagined a hard, bitter woman with an ever-present cigarette between her lips who spoke in a raspy voice. She had no idea why she'd pictured her this way, other than it helped ease her conscience over lying to Damien. The woman looking back at her from the screen was nothing like that. She was the type of woman you'd want to know, that you'd be proud to call your mother. She was precisely the type of woman that Trish had been worried would replace her.

Hannah hesitated before opening a website containing articles that dated back over forty years. It appeared that ten years ago someone had done a study of teenage rape victims and loaded the old newspaper articles as part of their report. There was a blurred photo of Janine as a teenage girl. An older man had his arm around her and looked like he was shielding her. She looked young and frightened. Reading the article, she realised it was a picture of Janine leaving the court where Calvin Deeks had been sentenced for rape.

Hannah clicked on the other articles, but there were no photos of Calvin Deeks. There was one more of Janine, in her school uniform and smiling for the camera. Hannah assumed it had been taken before the rape and supplied to the paper. The Rape Baby article was text only, just giving the details of the baby's birth.

> A healthy baby boy weighing 7lb 8 ounces was birthed by Janine Markinson this morning at 8.21am. The baby has already been placed with the authorities where adoption has been arranged.

Hannah leaned back in her chair. What a mess. Seeing Janine made her wonder whether she had done the right thing. Had protecting Damien from the truth meant he'd missed out on the opportunity to get to know his mother? She shook herself. She was being silly. No, it hadn't. If she hadn't hired Zane, she would never have found out any of this. The adoption authorities would not provide any information as Janine had requested that her file be sealed and no details released. Due to the nature of how she had become pregnant, her request for privacy had been granted. What Hannah hadn't counted on was Janine changing her mind and wanting to make contact with Damien.

When Zane had uncovered the truth about Damien's biological parents and seen Hannah's distress at the thought of telling her husband, he'd agreed to help her cover up the facts, for an additional fee. He'd come across a story around the time of Damien's birth that Hannah might want to present to him as his own story. A young couple and their newborn baby had been involved in a horrific car accident on their return from the hospital. The baby was only two days old. Although the baby had survived, both parents died at the scene, and with no other living relatives, the baby had been placed in foster care awaiting adoption. The article did not name any of the people involved but it happened in Albosta, a large town not far from Tallangetti, and it was the hospital in which Damien had been born. While of course he would be devastated to learn this about his biological parents, Hannah had reasoned that Damien would move on with life and have closure. If he'd discovered the truth, she'd thought he'd never recover and would struggle to come to terms with his gene pool.

She cleared her search history and closed the lid on her laptop. It was all very well thinking through the pros and cons of what she'd done, but deep down she still believed she'd done the right thing. But now, paying Zane off, which she had no idea how she would do without Damien noticing money missing, would take her deception to a whole other level and that was something she wasn't sure she could do. She fingered the heart-shaped pendant, wishing she could call her mother for advice. A lump formed in her throat as she thought of her mother, who always seemed to have a solution to any problem. She did her best to swallow it down, wondering instead if Phyllie would be home later. She could pop in and see her while Amy was at the party. She slipped her phone from her pocket and rang her number.

After organising to drop in on Phyllie later that morning, Hannah made her way down to the kitchen, where Damien was making coffee. It was only nine, but they'd all been woken early when a neighbour started his lawnmower at seven.

He raised a cup to her. 'Want one?'

She took a seat at the counter. 'Yes, please.'

'We should probably wait until Nat arrives, but I'm still half asleep.'

Hannah stared at her husband. They'd been awake for two hours and he hadn't mentioned Nat visiting. She hadn't spoken to her sister since the family dinner and had no desire to. 'Why's Nat coming over?'

Damien blushed. 'We discussed something last night that she wants further clarification on. Long story, but there's something I need to talk to you about.' He handed her a cup of coffee and sat down on a stool next to her.

Nerves swirled in Hannah's stomach. Did he know about Zane Fox? Had he guessed something was up with her? She waited, her hands clenching the cup tightly.

Damien cleared his throat. 'I've been keeping something from you because I was worried you might overreact.'

Hannah stared at him again. Wherever this was going, it wasn't what she'd expected. 'Okay, go on.'

'You know how I play solitaire and other card games online sometimes?'

Hannah nodded.

'I also play online poker.'

'You spend money on it?'

Damien nodded. 'A bit.'

Her husband played online poker? He squandered their savings on gambling? 'How much have you lost? You know the long-term odds of actually winning at something like that are very slim. You'll generally lose at least eighty-five percent of the time.'

Damien shook his head. 'Remember I said I hadn't told you because I was worried you'd overreact? Imagine your glass was half full. If it were, you'd have just asked me how much I'd won, not lost.'

Hannah put her cup back on the counter. 'Okay, how much have you won?'

'About the same as I've lost. Not a lot. I'm not playing it to win big, just to have some fun. It only costs a dollar to enter the cheaper games, so you don't need to worry. Losing our life savings is not something I plan to do.'

'No one *plans* to lose when they gamble, yet more than four hundred Australians commit suicide each year rather than face their gambling losses. That's more than one a day.'

Damien sighed. 'I knew I shouldn't have told you – and that you'd turn it into some statistical nightmare and take all the fun out of it.'

Hannah's mouth dropped open. 'Is that what you think I do?'

Damien took her hand in his. 'Not on purpose, but sometimes. My gambling isn't a problem, I just thought I should tell you about it. I've been playing for a few years and it seems strange to be keeping something from you.'

Hannah extricated her hand. 'Why tell me now?'

'Nat probably would otherwise. Matt mentioned online poker to her last night and also let on that I play. She was pretty horrified that I hadn't told you.'

'Really? Nat actually cared about me?'

Damien nodded. 'That's why she's coming over this morning. I promised I'd tell you and she's checking up on me. She was right, though. We shouldn't have secrets from each other. I'm sorry I didn't tell you, and promise I'll let you know if I ever think it's becoming a problem.'

We shouldn't have secrets from each other. She swallowed down the lump that kept filling her throat. Would he ever forgive her if he found out what she'd done? She wasn't convinced he would. She was, however, surprised by her sister's loyalty towards her. That was unexpected. 'How did Nat go last night? She can't afford to lose much at the moment.'

'She can now.'

Hannah's eyes widened.

'She cleaned us out, and Matt was betting big. Nat stayed with him in each hand, and nine times out of ten she won.'

'I didn't know she really knew how to play.'

'Phyllie's been teaching her.'

'Phyllie? I thought she was kidding when she offered to teach Nat. What does she know about poker?'

Damien laughed. 'Based on Nat's winning streak last night, I'd say a lot.'

Hannah was standing by the front door waiting for Nat to arrive and contemplating the information Damien had imparted about his online gambling habit, when the doorbell jolted her out of her thoughts.

She whipped the door open, realising she'd been so deep in thought she hadn't even noticed Nat's car turn into the driveway.

Nat raised an eyebrow. 'I wasn't expecting you to be waiting by the door. Does that mean you're excited to see me?' She held out a box to Hannah. 'Pastries. A thank you for Damien including me last night, and I figured after the other night at Dad's anything to make you a bit sweeter was a good idea.'

Hannah stared at her sister for a moment, still trying to get her head around this sudden revelation that gambling was an issue in her family and that Nat had stood up for her with Damien. She chose to ignore Nat's dig at her and took the box. 'Thanks. Come in, I'll make some fresh coffee.'

She led Nat down the carpeted hallway, past the many family photos that decorated the walls, through to the kitchen where Amy, having finished her homework, was sitting at the island bench, headphones on, staring at something on her iPad. Hannah tapped her on the shoulder and she removed her earbuds. 'Time to turn that off.'

Amy scowled at her mother but managed to muster a smile for her aunt. Nat leaned down and hugged her while Hannah busied herself with the coffee machine. 'How are you, princess?'

Amy rolled her eyes. 'Too old to be called that for a start.'

Nat laughed. 'Okay, *Amelia*. Is that better?'

'Yes, *Nathalia*, it is.'

Hannah smiled. Her daughter gave as good as she got. She never had to worry about Amy not standing up for herself.

'Did you hear we're getting a dog?' Amy asked Nat.

Hannah's smile slipped. *What?*

'Mum and Dad thought I was so good with Toby the other night, they decided to get me a dog for my birthday.'

'That's fantastic,' Nat said. 'What type are you going to get?'

Had Damien agreed to this, because she certainly hadn't. She liked dogs, but she didn't like all the work that went with having one.

'A rescue dog. I've been looking online.' She held up her iPad. 'There are so many to choose from. My birthday's still almost three weeks away, so there's plenty of time to make a decision.'

'Hold on a minute.' Hannah placed a steaming hot mug in front of Nat. 'Did Dad say you could have a dog? Because this is the first I've heard about it.'

Amy held the iPad in front of Hannah. A gorgeous brown face stared back at her from the RSPCA page, with a headline that read: 'Bear is looking for a home.'

Bear can keep looking for a home. 'Dad agreed to this?'

'Of course.' Amy slipped off the stool. 'He understands that we need to do our bit to support dogs in shelters, so adopting one is the first step.' She grinned at Nat. 'I've got a few weeks to convince them that Bear will need a friend. Two dogs would be perfect.'

'They sure would,' Nat agreed. 'They'd keep each other company when you're at school. That's exciting news.'

'I'm just going to go and chat to Skye,' Amy said. 'I was telling her about Bear yesterday and I want to show her a photo.'

Hannah shook her head as her daughter left the room. She picked up her coffee and sat on the stool next to Nat.

Nat looked at her and smiled.

'What?'

'Haven't you worked out that your daughter's playing you?'

'What do you mean?'

'The dog. Showing us cute pictures, saying that Damien agreed to it and then adding in the bit about convincing you to get two dogs. I'm guessing Damien knows nothing at all about getting a dog, and Amy's clever enough to make you think you're deciding between whether to get one dog or two, whereas the real decision is whether you are getting a dog at all. She's manipulating the situation beautifully.'

Hannah frowned. Would Amy do that? Would she be clever enough? She shook her head. 'No, she must have spoken to Damien. She's only eleven. She wouldn't come up with a plan like that.'

'Want to bet?'

Irritation overcame Hannah. 'Of course, you think you know my daughter better than I do.'

'Jeepers, no need to snap. I'm just saying I think she's up to something, that's all.'

'I definitely disagree, and anyway, bet what?'

'Let's call Damien in. If he knows about the dog, then you're right, and I'm giving Amy far too much credit for being deceptive. If that's the case, I'll babysit for an entire weekend so you two can get away.'

'And if I'm wrong?'

'Then Amy gets her dog. One, of course, not two, but she gets to pick a rescue dog for her birthday.'

The corners of Hannah's lips twitched. She'd be stupid not to accept the bet. A weekend away with Damien would be lovely, and seeing her sister's face when she realised she was wrong and didn't know her niece as well as she seemed to think she did would be the icing on the cake. She held out her hand. 'Deal.'

'Let's call in Damien.'

'He's popped out to the shops. He'll be back any minute.' Hannah pulled the box of pastries across the counter and opened the lid. 'Mm, these look delicious.' Glazed pecan Danishes, croissants and brioche au chocolat stared back at her. She pushed the box across to Nat. 'Hold on, I'll get us some plates.'

'Did Damien tell you what happened last night?' Nat asked.

'He mentioned you cleaned up, and I'm assuming from the box of pastries he was right.'

Nat grinned. 'Over two grand. Can you believe it?'

Hannah stopped, the plates held in mid-air. 'You're kidding? They bet that kind of money?'

'Damien said not usually, but I think Matt was showing off. Backfired on him.'

'But what if you'd lost?'

'I only took a hundred with me to start with. I just won the first few hands and turned it into more very quickly.'

Hannah placed the plates down in front of Nat. 'Did Damien lose much?'

'No, I don't think so. He said a hundred's his limit and he pulls out then, or before if he knows the night's not going well for him. I don't think he even got through that much last night. Both he and Pam stopped playing once the stakes got too high. Said it was a waste going into the hand as they couldn't keep up with the betting.'

Hannah nodded. That was good to hear at least. But this news that Damien was also playing online poker was worrying. It was gambling and gambling was addictive. The last thing she wanted was to see their life savings disappear. 'Thanks, by the way.'

Nat's eyes widened in surprise. 'For what?'

'For making Damien tell me about the online poker. I'm shocked that he kept it from me.'

'He said he didn't want you to worry. That you might think he was spending lots of money when it's only a hobby that he uses to practise for the real games.'

He was still hiding it from me played over in Hannah's head. She knew it was hypocritical, based on the fact she was keeping a massive secret from Damien, but it made her wonder what else he was hiding. That was not a conversation she was going to have with Nat though. She changed the subject. 'Damien said you were at Phyllie's for poker training on Friday.'

Nat nodded. 'I owe her a commission from what I won.'

Hannah smiled. 'I doubt she'll take it. Look, I know you and I disagree on many things, but Phyllie is one thing we do agree on. I'm really relieved that you're going to move in with her. I know it's probably not ideal from your perspective and might only be short term until you find something else, but she needs help. She's doing too much.'

Hannah was amazed when Nat nodded. She was so used to her sister objecting to everything she suggested.

'And there's that bloody goat too,' Nat said. 'It worries me.'

'What goat?'

Nat hesitated. 'It belongs to a neighbour, but I promised I wouldn't say anything. She thinks if you know, you'll be straight round there packing her bags and driving her to the assisted living place.'

'I wouldn't do that. I'm just worried, and if she's that against going into assisted living, then after you move out we need to work out a schedule for helping her. Get someone in to do the mowing and things like that. I know Dad goes round and does it occasionally, but Phyllie still gets out and does it herself if he hasn't been for a while.'

Nat nodded. 'Getting rid of the goat might be something we should add to the list too.' She met Hannah's eyes. 'When I arrived on Friday it had her trapped in the garden. It was only after her flowers, but she got in its way and it jabbed her with its horn. She needed a couple of stitches and was very shaken up. It scared me, so I'm not surprised it scared her.'

Hannah dropped her pastry on to her plate. 'What? She needed stitches! Jesus, Nat, how come this is the first I'm hearing about it? Did you take her to the doctor?'

Nat looked across the kitchen, through the French doors to the back garden, avoiding Hannah's gaze. 'I had a medical professional come to us. Don't worry, she got proper medical treatment.'

Hannah watched her sister. Nat was a terrible liar. Ever since she was little, she'd refuse to make eye contact and would look off into the distance when she was lying. It was easy to pick up on. 'Why are you lying about that? Was she hurt worse than you're saying?'

Nat sighed and looked back at Hannah. 'I'm not lying. She was attacked by the goat, had a cut that needed stitches, and I had a medical professional attend. There was nothing more to it. It meant we didn't have to waste our afternoon waiting to see a doctor, and she insisted we open the Prosecco I brought with me and get on with our poker training. You know what Phyllie's like. There's no arguing with her.'

'I'll speak to the council tomorrow,' Hannah said. 'See what can be done about the goat.'

'Don't. I suggested I'd speak to the council and Phyllie made me promise not to. She doesn't want to upset her neighbour.'

A key turning in the front door signalled Damien was home. He appeared in the kitchen moments later, a beautifully gift-wrapped box in his hands. He smiled at Nat. 'And the champion returns.'

She laughed. 'Beginner's luck, but it was fun and good timing.'

He put the present on the bench and placed an envelope on top. 'I got some books for Amy to give Mia. She said Mia's a bookworm, so hopefully she'll like them. There's a card there too. Amy just needs to write it. The bookstore wrapped the books, so that makes it easy.'

Hannah glanced at the rustic wooden clock on the kitchen wall. She'd need to leave soon to take Amy to the party. 'Would you mind taking the card up to Amy and asking her to write it? I just want to chat with Nat a bit longer. We're worried about Phyllie.'

Damien picked up the card, concern flooding his face. 'Why, has something else happened?'

'Else?'

'I mentioned the goat incident to Damien last night.' Nat didn't meet Hannah's eyes.

'Really?' Hannah turned to her husband. 'And you didn't say anything?'

'I didn't want to worry you.' Damien's cheeks burned red, something that happened when he lied. Neither her sister nor her husband were any good at lying. Ironic that she, who usually did everything by the book, was so effective at it.

Her eyes flicked between the two of them and they both looked away evasively. 'Okay, enough. Tell me what happened and why you're both lying about it. You're beginning to freak me out.'

Nat exchanged a look with Damien, a look that had Hannah's mind racing. Why were they exchanging secret looks? What was going on here?

Damien sighed. 'Nat rang me on Friday and asked me to drop into Phyllie's and sew up her arm. She was fine, the cut wasn't too deep but did need to be cleaned up. I examined her all over and other than minor shock, she was okay. We didn't tell you because Phyllie said she'd kill us if we did. She said it would be another nail

75

in her coffin regarding assisted living. She said she'd prefer the nail to go in a real coffin than be forced out of her home.'

Hannah tensed. Had she pushed it so far that Phyllie believed she'd force her out of her home? She was only trying to help. 'I'd never do that. I want to make sure she's looked after, that's all. And with Nat moving in I feel a lot more comfortable. We were also talking about putting a roster together to help Phyllie out.'

'Great idea,' Damien said. 'Feel free to put me on it. Anything handy that she needs doing around the house or garden. Now, I'd better get this card up to Amy as you two have to leave for the party soon.'

'Before you go,' Nat said, 'can you settle a bet for us?'

Damien raised his eyebrows. 'Sounds intriguing.'

'Did Amy mention to you that she wanted a dog for her birthday?'

'Really? I thought she wanted an Xbox, which we've both already agreed is not happening.'

'She hasn't said anything to you about a dog?' Hannah hoped he was about to remember that Amy had. She did not want to lose this bet.

Damien shook his head. 'Nope, that I would have remembered.' He frowned. 'Something we need to discuss, I guess. I'm not a total no, but they're a lot of work and a huge commitment. We'd need to weigh up the pros and cons.' He leaned across and kissed Hannah on the forehead. 'Which is what you're good at. I'll expect to see a spreadsheet weighing up all the factors by the end of the day.'

Hannah would have laughed at his light-hearted teasing if she hadn't been so shocked. The way Amy had spoken she was sure that Damien knew about the dog. She turned to Nat, her mouth hanging open.

Nat laughed. 'Guess Amy's getting her dog after all.'

Hannah shook her head. 'I can't believe she did that, and so convincingly.'

'Perhaps she'll be a lawyer. She certainly can lie.'

Hannah nodded. It appeared her daughter could. Considering the lie she was carrying herself, should she be so shocked?

Sparks of annoyance at both Nat and Amy stayed with Hannah as she drove Amy to the party. It wasn't Nat's fault that Amy had lied so convincingly but it was frustrating that her sister had seen through it and she hadn't. She stayed to chat with the other mums for a few minutes before excusing herself and driving the ten minutes from Donvale to Phyllie's house in Blackburn. With its proximity to Blackburn Lake Sanctuary, it was a beautiful leafy area; an unexpected oasis in the heart of suburbia.

Phyllie had been suspicious on the phone when Hannah had called her earlier.

'Why do you want to come and see me?'

'I'd like to talk to you about that in person, if you don't mind.'

'What has Nat or Damien said to you?'

Hannah realised Phyllie was worrying that she knew about the goat incident. 'Nothing. It's not to do with them.'

'Oh.' Phyllie's voice had been tinged with relief for just a moment. But then almost as quickly refilled with suspicion. 'What is it about then? I can tell you right now if it has anything to do with my living arrangements, I'll disinherit you immediately. Nat's moving in on Thursday, and that should keep you happy.'

'Phyllie,' Hannah had assured her, 'I need your advice. I've done something I probably shouldn't have, and I need to talk to someone. I thought you might be able to help me.'

'Why didn't you say so to begin with?' Phyllie instantly cheered up. 'This sounds very intriguing. I'll see you just after eleven. I'll have the kettle boiling.'

Now, as Hannah neared Phyllie's street, she wondered if she was doing the right thing. She probably shouldn't be involving anyone else in her lies. At the exact moment she had this thought her phone pinged with a text message.

Deadline's Wednesday. Time's ticking. Don't make me kill your marriage.

Hannah pulled up in front of Phyllie's house and took a deep breath. She knew unequivocally that Zane would kill her marriage if she didn't comply. As much as she knew she needed to be careful with what she told Phyllie, she needed to speak to someone.

By the time they were sitting facing each other Hannah's nerve had left her. She wasn't sure she could share this with anyone.

'Well?' Phyllie picked up a Tim Tam, her favourite biscuit, from the plate and dunked it in her tea.

It had always horrified Hannah that anyone would do this. It was practically a sacrilegious act.

She cleared her throat. 'I can't give you the exact details, but twelve years ago I decided to keep some information to myself. The information would have been devastating for the people involved, and while it wasn't my place to play God, I did.'

'To protect other people?'

Hannah nodded.

'It wasn't for your own benefit?'

She considered this question. She supposed it could be argued that she'd benefited from Damien not finding out about his father and potentially going into a deep depression, but there was no way of knowing whether that would actually have happened and it certainly wasn't the reason she'd done it. She shook her head. 'No, it was to protect two other people in particular. The information would have been upsetting and potentially changed a wonderful relationship.'

'And you can't tell me any more than this?'

Hannah shook her head. 'Not about what I've hidden, or from who, but I can tell you the next bit.'

She went on to tell Phyllie a condensed version of the facts about her meeting with Zane Fox. 'He's told me that he'll disclose the information I covered up if I don't pay him ten thousand dollars.'

Phyllie's eyes widened. 'He's blackmailing you? And you can't tell Damien? Or someone else who knows what this is about?'

Hannah shook her head, her eyes filling with tears. 'I wish I could, but it's too awful to reveal.'

'I can give you the money,' Phyllie said, 'that's no problem, but I'd be worried that he'll come back and ask for more.'

The tears rolled down Hannah's cheeks at Phyllie's kindness in her immediate offer to help.

'Thank you. I didn't come here to ask you for money. I can afford it, although I'm not sure how I'd pay without Damien noticing. It was just that I have the same concern. If I pay him once, what's to stop him coming back for more?'

'Can you get something legal drawn up that he has to sign?'

Hannah thought about it for a moment. That was quite a good idea. The reality was, if Zane Fox planned to tell Damien the truth then he was going to do it regardless. A legal document might at least deter him.

'You think I should pay him?'

Phyllie sighed. 'I'm not sure, love. I imagine you have two choices. Pay him off and hope he goes away, or you need to tell the people you're protecting exactly what happened twelve years ago and explain why you did what you did. Then you'll have to deal with the consequences. Paying this piece of scum, even with a legal document in place, may only buy you a bit more time if he decides to make the information public. It's impossible to predict how someone who will stoop as low as blackmail is going to act. Although past behaviour is usually a good indicator.'

They sipped their tea, both contemplating the situation.

Phyllie gave Hannah a wry smile. 'I must say, I can imagine Nat sitting across from me telling me something like this, but not you. You must have had excellent reasons for what you did.'

'They seemed like they were at the time.'

'Looking back now, with the benefit of hindsight, do you still think you made the right decision?'

Hannah nodded without hesitation. 'Definitely.'

Phyllie smiled. 'Good, then trust your judgement from back then and do your best to get rid of this guy. As I said, I'm happy to give or loan you the money if you don't want to explain to Damien where a large sum has suddenly disappeared to.'

Hannah sniffed back the tears that were threatening once again. She was so lucky to have a grandmother like Phyllie. Not having a mother to turn to in difficult situations, she'd always been able to rely on her grandmother. She didn't always provide the advice Hannah wanted to hear, but it was usually spot on. The fact that she'd offered to help her financially reminded Hannah how generous she was.

'It would make it a lot easier,' Hannah admitted. 'But can you afford it?'

'I have more money than I know what to do with. When I go, it will all be split between your father and you two girls. I keep a running tally of who has borrowed or been gifted what and I adjust the amounts accordingly.' She grinned, her eyes twinkling with delight. 'It's quite fun actually. You should be aware that I also add and deduct amounts based on your behaviours and actions towards me.'

Hannah's face flushed as Phyllie gave her a knowing look. 'I imagine I've had some huge deductions of late, with the assisted living suggestion. I'm fine with that. I'm trying to make life easier for you and safer, nothing more.'

Phyllie sighed. 'I know you think you're doing what's best for me but honestly, love, at my age what's best for me is being allowed to make my own decisions. I'm nearly ninety, and I have all my marbles. I'm much luckier than many. If I have a fall at home, I have a fall. Having Nat or anyone else living here isn't going to stop that happening. There's no point wrapping me in cotton wool just in case. We'll deal with things as they come. If they ever do. Who knows, I could go to sleep one night and never wake up. Then none of the planning for impending disasters will be relevant. You'd be much better filling your time thinking up nice things to do with that beautiful great-granddaughter of mine, rather than how to lock up an old lady.'

Hannah smiled. Phyllie's take on things was undoubtedly different from hers. She understood where her grandmother was coming from, but still wasn't convinced living alone was the best thing for her. It must have shown on her face.

'You're not convinced?'

Hannah shook her head. 'No, but as you say, it's your life, and I should do my best to stay out of it. Let's draw a line in the sand for now, while Nat's living with you. Agree to disagree and perhaps revisit it later in the year, if she's moved out and you're on your own again.'

Phyllie frowned. 'How about I give you the ten grand to pay off your mobster, and you consider that to be your payment to stay off my case?'

Hannah laughed. 'How about I think about it?'

Chapter Eight

Nat was still chuckling to herself as she drove away from Hannah's. Her sister's face when she realised Amy had played her was a classic. Poor Hannah, she was going to have problems in the near future if she didn't start thinking like a teenager and remember the tricks of manipulation. Although Hannah had probably never used them herself, so she wouldn't think anyone else would. It had been a quick visit, but that was more than enough when it came to her sister. And she was glad that Damien had been honest about the online gambling. As much as Hannah annoyed her, a secret like that had the potential to explode at some point. It was all fine while it wasn't costing Damien money, but if it ever did, he needed to keep it under control.

As Nat drove towards Shared, where she intended to spend the rest of her day, her thoughts reverted to the previous night. It had been amazing to win like that. It wasn't just the money – the whole atmosphere, the friendly camaraderie and the respect she'd seen in the eyes of Damien's workmates had shifted something in her. It was exactly what she'd needed at the end of a week of feeling like a complete loser. It was interesting that both Matt and Damien were playing online poker and winning. She wondered if the skills Phyllie had taught her would translate as well to the online environment as they had last night. Matt certainly seemed to think they would.

Her thoughts were still filled with poker as she pulled to a stop in the car park at Shared. As she went to exit the vehicle her phone pinged with a message from Pip.

> Hey stranger, what's happening? It's been too long. Let's catch up soon. Love ya.

She smiled, it had been a couple of weeks since she'd spoken to Pip, which was a long time in their world. She hadn't told Pip about her job or living situation, and right now didn't feel like going over it again. She sent back a quick text.

> Bit busy at the mo. Moving in with Phyllie to give her a hand. Hannah's worried about her and trying to get her to move into assisted living. I'm her last hope apparently! Just temporary but means I'll be a bit further out of town. How's the wedding planning? x

At least she was able to spin her moving in with Phyllie to be about helping her grandmother, rather than being thrown out of share accommodation. Nat remained sitting in her car, knowing Pip's response would come straight back.

> You're so sweet to be worried about Phyllie! Good on you and gets you out of that shitty share house too. Wedding plans ticking along. Crazy that it takes up so much time for something that's still months away. Bridesmaid dress fittings have to be organised soon by the way.

Nat groaned inwardly at the thought. At least Pip was allowing her and the other two bridesmaids to choose their dresses, but still, the whole thing seemed so out of date. Nat was surprised when Pip had said she was having a white wedding. Her friend had spent so much time fighting for women's rights and other female causes she'd assumed the feminist in her would rise up and say no to the traditional expectations of a bride, but she'd been wrong.

Another message came through.

Let me know when you're settled at Phyllie's and we'll organise dinner and a night out. Would love to see you.

Nat sent back an emoji blowing a kiss and slipped her phone into her bag. The one thing Pip was right about was the share house. It had been a shitty experience. She'd been fairly desperate when she'd moved in, having been evicted from her previous apartment, which she'd shared with a work colleague, after missing a rent payment. She'd been sure Angela would have understood that giving the money to a mother with three small kids, who she'd been speaking to while serving meals at Shared's soup kitchen, was a reasonable excuse for not having rent. It turned out Angela wasn't as charitable as she'd hoped. She'd moved into the share house with three others and hadn't clicked with any of them. They were all mature students living off assistance yet they looked down their noses at what she did for a living and her volunteer work. 'Surely you want to do something better with your life,' Yani, the oldest in the house, had said. 'If you went back to university you could do anything.'

Nat pushed open her car door, grabbed her bag and pushed all thoughts of her housemates from her mind as she headed towards Shared.

Nat found it hard to concentrate as she fed the leafy winter vegetables with fertiliser. Her mind kept flitting between the fact that she desperately needed to find a new job and the previous night's poker and how easy it had been to make money. She had a few days before she moved into Phyllie's and she'd intended to spend them split between working at Shared and looking for a paid job. Just the thought of a new job made her stomach clench. What was the point? It would most likely end up with the same result; fired for caring too much. But of course she needed an income. Maybe it would be better to invest her time in trying out the online rooms. If she only invested a percentage of the money she'd won the night before then she had nothing to lose really. As she thought about it the excitement that had sat in the pit of her stomach for most of the night before returned. Imagine feeling like this every day! And if she could make money from it, she'd have more time to volunteer. It could give her the flexibility she'd never had before.

'You look like you're miles away.' Robyn pulled her jacket around her as she approached Nat. 'How are you? You seemed a bit down the other day. Have things improved?'

Nat nodded and smiled. 'Kind of. I was just thinking through a business idea actually.'

'That sounds exciting. What type of business?'

'An online one. I haven't worked out all the details yet but I'm thinking it might be worth giving it a go. In fact' – Nat looked around – 'I've finished this area. Do you have anyone else who can do the rest of the beds today? I think I might head home and get a start on it.'

Robyn laughed and held out her hand for Nat's equipment. 'I can finish off. It's great to see you so excited. Once you're up and running you'll have to share with me what it is you're doing. I must say I'm intrigued.'

Nat handed over the equipment, said her goodbyes to Robyn and the two other volunteers working in the garden and hurried towards her car. She was intrigued too. Intrigued to know whether it was really possible to make an income from online gambling. She was well aware of the potential pitfalls and the stories of gambling addiction, but what about the people who actually won? They were out there. What was to say she couldn't become one of them?

By the next day Nat realised she could!

Her heart raced as she stared at the screen. She'd arrived home the day before from Shared and familiarised herself with the online poker sites Matt and Damien had mentioned. She started, as Damien had suggested, playing a few of the free tables first. She very quickly got a feel for how it worked and realised that a number of her competitors were complete amateurs. It was comforting to know her knowledge was superior to many she was playing against. She played five games, placing in all of them before moving on to a paid game. The buy-ins were only a dollar, so it wasn't much to lose, but Nat's hands had trembled throughout the game. Adrenaline surged through her each time she won a hand and she was euphoric when she won her first paid game. She spent the rest of the afternoon and evening increasing the amount she was betting until she found herself on the ten-dollar tables. By the end of the first day she was over a hundred dollars ahead. It wasn't a huge amount, but it was a profit. She'd found she was capable of having two tables open at a time, which increased her investment but also her potential payout.

She'd got up early that next morning and had done her best to smile at Ricky and Yani, who were in the kitchen drinking their morning coffee.

'When are you moving out?' Yani asked.

'Thursday, why?'

'Just thinking if you wanted to go earlier, we could give you a hand, that's all. Not that we're rushing to get rid of you, of course.' The two men exchanged a look and then laughed.

Nat chose to ignore them. She made herself a coffee, grabbed a banana and hurried down the hallway to her bedroom. Not for the first time she was grateful for the lock on her door. She locked it behind her and sat down at her small desk. She powered up her computer, excited that her workday was about to begin.

On Wednesday afternoon, Nat sat back and stared at the screen. She was going to have to start packing her belongings soon, ready to move to Phyllie's the next day. She'd played poker almost non-stop since returning from Shared on Sunday. Her plans to split her day between volunteering and looking for a new job hadn't come to fruition. Time had disappeared. She was winning enough to see the potential and know she *could* make poker work, but she was losing too. In fact, she'd managed to lose some of her winnings from the poker night. She wasn't too concerned. Like any new job, there was always a training period and that was what she considered this to be. She had to play with her head and follow the strategies Phyllie had taught her, not give in to her gut and go all in, as she'd done many times. Caught up in the excitement and thinking she knew better she'd been furious with herself when on more than one occasion she'd listened to her gut over strategy and lost the hand and the game. What was exciting, though, was she knew deep down she could win. Once she was at Phyllie's she intended to really commit her time and energy to the game. The potential upside was incredible. If she could make it work, she'd be able to pay off her credit card and her debts to her father, restart her charitable contributions and prove Hannah wrong.

Her credit card was linked to her account, which made it easier to transfer her winnings, and she intended to use them to pay off the small credit card debt she'd accumulated in the last few months. She owed just over five thousand on her fifteen-thousand-dollar limit. She didn't usually let it blow out like that but there had been a number of expenses she hadn't allowed for and she had donated a month's salary to UNICEF after watching a documentary on the Red Zone Hunger Crisis. Part of her knew she should stop giving her money away, but another part told her not to be selfish. There were people who needed her money a lot more than she did. She'd get by and had family to fall back on. She was incredibly lucky.

She turned off her computer and pulled her suitcases from her cupboard. She didn't have much to pack, just her clothes and the belongings in her room. Surprisingly, Yani had offered to help her move the next morning. He had a small van and assured her they'd be able to fit her bed, chest of drawers, desk and everything else. She was grateful for his offer, even though she was fairly sure he just wanted to make sure she actually moved out. It only took her a couple of hours and she was packed and ready to go. She sat on her bed, excited by the prospect of a new start. While her poker playing was still in the teething stages, she knew it had potential. Potential to replace her income if she was smart. Things were definitely looking up.

Chapter Nine

Hannah's hand trembled as she reached for the phone on her desk. She'd closed her office door, ensuring complete privacy, before dialling Zane's number. He picked up after three rings.

'Zane, it's Hannah Anderson.'

'Ah, Hannah.' The sneer in his voice made her gut churn. 'Got my money?'

She ignored his question. 'We should meet. I have what you want, but I need some guarantees from you. Are you available later today?'

'Sure. I can come to you again.'

'No!' The last thing Hannah wanted was anyone seeing her with Zane. 'I'll meet you in St Kilda. There's a small cafe in Grey Street near Acland Street. It's called Xpresso. Meet me at four.'

She placed the phone in the cradle, her hand still trembling. Was she really going to pay this guy off? She'd met with Lance Etheridge, a lawyer she'd found online, the previous afternoon. She'd decided to keep everything about this transaction separate from her current life. Therefore, she didn't talk with the lawyer she and Damien had used on occasion over the years. She didn't want to put anyone in a compromising position where they might feel obliged to tell Damien what was going on.

Lance had drawn up a contract for her to have Zane sign. It stated that once he received the payment from Hannah, he would under no circumstances discuss the nature of the transaction with anyone, nor would he ever try to contact Damien and divulge any of the information regarding his biological family.

Lance had, however, been sceptical. 'Look, he might sign it, but it doesn't guarantee anything. You're dealing with a blackmailer and, once again, I'd like you to reconsider paying him. Blackmail rarely ends at the first demand, and the fact he's only asking for ten thousand does ring alarm bells.'

'*Only asking for ten thousand?* Why do you say it like that?'

Lance shuffled the papers in front of him. 'In this day and age, ten thousand is loose change. Serious blackmail starts a lot higher. It's the sort of amount that makes me think he's testing you. If you can get your hands on that, you can probably get your hands on more.'

Hannah had excused herself during their meeting, only just making it to the ladies' room in time. With her head hanging over the toilet bowl and her lunch being flushed, tears welled in her eyes. She wasn't sure she had an option. If she didn't pay off Zane, he would tell Damien. There was no doubt about it. Lance's words had rung in her ears. 'Is what he has hanging over you really that bad? Would you consider telling your husband, so this guy has no power over you at all?'

Hannah immediately shook her head in response, but it was something she did need to consider. What if he was right? What if Zane did come back for more? She'd had over twenty-four hours to think about Lance's words. She couldn't see any good outcome at all if she was to confess to Damien. She doubted he'd ever forgive her. By doing what she'd done, she'd taken away his opportunity to meet his father. If she thought of it like that, it seemed like a terrible thing to have done, but then she'd reminded herself of exactly why

90

she'd made her choices – that they were to protect Damien, not hurt him – and she knew she was doing the right thing.

Following her discussion with Lance, she knew she wasn't going to hand over any money to Zane if her gut told her he'd be back for more.

Zane was sipping a coffee when Hannah entered the small establishment at four o'clock. Most of the tables were filled with a range of people from tourists to businesspeople to an elderly couple sharing a piece of chocolate cake. The classical music playing through the speakers was at odds with the metal tables and chairs, concrete floor and barista with piercings in his nose, lip, eyebrow and ears. But that was St Kilda for you, predictably unpredictable.

'Can I get you one?' Zane indicated to his coffee, as if this was a pleasant social catch-up rather than a meeting between a blackmailer and his prey.

She shook her head, did her best to control her trembling legs and sat opposite him. She pulled out the contract Lance had drawn up and pushed it across the table to him.

'These are my conditions.'

Zane raised an eyebrow before reviewing the contract. He looked up at her when he'd finished. 'Got a pen?'

'You understand the conditions then? That this is a one-off and you are never to contact me or Damien again?'

Zane grinned. 'Smarter than I'd taken you for. Covered *everything* by the looks of this.' He waved the contract at her. 'I'm not here to make your life a misery. I'll sign this, take my payment and be gone. You can go back to living your happy little life built on dishonesty. I really couldn't care less.'

The way he'd said *everything* alarmed Hannah. Had she overlooked something? Her eyes skimmed the contract for the hundredth time. It was straightforward, but if he agreed to the terms then, in theory, this would be the last time she'd have to deal with him.

Zane leaned back in his chair, his gaze trained on her as he sipped his coffee. A shiver ran down Hannah's spine as she met his eyes. There was something in them that unnerved her. In fact, he unnerved her altogether, but the taunting, mocking stare took it all a step further. She knew she couldn't trust him, and even though she'd promised herself she wouldn't hand over the money unless she were sure, she now realised it was a risk she was going to have to take.

She pushed the contract back to him and handed him a pen.

He put down his coffee and signed it. 'Okay. That part's done. What about the rest?'

Hannah glanced around the cafe. No one was paying them any attention.

She reached into her bag and took out an envelope. Phyllie had written a cheque for cash on Sunday when she'd visited her. The following day Hannah had cashed it at the bank. She'd been carrying around an envelope containing two hundred fifty-dollar notes ever since.

She held it out to Zane, not letting go when he clasped his hand around it. Their eyes met. 'I need you to tell me that this is the last time I'll ever hear from you.'

'Didn't I just sign a document that said that?'

'I want to hear it from you too.'

Zane rolled his eyes. 'Hannah, I promise this is the last time you'll ever hear from me.' He yanked the envelope from her hands. 'That good enough for you?'

No. But nothing he said ever would be.

Hannah's gut churned as she watched him flick through the notes. She picked up the contract and stood. 'It's all there. Goodbye, Zane.'

He grinned. A grin that suggested he'd won. And she guessed he had. But, if this was what it took to get rid of him once and for all, then she'd won too.

As she navigated the peak-hour traffic home an hour later, Hannah drew to a stop at a red light, conscious of her daughter chattering away but her thoughts were back at the St Kilda cafe. She still found it hard to believe that someone as risk-averse as she was had ever got involved with the private investigator. It was in her nature to protect those she loved. She just hadn't thought she'd do that at any cost.

'You're not listening, Mum.'

She glanced in the rear-vision at her daughter, who'd crossed her arms and was glaring at her.

'Sorry, hon, what did you say?'

'I said, it's time you and Dad listened to me about after-school care. I don't want to go anymore.'

'Neither Dad nor I feel comfortable with you being home alone.'

'No, Dad's fine with it. It's you that doesn't feel comfortable, because you're too overprotective and plan to smother me the rest of my life.'

Hannah's head whipped round and she stared at Amy. 'What do you mean Dad's fine with it?'

'Exactly that. He said if it were up to him, he'd say yes, but he knew you'd be too worried about me being safe, so it wasn't even worth talking to you about.'

Wasn't even worth talking to me about? But it had been worth telling their eleven-year-old what he thought about it.

She mustered a smile. 'Leave it with me. I'll chat to Dad, and we can discuss it again later.'

Amy's eyes widened. 'You'll think about it?'

Hannah nodded, although in all honesty her mind was made up. It was too dangerous to allow Amy to catch the bus and then be on her own in the afternoon. It wasn't like it was twenty years ago when she and Nat would let themselves in in the afternoon. And they were always together, which made snatching one of them much harder. She was buying herself some time. She didn't have the energy to live through one of Amy's epic *it's not fair* tantrums if she said no while they were in the car, and she also needed to talk with Damien. How dare he undermine her when it came to their daughter.

After they'd finished dinner Damien sat down on one of the kitchen stools next to Hannah, ready to continue the conversation they'd started as they prepared the meal. The discussion had stopped the moment Amy joined them in the kitchen. 'I'm sorry, you're right. Right in that I should never have suggested to Amy that you were overprotective. However, in my opinion you're not right that she's too young to get herself home. It would do her good to learn to become more independent, and it's not like she's got to change buses on the way home or do anything complicated. It's a dedicated school bus. We're the first stop on her way home, and if she caught the bus to school as well, she'd be the last stop before it goes direct to school. I can't see that it's a big deal. It would save us paying for after-school care too.'

'But what if something happens?'

'Then we'd need to give her an emergency plan. The neighbours would be the first port of call. I'm happy to go and speak with the Moores and the Rutherfords. If they know she's home alone in the afternoons, I'm sure they'd be happy if she went to them if there was an emergency of any kind. We'll reinforce exactly when she should ring for help and whether it should be us she rings or the emergency services. And if you're still serious about getting a dog for her birthday, then we get one that will help protect her. Not some silly little thing but a proper dog.'

Hannah smiled. *A proper dog.* She wondered what that consisted of compared to any other dog.

'A smile! Does that mean you think it could be a maybe?'

She sighed. 'I know I have to cut the apron strings at some stage and let her make her way in the world. Only, I wasn't expecting it to be at eleven.'

'She'll be twelve in just over two weeks and at high school after Christmas. She's growing up, Han.'

Hannah's eyes connected with her husband's. His were soft for a moment then clouded over.

He shook his head and stood. 'Anyway, I'm going to have a shower.'

She nodded absently, her mind racing as she tried to work out when Damien had distanced himself from her. She had no idea, but she knew she needed to find out.

'Can we talk after Amy goes to bed tonight?'

Surprise registered on Damien's face. 'Everything alright?'

Hannah swallowed. Asking him if they could talk was usually her code for 'something's wrong between us, can we work it out?' And he knew that. The fact he looked so surprised suggested he was unaware anything was wrong. How could that be? Hadn't he noticed they hadn't had sex for over a month? She opened her mouth to reply and shut it again. If he hadn't noticed, there would be a reason for that. He'd become distant, distracted and uninterested in her. She'd never imagined he'd cheat on her but was that what was happening?

'Hannah? Are you okay? You've gone completely white.'

She did her best to force a smile. 'Let's talk about it later.' Right now, she needed to gather her thoughts and think through what it would mean if he had.

Once Amy was in bed reading, and Hannah had had more time to think through what she wanted to say, she picked up the cups of green tea and walked through the French doors out to the backyard patio. The night air was crisp with a chill to it, but Damien had lit the patio heater, and its warmth made the outdoor space inviting. It also gave them complete privacy from Amy's eavesdropping ears. She placed a cup in front of her husband and sat opposite him.

'Thanks.' He placed his hands tentatively around the cup to warm them.

Hannah had rehearsed precisely what she wanted to say but always found asking these types of question nerve-wracking. What if she learned something she didn't want to know? What if there was a problem between them she was unaware of?

'Well?' Damien prompted. 'What is it?'

'I . . .' She hesitated. 'I wanted to ask if everything's alright? You've been very distant the last few weeks.'

He dropped his gaze, his eyes shifting to the heater.

'Is it work?' Hannah hoped it was. Damien's work did take an emotional toll and now and then she saw signs of him having trouble processing the distressing and sometimes tragic situations he had to deal with.

He closed his eyes and sighed. When he reopened them, he looked directly at her and smiled. 'No, it's not work, and I'm sorry.'

He was sorry? Her heart began to thump. There was only one thing she could imagine he would be sorry for. Her worst nightmare was about to unfold in front of her.

He took her hand, but she snatched it back. 'Why are you sorry? What have you done?'

He frowned. 'I haven't done anything.' His eyes widened, registering what she must be thinking. He reached for her hand again. 'God, nothing like that. You know I'd never cheat.' He smiled. 'Why would I? I love you to bits.'

Hannah felt herself relax. If that wasn't the problem, what was? She squeezed his hand. 'No, I'm sorry. I know you wouldn't, it's just you've been so distant with me the last few weeks. Longer probably. We haven't been, well, together, if you know what I mean, in ages.'

Damien ran a hand through his thick hair. 'I know, and I'm sorry. There's something I just can't get out of my mind at the moment, and it's affecting everything I do.'

'What is it?'

Pain flashed in his eyes as he looked at her. 'It was the anniversary of my biological parents' deaths a few weeks ago, that's all. I know it comes around every year, but this year, with me turning forty, I don't know, something feels missing. Maybe I'm having a mid-life crisis, and this is how it's going to play out.'

Hannah's stomach clenched. She'd just paid off Zane Fox that afternoon, and the reason for that payment was what was troubling Damien. Part of her wanted to scream. Would it never leave her alone? 'I hadn't realised you thought about them so much. I thought finding out about their deaths had been a type of closure. After all, you don't know anything about them.'

Damien sighed. 'I think that's the problem. I come from these people who would have had family, friends, jobs, interests, and I know nothing about them. I can't tell Amy anything about my heritage.'

Hannah frowned; she understood what he meant, but he did still have his adoptive parents.

'Don't get me wrong, Edward and Trish have been great parents, and I obviously talk to Amy as if their background is mine, but it isn't.'

Hannah stared at her husband. Since when did he refer to his parents as Edward and Trish? They'd always been Mum and Dad.

'Their heritage is yours too.'

He shook his head. 'Not in the way that matters. They're not part of my bloodline. I'm a random ring-in to the family. Of course, they've never intentionally made me feel like that, but I do. I hate that I know nothing about my genetic make-up. Who knows what illnesses are in the family? What things we should be aware of for both me and Amy?'

'You might be better off not knowing.' Damien had no idea how true that statement was. She cleared her throat. 'You might find out things about your family that you wish you never knew. Once you know the details, you can't unknow them.'

'I know. But I'd prefer to learn horrible things than live in ignorance the rest of my life.'

Hannah nodded. She needed to look supportive while at the same time drive him well away from this line of thinking. 'I guess we could try and do further explorations.'

He shook his head. 'There's no point. I think that's why it feels so hopeless. There isn't anyone left in the family to talk to. The investigator – something Fox – he made it pretty clear that as far as the bloodline went, it was just me. Although I guess there could be distant cousins around.'

A lump lodged in her throat as she thought of the enormity of what she'd done.

He reached for her hand and kissed it. 'I'm sorry, I should have told you what I was going through. I'm finding it tough to make sense of what I'm feeling.'

Hannah's eyes filled with tears.

'Oh, babe, I didn't mean to upset you. That's the last thing I want to do. It's exactly why I haven't said anything. No point in us both feeling miserable.'

Hannah shook her head. 'It's not that. I'm just gutted that you have to go through this. I wish there was something I could do to make you feel better.' This was his father's fault. Why did he have to turn out to be a rapist? She couldn't imagine any other scenario where she would have had to hide the truth from her husband. And now she was beginning to regret ever doing that. Damien was a mess, Phyllie was ten thousand dollars out of pocket, and there was the very real threat that she hadn't heard the last of Zane Fox.

Damien stood and held out his hand. 'I can think of something that might make us both feel better. Come on. It's been way too long.'

Hannah allowed herself to be led up the stairs to their bedroom. Damien shut the door behind them and pulled her to him. 'I'm so lucky to have you. You're always there for me. I really couldn't ask for anyone more supportive. I love you, Mrs Anderson.'

Hannah melted into his body and his kiss, wishing her mind would switch off and allow her to enjoy the moment, rather than being flooded with guilt.

Chapter Ten

'Now listen here, housemate, I thought we had a deal.'

Nat turned, her hand still holding the fridge open, and stared at Phyllie. There was a twinkle in her eye, but she looked serious.

'As much as I love the fact that having you living here gets Hannah off my back about assisted living, we agreed you could stay here while you looked for a new job and were in a position to house-hunt. You've been here for two weeks and you've hardly left the house. You haven't even been doing the volunteering I thought you were so passionate about. What on earth's going on?'

Nat retrieved the milk from the fridge and returned her focus to the coffee she was making. She glanced up at Phyllie briefly. 'I've been doing some work for a friend online.' Under no circumstances did she plan to tell her what she had really been doing. She'd had this story in the back of her mind just in case Phyllie or anyone else asked.

'What sort of work? You haven't been filming yourself and putting it on that blasted internet, have you? There are a lot of weirdos out there.'

Nat laughed. 'No, of course not. She has an online store selling kids' swimwear and needed some help with updating the site. They have hundreds of products and have just finished a photo shoot for the new season's stock. They needed someone to update all the product descriptions.'

'Oh,' Phyllie said. 'That's good then. You'll have to show me the site. It sounds fascinating.'

Nat poured the milk into the instant coffee, wishing for the millionth time Phyllie owned a coffee machine.

'What would I want a coffee machine for?' Phyllie had asked incredulously when Nat had mentioned it. 'Can't stand anything but instant. Those machines make it so strong I have to pour half of it out and add hot water. Can't think of a bigger waste of money.'

Nat thought of her friend Anita Green. She did run an online swimwear catalogue; that part was true at least. The part that wasn't was Nat's employment with her. She hadn't spoken to Anita in two years. She wondered momentarily how her old school friend was. She hoped Sandy Swimwear was still in business.

Phyllie cleared her throat, reminding Nat they were still having a conversation. She carried the two mugs across to the kitchen table and sat down opposite her grandmother, placing one in front of her. 'I've got at least two more weeks for Anita to do,' Nat lied. 'Then I'll have to get back out there looking for a permanent job. It's going okay having me living here, isn't it?'

Phyllie sipped her coffee and nodded slowly. 'It is, but it's not healthy being locked up in that room all day. You should be getting out with your friends or doing something else.'

Nat smiled. 'And I will. I need to get this work done first. Now, more importantly, what do you feel like for dinner?'

'Nothing for me, love. When I said you were to cook on the nights you were home, I assumed that might be two or three times a week. So far you've cooked every night you've lived here. That's not fair on you, and also, I'm getting fat. I'm not used to having proper meals every night. Quite often I'll have an egg or a tin of soup with some toast. All these plates of pasta, stir-fry and curry are delicious of course, but perhaps we'll change the rules to you cooking every second or third night that you're home. I'll look after myself tonight, and we've got Amy's afternoon tea for her birthday tomorrow, so neither of us will want a proper meal again until Sunday.'

Nat nodded. It suited her. The meals she was cooking added up too. While Phyllie had allocated a budget for their food, she was beginning to think she could utilise the money in better ways.

'Now, have you heard anything from that sister of yours?'

'Hannah? Why on earth would I hear from her?'

Phyllie shrugged. 'She has a few things going on. I thought she might have needed a shoulder to lean on.'

Nat snorted. 'I'd be the last person Hannah would turn to for anything. Surely you know that by now.'

Phyllie sighed. 'You two don't realise what you're missing out on. Having a sister is such a blessing. I'd give anything to have Isobel back. It's hard to believe eight years have passed since she died.'

'You and Great Aunt Isobel weren't like Hannah and me. You were both on the same page with things and enjoyed each other's company. Hannah and I are too different.'

'Not different enough to take an interest in each other and care about each other. She's having a hard time, and I think she could use a friend. The two of you seem to forget just how close you once were. Perhaps when we're there tomorrow for Amy's birthday you could make more of an effort.'

Nat smiled. She could just imagine how Hannah would receive any effort she made. It was utterly pointless but it was a conversation Phyllie had with her every year or so. She wondered if she spoke to Hannah too.

She picked up her coffee. 'I'd better get on with it. Anita's expecting me to finish a section of the site this morning.'

'Okay, love. And don't forget to show me what you've been doing later, will you?'

Nat wondered again how Anita was as she climbed the stairs to the second floor of Phyllie's three-bedroom home. The house was cosy, and despite Phyllie's initial eye-rolling at the thought of having a babysitter in the house, overall she had been very welcoming. As Nat had hidden away, saying she was *working*, she hadn't been in a position to interfere with Phyllie's daily routine, which she knew was one of her grandmother's biggest concerns.

She closed the bedroom door behind her and locked it. She didn't want Phyllie coming in unannounced and seeing what she was really doing. She hesitated as she went to sit at the small desk she'd set up in front of the window overlooking the back garden and the garden of the neighbour behind. Why did she care if Phyllie saw what she was up to? She wasn't doing anything wrong. Phyllie would probably enjoy trying out the site herself. Nat had asked for more instruction when it came to playing poker, and they'd spent many evenings with a pack of cards and Phyllie sharing her tips and strategies. Her thoughts flittered to the conversation they'd just had. Her grandmother was right that she hadn't been volunteering at Shared. But she had rectified the situation with her financial contributions. Just after moving in with Phyllie she'd had the inspired idea to donate half of the prize money from any game she won to Shared. As she'd moved on to more expensive tables, and the stakes for each game increased, so had her donations.

Her mobile rang as she placed the coffee cup on the desk and switched on the computer. It was Pip. Nat hesitated. Pip had called the previous day too and she'd let it go to voicemail. She didn't feel like speaking to her right now so she declined the call. She'd text her later and check that all was okay.

The computer made all sorts of noises as it started up. It was an old machine and always took ages to load. Once it was up and running, it was fine though. It had been a bonus to discover Phyllie had internet. 'Of course I do, you silly girl,' she'd said when Nat had asked. 'Everyone has it. How would I keep in touch on Facebook if I didn't?'

There had been quite a few surprises for Nat when she'd moved in with Phyllie. Discovering her glued to her iPad first thing in the morning and late at night had been a real eye-opener. It turned out Phyllie had more Facebook friends than she did. There was a large group she'd been to school with who had their own private group, and she was in there all the time, chatting or commiserating when another member died. 'Just a reality at this age,' she'd said. She logged in to the obituaries each morning and was forever sucking in breaths when she recognised a name. At eighty-nine, it was surprising there were still so many people in her school Facebook group.

'It's all that fresh air and socialising we had as children,' Phyllie had explained. 'We'll all live well into our nineties and beyond. Whereas your generation will all fry your brains with the radiation from your devices. Eventually, it will go full circle, and life expectancy will be thirty, not eighty. It'll be like smoking, where twenty years after it's encouraged, the authorities realise it kills you. Technology will be the same and you'll all die of brain tumours.' She'd chuckled at the thought. 'It will fix the ageing population issues in an instant.'

Nat hoped her grandmother was wrong.

Her computer finally booted, and she navigated to the web page. Time for her workday to begin. She had some losses that she needed to rectify to get back on track. She clicked on the link to Poker4Me and waited for the site to load.

Excitement built for Nat with each hand she played. The adrenaline rush when she won was so addictive. She'd found it exciting initially to win on the five- and ten-dollar tables, but the euphoric feeling dulled as she got more experienced and won more often. She quickly found that to retain that buzz she needed to up her stakes. She'd almost had a heart attack the first time she'd played a hundred-dollar table. She overanalysed every move and ended up being knocked out of the tournament in the first few hands. She realised the key was playing consistently. When she applied the same rules she'd used at the poker night and on the cheaper tables she usually placed in the game. She just had to stick with that strategy.

After only a few days of playing the hundred-dollar tables she found herself losing the buzz again. She'd win a game and open another, the high not the same as it was earlier in the week, so she upped the ante once again. It was unbelievable to think that only a couple of weeks after joining the site she was playing on the two-hundred-dollar tables. It was even more unbelievable that she was actually winning. Not every game, of course, but she was winning. And winning on a two-hundred-dollar table brought with it a much larger return.

Nat's heart raced as the final hand of the game was played and the *You Placed First* banner appeared on the screen. She was having a good day and had had an even better one the previous day. It was an incredible buzz to not only win a game but then log straight on to the Shared website and donate a substantial amount. The buzz of clicking on the donation button was almost as good as the buzz of seeing the *You Placed First* banner. Sure, gambling wasn't giving back to the community in the way her support officer role did, but financial contributions were the core of any successful charity, so she could still play her part. Hopefully, if things continued as they currently were, she'd be able to make a real difference.

Hours after her win a knock on the bedroom door jolted Nat into action. She minimised the screen and muted the volume on the computer.

'You alive in there, Nathalia?' The door handle rattled as Phyllie turned it. 'Why is this door locked? Is that necessary?'

Nat jumped up, unlocked the door and swung it open. 'Sorry, habit, I guess. I always used to lock it at the share house.'

Phyllie's eyes travelled around the room, settling on the computer. 'It's nearly three, and you haven't been out of here since breakfast. Surely you don't have so much work you can't stop for a break?'

Nat glanced at her watch. Phyllie was right, it was nearly three. It was surprising she wasn't starving. Although, the way her morning had progressed since she'd won the first game and made the donation to Shared had pretty much killed any appetite she might have had. Since then she'd lost the next ten games. It wasn't her best day on the tour.

'Come on down and I'll make you a sandwich. Can't have you locked in here all day without food. What would the neighbours think?'

'I'll be down in ten minutes,' Nat said. 'I've one thing to finish off first.'

Phyllie tutted. 'You're becoming a workaholic. That's not something I ever thought I'd have to say to you. Hannah yes, you no.'

Nat needed her grandmother to leave. She was mid-game, and she'd be lucky if she still had enough time to play the hand she'd been dealt. She was nearing the final three and needed a win to turn things around. 'I need to get back to it, Phyllie.'

Phyllie shook her head and shuffled out of the room and back down the stairs. Why had she even come up? It was one of her promises to Hannah that she wouldn't risk the stairs.

She quickly reopened the screen, frustrated to see her hand had automatically folded. There were only three other players left in the game. She needed to play her next few hands carefully to ensure she reached the top three. Coming third at least guaranteed she'd get part of her buy-in back.

The next hand was dealt. Adrenaline spiked as her cards were shown. The community cards were revealed, confirming she had a solid hand, more than a solid hand. So much for playing conservatively, she thought as she went all in. But that was the reality. Sometimes you had to have the confidence to play the bigger hands.

She stared at the screen as the other hands were revealed, her heart sinking. Fuzzy13 revealed a full house of aces and kings. The *Game Over, You Placed Fourth* message flashed on her screen. She banged her hands down on the desk. Shit. Two hundred dollars gone, just like that. She was about to open another game and restart when Phyllie's cry made her jump.

She rushed out of the room and down the stairs as words she never thought she'd hear from her grandmother's mouth reverberated around the backyard.

Nat followed the explosion of swear words to find her grandmother once again trapped by the goat. It was busily eating the flourishing clematis climbing a trellis by the small potting shed and had Phyllie pinned between it and the shed. She was pushing at the goat's side and swearing, but it didn't seem to be paying any attention.

'Thank God,' she cried as Nat grabbed the hose and ran around the shed so she could fire it straight into the goat's face.

Nat's heart was racing. What if this time the goat knocked Phyllie over or gouged her with its horns as it turned to flee? Anger boiled inside her. She'd be having a word with the goat's owner after this. 'Stay as close to the shed as possible. I'm about to spray it.'

'Like I have a choice,' Phyllie muttered. 'It's not exactly allowing me to get out.'

Nat turned the hose on the goat, who immediately whipped round and took off up the garden and around the side of the house, trampling the prolific star jasmine as it went.

Nat dropped the hose and hurried over to Phyllie. 'Are you okay?'

She nodded. 'I'm fine. It didn't hurt me, just ruined my clematis and the star jasmine by the looks of it.'

Nat studied her grandmother, whose hands were trembling as well as her voice. This bloody goat was probably stealing years from her life.

'This isn't on,' Nat said. 'I'm going to go and have a word with your neighbour. He needs to do something, or I will report him to the council. Let's get you back inside first and get you a drink. You're still shaking.'

'I'm a little dizzy. Stupid goat's got under my skin.'

Nat took Phyllie's arm and guided her up the small path that led to the back door. Once inside, she left her in her favourite armchair and went to turn the kettle on.

'I think whisky would be more appropriate, thanks, Nat. It'll calm my nerves and get rid of these silly head spins.'

Nat took the bottle from the small drinks cupboard and poured Phyllie a measure. She took it through to her.

'Don't go too hard on Leon. He's a lovely guy and has no idea what the goat has been up to. It didn't hurt me, so no real harm was done.'

'This time it didn't, but who knows what it might have done if I hadn't been here. It had you trapped against the shed.'

Phyllie laughed unconvincingly. 'I know, but it's so dumb who knows if it even knew I was there.'

Nat shook her head. 'Why on earth are you defending a bloody goat? It could push you over and you might break something. I'm beginning to think Hannah had good reason to be worried about you.'

Alarm registered in Phyllie's eyes.

'Don't worry. I'm not suggesting anything more than we need to get that goat under control. How many times has it been down here now?'

'Just one other time, I think. It didn't hurt me then either, just ate the roses.'

'What about a few weeks ago, when you needed stitches? Aren't you counting that?'

Phyllie's forehead creased with confusion. 'Stitches?'

'Yes, and the tetanus shot. Surely you haven't forgotten?'

'Um, no, of course I haven't forgotten.' Phyllie's tone was unconvincing. She sipped her whisky, appearing to be deep in concentration.

Did she really not remember the goat incident? Nat was about to say something when Phyllie spoke.

'Oh yes, when Damien dropped in and fixed me up.' She smiled at Nat. 'Sorry, love, you must think I'm a crazy old lady. I think the goat's visit this afternoon has given me a bit of a fright. Don't worry. I'm not losing it. I remember very clearly that bloody thing attacking me with its horn.'

Relief flooded through Nat. She stood. 'I'll go and chat to Leon and see if he can do something to keep it in or keep it tied up.'

Phyllie held out her tumbler. 'Before you go, can you refill this? There has to be some benefit in having a run-in with a goat.'

As she made her way along the footpath to number twenty-three, Nat wasn't sure whether to be worried about Phyllie or not. The previous incident with the goat was hardly one you'd forget. But she'd had a shock this afternoon, so perhaps that did explain the momentary forgetfulness.

Nat turned into the driveway of Leon's home. The lawn was neatly mown and flowerbeds lined the fence. She couldn't help but smile when she realised that the plants in the beds had mostly been chewed. Looking more closely she wasn't sure that any of them had been untouched by the goat. Served him right.

She was about to knock on the front door when she heard a deep laugh emanate from the back of the house. She walked around the side, through a carport to a small gate that blocked off the back garden. A man in his late thirties was holding out a carrot to the goat.

'Jesus, don't reward it.' Nat couldn't help herself. The goat could have done serious damage to Phyllie, and here it was enjoying what she assumed was a treat. 'You need to punish the bloody thing.'

The man's sandy-blond head snapped round at the sound of Nat's voice. His deep-blue eyes met hers. 'Sorry?'

She unlatched the small gate, pushed it open and walked towards him, her hands on her hips. 'Your bloody goat had my eighty-nine-year-old grandmother pinned against her shed a short time ago, and it's not the first time. She needed stitches a few weeks back when it came down to eat her garden and then gouged her with its horns.'

'Rainbow did that?'

Nat stopped. 'Your goat's name is Rainbow?'

He nodded. 'Is Phyllie okay? Why didn't she say something earlier? I received an angry note recently, but I know that wasn't from Phyllie. She'd be upfront with me, not hide behind an anonymous note.'

Nat felt her cheeks burn, deciding not to admit that the note was from her. She was slightly thrown by his good looks and concern. She'd been ready to have it out with the bloody goat owner,

110

picturing a yobbo who was too lazy to mow his lawn so had a goat to do it for him. 'It's been causing problems for her for ages. She said she didn't want to cause you any trouble when I suggested we talk to the council. She's just lucky I'm living with her at the moment and was there to help her. Surely you're not allowed to keep a goat in your garden?'

'Legally, on a block twelve hundred to twenty-four hundred and ninety-nine square metres, you are allowed one pet goat.'

Nat looked at Leon's garden. It was a reasonable size, but it wasn't huge. She doubted the block of land met these requirements. 'You say that like you're a real authority.'

'Of course I checked before I agreed to take on Rainbow.'

Nat nodded. 'Let me guess, you checked, realised your property wasn't big enough and thought, oh well, I'll look after it anyway.'

Leon laughed. 'You're pretty switched on, aren't you? Yes, you're right. My block is only a thousand square metres, so doesn't quite meet the requirements. I was thinking of moving when I agreed to take on Rainbow for a friend, but the right property hasn't come up yet.'

'You need to tie her up or do something to make sure she doesn't get out again.'

'You're right there too. I've found her in the front garden a few times but couldn't work out how she's been getting there. There are no gaps in the fence and the gate is always shut. I didn't realise she was visiting the neighbours until I received the note. I'll have a look now.'

He left and Nat watched him as he inspected the fences in the back garden. He returned a few minutes later looking puzzled.

'The fences are all intact so there's no obvious spot for her to escape.'

'Want to bet?' Nat nodded at Rainbow, who was heading to one side of the garden where a small tree stump sat at the bottom of a latticed fence. Rainbow jumped up on to the stump, giving her enough height to look over the neighbour's fence. She looked briefly before using the lattice like a ladder to climb the fence. When she got to the top, she slowly inched forward, made a clattering sound on her way down the other side and disappeared.

Leon and Nat stared at each other. 'Okay,' Nat admitted. 'If I hadn't seen her do that, I probably wouldn't believe it.'

Leon strode to the fence and looked over. 'There's a woodpile stacked about halfway up the other side. Nice and easy for getting down.' He shook his head. 'Unbelievable. But right now I'd better hightail it next door and get her. Don't want her causing any more problems.' He hurried to the gate leading through his carport and disappeared.

Nat took a quick look around the rest of the garden. There were a few climbing plants on other parts of the fence, but the only section with lattice was the one the goat had just scaled. It didn't look like there were any other places she could escape. She made her way back through the gate and up Leon's driveway. Nat met him leading Rainbow into the drive.

He grinned. 'Caught her, and thanks. If you hadn't come down, I wouldn't have realised she was causing such a problem. I'll remove the lattice as soon as I've got her into the garden. If she gets out again and you see her, can you let me know? I'd prefer not to tie her up, but it's always an option.'

Nat nodded. She could see now why Phyllie didn't want to report him. He was lovely. It made her wonder why Phyllie had never mentioned she had a gorgeous neighbour who Nat could quite easily enjoy getting to know.

'And tell Phyllie I'll pop down later today or tomorrow to apologise.' He glanced at his watch. 'More likely tomorrow at this stage.'

Nat nodded again. It was Friday night; he probably had plans. A hot date perhaps? She gave herself a mental shake. For all she knew he was married. She wasn't sure why her thoughts were going where they had. She'd been cooped up playing poker for too long. She needed to get out and have some fun. 'Okay, I'll pass on the message.'

She walked past him and the goat on her way out of the driveway, conscious that his eyes were on her.

'I'm Leon, by the way.'

She stopped and turned to face him. 'Nat.'

Leon raised an eyebrow. 'The mysterious Nat. Phyllie mentioned you a few years ago but I didn't realise you actually existed. Might have to let Rainbow escape so I have an excuse to come and visit you at Phyllie's.'

Heat rose up Nat's neck. 'Turning up with a goat definitely won't win you any brownie points. An apology for Phyllie will, though.'

Leon saluted. 'Right, boss. I'll keep that in mind.'

Nat's lips curled into a smile as she turned and walked back to Phyllie's. He was cute and funny. Once again, she wondered how come this was the first time she was learning of Leon's existence.

Phyllie was watching television when Nat returned. 'How did you go?'

'Good. We worked out where she's been escaping, and Leon's going to remove the lattice she's been using like a ladder, which should, in theory, keep her in the back garden. If that doesn't work, he's agreed to tie her up.'

Phyllie nodded. 'He's a good boy.'

Nat sat down across from her. 'How come you've never mentioned him before?'

Her grandmother grinned. 'Interested in my goat-loving neighbour, are we? The one you went to yell at and planned to dob in to the council.'

Heat crept into Nat's cheeks. 'Not really. Just intrigued as to why a guy like that is living on his own with a goat.'

'Who said he was living on his own?'

Disappointment flooded through Nat. She shook it off. This was ridiculous, she'd only just met the guy, and of course he'd have a wife or partner.

Phyllie laughed. 'You should see your face. The reason I've never mentioned my gorgeous and charming neighbour is that I don't want anyone ruining the rather lovely relationship I have with him. Leon pops in every couple of weeks and does all kinds of odd jobs for me. As a thank you I cook him dinner and we have a lovely evening. He's the grandson I never had.'

'And yet you've never mentioned him?'

Phyllie shook her head. 'He's mine, why would I? I don't want anyone else getting involved with him and ruining our friendship. Imagine if you did what you've done to many others – dated him for a few months then dumped him. That might be the last I'd ever see him.'

Nat couldn't believe her grandmother was admitting she'd deliberately kept Leon's existence a secret. 'It's highly unlikely he'd be interested in me to start with,' Nat said. 'But it's a bit disappointing that you think I'm not good enough for him.'

'I never said that.'

She couldn't quite work out why Phyllie had such a twinkle in her eye.

'I just said I didn't want you breaking his heart, that's all. Now, don't you have work to do? You said you had to get a lot done for Anita tonight.'

Phyllie was right. There's no way she'd get ahead today if she didn't get back to the tables soon.

Her phone pinged with a text message from Pip as she climbed the stairs to her room.

Call me. There's wedding stuff to organise and you seem to have disappeared. Is everything okay?

She sent Pip a quick message back saying she'd ring her the next day and then sat down at the computer. Weddings were the last thing she had time for right now.

It was close to midnight when Nat tried to enter one last tournament for the night, but a box flashed up on her screen saying she needed to deposit more funds into her account. That didn't make any sense. She'd set up her account to link to her credit card. Even with her donations to Shared she couldn't be out of funds.

She opened a new browser window and logged in to her internet banking. She stared at the screen in disbelief. There was no way her credit card statement could be right. Bile rose in her throat. It was maxed out. She started looking at the transactions. Playing the two-hundred-dollar tables, sometimes with two tables going at one time, could add up quite quickly. Of course, it only took one win every now and then to cover some of the losses.

She looked through the transactions, her stomach sinking as she realised what she'd done. How could she have been so stupid? Donating half of her winnings to Shared had been a noble idea, but she shouldn't have assumed she would be winning more often than losing. There were days when she'd played more than twenty games and only won three. Three wins was nowhere near enough to cover the losses. Donating from the winning games on top of that put her further back. Why hadn't she waited and worked out a percentage of profit to donate rather than rushing to fix the world and make herself feel good by donating after each win? She imagined what Hannah would say if she told her. Actually, she imagined that anyone would say the same thing. *You are a complete moron, Nat.*

Ten thousand dollars. An extra ten thousand added to the five she already had outstanding on her card. She'd blown through the entire credit card balance. She closed her eyes.

Rather than move into Phyllie's to save money and hopefully find a new job, she'd dug herself into an even bigger hole than before.

Chapter Eleven

Amy's eyes shone with delight as she picked up the last of her presents from the dining table; the one in gold wrap. Hannah had sensed Amy's disappointment when she'd surveyed the neatly wrapped pile of gifts, her eyes searching the garden, just in case. Hannah knew what she was hoping for, but she also knew Amy didn't really expect to receive a dog. She was glad to see her daughter still getting excited about her birthday, even though she believed she wasn't getting the present she had so desperately hoped for.

Amy had risen early, waking both Hannah and Damien as she rushed down the stairs, feet deliberately pounding to ensure the entire house was woken. It was a birthday and Christmas tradition, and turning twelve wasn't going to alter that. Hannah wondered if things would change when she became a teenager. Would they have to poke and prod her to wake up for the day?

Amy loved the books and clothes she'd unwrapped, particularly the antique copy of *Little Women*, but Hannah knew she'd be wondering what the special present was this year. Hannah always wrapped one item in gold paper. The one she thought Amy would like the best. It was usually a reflection of the most valuable present. Last year it had been an iPad, the first device they'd allowed her to have.

'What is it?' Amy shook the package, which gave nothing away. 'I bet it's jewellery or a watch. Am I right?'

Hannah was about to say no when Damien laughed. 'You could call it that.' He winked at Hannah. The studded collar could pass as jewellery, she guessed.

Amy slid her fingers under the wrapping, savouring the opening of the last present. She flipped open the paper revealing a collar and lead. A note was attached to the lead: *Time to go shopping!*

Amy looked up, her face flushed with pleasure. 'For real? I'm allowed to get a dog?'

Hannah nodded. 'After breakfast we'll head down to the shelter in Burwood East. We checked yesterday, and they've got quite a few to choose from.'

'Oh my God!' Amy threw her arms around Hannah. 'I can't believe you're letting me get a dog. I love you so much.' She squeezed her before turning and throwing herself at Damien. 'And you too. You must have talked her into it.'

'No, in fact, you can thank . . .'

Hannah shook her head. She did not want Nat getting credit for this present. She wanted Amy to believe it was her and Damien's doing, not a result of her losing a bet. And anyway, the bet was a bit extreme; she could still have said no if she'd chosen to yet she hadn't. The more she'd thought about it the more she realised that Amy was growing up and they would have to allow her to become more independent. A dog in the house would also give Hannah some peace of mind if they were going to allow Amy to be home alone.

'Can we go now?'

Hannah laughed and pulled Amy to her for another hug. 'They don't open until nine for adoptions. How about we get dressed and go out for breakfast first? I've booked a table for seven thirty at Franklin's. It's only a five-minute drive from the cafe to the shelter.'

Amy pulled away and was already running towards the stairs. 'Hurry up,' she called to her parents. 'We've got a birthday to celebrate.'

Hannah and Damien shared a delighted smile as they got to their feet, ready to follow Amy up the stairs.

He put an arm around Hannah's shoulders. 'Looks like we got it right this year.'

She smiled. Amy's excitement was contagious, and she had to admit, she loved birthdays. They reminded her of her mother, who'd made sure it was a day full of excitement and feeling loved. After her mother had passed, her father had done his best to carry on this tradition, which had made Hannah love him even more. It hadn't been easy for him, but he'd known what her mum would have wanted him to do, and he'd done it. A small part in making Amy's day extra special was carrying on this tradition of her mother's.

Rather than have a party with her friends, Amy had chosen to only invite her best friend, Skye, over for the afternoon. Hannah had suggested they celebrate by inviting the family and Amy had readily agreed to this, knowing it would mean more presents. She'd requested that the celebration not be for dinner, but in the afternoon instead. For dinner she wanted to order pizza and for her and Skye to watch movies in the media room by themselves. Hannah had agreed, grateful that Amy's requests made it the easiest birthday ever. Gone were the days of having fifteen screaming kids running around the house on sugar highs, with Damien trying to round them up and control them with party games.

Hannah had prepared a spread of Amy's favourite foods, appreciative of the fact that her daughter had a sophisticated palate. The family would be enjoying cheese platters, sushi, antipasto, dips and crackers.

Hannah smiled as she looked from the kitchen across the open-plan living area to the large bay window that overlooked the backyard. For the first time in weeks she felt like she could relax. The worry of Zane Fox's threats hanging over her were gone – for good she hoped – and her daughter was smiling in a way she hadn't seen for months. She was, of course, still worried about Damien and his up-and-down moods, but doing her best to be supportive and understanding was preferable to dealing with the fallout if he learned the truth.

Laughter erupted from the garden as Amy, Skye and Damien played with Bear, the chocolate Labrador Amy had chosen. Even though she had already shown interest in Bear when she'd looked at the dogs online a few weeks ago, she'd still surprised both Hannah and Damien when she bypassed a cage with three puppies and chosen the four-year-old dog. Hannah had been sure Amy would want a puppy. She'd been dismayed when she'd seen the enclosure housing the three ten-week-old pups. She'd assumed that all the rescue dogs would be older, and they wouldn't have to train a puppy. In saying that, they were so cute that the biggest issue would have been choosing one. They probably would have come home with all three.

But Amy had made a beeline for Bear, amazed that he was still available. She'd mentioned him over the birthday breakfast but had assumed he would have been adopted by now. The Lab, however, had sat patiently at the door of his cage, his tail wagging, his eyes locked on Amy. It was as if he knew that she'd come to rescue him. The moment the RSPCA worker opened the door, Amy had flung her arms around him, and he'd leaned into her, licking her face. When she'd let go of him, he'd rolled straight on to his back with his legs in the air wanting his belly rubbed. There had been no question as to which dog they were adopting.

Hannah smiled as she watched Amy throw a ball towards the back fence and Bear rush to get it, return to Amy and drop it at her feet. He was already well trained as he'd belonged to an elderly man who'd had Labradors all his life. He'd raised him from a pup and taught him to be incredibly obedient. But according to the manager at the shelter, he was a man without any family and when he'd surrendered Bear the previous month it was because he'd had a stroke and been moved into a care facility.

Tears had welled in Hannah's eyes when she'd heard this story. She thought of Phyllie and imagined her without any family. It was so sad to think of getting to the end of your life and having no one at all. She'd asked the manager if it was possible to get a message to the man to let him know that Bear had gone to a loving home, but the manager shook her head. Bear's owner had died the previous week.

Hannah glanced at her watch. It was nearly three. Her parents, Nat and Phyllie would be here any minute.

Hannah's eyes travelled over to her sister as they sang 'Happy Birthday' and Amy blew out the twelve candles on the mud cake they'd picked up from Sweet Treats on their way back from the shelter.

Damien stepped forward to cut the cake after Amy finished blowing out the candles, smiling as Phyllie checked she'd made her wish. Hannah was smiling too, but she couldn't help but focus on Nat. Her sister had hardly said a word since she'd arrived. She'd also forgotten to bring Amy a present, which was so unlike her.

When the formalities of the cake-cutting were over, Amy and Skye went back outside to play with Bear. Hannah had agreed that the dog could come inside, even though initially she'd said he was to be an outdoor dog. But even she couldn't imagine being rel-egated to the yard with the temperature falling to low single digits overnight. They'd bought Bear a bed, which had been set up in the laundry, although Hannah had a sneaking suspicion that Amy would get her way and Bear would sleep with her.

She'd insisted her dad, Sue and Phyllie move through to the lounge room, and Damien was refilling their champagne flutes as Hannah stacked the dishwasher with the plates from the cake. Nat excused herself to use the bathroom, but Hannah noticed that rather than join her parents and Phyllie on her return, she'd slipped out into the garden and was sitting huddled on the small bench under the rose arbour watching Amy, Skye and Bear.

Hannah wiped her hands on a towel and decided it was time to get to the bottom of Nat's strange mood. She poured two glasses of Pinot Noir, knowing Nat would prefer the light red over cham-pagne, and carried them through the French doors to the patio area where her sister sat.

Surprise registered in Nat's eyes as Hannah passed her a glass. 'Thanks.'

Hannah sat down next to her, a smile playing on her lips as Bear ran after Amy as she tore across the garden. She couldn't remember the last time she'd seen her playing in the backyard. She was usually holed up in her room, reading or on her iPad.

'You were right about a dog being good for Amy.' Hannah laughed as Nat's mouth dropped open. 'What?'

'I just can't remember you ever suggesting I was right about something, that's all. You're usually very good at telling me what I've done or said that's not right.'

Hannah chose to ignore the bitterness in Nat's voice. She was going to do her best to rise above the little digs today and find out what was going on with her.

'You okay?'

Nat broke eye contact and sipped her wine.

Her evasive stance immediately had Hannah on alert. 'What are you keeping from me?'

'What? Why do you automatically think I'm keeping something from you?'

'Because you're a terrible liar and I know your body language. It's Phyllie, isn't it?'

Nat shook her head. 'What the hell are you talking about? I'm tired from working long hours and you interpret it as something's wrong with Phyllie?'

Hannah folded her arms across her chest. 'So Phyllie seems okay? She can manage everything?'

Hardness replaced the surprise Nat had previously shown. 'What are you getting at? You're not still trying to put her in a home, are you?'

Hannah stared at her sister. They'd had this discussion when she moved in with Phyllie. It wasn't about putting her in a home, it was about working out whether she could cope alone if Nat were to move out. Why was she being so obtuse? 'No, I'm not trying to put her in a care home. I'm just checking that you think she's still fine to live at home, that's all. You're there every day, you'd know if she wasn't coping or needed extra help. There are all sorts of services she's entitled to. Meals on wheels, gardening help, even cleaning. She won't let on to me, and with the way you're acting I can only assume she does need help but has made you promise not to say anything.'

'She hasn't asked me to promise anything, but she is still convinced you're going to do everything you can to run her out of her house.'

Hannah sucked in a breath. 'She still thinks I'd do that?'

'More or less. She wants you to mind your own business, which I'd appreciate too. If I'm not feeling sociable I don't need the third degree from you.'

Hannah took a deep breath and moved her gaze to watch Amy and Skye, who were doing their best to train Bear to shake hands. Why was Nat always so prickly? She'd only asked her if she was okay because it was very obvious she wasn't, and then it had to be turned into another argument. She didn't know why she even bothered sometimes. She was surprised, though, that Phyllie thought she was still trying to remove her from her home.

'Amy, you can't give him too many treats,' she called, realising the process Amy was following seemed to involve a lot of laughter and, from the looks of it, a lot of dog treats. 'The book said only ten percent of his daily calories, remember.'

'They're not treats,' Amy called back. 'Dad said to just use his normal dry food as a reward.' Bear was sitting gazing lovingly at Amy. 'He loves it, by the way.'

'He loves her too,' Nat said. 'I'm glad you lost that bet.'

'About that,' Hannah said. 'I don't want her to know about the bet. She's so happy about having Bear. I think from her perspective it's the best present we've ever given her, so I'd prefer her to think it was our idea.'

Nat stood. 'Even though you said *absolutely no way*, you're going to let her believe you've given him to her out of the goodness of your heart?' She shook her head. 'You've always been a piece of work.'

'Me? Jesus, listen to yourself. I don't know why you even came today. We would have preferred it if you and your bad mood had stayed away.'

'Next time don't invite me then. Having to spend part of my weekend around you is hardly something to look forward to.'

Hannah's mouth dropped open as Nat turned on her heel and walked back inside the house.

When she came back inside, Hannah found Phyllie boiling the kettle. 'Let me do that for you. You go and sit down, and I'll bring it through to you.'

'I'm perfectly capable, Hannah. There's no need to treat me like an invalid.'

Hannah frowned. Nat appeared to be right, Phyllie was still angry with her. She was sure they'd cleared the air when she'd given her the money for Zane Fox. 'I was treating you like a guest, not an invalid. But if you insist, I'll have one too thanks.' She placed her empty wine glass on the countertop and sat down on one of the stools, doing her best to hide a smile as Phyllie, looking somewhat taken aback, placed a second cup next to hers.

'The others are still drinking champagne. It's too cold for champagne. I'd much prefer something warmer.'

'There's a nice Pinot Noir if you'd prefer,' Hannah said.

Phyllie shook her head. 'No, I'd better keep what little of my wits I have about me. I'll stick to tea.'

'Phyllie' – Hannah lowered her voice – 'I thought we'd agreed when you gave me the money that I wouldn't push the assisted living idea anymore.'

Phyllie's eyes widened in surprise. 'It's my understanding that you think I'd be better off locked away. It's what you keep saying. And what money?'

It was now Hannah's turn to be surprised. They'd had this conversation, and it appeared Phyllie didn't remember about the money. She swallowed. If this was the case, she did need to be worried.

'Do you remember me visiting you when Amy went to her friend's party? We discussed a problem I was having. You helped me out?'

Phyllie's eyes clouded over for a moment and then cleared. She looked around and lowered her voice. 'Of course I remember, I just didn't think you wanted it to be talked about.'

Hannah wasn't sure whether to be relieved or not. 'Then why are you acting like I'm still trying to ship you off to a home? We agreed that I'd back off.'

Phyllie poured hot water into the cups and grinned. 'Just teasing you of course.'

'Nat seems to think I'm still on your case about it too. She's quite snarky today.'

Phyllie laughed. 'Yes, I think she got out on the wrong side of the bed this morning. I'll set her straight that you and I have struck a deal and you plan to leave me alone.'

'The arrangement's going well then? With Nat?'

Phyllie frowned. 'It is.'

'But?'

She looked up. 'But what?'

'You had a look of concern on your face, that's all. Like everything wasn't okay.'

Phyllie passed a teacup across to Hannah, came around the island bench and sat on a stool next to her granddaughter. 'I'm a little concerned about this new job of hers, if I'm honest.'

'Oh?'

'She's working very long hours. In fact, since she's been living with me, she's hardly been out. She's been here and to your parents, but other than doing some grocery shopping and running a few errands I don't think she's seen any of her friends or done anything. Does that seem strange to you?'

Hannah had no idea how social Nat was before moving in with Phyllie, but yes, it sounded odd. 'Perhaps she wants to make a good impression with the company she's working for.'

'Mm,' Phyllie nodded. 'Possibly. It is a little unusual though. Even in this day and age of computers and virtual meetings, I would have thought she'd need to go and meet with the company more. Being holed up in her room all day and night isn't healthy. I'm also not convinced she's earning much from it.'

'What makes you think that?'

Phyllie looked away, suddenly evasive. 'I've said too much already. I should leave Nat to talk to you, if she decides she wants to.'

'Nat's hardly one to stick with a job if it doesn't suit her. I'm sure she'll find something else if she gets sick of this new one.'

'I'm not so sure.'

Hannah raised an eyebrow. 'What makes you say that?'

Once again Phyllie avoided her gaze. She picked up her teacup and nudged Hannah. 'Come on. Your parents are probably wondering where you've got to. With the mood Nat's in I can't imagine her entertaining skills are at their best.'

Hannah got to her feet. 'Any idea what the mood's about?'

Phyllie shook her head. 'No, but I'm sure we'll find out when she's ready to talk.'

Her father smiled as Hannah and Phyllie entered the living room. 'Can you believe she's twelve already? It's crazy. I remember when you turned twelve, it doesn't seem like it was that long ago.'

'She's a lovely girl,' Sue said. 'You should both be very proud.'

Damien smiled. 'She makes it pretty easy. She tries hard at everything she does, and everyone seems to like her at school. Hopefully the transition to high school next year won't be too hard.'

Hannah noticed Nat had refilled her wine glass and it was practically overflowing. She turned to her father. 'Did you bring Nat and Phyllie today?'

'No, why?'

'You might want to slow down, Nat,' Hannah said. 'You'll be driving Phyllie home soon.'

Nat's eyes narrowed. 'Trying to get rid of us already?'

'Of course not! But today was for afternoon tea, not dinner. Amy's got Skye staying, and we'll be ordering pizza for them later. I wasn't planning to cook a meal, but I'm happy to order pizza for everyone if you want to stay.'

Amy and Skye entered the room with Bear bounding after them before Nat had a chance to answer.

'Is it okay if we take Bear upstairs with us? I want to show him my room.'

'He's sleeping in the laundry, Ames,' Damien reminded her.

Amy rolled her eyes. 'I know that. But if he's clever enough to open the door, then he'll need to know where to find me so I can return him to the laundry, won't he?'

Hannah's father laughed. 'You can't argue with that logic, can you.'

'Of course you can take him upstairs,' Hannah said. 'We might as well get used to Bear being part of the family. Considering he's only been here a day he's fitting in already.'

Bear barked, causing further laughter around the room.

'He knows you're talking about him.' Skye rubbed the dog's ears. 'You're so lucky, Amy. There's no way my mum would let me have a dog. She goes on about what a commitment they would be and how we could never go away if we had one.'

'My mum's the best.' Amy shot Hannah a smile so full of love that she had to blink to stop the tears.

Nat snorted. 'Now that's a joke.' She took another large swig of her drink.

Amy's face fell. She looked at her aunt. 'What do you mean? This is the best birthday I've ever had, and it's because of Bear.'

'Let's just say your mum should never gamble and leave it at that.'

Amy looked to Hannah for help.

'Nat.' Sue's voice was sharp. 'That's enough.'

'Yes,' her father added. 'No need to spoil a lovely afternoon.'

Hannah was grateful for their support but couldn't believe Nat had said anything, especially after she'd specifically asked her not to. She stood. 'Why don't you girls take Bear upstairs and get settled with the movies you want to watch. I'll come up soon, and we'll work out what toppings you'd like on the pizzas before I order them.'

'Okay.' Amy was still staring at Nat.

'I'm glad it's the best birthday you've ever had, sweetie.' Hannah lowered her voice and smiled conspiratorially at Amy. 'Ignore Aunty Nat, she's in a bad mood, that's all.'

Amy nodded, and with Bear at her heels she and Skye left the room whispering together.

'What?' Nat shrugged when Hannah turned and glared at her. 'I didn't say anything.'

'You said more than you needed to. Why spoil her day? Just because you're in a foul mood doesn't mean you need to bring a twelve-year-old down on their birthday. Did it make you feel better?'

Nat stood and looked at Phyllie. 'I think it's time we left.'

Damien stood at the same time. 'I'll drop you home.'

'What? I'm perfectly capable of driving. I've only had a couple of glasses.'

'No arguments, Nat. You've had more than a couple, and you have precious cargo on board.' He nodded towards Phyllie.

'We can drop them,' Sue said. 'It's not out of our way.'

David cleared his throat. 'It is actually. I've booked us some Gold Class tickets at the cinema at Doncaster for eight.' He blushed. 'I was going to surprise you with dinner and a movie tonight once we left here.'

'That's so nice, Dad,' Hannah said. She loved that her father had a romantic side and constantly surprised Sue with little gifts and outings.

Sue smiled and slipped her hand into her husband's. 'Your father is the most wonderful man on the planet. No offence, Damien.'

Damien laughed. 'None taken. If anything, I should follow his lead.' He smiled at Hannah. 'I promise to do better. But for now, I'll drive Phyllie and Nat home in Nat's car and get an Uber back.' He looked over to Nat. 'That way you don't have to come back tomorrow to collect it.'

Nat snorted. 'I can't imagine I'd be welcome.'

Hannah stared at her sister. Surely her nastiness wasn't just because of the dog? She glanced at Phyllie, who looked as bewildered as she did.

'Come on.' Damien hooked his arm through Phyllie's. 'I'll escort you out.'

'I'd like to say goodbye and happy birthday to Amy,' she said as they neared the front door. 'But' – she turned to Nat – 'I suggest you go and wait in the car while I do that.'

Nat opened her mouth to object but then seemed to think better of it. She swung open the front door and made her way down the drive towards her car.

'She won't try and drive, will she?' Sue's voice was full of concern.

Damien took a set of keys from his pocket and rattled them. 'I took care of that about an hour ago. I had a feeling something was off.'

'Thanks, son.' David clapped Damien on the back. 'Nat's lucky to have everyone looking out for her.' He frowned. 'It's not like her to act like that in front of Amy. I hope she's alright.'

Hannah shook her head. Her sister had acted like a prize bitch, almost spoiling Amy's birthday, and her father was worried about Nat? Yes, she didn't normally act that way in front of Amy, but she always tried to undermine Hannah. Tonight was another example. For now, she just wanted her gone. She turned to Phyllie. 'You wait here and I'll pop up and get Amy to come down and say goodbye. There's no point risking a journey up those stairs.'

She did her best to ignore Phyllie's eye-roll as she hurried out of the room to fetch Amy.

Following Nat and Phyllie's departure, Hannah was pleased to find Amy and Skye chatting and giggling when she brought their pizzas to the media room. It appeared Nat's little outburst hadn't ruined their night. They were lying on the mattresses they'd prepared for their sleepover and Bear was fast asleep, his head resting against Amy's outstretched foot. The way the dog attached himself to her you'd think he'd been living with them for years. It was quite special.

'Pizza's up.' She put the tray containing the two pizzas and a bottle of mineral water on the coffee table the girls had pushed to one side.

'We'll never eat all that.' Skye eyed the pizzas. 'They look delicious. Thank you, Hannah.'

Hannah smiled. Skye was one of those kids you couldn't help but love.

'Thanks, Mum,' Amy added. 'And don't worry, I'll make sure Bear doesn't eat any. He had his dinner before we came up here.'

'You're doing an amazing job with him.'

'So he can stay?'

'What do you mean?'

'Aunty Nat was acting strange, and I thought that was because you'd decided Bear had to go back.'

Hannah sucked in a breath. She could kill Nat. 'Hon, Bear's not going anywhere. He's your dog now. Dad and I will help out, of course, but overall you're responsible for him. We don't buy a pet one day and take him back the next. You don't have to worry, just enjoy him. He's an Anderson now, whether he likes it or not.'

Bear opened one eye and gave a little yelp.

Amy and Skye laughed.

'What was wrong with Aunty Nat?'

Hannah shook her head. 'I have no idea. She mentioned a bad day, but that was no excuse for how she behaved.'

'Next time you speak to her tell her to stay away from Bear and me,' Amy said. 'She must hate dogs or be jealous or something.'

Hannah opened her mouth automatically to defend Nat, but then she closed it again. Why should she? Amy was old enough to recognise that Nat's behaviour was not only unacceptable but mean. The lack of a birthday present also hadn't gone unnoticed. Where she previously would have told Amy not to think like that, tonight she didn't have the energy. She didn't owe her sister anything right now.

'I'll let her know. Now, why don't you two put on one of the movies and enjoy the pizza? It's still early, so you should have time to watch two if you want to.'

Amy grinned. Her usual eight thirty bedtime was not coming into play tonight. 'Thanks, Mum.'

Hannah walked back downstairs, grateful to find her father and Sue had stacked the dishwasher before they'd left. It hadn't turned out to be the relaxed family afternoon she'd been hoping for. She sighed, sat down at the kitchen counter and just as she reached for the bottle of Pinot Noir, her phone pinged. It'd better be Nat with an apology. She picked up the phone and swiped up to see the message. Nausea swept over her. The text was from Zane Fox.

We need to meet.

Chapter Twelve

Nat leaned her head against the side window as Damien drove the ten minutes back to Phyllie's house. God, Hannah had overreacted. Amy knew she was only mucking around. As if she'd spoil her niece's birthday. It was just like Hannah to take credit for a present she only bought because she lost the bet.

'You know,' Damien's calm voice broke into her thoughts, 'while the bet certainly helped give Hannah a push in the right direction about the dog, she had already decided that it was the right time for Amy to have a pet. Her wanting Amy to believe she'd changed her mind did have some truth in it.'

'Whatever.' Her sister always came out looking good. She probably weighed up the risk factor of every situation and worked out how to manipulate it in her favour.

'What on earth is wrong with you tonight, my girl?' Phyllie swung round from the front seat and stared at Nat. 'It's not like you to be so moody. Is it this new job? I can't imagine it could be anything else as you've hardly left the house since you moved in.'

Nat sighed. 'Something like that. I don't want to talk about it.'

'Fine, but don't be so down on your sister. She had us over for what should have been a lovely afternoon. You have no excuse for behaving so badly.'

They travelled in silence for a few minutes as it began to rain, the swish of the windscreen wipers the only distraction.

They reached the house, and Damien jumped out of the car and ran around to open Phyllie's door. He looked through to Nat, who hadn't moved from the back. 'Stay there. I'm going to walk Phyllie in and then I want a word.'

Nat sank back into the seat and closed her eyes. Her head swam a little as she did. It was probably a good thing that Damien had insisted on driving them home. The way everyone was acting you'd think she'd done something awful, not just stirred up her sister by pointing out the truth.

She blinked as the passenger door across from her opened and Damien slid in beside her.

'Is everything alright?'

Nat's eyes instantly filled with tears. His voice was so gentle and caring. Not accusatory like Hannah and Phyllie had been.

He handed her a tissue. 'I'm here if you want to talk. I won't say anything to Hannah or anyone else.'

Nat gave a little laugh. 'You're not the best at keeping secrets. Hannah found out you were the medical professional who attended to Phyllie over the goat incident within minutes of it being mentioned.'

Damien shrugged. 'That was a bit different as it affected Phyllie and she was worried. She won't expect me to know anything about what's going on with you. Anyway, you don't have to say anything, I just thought you might need a friendly ear.'

Intense gratitude flooded through Nat. Hannah was lucky to have him. The tears that had threatened began rolling down her cheeks as she thought of how badly she'd messed up. Nothing was going right at the moment. No job, no relationship, living rent-free with her grandmother because she couldn't afford to live anywhere else, and now she was in debt.

'I've got myself into some financial trouble,' Nat admitted.

The small lines around Damien's eyes creased with concern. 'Can we help?'

The tears continued to flow. He hadn't done what Hannah would have; she'd have demanded to know the details, whereas he'd simply offered help.

She shook her head. 'No, I'll need to get myself out of it. It's just very stressful without an income.'

Damien nodded. 'I attended a job at the Walton House Shelter yesterday. They were understaffed. You've worked there before, haven't you?'

'And hated it,' Nat said. 'But it might be worth talking to them; I probably can't be choosy.' She sighed. Part of her thought if she could just get back on the tables, she could turn things around very quickly.

Damien was studying her. 'I know it's none of my business, but are you playing the online poker tables?'

Heat rushed to Nat's face. 'Why would you want to know that?'

'Just curious. As much fun as they can be, they're a quick way to lose money.'

'You're telling me.'

'Poker's the problem then?'

Nat shook her head. 'It's not a problem. I just need to get back to where I was. I got greedy and started playing the more expensive tables. The return is so much bigger when you win or place.'

'But so is the competition. There would be at least four professionals sitting at each table. Winning is virtually impossible.'

'That's the thing. I did win to start with. I just need to work out what I was doing in those games and try and replicate it.'

'Can I ask how much in debt you are?'

'Fifteen grand. That's not all poker though. I'd already clocked up five grand before I started playing.'

Damien's face paled at her admission. 'I'm sure Hannah and I can help you, but if you're going to keep playing poker, it would be a hard sell for me to get her to agree.'

'Hold on. I don't want you saying anything to Hannah. You can hardly ask her to give me money without explaining.'

Damien was deep in thought. Nat loved him for the fact he seemed to be genuinely considering how he could help her. 'Damien, I can't take your money and certainly couldn't ask you to be deceitful with Hannah. She'd never forgive either of us if she found out. The best option is for me to get a job and pay it off slowly.' This was the most sensible option, of course, but not necessarily one she intended to carry through.

'Hopefully, the swimwear business will start to make some money for you soon. From what Phyllie said you've been working long hours on it.'

She saw the question in his eyes. He'd seen right through her but was too polite to ask her outright if there actually was a swimwear business. She reached for the door handle. 'I'd better get to bed. Tell Hannah I'll drop in and bring Amy's present with me. I still can't believe I turned up empty-handed. A big fail on my part tonight.'

Damien opened his door and walked around to meet Nat. 'I'll come in and call an Uber. And don't worry about tonight, you've got a lot on your mind, and I get that you're stressed. The one thing I'd suggest is that you go into the house, get on to the poker site and deactivate your account. It can be addictive, and I've read stories about it ruining people.'

Pity you didn't mention this when you introduced me to the site. The bitterness in Nat's thought was unfair, she knew that. For a start it had been Matt, not Damien, who'd suggested online poker.

Damien played poker for some light entertainment and an escape from everyday life. Neither he nor Matt could have anticipated she'd have a problem with it, but, to be fair, neither had she.

Damien's words stayed at the front of Nat's mind for the next few days after admitting her situation to him on Saturday night. *Get on to the poker site and deactivate your account. It can be addictive, and I've read stories about it ruining people.* Yes, but for every story of someone being ruined, there were stories of it being life-changing for others. And she'd done so well at the poker night and initially online. She must have changed something in her game. That was probably the issue, she realised as she drove through the leafy streets near Phyllie's house on her way back from the supermarket. She needed to go back to basics. Get back on the free tables and check her strategy and stick to it. But even if she refined her game play, she still had the issue of being fifteen thousand dollars in debt and having no money to add to her poker account. She'd thought this through and decided she'd try one last approach before seriously considering looking for a regular job.

Nat climbed out of her car and took the shopping bags from the boot.

'Need a hand with those?'

She turned to find Leon standing a few metres behind her. She shook her head. 'No, I'm good, thanks.' Her heart rate quickened as she took in his lopsided grin. She took a deep breath, doing her best to ignore the attraction she felt towards him. 'You're not looking for your escaped goat again are you?'

Leon shook his head. 'No, just going for a walk. Want to join me?'

'Yes, I'd love to.' The words came out of Nat's mouth before she had a chance to bite them back. Yes, she would love to, but Phyllie's words came flooding back to her: *Imagine if you did what you've done to many others – dated him for a few months and then dumped him. That might be the last I'd ever see him.*

'Actually, I can't, sorry.'

Leon raised his eyebrows in question. 'It's just a walk, Nat. No big deal.'

Not for him, perhaps, but Phyllie was right. Her track record was terrible and right now, when she was unemployed and sinking further into debt, it was best to keep to herself. While he might not be offering more than a walk, if it turned into something else, she'd have Phyllie to answer to. It was best to be friendly and keep him at a distance. 'I forgot that I've got a few things to do for Phyllie.'

Leon pushed his hands into the back pockets of his jeans. 'No worries. Another time, perhaps?'

Nat nodded and watched, disappointment filling the pit of her stomach, as he continued on down the road. She wondered if there would be another time.

She turned with her shopping and made her way towards the house. She planned to talk to Phyllie that night and had decided to make her favourite dinner. Hands full, she stopped at the front door, surprised to find it ajar. She smiled, thinking of Phyllie's constant reminders to 'keep the bloody door shut so that blasted goat doesn't waltz on in'. Still, it saved her having to put her shopping down to unlock it.

She pushed it open with her foot and took the bags through to the kitchen, winding her way around the ironing board and iron that Phyllie had left in the middle of the living room, a skirt hanging over it looking like it had been half ironed.

'Phyllie, are you here?' Nat assumed she was probably in the bathroom. She would hardly go out halfway through ironing something and leave the door open.

There was no response.

Nat left the shopping bags on the bench and walked through to Phyllie's room. She knocked, poking her head around the door when there was no answer. The door to the en suite was open, and Nat could see Phyllie wasn't in there. She went back to the living area and switched the iron off at the wall. She could imagine the lecture she'd receive from Phyllie if she left the iron on when she went out.

Perhaps the goat was back and Leon hadn't realised it had escaped. She hurried to the back door and flung it open, half expecting to find Phyllie pinned against the back fence by the goat. But other than a noisy miner splashing in the birdbath by the rose garden, the area was empty.

She went back inside. Perhaps Phyllie had ducked out to see one of the neighbours. Still, to leave the iron on and the door open wasn't very smart. She unpacked the groceries, putting the perishables in the fridge, and returned to the living area. She switched the iron back on. She would finish ironing Phyllie's skirt and then she'd start dinner.

She was packing up the iron, having laid the neatly pressed skirt on her grandmother's bed, when the front door flew open and Phyllie hurried into the house.

'What's the rush?' Nat called.

Phyllie stopped, her eyes wide as she stared at Nat. 'What are you doing here?'

Nat laughed. 'What do you mean? I live here, remember?'

Confusion flashed across Phyllie's face for a split second, then she smiled. 'I know that, I mean what are you doing *down here*? I thought you'd be busy working. You've hardly left that top floor since you've been here.' Her eyes moved to the ironing board. 'Although, that's a good sign if you're ironing something to go out in.'

'No, I finished ironing your skirt. I put it on your bed.'

Phyllie laughed. 'Why are you ironing my clothes? I'm sure I can manage that when I need them. Mind you, I hardly ever get that blasted thing out. I usually cheat and throw my clothes in the dryer for a few minutes. It gets the creases out.'

'Phyllie, you left the iron on with your skirt half ironed before you went out. I was finishing it for you so I could put the ironing board away.'

Phyllie's forehead creased as she frowned.

Nat stared at her grandmother. Had she forgotten she'd been ironing? No, she'd probably just been in a hurry to do something. She was still in her gardening trousers so couldn't have gone far. 'Where did you go?'

'What, just now?'

Nat nodded.

'Down to the charity shop. It's Joan Margaret's birthday today, and Bev organised a cake for afternoon tea. I promised I'd go down and join them, but when I got there, the shop was locked up. I'm about to ring Bev to find out what happened. I'm praying that no one has had a fall or anything worse.'

She'd gone for a birthday celebration in mud-covered trousers? That was unheard of for Phyllie.

'Were you in a hurry to get down there?'

'Not particularly, why?'

Nat pointed at her trousers. 'It's just that you'd normally get changed for social events. Your blouse is nice, but you're wearing your gardening trousers. And it's Tuesday. Unless they've changed their opening hours, the shop's closed today.'

Phyllie looked down at her legs, her eyes widening. She gave a little laugh. 'Silly me, I thought it was Wednesday. And anyway, it's only the op shop. No one dresses up to go there.'

Others might not dress up, but Phyllie certainly did. She always presented herself nicely. There's no way she'd leave her house voluntarily wearing her gardening trousers. Nat realised there was no point discussing it further. Phyllie was looking distressed.

'How about I put the iron away and start on dinner while you make your phone call,' Nat said. 'I've got a special treat for you tonight.'

Phyllie eyed her suspiciously. 'Why?'

Nat laughed. 'What do you mean why? Can't I do something nice for my grandmother? After all, you're letting me stay here rent-free.'

Phyllie nodded. 'Okay, well, that's very nice of you. Although I don't need to make a call if it is Tuesday. I'll pop back down to the shop tomorrow for the birthday celebration. But I will go and change out of these trousers. I've had a silly headache all day, which I blame for all of this.'

Nat watched as she walked through to her room, Hannah's concern about their grandmother playing on her mind. Was there something wrong with Phyllie or was it just old age? She seemed confused and was behaving entirely out of character. A headache wouldn't usually cause that. It reminded Nat that she hadn't mentioned the door being open.

She returned the iron and ironing board to the laundry and set about making dinner, trying to push aside Hannah's concerns that there was something not quite right about Phyllie and she needed to be examined. Hannah overthought everything and worried unnecessarily. Irritation surged through her. Why was it that Hannah always managed to annoy her? She took the lamb cutlets from their bag, ready to crumb them. A sick feeling replaced the irritation of moments before. Hannah's concerns weren't so much annoying her as they were worrying her. What if her sister was right? What if there really was something wrong with Phyllie?

'Let me get this straight.' Phyllie pushed her knife and fork together on her empty plate. 'Your friend wants you to invest in the company and you need five thousand dollars to do this?'

Nat crossed her fingers beneath the kitchen table. She seemed to be doing this a lot lately. She'd let Phyllie enjoy her lamb cutlets before launching into her story about the expansion of Anita's swimwear website and how Nat had an opportunity to become a partner in the business. There was no way she could tell Phyllie the truth – that she planned to use the five thousand dollars to invest in online poker. She needed to win enough to pay off her credit card and repay Phyllie, assuming she loaned her the money. She nodded. 'Yes, it's not a lot, but more than I currently have. I'll own ten percent of the business, and Anita has guaranteed me work for the foreseeable future if I'm a partner.'

Phyllie narrowed her eyes. 'But what about your work as a community support officer? I thought you loved it and that you found it rewarding.'

'I do enjoy it, but I'm enjoying a change too. I'll go back to it at some stage.' Nat did her best to plant what she hoped looked like a genuine smile on her face. 'It's an exciting opportunity to do something that's mine. But I completely understand that you might not be in a position to loan me the money.'

Phyllie's features remained set in a frown. 'Of course I can loan you the money, that's no problem, I'm just not sure it's a good idea.'

Nat's heart began to race. She needed this money. She didn't want to ask her father. She still owed him money from other occasions, and the way he and Sue had been speaking it sounded like they were scrimping every cent for their retirement. She did her best to remain calm. She couldn't let Phyllie see how desperate she was. 'Why do you think it's not a good idea?'

Phyllie pushed her plate away. 'You've been living here for over three weeks, Nathalia. In that time, I've only seen you leave the house to get groceries and to attend Amy's birthday celebrations. You've not been on any dates or out with your friends, and you don't seem to be getting any exercise either. I seem to remember you talking about a run of some kind you were training for. Something for cancer. And what about Shared? You usually volunteer in both the gardens and soup kitchen every week. You haven't even mentioned the place since you've moved in. Whatever you're doing on that computer has become a total obsession, and it worries me.'

Nat realised her mouth had dropped open. She'd had no idea Phyllie was paying such close attention to her. She was also right. Nat had hardly left the house since she'd moved in. She swallowed. She loved playing poker, well, she loved it more when she was winning, but she did love it. There was something that drew her back to it every day and kept her up late at night. God, she'd better not mention it to Hannah, or she'd be telling her she had some kind of addiction. Nat almost laughed at the thought, but the amusement was quickly replaced with concern. She didn't have a problem, did she? The time she'd initially dedicated to it was because she wasn't working so didn't have anything else to do. She'd start work again, and it would just fall back to being a hobby she spent a few hours on here and there.

Phyllie's eyes were drilling into hers, waiting for an answer.

'I haven't got the money to be going out at the moment,' Nat said. 'Even going to Shared costs me money in petrol. And I'm not interested in dating right now.'

'You've been working day and night for weeks on this website business. You're being paid for that aren't you?'

Nat paused. How did she talk her way around this one? 'I'm being paid in kind initially. The hours I've worked so far have given me an additional ten percent ownership, so if I invest I'll own twenty percent. Anita doesn't take a wage at the moment either, but that will change next month as she has a large order from China to fulfil.' Nat wasn't sure where all this made-up information was coming from and a sick feeling expanded in her stomach. She was lying to her grandmother!

'You'll get paid next month?'

Nat nodded. There was no turning back now. 'Yes. Keep in mind it's a start-up business. Often the income received needs to be reinvested into the business rather than paid out as wages. This is why the five-thousand-dollar investment will help tide the cash flow over for another few weeks before the money from the China contract comes through. And you're right, I've been a bit obsessed with it all.' She gave a small laugh. 'I'd better get back into my running, or I'll be no good at all in September for Relay for Life.'

'I'll do you a deal. You start running and getting away from that computer, and I'll help you invest in the swimwear business.'

'I'll pay you back as soon as possible. I don't think it will take very long.'

Phyllie patted her hand. 'No need to do that. I'm happy to help you out.'

'That's very kind of you, but I'll definitely pay you back.' There was no way Nat was going to let Phyllie help fund her poker career without paying her back. The sick feeling in her stomach expanded to a feeling of unease that settled over her. She wasn't someone who usually lied as she'd just done. But then, it was a one-off. She'd win the money back quickly and repay Phyllie. She'd probably be able to pay her back with interest.

Chapter Thirteen

Hannah had hardly seen Damien since he'd returned from taking Nat and Phyllie home from Amy's party. He'd been on call on Sunday and had ended up working from lunchtime until close to ten o'clock. And with him on afternoon shifts Monday and Tuesday, they'd been like ships in the night, rolling over briefly in the morning to discover they were both in the same bed, then Hannah crept out, leaving him to sleep before his next shift while she got Amy ready for school and herself for work.

Not seeing Damien had been a blessing. Zane Fox's message had left her on edge. She hadn't called him or replied to his text but knew that any day now he was likely to contact her again. Her stomach lurched at the thought of him. So much for signing a contract saying he wouldn't contact her again. What could he want, other than more money? She couldn't pay him any more, that much she knew.

'Mum.' Amy came bounding into the kitchen with Bear beside her. Hannah couldn't help but smile. The two of them had become inseparable. Seeing them, she now wondered why she'd ever objected to having a pet. For an only child, it had been like providing a sibling. 'Have you seen my school diary?'

Hannah nodded towards the kitchen bench where Amy's lunch sat, along with her diary and music book. 'You left them on the kitchen table last night.'

Amy grinned and scooped them up, ready to pack her school bag. 'And you're not changing your mind about today?'

Hannah gave a wry smile. As much as she would like to change her mind, she knew that she couldn't. She and Damien had agreed to give Amy a trial run of letting herself into the house after school on her own. Hannah would be home by five thirty, but it did mean Amy would be home alone for at least two hours. 'No, I'm not changing my mind, but you have to promise to ring me if there are any problems. It doesn't matter how big or small.'

Amy smiled. 'You need to relax. Bear and I will be fine.'

Hannah's phone pinged with a text message, and she slid the phone across the counter and looked at the screen. Her heartbeat quickened.

Ring me if you know what's good for you. ZF.

She'd known ignoring him wasn't going to achieve anything. She'd even contemplated changing her phone number, but as he knew where she worked and lived, it seemed futile.

Amy was staring at her. 'Your hand's trembling. Are you okay?'

Hannah shoved the phone into her pocket and smiled. 'Of course I am. Now, go and finish getting ready. We need to leave in ten minutes.'

Amy frowned. 'Are you sure you're okay? You've gone very pale.'

'Just a difficult client. Nothing for you to worry about, but it does mean I'm going to have a more challenging day than I'd thought.'

Amy seemed to accept this explanation and hurried off, Bear at her heels, to clean her teeth and find her shoes.

Hannah sank on to a stool at the counter. She would have to face Zane Fox. She slipped her phone from her pocket and typed a message.

Will call you from work this morning.

She hit send and sighed. How on earth had she got herself into this situation?

Hannah pulled into her driveway a little after five that afternoon. She'd managed to get away early, which was a relief. She'd spoken to Amy briefly on the phone, and while it sounded like everything was fine, she found it difficult to concentrate on her work while worrying about all the potential dangers Amy could be facing. She was being ridiculous. She knew that. Well, part of her knew that, and the other part, the part that couldn't help but assess risk, knew otherwise. She opened her car door and was greeted by the sound of Selena Gomez blasting from the top floor of the house.

She grinned. She remembered doing precisely this when she was twelve and she and Nat would let themselves in after school and look after each other until their parents arrived home from work. Except it was the Backstreet Boys blaring from the speakers.

She pushed open the front door and walked through to the kitchen. She wasn't going to let Amy know she was home. She was interested to see whether the music would stay on until just before five thirty, when Amy was expecting her home, or whether she would just leave it blaring.

Hannah stopped as she entered the kitchen and found Damien sitting on one of the stools sipping a glass of mineral water. He put his finger to his lips signalling for her to be quiet.

'I want to see what she does,' he said. 'She's certainly having a good time.'

They exchanged a conspiratorial smile.

Hannah kept her voice low. 'What are you doing home? Aren't you in the middle of a shift?'

He nodded. 'This is my break. We were in the area, so I had Pam drop me off. She's gone to pick something up in Doncaster and will be back to get me in about twenty minutes.'

'So you thought you'd spy on Amy? I thought you said we should trust her and that she'd be fine?'

Damien smiled sheepishly. 'Doesn't mean I can't worry about her.'

Hannah nodded, glad it wasn't just her being overprotective. 'She'd kill us if she knew we were both down here.'

'I doubt she'll have any idea with that racket going on. Although when I opened the front door Bear came straight down to see who it was. That was good at least. He went back up to Amy after sniffing around me for a couple of minutes.' He slid from the seat. 'Now, can I pour you a glass of wine? I assume your day has left you feeling the need for a nice Pinot Gris?'

Her workday had been relatively straightforward, but yes, the added stress of worrying about Zane Fox meant a glass of wine was in order. She nodded. 'Thanks, that would be lovely.'

She'd called Zane when she'd arrived at work. She'd reminded him about their contract and his verbal promise not to contact her, but he'd just laughed, sending chills down her spine when she realised how worthless the contract was. He wouldn't tell her what he wanted over the phone. Instead he insisted they meet. 'I have a proposition for you, Hannah. Nothing to be concerned about, just something that I believe could be mutually beneficial.'

She'd reluctantly agreed to meet him at a cafe in Doncaster on Friday afternoon, figuring if she did it last thing before returning home, it would have less impact on her working day. Dread filled her every time she thought of him.

She watched as Damien poured her glass and handed it across the counter.

'Thank you.'

He smiled, but she noticed that his smile didn't reach his eyes. He'd been like this for the past few days. 'Is everything okay?'

He looked surprised at the question. 'Of course, why?'

'You just look a bit down, that's all. Are you thinking about your biological parents?'

Damien sighed and sat down beside her. 'No, it's not that, although they constantly play on my mind.' He stared at her for a moment, as if he was carefully choosing his words. 'A friend's in trouble.'

'Who? Someone from work?'

He shook his head. 'I can't say.'

'Okay, well, what kind of trouble?'

'She's got herself into debt, and I think she might have an addiction that will make it very difficult to turn things around.'

'An addiction? To what?' Alcohol and drugs immediately came to mind.

'Gambling.' Damien's eyes fixed on his glass of water. 'She's lost a lot of money in the online poker rooms.'

Hannah's mouth dropped open. It was someone from his poker night proving precisely what she'd been worried about. 'I thought you said it only cost a dollar to enter and would be almost impossible to lose much money.'

Damien pushed a hand through his hair. 'It is if you're sensible. I said the free and one-dollar tables were what I play, but if you move to the more expensive tables, then I guess you can lose a lot.'

'And she has.'

He nodded.

'Does she have a partner? Do they know?'

He shook his head. 'No, she's on her own. I'm not sure if that's better or worse, to be honest. The problem is she seems to think she can dig herself out of the hole she's in by spending more money.'

Hannah watched her husband as he spoke. While words were coming out of his mouth, he wasn't making eye contact. He seemed to be deliberately avoiding it, in fact. Why wasn't he able to look at her? Her mind snapped into analysis mode. He was hiding something, and she could only come up with one valid reason for doing this: there was no friend. *He* was the friend, and he was hiding behind his lies. 'Did she say how much she'd lost? Are we talking hundreds, thousands, tens of thousands?'

'Fifteen thousand. Although I'm not sure it's all gambling-related, but it's still a lot.'

Hannah sucked in a breath. If her suspicions were right and there was no friend from work, did this mean Damien had lost fifteen thousand dollars of their savings? He'd have to have transferred it from one of their accounts or cashed an investment. Surely he wouldn't do that behind her back?

An uneasy feeling hung over her as she thought of her own recent deception. Borrowing money from Phyllie to pay off a thug was hardly something he'd be expecting her to do either.

'Are you planning to help her?'

This time he did meet her gaze. 'What, with money?'

She nodded.

'God no, that would be the worst thing I could do. There's no point handing over our money for her to lose.'

Hannah nodded. On the surface, they appeared to be having a reasonable discussion, but everything about Damien's body language and lack of eye contact confirmed that they weren't. He was hiding something. Something she intended to get to the bottom of.

She lapsed into her own thoughts, the loud bass of Selena's song abruptly coming to a halt. She glanced at the clock. Five twenty-five.

'I guess she's expecting you home any minute,' Damien said. He stood and planted a kiss on Hannah's forehead. 'I'll go outside and wait for Pam. Amy doesn't need to know I was here checking up on her.'

'Actually, I'll come out with you and pretend I just got home too. I don't want to spoil her first day of independence.' She picked up the barely touched wine glass and put it in the fridge before following Damien to the front door.

They slipped outside, closing the door quietly behind them.

'I hope your friend can work out her problems,' Hannah blurted out. She'd said it for no other reason than to gauge his reaction.

His eyes immediately flitted to the road, as if he was watching for his ride. 'Thanks, so do I.'

Hannah pulled the front door shut with a loud bang, ensuring that Amy would know she was home. Bear barked, and moments later was in the hallway, tail wagging. She rubbed his head, smiling as she heard Amy on the stairs.

'Hey, Mum.'

Hannah pulled her into a hug. 'Hi yourself. How did you go this afternoon?'

'Good. Bear and I have been upstairs doing my homework. I'm almost done.'

Hannah opened her mouth, tempted to say that studying with loud music on would hardly be productive, but shut it again. She, of course, wasn't supposed to know about the music. Instead, she squeezed Amy tight. 'Well done, I'm very proud of you.'

Amy blushed and pulled away. 'The afternoon went fine. There's nothing to worry about. Now, I'd better finish my homework before dinner.'

Hannah watched as her daughter left the room. *Nothing to worry about.* How she wished this statement was true. She had plenty to worry about – Zane Fox and now Damien.

She continued down the hallway into the kitchen and opened the fridge, retrieving her wine glass and scooping up her computer from where she'd left it on the countertop, then went upstairs to her office.

The evasive conversation she'd had with Damien worried her, as did his behaviour during the last month. While he'd said that he was sad about his biological parents, Hannah was now wondering if there was more to it, or if that sadness had led him to look for an escape. An escape in the form of online poker.

She powered up her laptop and opened their online banking accounts. She clicked on their savings account first, scrolling through the line items. There was nothing out of the ordinary. The credit card proved to be the same.

She pulled open one of their drop files, looking for the investment accounts they held. She was pretty sure they required them both to sign to withdraw any money, and she really couldn't imagine Damien forging her signature. But she needed to check. They had accounts with three different investment funds. She found the account details and logged in to each one. There was no unusual activity in any of them. All were slowly increasing in value, not at the speed high-risk funds might, but Hannah certainly wasn't going to jeopardise their savings in high-risk ventures.

The only other investment they had was the one Damien's parents had given them on their wedding day. It had been left in Damien's name with the plan to add Hannah's once she'd legally changed her surname to Anderson. By the time she'd done that it hadn't seemed like a priority to add her name. They'd earmarked that investment for Amy's future and had chosen to leave it accumulating. Hannah checked it when she prepared their tax documents for the accountant each year. She hadn't prepared the previous year's accounts as yet, so hadn't looked at the figure for over twelve months. She pulled out the drop file with the login details and opened a web browser. She keyed in the details and waited for the account balance to appear. When she'd done their taxes the previous year the account had close to thirty thousand dollars in it.

She stared at the screen. The balance was just over eighteen thousand dollars. Hannah's stomach churned as she clicked on the transaction history. A withdrawal had been made for fifteen thousand dollars two months ago. Interest of three thousand was the only other transaction for the year.

She continued to stare at the screen. No wonder Damien was feeling down. She doubted his mood had anything to do with his adoptive parents at all. He'd told her outright that he played the free tables or the cheap ones and had only deposited a small amount of his winnings from one of the poker nights. So much for *a friend was in trouble*. When had he become such a good liar?

She logged out of the account and returned the file to its drawer. She'd thought her problems with Zane Fox were bad, but this took things to a whole other level. Not only had her husband lost a substantial amount of their savings, but he'd also lied on numerous occasions directly to her face. At this stage, she wasn't sure which was worse.

Hannah operated on autopilot for the remainder of the week. Damien was working odd shifts and she'd barely seen him. She put her focus on getting Amy to school and getting through the workday. Her mind had been a jumble of thoughts on how to approach him over the gambling debt, and she'd worried endlessly about her meeting with Zane Fox. She'd arrived a few minutes early on Friday afternoon at the cafe in Doncaster, only to receive a text message from Zane saying he'd been delayed and would contact her to reschedule. She'd stared at her phone, not sure whether to be relieved or annoyed. By Saturday morning the one thing she'd concluded was that she needed some advice with the Damien situation.

Late on Saturday afternoon, with Damien and Amy having taken Bear to Aranga Reserve dog park, as according to Amy he needed 'socialising with other dogs', Hannah used the opportunity to visit her father. She pushed open her car door and pulled her coat tightly around her as she stepped into the cold winter air. A welcome waft of smoke puffed from the Edwardian brick chimney, and she hurried up the driveway to the front door. She shook off the sense of disappointment when she saw that the hydrangeas were no longer in flower and many had been deadheaded. It was silly really, but they did evoke strong memories of her mother.

She lifted her hand to ring the bell as the door opened – her father, dressed in a warm grey knit jumper, beamed at her.

'What a nice surprise!'

Hannah laughed. 'Hardly a surprise. I did text you to let you know I was dropping in.' She stepped in out of the cold, the warmth of the house an instant comfort.

'I know, love.' Her father took her coat and hung it on the wooden coat stand next to the front door. 'I meant it was a nice surprise to get your text. Come through. Sue's in the kitchen, putting a little snack together for us.'

He led her through to the kitchen, where Sue was putting the finishing touches on a fruit and cheese platter. She looked up, a delighted smile spreading across her face. She was quick to round the kitchen island and draw Hannah into a hug. 'How are you, hon?'

Tears welled in Hannah's eyes. A simple question had the potential to open the flood gates. She blinked back the tears and did her best to appear unflustered. 'I'm good, thanks. How are you?'

Sue released her from the hug and sighed. 'Good, but things have been better. Your father and I have something we'd like to talk to you about too.'

Hannah turned to her father. 'Is everything okay?'

'Let's talk about us later; it's nothing to worry about, just an idea we wanted to float by you. Now, how's that dog of Amy's going?' He poured them each a glass of wine. 'Have you sent it back yet? Sue and I have a bet going as to how long he'll last.'

Hannah smiled. 'If either of you said he'll be sent back then you've lost. It's like he's been part of the family for years. We're lucky she went for one that was a few years old rather than a puppy. Bear is not only toilet trained, he's been properly trained and is very obedient. Hasn't even chewed a shoe. I don't think Amy's stopped smiling since her birthday.'

'And she's been okay letting herself in after school?' Sue asked.

'It's only been three afternoons so far, but yes, she's doing fine.' She laughed. 'Although the neighbours might not agree.' She went on to tell them about coming home early on Wednesday to blaring music that was turned off five minutes before her expected arrival time.

They took the wine and cheese platter through to the living room and sat down in front of the crackling open fire. Hannah looked to her father as she inhaled a sweet smell of citrus. One of her mother's tricks had been to add dried apple and orange slices to the fire to fill the room with a sweet scent. At other times she'd burned pinecones or cinnamon sticks. It was only smelling the fragrance now that reminded Hannah that her mother used to do this. It wasn't something she recalled her father doing at all since her death.

'The room smells gorgeous. Exactly like Mum used to have it.'

Sue nodded. 'She had a knack for creating an inviting space, didn't she? We felt that we needed her with us today. To provide us with some advice. We hoped filling the room with a reminder of her might give us some inspiration.'

'Anything I can help with?' The concerned look on her father's face as Sue spoke wasn't something Hannah saw often.

'Possibly, but let's talk about you first and why you wanted to see us. As much as we love you dropping in, it's not exactly a regular occurrence. Did you need some help with something?'

Hannah nodded, not quite sure where to start. Her hand automatically reached for the comfort of her heart-shaped pendant.

Her father smiled encouragingly. 'I'm flattered, I must admit. You normally have everything worked out so clearly with your risk assessments helping you find your way.'

'This is a bit different.' Hannah took a deep breath. 'I discovered Damien has secretly been playing online poker and losing. He's run up a debt of fifteen thousand dollars using funds from an investment we have.'

Sue gasped as her father's mouth dropped open. 'You're kidding?'

'I wish I was. I'm here because I don't know what to do, and I remembered how you and your friends had that intervention for Troy Mitchell when he was gambling a lot.'

Her father nodded slowly. 'We'd all spoken to Troy many times, so the intervention was a last resort rather than a starting point. Have you spoken to Damien about this?'

'Not yet. I only found out on Wednesday and his shifts this week haven't left us much time to have a proper discussion. I need a plan, a strategy for talking to him rather than just confronting him with it. Any suggestions for how I handle it?'

'It depends on how he reacts,' her father said. 'Which of course is highly unpredictable.' He shook his head. 'I can't believe it, to be honest. With Troy it wasn't surprising. He had an addictive personality. Drank too much, regularly took drugs and had been gambling on and off for years. He always had a vice. Damien doesn't strike me as someone with those kinds of problems.'

'Me neither,' Sue added. 'You can take Damien at face value, I'm sure of it. Are you sure you haven't made a mistake? That there isn't something else going on?'

Hannah shook her head. 'The gambling is the first sign of any problem at all. Although . . .' she frowned. 'He's been depressed about his birth parents and not having had an opportunity to get to know them. I think the poker has been a distraction from his own thoughts.'

'There's not a lot you can do to help him with his birth parents. It certainly isn't your fault,' Sue said.

If only she knew. 'Any ideas on what I should do?'

Her father nodded. 'Yes, the first step is to talk to him. Let him know that you know about the situation and that you need to put steps in place to minimise the damage for him.'

'Steps?'

'With Troy, we organised for the bank to cut off access to money. It was the only way. The investments that he hadn't already spent were frozen so he couldn't access them, and other than a savings account that he could deposit into, all his credit cards were removed.'

'I think that's what's shocked me,' Hannah admitted. 'That not only has he been running up a huge debt, but he's done it so sneakily. It's the only account I don't check regularly. Just annually for tax.'

'Before you talk to him, I'd look into some support groups. See what advice you can get. We found this invaluable with Troy. Not only were there groups to support him directly but there was one for us too, to ask questions and get a feel for how we needed to speak to him.'

Hannah nodded. 'That's a great idea. I've done plenty of searching online for signs that your partner is in trouble and things like that, but I haven't searched for support groups.' She sighed. 'I don't need this right now.'

'We don't need things like this at any time, believe me,' Sue said. 'Finances can cause so many problems.' Her eyes glassed over with a far-off look.

'Is that what you needed Mum's advice for?'

Her father nodded. 'As you know, we're planning to retire next year. The managed fund all of our superannuation is in hasn't performed well in the last four years. If we do retire next year, the amount we'll have is much less than we anticipated. We'll have to manage our money very carefully.'

'Will you still be able to travel?'

'Not very far. Certainly not overseas, as we'd planned.'

Hannah fell silent. That was so unfair. Her father and Sue had worked hard their entire lives and had been looking forward to retirement.

'The fund will most likely come good again over the next few years,' Hannah said. 'You don't need to worry too much. They usually perform on a cycle.'

'Yes, but I'm worried we've invested in funds that are too high-risk.' His cheeks flushed. 'I was hoping to add a lot in the last few years but instead have done the exact opposite.'

'I'm surprised your fund manager let you,' Hannah said. 'Usually the closer to retirement you get the lower the investment risk.'

'I gave instructions and they followed them. Now we need to decide whether to leave it in the high-risk option and hope that on the next up cycle we not only recoup our losses but move ahead, or whether we pare it back to the lower risk and accept the loss.'

'We work with a number of fund managers at No Risk,' Hannah said. 'Would you like me to organise for one to provide some independent advice on how you move forward?'

He let out a huge breath. 'Would you, love? That would be terrific. Our biggest concern has been that the fund continues to lose money. It will leave us in an awful position if it does. Selling the house might be our only option.'

Hannah looked from her father to Sue. 'Would that be so bad?'

'I'd feel awful if it came to that,' Sue said. 'As you know, I lost most of my savings during the global financial crisis. If only I'd owned real estate at the time and sat on it rather than holding shares that never recovered. Selling the house would seem very unfair. It was your mother's house and ultimately should be yours and Nat's inheritance.'

Hannah smiled. 'I wouldn't worry about us. We'd much rather you and Dad enjoy your retirement the way you want to.'

Her father shook his head sadly. 'I appreciate that, love, but I don't think Nat would feel the same way.'

Hannah was deep in thought as she drove from East Malvern back to Donvale. She felt awful for her father and Sue and would have one of the fund managers contact them on Monday to see if they could help. She would be surprised if Nat objected to them selling the house. For all her flaws, she was the first to come to people's aid. She wasn't materialistic and flitted from one home to the next. She doubted Nat would have any emotional attachment to the house or any expectation that she would one day inherit it. She sighed. Hopefully they could get their investments back on track and selling the house wouldn't be necessary.

She'd sent Damien a text saying she'd pick up some Thai food on the way home, but was surprised when he responded with:

Don't. Amy and I have prepared something. See you soon x.

She continued mulling over her situation and her father's advice about looking into support groups. It was a good idea. Fifteen thousand dollars wasn't a small amount. If it had been one or two thousand, she would have been concerned but also have believed that it was something they could rein in quickly. Fifteen thousand was out of her depth.

Her phone pinged as she turned into her street. She glanced down and saw Zane Fox's name appear on the screen. Her stomach lurched and she pulled over. She picked up her phone with shaking hands.

Meet me at Chinwags in Prahran on Monday at eleven a.m.

Hannah sank back into her seat, her heart thumping. She'd already spent Phyllie's money getting rid of Zane, and by the looks of it, it certainly hadn't achieved that. She couldn't give him any more money. He'd never stop asking if she did.

She took a deep breath and pulled back out into the street, driving the last hundred metres to her house. What a ridiculous situation. She was hiding a massive secret from Damien, and Damien thought he was hiding his financial debts from her. So much for their promises to be upfront with each other and not harbour secrets.

Chapter Fourteen

Adrenaline pumped through Nat's body. She held her breath while the last card, 'the river', was dealt. An ace. She now had two pair – aces and kings. Unless her competition had two aces in his hand, she should win. Would he raise again? Damn, he'd gone all in.

Nat's hand hovered over her mouse, the arrow pointing at the 'Fold' button. Her strategy said to fold and wait for a better hand, but her gut said no. She pushed her mouse to the right, the 'All In' button now highlighted, and clicked it.

The cards were revealed. He had a king and a four. Nat sighed with relief. She was starting to win again at fifty-dollar tables. While the buzz wasn't as great as the two-hundred tables, she seemed to be able to win or place more consistently. If she could continue like this for a few more days, she would begin to recoup her losses quickly. She'd also banned herself from donating to Shared or any other charity until her debt was repaid.

She opened a new table and a second. She'd played more than one table at a time before, and when she was winning it worked well. She knew other players played as many as twenty-four tables at once, but she didn't have the confidence to play more than two yet.

The games began. She heard Phyllie call out to her at one stage, asking if she wanted a cup of tea, and she called back that she was busy but would be down within the next forty minutes. That was being optimistic, of course. It meant that she was going to play through to the final round of the tournaments.

Thirty-five minutes later, Nat appeared in the kitchen, a broad smile on her face. The games had resulted in second and third places – prize money of two hundred and fifty dollars. With an additional two hundred from her first place in the earlier game, things were looking up.

Phyllie glanced up from the kitchen table where she was doing a crossword, dwarfed by a large arrangement of lilies. 'You look like you're having a good day, love. What's the goss in the world of online swimwear?'

Nat moved across to the bench and flicked on the kettle. 'Not a lot to report. Things are coming along nicely, though. It looks like China isn't the only big deal that's about to come off.'

'Your investment is safe then?'

Nat nodded and unscrewed the top of the biscuit barrel. She helped herself to a Scotch Finger and held out the container to Phyllie.

Phyllie shook her head, waiting for Nat to respond.

'The investment is safe. It'll be turned into gold before you know it.'

Phyllie laughed. 'That's good to hear.'

'Where did the flowers come from? They're beautiful.'

'Leon. That's why I called you down for tea earlier. I thought you might like to say hello.'

Nat did her best to ignore the flutter in her stomach whenever Leon's name was mentioned. Part of her would have liked to have said hello but another part of her knew it was sensible to stay away from him. 'Were the flowers his apology?'

Phyllie nodded. 'Yes, and a two-hundred-dollar voucher for the nursery so I can replace the plants Rainbow enjoyed. It was very generous of him. We had a lovely chat. He's right into reading thrillers, did you know that?'

Nat shook her head. 'I don't know much about him at all.'

'I promised he could borrow my copy of *Murder on the Orient Express*. Can you believe he hasn't read it? And I have that lovely first edition sitting on the shelf in my sewing room.'

'Did you give it to him?'

Phyllie shook her head. 'No, I said you'd drop it in this afternoon. I didn't want to come upstairs and disturb you. You don't mind, do you?'

Nat felt her cheeks colouring. Why was Phyllie sending her to see Leon after being so adamant she didn't want her messing things up with him?

'It's just dropping in a book, Nat, nothing more. Now, enough about Leon. I want to talk about you and your workaholic tendencies. It's Saturday afternoon. You're working seven days a week. Whether you're spinning swimwear into gold or not, you need to get out and do something else.'

Nat poured her tea and brought it across to the table to sit with Phyllie. 'In approximately two hours from now, I'll be catching up with Pip. I haven't seen her since before I moved in here. She's invited me for drinks before seeing a comedian, Grant Lacey. She received two free tickets for the show and her fiancé, Richard, is away, so she needs someone to go with her. I imagine half the night will be taken up talking about her wedding and her locking me down for bridesmaid fittings and the rest of it.'

Delight crossed Phyllie's face. 'That's wonderful. A perfect end to what looks like a great day for you.' A wicked glint appeared in her eyes. 'But remember my rule – no houseguests. I don't want to be woken in the middle of the night by thumping, or should I say humping, coming from your bedroom. Do you understand me?'

Nat laughed. 'Don't worry. Pip's about to get married and won't be happy if I abandon her to hook up with someone. I'm just looking forward to a few laughs. Grant Lacey's supposed to be hilarious.'

As instructed, Nat took the first edition from Phyllie's bookshelf and walked to Leon's house. Butterflies flittered in her stomach, which annoyed her. She was delivering a book, nothing more.

Leon opened the front door seconds after Nat knocked. His hair was wet, his white t-shirt, crisp and clean, hung loosely over his snug-fitting jeans.

She held up the book. 'Special delivery from Phyllie. I believe you're expecting this.'

Leon smiled. 'Thanks, come in. Perfect timing actually, I just opened a bottle of wine.'

Nat hesitated before stepping through the doorway and into a living area. With a fireplace on one side, three navy couches and a large wooden coffee table, the room was homey and inviting. The carved artwork on the walls added a unique and interesting feel. Nat walked over to one of the carvings.

'These are nice.'

'Thanks.'

She glanced over at him, noticing his cheeks had coloured. 'Did you do them?'

Leon nodded. 'A hobby. I usually sell them and donate the proceeds to charity, but every now and then I keep one.'

Nat moved to the next carving, a sailboat travelling through rough seas. 'They must take you ages. The detail is so intricate.'

'There's no hurry to finish them. Some take me days, some take me weeks.' He winked. 'They keep me out of trouble. Now, how about that glass of wine?'

'Just a small one, thanks. I need to be going soon to get changed. I'm going out with a friend tonight.'

A shiver went down her spine as his eyes looked her up and down. 'You look pretty good to me as you are.'

Nat smiled. 'Not sure an old t-shirt is considered appropriate for a night out, but thanks all the same.'

Leon grinned and motioned for her to follow him through to the kitchen. He poured them a glass each from the bottle of Merlot he had breathing on the kitchen bench. More wood was featured throughout the kitchen, but it was the large window overlooking the back garden that Nat's eyes were drawn to.

She clapped her hand over her mouth to stifle her laughter.

Leon followed her gaze and laughed too. 'Bloody goat. I fixed the trellis so she can't get out, but she was so bored I had to give her something to do.'

A number of wooden blocks looked to have been hammered into the grass. Rainbow was currently balancing halfway along the ten metre row, tentatively placing one hoof forward.

'She's been walking up and down it for ages. She'll be good enough for the circus soon.'

Nat's phone pinged with a message as they watched the goat. It was Phyllie.

Just drop the book off, my girl. No breaking my Leon's heart.

Heat rose in Nat's cheeks and she placed the wine glass on the kitchen counter.

'Everything alright?'

'Sorry, I have to go. I hadn't realised how late it was already. The text was a reminder that I'm being picked up soon.'

Nat's own disappointment was reflected in Leon's expression.

'No worries, let me walk you out.' He walked her to the front door and held it open for her. 'Thank Phyllie for the book, won't you?'

Nat smiled. 'Will do.' She turned and headed back up the path and out of Leon's garden. What was Phyllie playing at? One minute she was sending her to see Leon and the next dragging her back. If she didn't want her breaking Leon's heart, why even suggest Nat have anything to do with him at all?

Two hours later, Nat sat across from Pip at Trambos, a quaint pub in Carlton. It was buzzing with the relaxed laughter and chatter of the Saturday night crowd, reminding Nat that she'd isolated herself in the previous weeks.

They'd met half an hour ago and Nat was genuinely delighted to see her friend. She was also in an excellent mood, having won another game before coming tonight. It was as if her lucky streak was back again. Maybe she would be able to dig herself out of the hole she was in. And at this rate, a lot quicker than she'd previously imagined.

'What the hell, Nat?'

Nat's hand froze, her mojito halfway between the table and her lips. She'd never seen Pip so annoyed, and she assumed she was about to learn why.

Pip was shaking her head. 'You've ignored my calls and hardly answered my texts and now you're unsuccessfully trying to build a career playing online poker? That's ridiculous.' She took a huge sip of her cider. 'You've done some bizarre things, but this one tops it all.'

Nat put her mojito down on the table and laughed. She couldn't help it. The way Pip was looking at her and talking to her was so out of character it was hilarious. She'd hardly packed herself off to a convent or started taking drugs or doing something way out there.

'It's not funny. I've known you for years now, and you flit from one thing to the next, never spending more than a few months at it. I guess that's a positive on this occasion in that you must already have itchy feet and be thinking of moving on to something else. I also can't believe that I had to hear from that arsehole Todd that you'd been fired. I bumped into him a couple of weeks ago; I was surprised he remembered me actually, but he obviously paid attention to who you took to the Christmas party last year. He was practically salivating with excitement when he filled me in. But gambling, Nat, are you crazy?'

'Jeez,' Nat said. 'Where's nice, lovely Pip gone? Let's talk about you and Richard and how that's going and where the wedding planning's up to. It will make for a nicer night than having an opinion on something you know nothing about.'

'I know enough about gambling to know it's something to stay right away from. You remember Dean, Wendy Hollis's husband?'

'Of course.'

'Wendy found him in his car in the garage after he'd used a pipe and the car's exhaust to kill himself.'

Nat did remember. It had been an enormous shock. Dean was one of those guys who'd always been the life of the party. A loving husband with a baby on the way.

'He'd maxed out all their credit cards, spent all their savings and even had the house remortgaged. We, including Wendy, all thought he was doing well in his position at Reuters. It turns out he'd been fired over six months earlier and was spending his work hours at the casino. Imagine the position that left Wendy in. Not only grieving for the loss of her husband and father of her baby but with huge amounts of debt as well. She had to sell the house and move back in with her parents. Gambling can become a disease. It's addictive and ruins lives.'

Nat wasn't sure how to respond to any of this.

Pip studied her. 'How much have you won, if this is now your career?'

'Overall, I'm not sure, to be honest, but to give you an idea of how lucrative it can be, I've won over seven hundred dollars today.'

'Profit or winnings only?'

Heat crept up Nat's neck. 'Winnings. Profit would be about five hundred. Still, not a bad result for the day.'

Pip nodded. 'Okay, so in the four or five weeks you've been doing this, how much profit have you made?'

'God,' Nat said. 'I wouldn't ask you such a personal question about your finances.'

Pip rolled her eyes. 'That tells me exactly what I thought – you've made none and are probably in debt. How much?'

Nat took a large sip of her drink. 'It's none of your business. All you need to know is I'm enjoying what I'm doing, and I'm not in huge debt.' Okay, so that was a lie, but it really was none of Pip's business. She hadn't volunteered the information, and had no intention to.

Pip reached across the table and squeezed her hand. 'Sorry. I'm not trying to be a bitch. I'm genuinely worried about you. If this were a part-time hobby, I'd still be a bit worried, particularly after what happened to Dean, but you're doing this full-time. What about the work you love? Sitting inside on a computer all day playing poker with random strangers can't be good for you. Surely you want to be doing something that matters? When did you last volunteer at Shared? I helped out in the soup kitchen after work on Wednesday night and Robyn said she was worried about you. That you usually put in an appearance at least twice a week and she hadn't seen you for about three weeks. That's not like you to let people down.'

Nat sighed. Part of her was tempted to tell Pip that she had contributed to Shared via donations, but she decided to keep this to herself for now. 'I just need a break for a while, that's all. If anything, I'm the one who's been let down. I didn't do anything wrong at Benedict's and look how that worked out. I can't imagine I'll get another job very easily without a reference.'

Pip grinned. 'Actually, I think you can get another job just like it. One of my clients is the HR manager at Endeavour Trust. They're about to advertise for a community support officer. I told Col, the HR manager, to hold off until I'd spoken to you. He's willing to interview you next week before he advertises. If you're suitable, you'll save him the headache of going through the whole recruitment rigmarole. I think he's away for the first few days of the week so it would probably be Thursday or Friday.'

Nat stared at Pip. As much as she knew she should probably be thanking her friend, she felt annoyed. She'd explained she had a full-time job and wasn't looking for another one. Just because Pip didn't approve of poker didn't mean she shouldn't be doing it.

'And,' Pip continued, 'you don't need to worry about him finding out about the guy you took home while you were at Benedict's. I already told him.'

'You what? How's that going to help my chances of getting a job?'

Pip laughed. 'Col's cool, you'll like him. He rolled his eyes and said he couldn't believe they hadn't just given you a warning, that he'd probably do the same thing himself if put in that position. It's against the contract terms at Endeavour Trust too, but he's not going to penalise you for something you did at another job. He said doing something like that showed your heart was in the right place. As I said, he's a great guy.'

Nat couldn't help but smile. It was a shame he wasn't the HR manager at Benedict's. If that was his attitude she probably wouldn't have been fired.

'Now that you're smiling, I'll take it as a sign you're interested in the job?'

Nat shook her head. 'I never said that. I'm grateful you've gone to the trouble but the timing's not right. I'm going to make this poker thing work.'

Pip stood. 'I'm going to get us some more drinks, and when I get back, I'm going to convince you otherwise. Even if I have to blackmail you, you'll be applying for this job.'

Nat watched as Pip wove her way through the wooden tables to the bar. Underneath the tough act she seemed to be trying on, they both knew that Pip was too nice; there was no way she'd resort to blackmail or anything underhand. It just wasn't how Pip operated.

Nat's head was a little fuzzy as she powered up her computer the next morning, ready to start her workday. Phyllie had gone out with her friend Verna for the morning to visit Verna's son's farm in the Yarra Valley. She'd probably return with amazing fluffy scones or slices of one of Verna's legendary sponges. Her mouth drooled at the thought. She'd woken late after getting home just after one. The Grant Lacey show had been fabulous. She and Pip had laughed until their sides hurt, which had surprised Nat as she'd been feeling angry when they'd arrived at the theatre. Pip had stooped to the lowest of lows when it came to convincing her she should interview for the job.

'Fine, if you're going to ignore all my compelling arguments as to why working for an organisation like Endeavour Trust would be beneficial for both you and them, then you leave me no other option.'

Nat had waited, wondering what on earth Pip was going to come up with. What came out of her mouth had shocked Nat.

'No way. Why would you do that?'

'Tell your family you're gambling full-time? Why not? If it's a legitimate career and you're winning money, why wouldn't you share this news with them?'

'Because it's none of their business.'

Pip shook her head. 'I think it is. I don't want to be the friend who knew all about this and then discovers you've run up debts of thousands of dollars and I could have done something to prevent it.'

We're already at that point.

'I think I should probably tell them whether you interview for the job or not, but at least I'll know if you're working full-time, you won't have the same amount of time to ruin your life by losing all your money. You'll also have another income to fund your hobby, which will hopefully minimise your losses.'

'You'll only tell them if I don't interview for the job?'

Pip nodded.

'But what if I don't get it?'

'You're qualified, likeable and I've already twisted Col's arm. You'd have to do or say something wildly inappropriate not to get the job.'

Nat nodded, draining the last of the mojito from her glass. 'I guess you aren't giving me a choice then.'

As she opened two tables, ready to start the day, she smiled. Pip had been uncharacteristically persuasive, if you could call blackmail that, but she hadn't accounted for Nat's strong aversion to being told what to do. Yes, Nat would go to the job interview but she would ensure she presented herself so badly there was no way Col would give her the job.

As Sunday morning ticked by Nat only stopped to give herself enough time to make coffee and grab a banana. It was easier when

Phyllie was out not to get as distracted or have her wanting to sit and chat. While the arrangement was working well, Phyllie still wanted to know her business. It was lunchtime when she heard the front door open.

'I'm home bearing cake. Come and get it whenever you're hungry.'

Nat watched as her hand folded in front of her and she was bundled out of the tournament. It had not been a good start to the day. She'd lost everything she'd won yesterday and more. How could it go from one extreme to the other so quickly? There didn't seem to be any proper reasoning behind her winning or losing streaks. Was it all down to luck? Surely it couldn't be. She checked her account balance. She still had two thousand dollars of the five Phyllie had given her, but that meant she had lost three thousand in only five days.

'Nat? Are you home?'

She heard Phyllie's feet on the stairs. 'Yes, coming down now. No need to come up.' The last thing she wanted was to be responsible for Phyllie taking a tumble on the stairs, as well as her substantial financial losses. She closed her computer down and walked out of the room to the landing at the top of the stairs.

Phyllie beamed up at her. 'Let's be incredibly decadent and have cake for lunch. Verna gave us the rest of a delicious hummingbird cake. The passionfruit is to die for. Let's celebrate, shall we?'

'Celebrate?' What on earth was there to celebrate?

'You going out last night,' Phyllie said. 'You're back in the land of the living, which is just wonderful. Now, I hope you're not planning to work all day. You must start taking some time for yourself on the weekend.'

Nat moved down the stairs in a trance. She couldn't even begin to imagine how Phyllie would react if she discovered what she was really up to. And if she was honest, she wasn't sure she would be able to handle her finding out.

Chapter Fifteen

Damien and Amy disappeared with Bear for most of Sunday morning, giving Hannah plenty of time to trawl through websites on addiction. When she read through the online questionnaires with titles such as 'Do you have a Problem?', she wondered how many of the symptoms listed Damien was suffering from. It was quite likely he was experiencing extreme guilt, and what he'd told her about feeling low because of his birth parents could be a lie. The articles all began to blend into one: the same lists of likely symptoms addicts would be suffering, along with advice to get help. *You are not alone.* It appeared there were thousands of people who were being ruined by gambling, and there were plenty of support services.

She read through the Gambler's Aid website, discovering it offered a full range of support services, including daily meetings. A bit like AA, she assumed. You could speak to psychologists, and there was a chat room to talk with like-minded people. She couldn't enter a chat room and pretend to have a problem. They'd see through her straightaway. Well, they would if they asked her anything at all about poker. But would they? And anyway, was there any reason to say it was her? She could always ask for some advice about confronting someone with a gambling problem.

She hesitated before creating an account. Other than an email address, it wasn't like she was giving any of her real details. And even if she was, what did it matter? This wasn't anything dodgy. She was looking for some guidance on how to handle something she felt out of her depth with. There was no point confronting Damien without a plan in place for moving forward. She'd read enough that morning to know that he was likely to lie about his gambling habit when confronted.

She thought about a username. She could use Bear. People often used their pets' names, didn't they? But what if there was someone online who knew about Bear? She gave herself a mental shake. It was hardly a unique name. But, to avoid the risk – as slim as it might be – she used *BrownDog40*. A combination of Bear and Damien's age.

Once she'd verified her account, Hannah started to read through the various chat threads. It seemed on most chat screens two or three people were having a conversation. She hadn't been sure how it would work. She'd almost imagined that, like social media, there might be a large number of people commenting on a single post. These smaller interactions made it more personal and meant a proper conversation could be had.

She sat back and read through the conversation notes of a woman, *Jazbelly70*, who was asking for help. She woke each morning vowing to stay away from the poker rooms and could often get through most of the day without going near them, but at around five o'clock the urge was so great she found herself back on the tables for most of the evening. She'd maxed out six credit cards and spent all the savings she and her husband had accumulated. Hannah sucked in a breath as she read on. The woman's husband knew nothing of the debt, or that she was in trouble. She'd convinced him that she just played for fun, mostly on the free tables, and he shouldn't be concerned. He was now planning a trip to

Europe for the two of them to celebrate her fortieth birthday, completely unaware of their financial situation. In her day job she was a bookkeeper, so had always looked after their finances. He trusted her implicitly, and she had no idea how to break the news to him.

Two people were in conversation with her. Both were incredibly sympathetic, reassuring her she'd get through this. One had what looked like good, practical advice.

> You need to install gambling blockers on all of your devices. Use Gamblock and PokerProblem as a start and then research what else is available. Put as many on as possible to help lock you out. This will at least stop you from getting further into debt.

The other person concentrated more on the issue with her husband.

> As hard as it may seem right now, you need to tell him. He's going to find out at some stage, perhaps when he goes to pay for the trip to Europe. You've said earlier how much he loves you. Prepare for him to be shocked and disappointed, but hopefully, he'll be supportive too.

Hannah wondered how supportive she'd be if Damien lost all their savings. From everything she'd read, gambling addiction was no different from alcohol addiction or substance abuse. If he had problems with either of those, she'd be beside him, trying to help. Gambling *was* different though. The financial stress it brought was just awful.

As she watched the conversation unfold further, she was surprised that neither of the people chatting to Jazbelly70 had suggested she see a therapist or go to a meeting. Her fingers hesitated only momentarily before she typed a message.

BrownDog40

Hey Jazbelly70, feel your pain right now. Wondered if you'd considered speaking to a psychologist or joining one of the GA meetings? You might find it helpful.

She sat back, her heart beating a little faster. She felt like a fraud dishing out advice.

Jazbelly70

Hi BrownDog40. Thanks for the suggestion. Yes, I've looked at GA meetings but have been too scared to take the plunge and go. What if I knew someone there? How on earth would I explain what I was doing?

Hannah smiled, her fingers already typing.

BrownDog40

The meetings are confidential, and if you met someone you knew would it be a bad thing? If they're there too then they're struggling and need help. You might find a kindred spirit who you can confide in. And if there's no one there that you know, that's a great outcome too.

Jazbelly70

Good point, BrownDog40. Thanks, I'll look
into it.

A surge of adrenaline pumped through Hannah. That felt good, really good. Giving a gentle piece of advice. She hoped Jazbelly70 did take her up on it. She shuddered. While she agreed that Jazbelly70 needed to tell her husband, she didn't envy either of them. Breaking that sort of news would be traumatic enough but being on the receiving end of it would be even worse.

A knot twisted in her stomach at this thought.

She read through a number of other conversations that were taking place. The daily struggle to stay away from the online rooms seemed to be one of the major battles addicts were facing.

Two hours passed in a flash and she heard the automatic garage door open. Damien and Amy were home. She quickly cleared her browsing history and powered down.

The chat room had been eye-opening. A window into a world that until a few days ago she'd given very little thought to, and it wasn't one she'd ever thought she'd need. She hadn't even had a chance to ask for any advice on how to approach Damien. She could already guess from what she'd read that people would suggest she be diplomatic and supportive and have help options available. She needed something more specific though. She'd get back online later and ask the question. Ideally, she'd like to speak with someone who'd been through this. Either as the gambler admitting their downfall, or the partner hearing about it for the first time.

Hannah didn't have the opportunity to get back online to the chat room on Sunday. Damien had suggested the three of them head out after lunch to Stiggant Park in Warrandyte and take Bear for a walk along the upper Yarra River. They all loved it there, and Amy was delighted with the thought of introducing Bear to the river and bush.

As she got dressed for work on Monday morning, she thought back to their afternoon. To Damien squeezing her hand as they'd walked along the picturesque river with Amy and Bear bounding along in front of them. From the smile on his face she assumed he was thinking just as she was, that their child had had a complete transformation. The broody pre-teen had disappeared, and their happy, fun girl had returned. Hannah just hoped the shine wouldn't wear off as Bear became less of a novelty.

'I'm sorry,' Damien suddenly said.

Hannah stopped in her tracks. While she'd been mulling over various ways she could approach him about the gambling and his debt, she hadn't considered the scenario of him admitting the problem. Maybe he'd been in the chat room and received the same advice she had been giving out early that morning.

She waited for him to continue.

'I know I've been moody and distant. The thing is, I've been doing something that I haven't felt comfortable telling you about.' His eyes shifted from her face to the river. 'As I said to you, I've found this year particularly hard, dealing with the loss of my biological parents and having no knowledge about who they were.'

She was right; he had used the poker to try and numb his pain.

'I didn't know how to deal with it. The fact that it's so final, that I'll never know anything about them is tough to wrap my head around.'

If Hannah weren't wracked with guilt, she would have drawn her husband to her to comfort him. But her legs were trembling, and she had no idea how she'd explain that away.

He took a deep breath and made eye contact with her again. 'Last week I started seeing someone. A psychologist.' His cheeks reddened with the admission. 'I didn't want to say anything, but I feel uncomfortable keeping such a big secret from you. I hope you don't think I'm a big baby or that I'm wasting money.'

Hannah stared at him. What? She tried to compute what he'd just said. That he hoped she didn't think he was wasting money. What about the fifteen thousand?

'Han? You think I'm an idiot, don't you?'

She shook her head, realising she needed to react to his admission. 'God no, of course I don't. I think it's a great idea. Hopefully, it will help you get some closure. And no, I don't think it's a waste of money at all.' *The fifteen thousand, on the other hand . . .*

Relief flashed across his face. He pulled her to him and hugged her tight. 'That's why I love you. You're always there for me. It's probably the most important thing to me about us. That you'd support me no matter what. I'll let you know when I have my sessions, as the first one left me feeling a bit down afterwards just dealing with it all. I wouldn't want you or Amy thinking there was something else wrong.'

Hannah returned his hug, feeling like a massive fraud. Yes, she supported him, but her version of support was the very reason he was now in therapy.

'Mum!'

Hannah was brought back to the present and the fact she should be getting ready for work as Amy poked her head around the bedroom door.

'Could you drop me a bit earlier this morning? I need to go up to the music room and see if I can get a new reed for my saxophone. If they don't have any, we might need to get some after school.'

'Of course. I'll be ready in five minutes. Your lunch is down on the bench. Get your bag packed and leave Bear some fresh water and biscuits and we'll get going.'

An hour later, after dropping Amy at school and grabbing a coffee, she sat at her desk checking her emails. Her phone pinged. Zane Fox reminding her of their eleven o'clock meeting. Her heart rate increased, as did her distaste for the man as a second text arrived demanding she confirm her attendance. Did he really think she'd forgotten?

Hannah allowed thirty minutes to travel from No Risk to Prahran. While it would typically only take ten to fifteen, she needed time to try and calm her nerves. She had thought through a million different scenarios as to what Zane wanted to see her about, but each scenario wound itself back to the same thing. He wanted more money.

She was right.

Zane stirred sugar into his coffee as if he didn't have a care in the world. 'I need another payment if you want me to continue to keep quiet.' He slid a piece of paper across the desk. 'I received this last week. As I mentioned at our first meeting a few weeks back, Janine was put in touch with me by Family Information Networks and Discovery. I spoke to her initially confirming that I was unable to provide any details for her, and now I've received that.'

Hannah lowered her eyes to the page, scanning the words.

While I understand you are in an awkward
position, please be assured I only wish the best for
my son. I have no intention of creating problems

in his life but would love an opportunity to meet him and at least express my wishes of getting to know him. Of course, I understand that he may not feel the same way and that is something I'll need to deal with if it is the case. I would be very grateful for your help in relaying my wishes to him. If a fee is required to make this happen, then please let me know.

'As you can imagine, I'm in quite an awkward position. We have a woman, who in my opinion sounds decent and nice, wanting to make contact with the son she birthed. Imagine what this poor woman went through. Not only the situation that led to her getting pregnant but then having to live with the shame of everyone knowing. Giving up a baby in any circumstances is difficult, so don't think because she was the victim of a crime it was any easier for her than it is for others.'

Hannah shook her head. If you'd never met Zane before you might believe his heartfelt words. But she'd seen enough of him to know that he didn't mean any of them. 'What do you want, Zane? How much are you planning to charge me to get rid of her?'

Zane's eyes widened. 'You want me to kill her?'

'Oh, for God's sake, of course I don't. I want you to get rid of her from our lives. As in I don't want to hear you mention her again or for you to ask me for more money. Go back and ask her what she's willing to pay to get the information, and I'll pay you the same not to give it to her.'

He smiled. 'Now, that's more like it.' He slipped another sheet of paper across the table to her. It showed further communication between him and Janine.

I'd be willing to pay up to ten thousand dollars to be reunited with my son. Unfortunately, I am not in a position to pay more than this. This is my accumulated life savings. If I had more, I would, of course, offer it.

Another ten grand? Where was she supposed to get that from? She certainly couldn't ask Phyllie, and she couldn't tell Damien. And even if she did, it was almost guaranteed Zane would be back a few weeks later asking for more.

'When I gave you the first payment you signed an agreement and said you wouldn't contact me again. Yet here we are. How can I trust that you'd go away once and for all if I paid you more money?'

Zane sipped his coffee, licking the foam from his lips. 'Janine's offered me money, I'm not going to say no to her.'

'If I pay you another ten thousand it will close this down once and for all?'

He nodded.

Hannah thought back to what her lawyer had said when she'd asked him to draw up the initial agreement. That she was dealing with a blackmailer and a legal contract was probably going to mean nothing to him. He'd been right.

'Can I have some time?' Hannah needed time to think about her next steps. With all Damien was going through right now, perhaps the best scenario was that she tell him about Janine and what she'd done. But the fallout could be disastrous. He'd taken to gambling and run up a huge debt just because he was feeling sad about not knowing his biological family's history. She hated to imagine what lengths he'd go to, or debts he'd accumulate, if he knew the truth about them and what she'd kept from him.

Zane nodded. 'I'm going away, which is lucky for you. Normally I'd give you a week maximum, but on this occasion, I'll expect an answer on Friday of next week, the thirtieth.'

Hannah nodded. That would give her plenty of time to work out the best solution, and to get a credit card in her name if she decided to pay him off.

With Damien working afternoon/evening shifts that week, Hannah found the Gambler's Aid chat room a welcome distraction from her thoughts of Zane and what she was going to do about him.

She'd plucked up the courage to ask the members for advice on how to confront her husband and had received a number of responses. She'd ended up chatting with a woman who had faced a similar scenario only a few months before. She'd noticed her husband's gradual decline into depression and hadn't been able to work out what was causing it. It had come to a head when she'd gone to pay the school fees for the start of the new term for her two children only to discover their bank account was overdrawn.

LizaE

It's my fault. I should have paid more attention to our finances. Although to be fair to me, he was using credit cards I didn't even know about to fund his addiction. He'd also convinced me to invest large amounts of our savings on what he told me was the advice of a financial planner. I trusted him, of course.

184

Stupid me. There was no financial planner. That money was a one-way investment straight into the casino.

Hannah had enjoyed chatting with LizaE, as her tag called her. When she'd asked how she'd approached her husband, the woman had some interesting things to say.

LizaE

I didn't know where the money had gone to start with, only that it wasn't in the account any longer. I was hoping there was a reasonable explanation for where it was. I think I had my fingers crossed so tight that they almost fell off.

According to LizaE, the next few months were about keeping afloat. Her main concern was for her husband's safety. She worried every time she went out that she'd come home to find he'd taken his life.

LizaE

He knew he'd let us all down. We had to take the kids out of private school and put them at the local state one. That is probably the one upside of the whole situation. Suddenly we're saving thirty grand on school fees. Imagine what you could do with thirty grand if it fell in your lap. But, of course, at the moment it isn't falling in our laps, it's just paying off a ridiculous amount of debt. I never thought I'd be in my thirties with kids and be on the verge

of bankruptcy. But staying strong and supporting Doug means we've had some great times
since. He's seeing a psychologist and attending GA meetings daily. He's still holding down
his job, so we'll get out of this mess at some
stage. Our savings are gone and the house is
remortgaged to the hilt, but we haven't lost it
yet. Crazy to think how quickly one person can
blow two hundred grand!

LizaE was certainly going through a tough time. At least Hannah
had caught this reasonably early. Fifteen thousand, assuming
that was the total Damien had lost, was manageable. Their bank
accounts and investments were still intact, and no mortgage had
been taken out on their house. The fact she was across all their
finances certainly helped. LizaE's story was interesting, but she still
hadn't shared with Hannah how she'd approached her husband.
Hannah had done her research and knew that she was going to
have to handle the situation delicately, but she'd still like to hear
how someone else had done it. She clicked on the chat window
and started to type.

Chapter Sixteen

As Nat waited for the kettle to boil, she did her best to push all thoughts of online poker from her mind. But she couldn't. Nor could she believe it had taken losing the five thousand dollars Phyllie had given her to push her towards looking for some help. She'd lost it all in a matter of days. She had a problem. Her first thought when she saw her bank account once again empty was: where could she get more money from? In retrospect, she should have felt the horror that she'd now burned through fifteen thousand dollars in the poker rooms and still had no means to pay back the credit card. It had to stop. As much as she loved the buzz when she was winning, the extreme despair she felt when she lost told her it was not okay to continue.

She contemplated talking to Damien again, but if it got back to Hannah, she'd be mortified. Instead, she started with online research. She'd heard of Gamblers Anonymous but wasn't sure she was ready to face people in public by going to meetings. She'd now read plenty of articles about gambling addiction and taken numerous questionnaires that all told her what she already knew: she had a problem. What had interested her was a site called Gambler's Aid. It offered all sorts of advice, the opportunity to talk to experts, and it had a chat room.

She'd spent a few hours reading through chat conversations. The people were incredibly friendly and supportive. The first tip, after deactivating her poker account, appeared to be to put blockers in place to prevent her accessing any sites. Was she so weak she'd need to put blocks in place?

She searched in the chat room hoping to find someone who said they'd turned their losing streak around and were now winning. Imagine if she could do that too. Just a few decent wins would get her back on track and start her kitty again. She shook herself as the thoughts plagued her and confirmed, yes, she was weak enough to require blocks to be put in place.

She watched one conversation with interest. Two women were discussing the fact that their husbands were the gamblers, not them. One, BrownDog40, was asking how she should confront her husband. That was one thing Nat had in her favour at least; she didn't have to answer to anyone. Imagine admitting to your partner or family that you'd spent their life savings. It seemed that's what LizaE had gone through. Her thoughts shifted to Hannah as she thought about having to tell people. There was no way she'd ever tell Hannah, she could imagine her reaction. She'd be shocked but in a smug way. She'd give her the *you're such a loser* look she managed to convey so frequently without even speaking. It must be nice to be Hannah, to have everything streamlined. Her finances in order, a well-paid job and a husband who earned good money. They were living the life of a perfect fairy-tale family. Even Amy had smartened up according to Phyllie, since Bear's arrival. The *perfect* nuclear family. It made Nat's skin prickle with annoyance just thinking about it. She was sure she wouldn't feel that way if she had a sister she could relate to or even talk to without feeling judged.

She wondered, watching the conversation unfold, why LizaE was still visiting the chat room months later if it was her husband that had the issue rather than her. It seemed a little strange. She also noticed that BrownDog40 had asked her for details of how she'd confronted her husband and what his reaction had been. LizaE was providing a lot of details, but she still hadn't answered this question. Maybe she was pretending it was her husband who had the problem when it was actually her, so a confrontation had never happened? She decided to ask.

PinkFish88

Hey LizaE, I'm intrigued by your understanding of gambling addiction and the advice you're giving BrownDog40. Are you sure it isn't you that had the problem?

LizaE

Hey to you too, PinkFish88. No, not me with the gambling problem. Although I guess you could argue it is as my financial ruin is a result of gambling addiction. This chat room has given me great insight into what addicts are facing. My husband doesn't like to talk much about what's going on in his head, so this helps me at least have a vague idea. What's your story? Why are you here?

Nat stared at the screen. That served her right. She didn't want to get into a conversation about herself; she'd just been interested in finding out whether this person was misrepresenting who they were. It was so easy to do in the online world. But her explanation did sound reasonable. And even if she was lying, what did Nat care? She was only lying to herself. Another message appeared on the screen.

BrownDog40

Welcome, PinkFish88!

They knew she'd been eavesdropping. Not that she really was. If you posted in a public forum, then anyone could read it and join in. She took a deep breath, reminding herself she had come here for help. Her fingers glided across the keys.

PinkFish88

Thanks for the welcome. I've only recently been introduced to online poker but have managed to run up a debt of fifteen grand since I have. Quite an accomplishment really in less than five weeks. I came here partly looking for help in quitting and partly hoping someone would have a miracle solution as to how to win! Yes, I realise that even admitting that makes me look bad.

LizaE

Not bad, PinkFish88, just honest, which is refreshing. Have you told anyone?

PinkFish88

Just my new chat room buddies, being you two. My brother-in-law knows that there's a problem, but he hasn't pushed it too much with me.

LizaE

I found confiding in someone else helped. The chat room support is great, but having someone you can sit down and have a coffee with is better. I told my brother. He's been a fantastic support.

PinkFish88

It's not your problem though. You're asking for support for something your husband has done rather than admitting you've completely stuffed up. Has your husband told anyone or is he too ashamed?

LizaE

Fair call. I think the people at the GA meetings are probably the only ones Doug's told. He's embarrassed and would be mortified if he knew my brother was aware of all the details. But I've needed him. He's the one person I can rely on to be positive, no matter how things unfold. He's not judged Doug either, which I love him for. He recognises his problem as an illness, which it is. He's helped me see this too. At first, I was just angry. I even considered leaving him.

BrownDog40

I'd want to know if my sister was in this kind of trouble. I'd be shocked, but I'd do everything in my power to get her help. I'd hate to think she was going through something like this alone.

PinkFish88

It sounds like you have much better relationships with your siblings than I do. My sister would shake her head in disgust and reel off a list of all of my failures to date. I'll admit, it's a reasonably long list, but I'm not sure what she thinks it achieves to rub it in my face. Perhaps it makes her feel better about her boring life.

BrownDog40

She sounds like a bitch. What about a friend then, or someone more supportive in your family?

Nat thought for a moment. Aside from Damien, the one person she probably could confide in would be Phyllie, although she'd be gutted to tell her about the five thousand. But Phyllie was practical in her approach to life. She'd help Nat put in steps to make sure she never revisited the poker sites. But she'd lied to her about so many things. She hated to disappoint her grandmother.

PinkFish88

Maybe. I'll think about it. But I've hijacked this thread. Sorry. BrownDog40 was asking for advice on how to confront her husband. Any thoughts, LizaE?

LizaE

Just listen to him. Let him cry if that's what he needs to do and try not to be too judgemental. He's messed up in more ways than one, but if you love him, you'll need to look after him now. You don't want to lose him altogether. From what I've seen in chatting to people, addicts aren't honest. There are very few stories of people who lost everything and their spouses or partners knew all about it. They lie to cover their tracks or are dishonest to start with, like your husband hiding his investment. He'll be humiliated and quite possibly distraught when you talk to him. He'll most likely deny there is a problem. You'll need your evidence, the investment statement, to present him with and I guess try and do it with as much love for him as you can muster. Show him that you're there for him and will support him through this. I don't want to alarm you, but a lot of people who get into difficulties consider taking their own lives.

BrownDog40

My research has been scaring me. That's why I'm here asking for help. It's terrifying when you read the statistics. Forty-nine percent of people attending GA say they've contemplated suicide.

PinkFish88

Wow, that many?

BrownDog40

Yes. That's a global statistic, but in Australia it is believed one gambling addict a day commits suicide. It's not all online gambling. Poker machines are one of the worst culprits. Did you know that while we only account for 0.5 percent of the world's population, we have a fifth of the world's poker machines? No wonder so many people are in trouble. It's so irresponsible of the government. But then they make $5.8 billion a year from it, so you can see why they're not rushing to stop it.

Nat smiled at BrownDog40's message. She'd get along well with Hannah. She bet if she asked Hannah anything about gambling addiction, she'd have all the figures at her fingertips too. She wondered if BrownDog40 was a risk advisor?

LizaE

Lol! You certainly know your stats!

BrownDog40

A lot of research. I wanted to find out as much
as possible before I talk to my husband. I'm a
facts and figures kind of person. When something's out of my control, I think it gives me a
sense that if I know enough about it, I can help
control it in some way. Not sure on this occasion it will be any help to him, but it helps me.

BBrooter

I've got something that could help you
BrownDog40. Would relax you and make confronting your husband a lot easier.

BBrooter? Who was this? Nat was enjoying talking to the other two
women and had forgotten that their chat was public.

BrownDog40

What would that be?

BBrooter

Hold on. I'll post a pic.

Nat waited, and seconds later a photo appeared on her screen of an
enormous, very erect penis. Her hand flew to her mouth, a horrified laugh mingled with a gasp erupting from her.

BBrooter

Want some? It'll take your mind off that husband of yours. Turn you into a nasty wife.

LizaE

You'll be shut down any moment, you arse.
Have reported you to admin.

BrownDog40

Bye ladies, that's my cue to get going. Thanks
for the chat.

BBrooter

But BrownDog40, we can do it doggie if you
want. I bet you've got huge tits . . .

Nat closed the chat room screen, shaking her head. What an arsehole. Lurking in a chat room waiting to hijack conversations in
such an offensive way. It was a shame; she'd felt a sense of relief
being able to talk to the women about her problem. While neither
of them were gambling addicts, they were still dealing with it in a
big way.

The next morning, Nat's original plan to sabotage the job interview at Endeavour Trust went out the window the moment she
entered the not-for-profit organisation. The energy and vibe were
infectious, as was Col Fletcher. The human resources manager was
in his mid-forties and came across as one of the most contented

people Nat had ever met. He spoke about Endeavour with a passion that she admired and desired to feel herself. He'd been with the organisation for five years, having previously worked for Qantas. It had been a big change, mainly when it came to salary, but one he didn't regret.

'You come with glowing references from Pip,' Col said. 'Some incidents she mentioned are a little more colourful than others, of course.'

Nat blushed.

'But we won't hold any of that against you. We're looking for passionate people who put the client's needs above and beyond anything else.' He winked. 'And funnily enough, the reasons for dismissal from your previous job confirm that you go all out in that regard. Of course, we have the same guidelines as Benedict's as far as not taking clients home, but the fact that you put your own job at risk to help someone says a lot about your character.'

Nat grinned. She couldn't believe what got her fired from Benedict's was working in her favour here.

'If you're up for it, you can start Monday.'

Nat's mouth dropped open. 'What? Are you giving me the job? I didn't even bring in my résumé.'

'I trust Pip's judgement, and I can read people pretty well, Nat. You're someone who's given an amazing amount to the community in your previous paid and volunteer positions. You're a good person and, aside from everything else, that's what I'm looking for.' He pushed a piece of paper across the table. 'Here are the employment conditions and salary. I'd say it would be on a par with Benedict's, or possibly slightly better as we have a little more in our budget than they do.'

Nat glanced at the figure. It was indeed more. Six hundred dollars a month more. Living at Phyllie's meant her current expenses were minimal. With this type of salary, she'd be able to pay off her debt comfortably within the next six months, if not earlier.

'What do you say? Are you coming on board?'

Nat nodded. 'Definitely. Thank you for the opportunity. I won't let you down.'

Col stood and held out his hand to Nat. 'Welcome to the team.'

Nat's smile was wide as she pulled up in front of Phyllie's house and got out of the car.

'You look happy.'

She turned to find Leon walking towards her. Her heart raced as he approached. *Get a grip, Nat, he's just coming to say hello and he's off limits.*

'Good news?'

She nodded. 'I was offered a new job. It's with a company that's doing amazing things in the community, so I'm really happy.'

A delighted smile spread across his face. 'That's fabulous, Nat. Really terrific. I'm sure you'll do a fantastic job.'

Her smile slipped, causing concern to flicker in Leon's eyes. 'Did I say something wrong?'

She shook her head. 'No, it's just that I have a track record of doing the wrong thing and getting fired. I just hope that doesn't happen this time.'

'Don't let it happen.'

Nat laughed. 'It's not that simple.'

'Yes, it is. Anytime you know you're about to break company rules, go and see someone higher up the ladder than you. Ask them what you should do. It shows you're taking initiative and looking for a solution when one might not already exist. Believe me, it works. No one's going to fire you if they see you're genuinely passionate about making a situation better.'

Nat nodded. It was actually good advice. She'd tended to make decisions by herself, even when she knew they would land her in trouble. Col Fletcher was definitely someone she could talk to if a problem did need to be dealt with.

'See, I'm a good sounding board. You should consider dropping in and having unsolicited advice thrown at you more often.' He winked. 'I'm a leader in unsolicited advice. I think it's my calling.'

Nat laughed. 'I'll keep it in mind. Now, I'd better get going. I promised Phyllie I'd come straight home and tell her how it went.'

Leon pushed his hands into his pockets, the smile was still on his face but there was something else. He looked nervous. 'Don't forget about that advice,' he said. 'It's always there and usually comes with a glass of wine, sometimes even dinner. Drop in anytime.' He gave her one last smile and turned and headed back towards his house.

Nat hesitated. Had he just asked her out? She wasn't really sure. He was very friendly, but maybe that was just his way. They were neighbours and of similar age, so it made sense he'd want to be friends. And with Phyllie's warnings playing over in her head, that was all he was ever going to be.

Phyllie appeared to be pacing the lounge when Nat opened the front door and stepped inside. She stopped, her face breaking into a wide smile as Nat entered.

'Now, this is a wonderful surprise. I was thinking about my lovely Frederick, so I could use a distraction.'

Nat laughed. 'What's a surprise? That I've been out or that I've come home?'

199

Phyllie's smile dropped. 'Come home? Is that what you call a visit these days?'

'What are you talking about? I didn't think I was still considered a visitor. I thought you wanted me to stay as long as possible to keep Hannah off your back?'

'Hannah? That interfering pest. Well, yes, keeping her off my back would be a good idea. She wants to put me in a home, you know.'

Nat stared at her grandmother. She was behaving very oddly, and her eyes were glazed, certainly not their usual bright blue.

'Phyllie, where do you think I've been this morning?'

'How on earth would I know what your movements are, you silly girl? I assume you're about to tell me all about whatever it is you've dressed up so nicely for.'

Nat crossed the room and took her grandmother's arm. 'Come and sit down. I think there's something wrong with you.'

Phyllie allowed Nat to guide her to her favourite armchair. The dazed look in her eyes cleared almost instantly, and she stared at Nat.

'Sorry, love, I'm feeling a little odd this morning.'

'Perhaps we should get you to the doctor?'

Phyllie shook her head. 'No, they'll just diagnose me with old age.' She smiled. 'I was lost in thoughts about Frederick, that's all. I was confused for a split second but I'm fine now. You had the interview this morning, didn't you? How did it go? You didn't offer to take any of the clients home for the night, did you?'

Nat laughed, relieved to see Phyllie back to her regular self. Perhaps at her age it was normal to be a little forgetful and confused at times. Nat tucked away a reminder in her mind to consult Google later.

'No, I said and did nothing inappropriate at all. It was the easiest job interview I've ever been to. The company has a great feel to it, and I start on Monday as their new Community House Support Officer.'

Phyllie clapped her hands together. 'That's marvellous news! Marvellous. Give me five minutes to change, and we'll head out to Ms Jones's for a celebratory lunch. It's my treat.' She stood up. 'How exciting. A trip to Ms Jones's with something to celebrate. We couldn't ask for a nicer day.'

As she sat across from Phyllie, sipping champagne and enjoying a cucumber sandwich, Nat had to agree. It was an excellent way to celebrate. While the pull of the poker rooms was still with her, the fact that she now had a way to pay off the debt removed a tremendous amount of stress. There was no reason anyone would ever need to know what trouble she'd got herself into. She was also giving strong consideration to the suggestions from both Damien and the chat room messages to deactivate her account and put poker blockers on her computer.

'What exactly will the new job entail?'

Nat explained what a community support officer did, and the specifics of the position based on what Col had told her.

'What will you do about the online swimwear company?' Phyllie asked. 'You've put so much time and effort into that. Will you be able to do both?'

Nat nodded. 'I'll still have evenings and weekends.'

Phyllie frowned. 'But you've been working seven days a week on that business. Won't they notice you suddenly disappearing?'

'I'll chat to Anita tomorrow,' Nat said. 'She'll understand. Most of the systems are in place now, so my role would have reduced anyway.'

'And you'll get an income from both jobs?'

Nat nodded. 'And I'll be able to pay you back soon.'

Phyllie shook her head. 'Don't be silly. That money was a gift. I'm just glad the investment looks like it was a success.' She leaned forward and lowered her voice. 'There's a woman in a very flashy yellow shirt over by the fireplace waving at us. She's about your age. I have no idea who she is, do you?'

Nat glanced across the room to the fireplace. Her heart caught in her throat. *Anita Green.* She wanted to dive under the table and disappear.

Chapter Seventeen

Hannah watched her husband as he sipped his coffee, the paper spread out on the island bench. He looked happy and content, not like a man who'd recently lost fifteen thousand dollars gambling. He'd had a session with the psychologist the day before and it seemed to be helping with his issues surrounding his parents. *His parents.* She felt sick to the stomach just thinking of them and Zane Fox's threats hanging over her.

Damien looked up, breaking her train of thought, the corners of his eyes creasing as he smiled. He reached out his hand and pulled her to him. 'Don't you need to get to work? As lovely and unexpected as it is to have morning tea with you on a Friday, you did say you needed to be in by lunchtime.'

Hannah nodded. She did, but she also needed to talk to him. It was the reason she'd called the office and said she was working from home this morning. She wanted to talk to him before he started his afternoon shift. She wasn't sure how much longer she could go on without knowing the truth behind the money. As LizaE had suggested, she'd put together a lot of information on gambling addiction and where he could get help. She just hoped he was open to her talking to him about it.

'What's the matter?' Damien held her at arm's length, searching her face. 'You look like something's bugging you.'

'There's something I need to talk to you about.'

He dropped her hand. 'Okay, let's talk.'

'I have to get something first.' Hannah climbed the stairs to her office and took the folder she'd prepared from one of her drop files. She wasn't sure at all how this was going to go.

Returning downstairs, she saw that Damien had moved into the living room and made himself comfortable on one of the reclining chairs. He grinned. 'Thought we might as well settle in. The fact you have a folder makes me think we're here for a long session. It's not about horse riding, is it?'

It wasn't, although it would be very justifiable if it were. Hannah still found it hard to believe that Damien had gone behind her back and signed Amy's permission slip, which in effect enrolled her in the equestrian classes Hannah had said no to.

'It's not a big deal,' Damien had tried to convince her. 'We can't mollycoddle her forever. I've spoken to the school about the safety equipment and how the sessions are supervised, and there's no reason to worry. She could just as easily have an accident playing tennis and smash her head on the court. At least with horse riding she's wearing a helmet.' He'd pulled Hannah to him. 'It won't happen again, babe. Your mum was incredibly unlucky. You need to let Amy experience things.'

Hannah's anger had left her eventually, and she did see that she was being overprotective, but could anyone blame her? If you knew someone who'd died in a motorcycle accident would you encourage your kids to get one? Of course not. So why was it any different with horses?

Because they're not at risk from other traffic like motorbikes are. Damien's sensible words filled her head. He'd had an answer for every objection she'd raised, and in the end, she'd conceded.

Now she looked at him and remembered LizaE's advice on showing him how supportive she was planning to be. That the money he'd lost wasn't the problem, but ensuring he quit gambling was. She sat across from him on the couch with the squishy blue cushions that Bear appeared to have claimed as his.

'I'm worried about your online poker games.'

Damien stared at her for a moment and then laughed. 'That's what this is about? Poker?'

She nodded. 'It's addictive, and many people get into trouble with it. I don't want that to be us.'

'You want me to stop playing?'

'Definitely. As of right now I'd like you to deactivate your account and consider putting blocks on your computer to stop you from accessing poker sites.'

Damien kicked the footrest down and sat forward in his chair, an incredulous look on his face. 'Is this a joke?'

Hannah shook her head. 'I don't want you using our savings for your habit. It worries me.'

'My habit? I don't have a habit. I play after work a couple of times a week and on a weekend if there's time. I don't even bet half the time. I play the free tables because it's fun. Jesus, you spend more on boots than I do on poker.'

'How much money have you lost to date?'

Damien shrugged. 'As I told you last time, I haven't lost anything. I had a gift card with free starting credits. Since then I've been winning here and there, and the overall balance is in credit.'

'You haven't run up any other debts with it? Used money from our investments for your gambling?'

He shook his head. 'Nope, and anyway, you'd see it on the statements if I had. I'm pretty sure it would show up as Poker4Me or something similar.'

Was he really going to lie about it?

She handed him a piece of paper she'd printed with the balance of their investment account.

His face immediately paled.

'Fifteen thousand dollars was withdrawn from this account a couple of months ago. Did you think I wouldn't notice?'

Damien shook his head. 'It's not what you think.'

She waited for him to continue.

He ran his hand through his hair. 'I'm sorry, okay. I had to use this money for something, and I promised I wouldn't tell you what for. It will be paid back by the end of August. As you don't do the accounts until September, I thought you wouldn't notice. You only ever use that one-page summary they send you, without looking at the transaction history.'

'That's because we never make any transactions. Where did the money go?'

He shook his head. 'I told you. I made a promise.'

Hannah stared at her husband. Who could he be giving that kind of money to and wanting to hide it from her?

He sighed. 'You're not going to let it go, are you?'

She shook her head. 'How can I? Would you if you suddenly discovered I'd spent thousands of dollars without telling you and had done my best to hide it from you?'

'If I tell you, I need you to promise me you won't say anything to the person I loaned the money to. She would never forgive me.'

Hannah nodded, not having any idea who he could have given the money to.

'I gave it to Mum.'

'Trish?'

He nodded. 'They got themselves into a bit of financial trouble a few months back. They received a tax bill on the investment property they sold last year that they weren't expecting. It turns out my father, the savvy investor, didn't realise he had to pay capital gains tax.'

'Couldn't they use the money from the sale of the property?'

Damien shook his head. 'They invested it in a six-month investment that has hefty penalties if they withdraw the money early, so I suggested I loan them the money as our account allows one withdrawal without penalty. I was going to tell you, but Mum made me promise not to. She said they were so embarrassed to be in a situation of needing to borrow from us that she would be mortified if you knew.'

'But that's ridiculous. Of course I would have been fine with it, especially as it's being paid back. Even if it wasn't being paid back, I would be fine with helping your parents.'

Damien crossed the room and took Hannah's hands. 'And that's why I love you. I'm sorry, Han. I was put in a horrible position. Mum was really upset about it, so I thought it was easier to just do what she asked. You know what Dad's like, he would hate you to know that he'd messed up something like that.'

'So, all of the money went to your parents and none to online poker?'

Damien's face softened and he smiled. 'Yes, all to my parents. You have nothing to worry about with me and poker.'

Hannah stared at him for a moment.

Damien's smile slipped. 'You don't look convinced.'

'It's just very convenient, that's all. You've loaned your parents the exact amount you told me a friend owed to a gambling debt and I'm not allowed to ask them about it because they'll be embarrassed. I'm not sure I buy it.'

Damien ran a hand through his hair again. 'I can't stop you from asking Mum about the money, I'm just asking you not to. If you really don't trust me then go ahead and ask.'

Hannah hesitated. Up until now she'd trusted him implicitly. Whether his reasoning was justified or not, he'd still deceived her.

'I know how I can prove it.' He held out his hand to her. 'Come with me.'

She took his hand and allowed him to lead her up the stairs to the office. He sat at the computer and pulled her down next to him. 'Let me drive for a minute.'

Hannah watched as he opened and logged in to one of the poker sites he played.

'Let's look at my balance. Like I told you, I was given a hundred dollars of free credit from the gift card I won at one of the poker nights. You'll be able to see my current balance, and then the daily transaction lists that show if I've won or lost. It's quite an interesting document to study. You can see different patterns in the results for different days and times.'

He opened the balance page, turned the screen slightly to face Hannah and relinquished the mouse. 'Scroll through and see what I'm talking about.'

Hannah did. The available balance was six hundred and thirty dollars. She started to scroll through the daily transaction history. It showed each game he'd entered, what he'd invested and his net result. Most of the games he entered were free, or a maximum of a two-dollar buy-in. As she scrolled down further, she stopped when she found a fifty dollar buy-in.

'Oh, that freaked me out! I entered by mistake. I'd been doing well the previous few games I played on the two-dollar tables and decided to be adventurous and try a five-dollar table. Except I clicked on the fifty by mistake. By then it was too late.'

Hannah looked along the transaction line. 'You walked away with a hundred dollars?'

'I was lucky. Placed third. Pure luck, as I was dealt some very favourable hands.'

'That must have felt amazing to win?' Hannah wanted to gauge his reaction. Was he going to launch into a monologue of just how wonderful it was and how he couldn't wait to play more?

'Amazing? More like terrifying. Imagine if I'd lost or if I was playing those tables all the time. For a one-off, it wasn't the end of the world, but I was gutted at first when I assumed I would lose. You're up against professional players on those tables. Your odds are so bad you might as well just set fire to the money to start with. I can't imagine anyone, other than the professionals, enjoying those tables. It would be soul-destroying, let alone financially crippling losing such large amounts.'

Hannah continued scrolling down the huge list of transactions. When she got to the bottom, she realised it went back three years. She looked at Damien. 'You didn't spend anything the first six months you played?'

He laughed. 'I was too scared to lose, even if the money wasn't mine to start with. I moved on to the paid tables when Poker4Me sent me a message saying the free dollars would expire unless I started using them. I stuck to the one-dollar games for most of the time and occasionally played a two-dollar one.'

The transactions matched what Damien was saying. It was surprising looking along the line items to see how often he'd walked away with more money than he'd invested. That he'd built his original investment to over six hundred was impressive, especially when you saw the consistent wins and adding of small amounts to up the total.

'This is quite fascinating,' Hannah said. 'Your win rate is high. Doesn't that make you want to play more often or for higher stakes?'

'My win rate isn't that high. I tend to place second or third a lot. Like I said before, the higher-staked tables have professionals on them. If I'm coming second or third on a one- or two-dollar table, I'm unlikely to place in the money at all on the higher-staked tournaments. The fifty-dollar one was a fluke that I'm happy to take and not risk again. And no, I wouldn't play more often. It's a fun thing to do occasionally after work with a beer. I usually only play two or three games.'

Hannah leaned back in the chair, relief flooding through her. Damien didn't have a gambling problem, and he hadn't lost fifteen thousand dollars. She turned to him. 'I'm sorry I thought you were doing something deceptive. I was really worried about you. When you said you knew someone in gambling trouble, you looked suspicious, and I just assumed it was you.'

His eyes dropped as the words left her mouth.

Okay, this didn't add up. 'Why can't you look at me when I mention someone being in trouble with gambling?'

He lifted his eyes to meet hers. 'Because I promised the person I wouldn't say anything to anyone, and making promises like that always makes me uncomfortable. You know what I'm like. I hate keeping secrets.'

Hannah nodded. It was true. Damien preferred not to know a secret at all than be expected to keep it.

'I don't need to worry about you?'

'Of course not.' He took her hand. 'I'm sorry now I didn't tell you about the poker. If I'm honest, I knew you wouldn't like it, but I also knew it wasn't doing any harm. We should never have secrets, not ones that could lead to hurting each other.'

Hannah nodded again, not daring to speak. It was bad enough she'd held the truth about his birth parents from him but paying off Zane Fox made it a million times worse. She couldn't imagine any scenario where telling him the truth now would work out well.

He pulled her to him and kissed her softly on the lips. 'I love you, Han. I'm sorry I made you worry. I'll do my best to always be open from now on.'

She kissed him back, wishing she could go back twelve years and change what she'd done.

The rest of Friday dragged for Hannah. She'd double-checked the clock on her office wall numerous times, willing it to be five thirty, but it was still only early afternoon. She had too many personal issues plaguing her at the moment, uncharacteristically drawing her attention from her work. She was relieved to have spoken with Damien and even more relieved to realise he didn't have a gambling problem and they weren't in financial trouble. However, Zane Fox's beady eyes and smirking face continued to dominate her thoughts. She had seven more days to decide what to do about him, and so far all she'd done was try to push the situation out of her mind, hoping it would miraculously solve itself.

She needed advice. She needed a chat room that wasn't gambling specific, that just gave life advice. She wondered momentarily if such a place existed. But LizaE and PinkFish88 had been fantastic in making her think through her approach to Damien on the gambling issue. Maybe they'd be able to help her with this too?

The universe was obviously tuned into her situation, as just as Hannah had the thought, an email arrived on her screen. It had come via Gambler's Aid, telling her to log in to her account as she had a private message. After BBrooter had hijacked their chat room conversation, Hannah had been reluctant to revisit it. Although hopefully he'd been blocked from the site by now.

She logged in to Gambler's Aid and clicked on the envelope icon. An inbox appeared. There was one message from LizaE.

LizaE

Hi BrownDog40, really enjoyed talking to you the other day. What a shame that idiot hijacked our chat. It is a problem with an open forum. Lots of legit people and then losers like that. Wondered if you wanted to keep chatting? We

211

> can set up a private account and invite in peo-
> ple we'd like to include. PinkFish88 might like
> to join us? Let me know what you think. Hope
> you are having a good week, and if you con-
> fronted your husband, that it went well. Eliza.

So LizaE was just a mix-up of her name. Hannah smiled. Even though they were only messages, she'd felt a connection with LizaE. She seemed easy to talk to and non-judgemental. She had her share of problems to deal with, of course, but that was the beauty of it being online and anonymous. Although it appeared Eliza was happy to out herself – as far as her first name went, at least.

She sent back a message.

> BrownDog40
>
> Would love to continue chatting, and yes, invite
> PinkFish88 in too. I wonder if she's stopped
> gambling yet?

She went to sign off but decided against putting Hannah. She wanted to keep this as private as possible. She hesitated for a moment, thinking of a suitable name. She thought back to a conversation she'd had earlier with Amy, who was reading a modern book series rather than her usual classics. She'd become completely enthralled by a character named Suze Simon. It was as good a name as any, as long as she didn't have to answer to it in public, when she'd probably forget.

Eliza came back with a message almost immediately.

> LizaE

Great! So, how are you? Have you spoken to your DH yet?

BrownDog40

DH?

LizaE

Darling Husband!

BrownDog40

Sorry! I should probably know the abbreviations! Yes, it turns out he'd loaned the money to his parents. They had an unexpected tax bill and it saved them paying fees to break other investments to pay for it. We'll get the money back next month. He showed me through his poker account, and he's not in debt. He's only playing the one- and two-dollar tables and is ahead. I've overreacted big time. But things still aren't perfect. I've done something he'll never forgive me for, and I don't know how to move forward.

LizaE

Anything I can help with?

BrownDog40

Only if you know how to get rid of a blackmailer.

LizaE

Oh no, what's happened?

Hannah stared at the screen. Some advice would be good right now, and no one would ever know it was her. She hesitated, took a deep breath and began to type.

Chapter Eighteen

Nat braced herself as Anita approached the table. Could she jump up and intercept her, drag her away before she had to introduce her to Phyllie? In the time it took to even have this thought Anita was standing next to her table.

'Nat, it's so good to see you! It's been too long.'

Nat stood and hugged Anita. 'It has. You look fantastic, by the way. So tanned.'

Anita laughed. 'Perk of the business. We're developing a range for adults alongside the children's products so I wear the merchandise as much as possible, which means I'm hanging by the pool or beach when I can.'

Nat shivered. 'Bit cold for that, isn't it?'

Anita slapped her playfully on the arm. 'Here yes, not on the Sunshine Coast. Luke and I moved eighteen months ago. Shows how long it's been since we've been in touch.' She turned and smiled at Phyllie.

'Sorry.' Nat intercepted before either woman could introduce themselves. 'This is my grandmother, Phyllie. Phyllie, this is a friend of mine from years back.'

'A pleasure to meet you, dear.' Phyllie didn't seem to notice that Nat had deliberately avoided using Anita's name. 'Would you like to join us?'

Anita shook her head. 'Oh, no, thank you. That's very kind of you though. I'm meeting my sister for high tea. I'm only down from Noosa for a couple of weeks, so I'm making the most of it.' She patted her stomach. 'Although I'm going to have some work to do when I get home before I dare put on any of our swimwear. I don't think I'll be doing us any favours with this stomach on me.'

Phyllie's eyes lit up. 'You have a swimwear business? What a coincidence. Nat's been involved in an online swimwear business for a friend.'

Anita turned to Nat. 'Really? Who? We don't have much competition in Australia.'

'It's nothing compared to yours. Now, how's Luke? Is he still training for triathlons?'

Anita nodded. 'Ironman now we're up in Queensland.' She stopped. 'I'm intrigued about this swimwear business you're involved in. What's their name?'

'Sandy Swimwear,' Phyllie piped up. 'Nat's a partner in the business.'

'Are you for real?' Anger clouded Anita's face. 'You're a partner in a competing business that's using the same name? How is that even possible? We're trademarked for a start.'

Phyllie was looking from one woman to the other. Nat knew her face was bright red, and she couldn't look at Phyllie. She just needed Anita to leave. She could explain it to her later. She stood. 'Why don't we pop out for a minute and I'll fill you in. Phyllie can enjoy the surroundings on her own for a minute or two.'

'Oh, I'm sorry.' Anita looked apologetically at Phyllie. 'I didn't mean to interrupt. I'm just a bit surprised, that's all. It's one thing for another business to start up with your concept and name, but to find out a friend is involved is very strange. Yes, Nat, I'd like you to explain more. Either now, or I'm happy to wait until you've finished your lunch.'

Phyllie's smile didn't reach her eyes. 'What's your name, love?'

'Anita. Anita Green.'

Phyllie turned to Nat. 'The Anita you've told me you've been working for the last month or so?'

Nat nodded.

Anita's eyes widened. 'What? I haven't spoken to you in over two years. What on earth's going on?'

'Yes, Nat.' Phyllie crossed her arms. 'I have five thousand reasons why I'd like you to explain exactly what is going on.'

Nat promised Phyllie she'd be back in a minute and would explain everything. She couldn't do this in front of Anita, who looked as confused and angry as Phyllie. She needed to deal with her first. Heart thumping, she led her out of the front door, down the short flight of entrance steps and on to the footpath.

Anita turned and faced her. 'Well?'

'Look, I'm sorry. I've been working on an investment scheme that I didn't want Phyllie to know about. I'm living at her house at the moment and had to use a cover story. One of your ads popped up in my Facebook newsfeed, and it gave me the idea to say I was working with you. There's nothing more to it than that.'

Anita nodded slowly. 'Okay, so there's no competing company, and your grandmother believes you're a partner in my company?'

Nat nodded.

'What percentage?'

'What do you mean?'

'I mean, what percentage does your grandmother think you own?'

'Twenty.'

'Okay, to give you an idea, the company is currently valued at sixteen million dollars. So, your share in the business is valued at around three point two million.'

Nat's mouth dropped open. 'Sixteen million? How on earth did you grow it to be that big?'

'International sales mainly. We have a Californian company looking to buy us out at the moment. But that's not relevant. We don't have any business partners and don't want people claiming they own part of our business. I'd appreciate it if you cleared that up with your grandmother and anyone else you've led to believe this. The buy-out is getting some media interest, and we don't want anyone providing incorrect information.'

'Of course. I'll put her straight now. And Anita, I'm sorry, I should never have made up such a story.'

They were approached by a tall woman with flaming red hair, dressed entirely in black and the sort of knee-high boots Hannah would drool over.

'That's my sister. I have to go, but please sort this out quickly and don't use our business name again. Okay?'

Nat nodded and watched as Anita turned and hugged her sister. She didn't introduce them, and the pair disappeared inside the restaurant. Nat followed them, forcing one foot in front of the other. She was dreading the conversation she was about to have.

Phyllie was topping up their champagne flutes when Nat sat down at the table. She couldn't even look at her grandmother.

Phyllie reached across the table and patted her arm. 'I've had a few minutes to calm down and realise that whatever you've done, you've got a good reason for it. I'm here to listen.'

Nat's eyes filled with tears. She wasn't going to react so reasonably when she heard what she'd done. Of that Nat was certain.

'Come on, love, drink up and then tell me. What on earth have you been doing up in that room all these weeks if it wasn't this online swimwear business?' Phyllie's face paled suddenly, and she looked around the restaurant before lowering her voice. 'It's not porn, is it?'

Nat clapped her hand over her mouth. Why did Phyllie automatically assume porn was the only way to make money on the internet? She shook her head.

Phyllie leaned back in her chair. 'Thank goodness for that. In that case, there's nothing I can imagine that you would have reason to be ashamed of or hide from me. You're not writing a book, are you? Hiding away while you belt out the first draft? I've heard writers can be reclusive; you'd fit the bill perfectly. We might need to get you a cat, if that's the case. Apparently, they make good companions for authors.'

'No, although that would be a more desirable option than the reality.' She took a deep breath. 'You know before I moved in how you gave me some pointers on poker, and I went to Damien's poker night?'

Phyllie nodded. 'And cleaned up, from what you said.'

'Well, it got me excited about poker. I heard about some online poker sites and I set up an account.'

'Oh no.' Phyllie shook her head. 'I can already see where this is going. Please tell me it was just five thousand.'

Nat shook her head. 'A credit card too. I've lost fifteen thousand.'

Phyllie picked up her champagne and knocked it back in one large gulp. She replaced the glass on the table and fixed her eyes firmly on Nat. There was no looking away when she eyed you like this. 'Okay, so we now know what's going on. What's the plan to get yourself out of this situation?'

'Your five thousand was the first part of my plan. I honestly thought I'd be able to turn that into profit and pay off the credit card.'

'Let me get this straight, after losing ten thousand you thought the best idea would be to throw more money into the fire? It didn't cross your mind that if you'd lost ten, you were likely to lose another five?'

'Not at the time. I thought I'd veered away from my strategy, so just needed to get back to it. I did start to win again, and it gave me false hope. I also got greedy and played tables that were expensive but had good returns if you won. I thought that would be a quicker way to build up my winnings.'

'But instead, you lost everything?'

Nat nodded.

Phyllie leaned back, deep in thought for a few moments. 'In this day and age, fifteen thousand isn't the end of the world, and you only need pay back the ten you owe on the credit card. I'm not expecting my money back. I gave that to you to invest. You didn't exactly invest it where I thought you would, but that's not my concern. You've got your new job and you don't pay any rent so, in theory, you should be able to pay it off in a matter of months.'

'As long as I don't lose any more. And I already owed five on the credit card, so my credit card debt is fifteen thousand.'

'How can we make sure you don't lose more? Is there something I can do to help you?'

'I need the willpower to deactivate my account and put blocks on my devices to stop me from accessing the sites. Even though I know it would be disastrous to get back on, there's part of me that still thinks if I could win a few hundred dollars, I'd be back on track.'

'Okay. As soon as we get home, we do that. Also, I think you should bring the computer out of your room and set it up in the living room. That way I can monitor what you're doing. Any suspicious activity and I'll do the one thing I know will drive you mad.' Phyllie grinned. 'I'll tell Hannah.'

Nat stared at her grandmother, a small smile forming on her lips. 'Two can play at that. You do that, and I'll tell Hannah you're getting forgetful and I'm worried about you.' As the words came out of her mouth, Nat realised with a shock that they were true. Phyllie was showing signs of memory loss or something that wasn't quite right.

'You do that and the house will be sold, and you'll have nowhere to live. How about this – I won't tell Hannah anything. But you are to deactivate the account and show me how these blocks work as soon as we get home. Let's set up a joint bank account where you can have your pay deposited. That way I can help monitor what you're doing with it. You'll want to pay off that fifteen thousand as quickly as possible, so you don't pay too much interest. Agreed?'

Nat nodded. She needed help, that much she knew, and answering to Phyllie was an easier solution than many others she'd considered.

Phyllie poured the last of the champagne into her glass and raised it. 'No more secrets. I'm drinking the rest as you have to drive, and you'll be over the limit if you have any more.' She winked. 'Also, I'm older, and with the stress you're putting me under I need it more than you do.'

An hour after arriving home, Nat looked at the new computer area in Phyllie's living room. 'Are you sure this isn't too intrusive?' Under Phyllie's strict instruction, Nat had moved her small desk and computer downstairs.

Phyllie looked up from her television show. 'Not if it's going to help you stop. Once you've got everything set up, I want to see you deactivate your account and put those blocks on the computer.'

Nat nodded. She'd already set everything up, so it was now time to do as Phyllie said. She took a deep breath. 'Come and sit beside me and we'll do it together.'

Phyllie muted the television and hauled herself up out of the armchair. She came and sat on the computer chair while Nat got another chair from the kitchen.

'Do you have Facebook on this?' Phyllie asked as she returned. 'It's the one program I understand.'

Nat laughed. 'I do, but I don't use it very often. I'm not that interested in what people I hardly know ate for breakfast.'

Phyllie raised an eyebrow. 'Really? What if they had something delicious you'd never heard of? You could be missing out. Like me and avo smash.'

'Avo smash?'

'Yes, you know – mashed avocado on toast with a poached egg and tomato salsa or bacon. It's delicious.'

'I know what it is. You mean you only learned about it through Facebook? It's been around for years.'

'I'm not someone who ever goes out for breakfast. How on earth would I know of it otherwise?'

Nat laughed. 'Guess you've proved there is a global culinary need for Facebook.'

She logged on to the poker site and went to her account settings. Cancel Account stared back at her.

'Hold on a minute.' Phyllie put her reading glasses on. 'What does this say exactly?'

'It's pretty straightforward. You just press cancel account.'

Phyllie shook her head. 'No, in this fine print it says if you are experiencing issues with gambling you can cancel your account and also be blocked from setting up a new one. I think you should tick this box.'

'I doubt they can really block me. I could set up another account with fake information.'

Phyllie shook her head. 'Not easily. From the sounds of this, you'd need a different credit card and a valid driver's licence with the name matching that on the credit card.'

As she said it, Nat remembered the sign-up process, thinking it was more elaborate than she had anticipated.

'Good,' Phyllie said. 'They've made this very difficult. Make sure you tick the box.'

Nat ticked the box, her mouse then hovering over the 'Cancel Account' button.

Phyllie gave her a nudge. 'Come on, you can do it. This site has brought you nothing but misery.'

Actually, it had brought Nat incredible adrenaline bursts and happiness at times, but yes, overall, she'd spiralled down a dark hole of misery because of it. She clicked the 'Cancel Account' button and a screen confirming the cancellation and blocking of PinkFish88 appeared. She shut it down and searched *Poker site blockers*.

It only took ten minutes, and they'd installed enough blocks to lock out all the main poker sites. When she searched now and clicked on any of the websites, she was instantly blocked.

'We need to update those every few weeks,' Phyllie said. 'They'll add any new sites that have popped up that might lure you in.'

'We're done then,' Nat said. 'I should log in to Gambler's Aid and tell the women I was chatting to the other day that I took their advice on board. They'll probably have tips on how to overcome any cravings I have.'

Phyllie stood and slowly moved back to her armchair. Her face was serious.

'What? The group is for addicts. No one's going to be encouraging me to gamble.'

'It's not that. It's this new job of yours. It is real, isn't it? You're not just planning on heading out to work each day and going to the casino, or somewhere else you can play the pokies or join a poker tournament?'

'It's definitely real. In fact, why don't you come and have lunch with me one day next week? I'll show you around the offices, and you can see exactly what I do. I'm sure they won't mind. Just give me a day or two to settle in first.'

Phyllie nodded. 'Okay, but probably not for lunch. I'll drop in when I'm free. If you're available that's great, if not you can say a quick hello and get back to it.'

Nat was about to object when she realised Phyllie was going to drop in at a random time to make sure she was there. If they pre-planned lunch, Nat could conveniently turn up whether she worked there or not. She felt awful that she'd put her grandmother in a position of not being able to trust her.

She didn't say anymore, instead turned her attention back to the screen and logged in to the chat room. She had a message flashing and clicked on her inbox.

LizaE

Hey, PinkFish88. BrownDog40 and I have set up a private group for the two of us. After the 'dick' ruined our last chat, we decided to make it less public. Would love you to join us if you would like to. Just click on the 'accept' button on my name in your private groups tab. It should bring you into our chat. Eliza.

Nat smiled. Eliza, hey. A clever use of her name for her username. She'd quite liked the brief conversation she'd had with the two women. She clicked on the 'Accept' button, and the screen changed to another chat screen. This time it had a highlight at the top that said 'Private Conversation'. LizaE and BrownDog40 were already chatting, and it appeared their real names were Eliza and Suze. She wasn't sure she wanted to share her real name. She needed anonymity. Lia. It was perfect. She and Amy often joked that as it was the last three letters of their full first names, they actually shared a name.

She quickly read through their conversation. Her eyes widened as she read Suze's comments about having done something her husband wouldn't forgive her for and not knowing how to move forward. This probably wasn't to do with poker, but it was indeed intriguing. From Suze's earlier comment that she tended to over-react, Nat assumed this might also be the case.

PinkFish88

Hi ladies, thanks for the invite. Touched to be included. Lia.

BrownDog40

Great to see you here, Lia. How are you doing? Thought we'd get away from the 'dick', as we are now calling him.

Nat laughed. A perfect name for BBrooter.

PinkFish88

Good plan. I have lots to tell you both but can see you were mid-conversation. I've read through and am all caught up. I'm intrigued, so don't let me interrupt. You sounded like you were about to get something off your chest, Suze?

Chapter Nineteen

Hannah had already started her message when PinkFish88, otherwise known as Lia, had joined the chat. She continued typing, realising it was going to be a long message. Part of her found it difficult to believe she was going to share what she'd done with two strangers. While she'd never met them, she still agonised over what they would think of her. She hit send on the message and waited. It would take them some time to read and digest everything she'd said. Would they come back telling her what an awful person she was and that it served her right that she was now being blackmailed?

She checked the clock on her office wall. It was almost six. She should get packed up and head home. She needed to relax before she picked up Amy and Bear, who had been invited to Skye's after school. She posted another quick message.

BrownDog40

Leaving work now. Completely understand if you think I'm an awful person. No need to sugarcoat your thoughts, I probably need to hear them. Will check messages when I get home. x

She switched off her computer and quickly tidied her desk. She had a big week next week, presenting to Halpin and Sons, and she would need part of the weekend to prepare. She slid a number of files into her briefcase, picked up her bag and left her office. The reception area was deserted, as was the rest of the floor. She pressed the button for the lift, her mind still in the chat room. She shouldn't have told them. She could imagine how she would have reacted if either of them had posted that message. She would have considered their actions not only irresponsible but downright deceitful. Would she have been able to see past this and realise they'd been protecting their husband and his adoptive mother?

It was close to seven by the time Hannah pulled into the driveway. She waited for the automatic garage door to open before driving into the space. She had two hours before she needed to get Amy. Two hours to get out of her work clothes, eat something, have a glass of wine and maybe even a bath. She felt like she needed to soak her mind if nothing else. It was always on the go, worrying endlessly about the Zane Fox situation.

She walked through the internal access and into the kitchen, dumped her bag and briefcase on one of the stools at the island bench and went straight to the fridge. The Pinot Gris she'd put in to chill earlier in the week would be very welcome right now. She poured herself a glass and took it upstairs to her office. She took a large gulp, hoping to quash the nerves that had risen in her. It was ridiculous to be worried about what two strangers thought of her; they weren't even friends. But she was worried. She knew that their reactions would be a reflection of how those close to her would react.

She switched on her computer, left her wine on the desk and walked through to the master bedroom. She'd get changed while it was starting up. She hung up her charcoal pencil skirt and jacket, pulled on her sweatpants and a hoodie and went back to her office. She sat down in the chair, pulling the wine close to her.

She logged in to the chat room and held her breath. There were two responses to her message already.

LizaE

OMG, you poor thing. How on earth are you keeping it together? That private investigator sounds like he should be in jail. Will give some thought to what you can do. So sorry to hear you're in this position.

PinkFish88

Agree with Eliza, the PI should be shot. I think you've done something courageous to protect your husband and his adoptive mother. You guys sound very close. Do you think if you told him the truth, he might understand why you did it?

Hannah breathed out a huge sigh of relief as she read the responses. Neither of the two women had told her she was a terrible person; in fact, they'd been incredibly supportive. How amazing that with just a few communications she felt like she'd made close friends. There was no one else in her life that she felt she could talk to without judgement. She knew why she'd been so worried about their reaction. She wasn't comfortable with what she'd done so how could anyone else be?

BrownDog40

Phew, I thought you'd tell me I was awful and ban me from the chat. Thank you. Your messages have made me feel a lot better. Yes, Lia, we are close, but I'm worried that DH has been going through so much emotional trauma over this, to the point he's now seeing a psychologist, that I could have helped him avoid this.

PinkFish88

Hon, finding out your father was a rapist and your mother only seventeen at the time would guarantee he'd be seeing a psychologist. I'm with you, knowing you share your gene pool with a rapist would have me wishing I never knew my background. I think, even if your DH is mad to start with, he'd understand this pretty quickly.

LizaE

Perfectly stated, Lia. There's no way I'd want to know that was my heritage; however, that puts you in an awful position. You can't give this investigator guy any more money. He's blackmailing you, and my gut tells me it won't end well. Also, how do you explain the money you're giving him? You were pretty quick to notice the fifteen thousand your husband spent, and you said that wasn't even in your regular accounts. I can't imagine you have a spare 10K just lying around?

BrownDog40

No, I don't, and I can't go back to my grandmother for more. She gave me the first 10K no questions asked. I don't think she'd be quite so generous if I ask her again. And I agree, he's just going to keep asking for more.

PinkFish88

You said in your original message that he'd threatened to tell the biological mother about your husband and where you live. Do you think he'd tell her that you paid him not to say anything? I'm just wondering if you can spin it that he's the one who gave misleading information to start with. What if he had told you that your husband's biological parents had been killed? Would you have had any reason not to believe him? Can you wait and see how it all plays out? You might get lucky.

Hannah stared at the screen. It was a gamble, but Lia might be right. If Janine contacted them and she acted as surprised as Damien, he might just buy it. She sighed. More lies. She'd woven such a complicated situation and every day it was being made worse.

LizaE

I like Lia's idea, but I worry that this guy will make life difficult for you. I'm sure he'd tell the biological mother what you'd done and possibly even contact your husband out of spite. Be careful if you go down this route. I've learned over the years that while it might be the hardest road you take, the honest road is the easiest in the long run.

BrownDog40

Thanks, ladies, I'll give your suggestions a lot of thought. Now, Lia, you said you had news for us. Fill us in. What's been happening?

Hannah enjoyed the distraction from her thoughts as she read through Lia's story. She gasped out loud when she read that the woman who Lia was pretending to be in business with had turned up at her celebratory afternoon tea. She had to say, Lia's grandmother sounded like quite a character. She reminded her a bit of Phyllie. Although she couldn't imagine Phyllie being quite so understanding about the online poker. The practical steps of the computer being moved to the lounge and the grandmother watching as Lia deactivated her account and put blocks in place did sound like something Phyllie would do. She was pleased for Lia though. She'd landed herself a new job, and without huge living expenses, it sounded like she'd be able to get herself out of debt reasonably quickly.

LizaE

I've got some exciting news to share too, ladies. I hope you don't find this inappropriate considering the difficult financial situation you are in Lia, but it's a bolt out of the blue for us. As you know, we are in a huge financial hole with debt up to our eyeballs. Well, last week, my brother Jacob mentioned a short-term investment for us. Like really short term. They needed the funds for four days while some massive investment was made, then they'd sell again and divide the profit between shareholders. He knew we didn't have any money so said he'd spot us the initial 7K. He said that he'd give us any profit above and beyond the 7K he invested. I mean, I know he's my brother, but who does that? People aren't that kind or generous, are they?

Hannah thought of Nat. No, they weren't that kind or generous. She thought back to Nat deliberately trying to spoil Amy's birthday and take credit for Bear. If she was like that, she could hardly imagine her helping her out financially with no strings attached.

PinkFish88

What was the deal if the 7K was lost?

LizaE

A bad deal for my brother. He was going to bear the loss. This is what I mean, other than being genuinely beautiful, there was no benefit in this at all for him. Anyway, it went ahead, and he contacted me yesterday to say he'd transferred an amount into our account. It was for twenty-seven thousand dollars! Can you believe that? Do you guys have siblings? Would they do something so amazing for you?

BrownDog40

No Way.

PinkFish88

You have to be kidding. My sister would throw a dagger straight into my heart before she helped me out.

Hannah laughed. It sounded like she and Lia had similar experiences with their sisters. She glanced at the clock on her computer screen. It was eight forty-five already. She hadn't even eaten, and she needed to go and get Amy. She typed a quick congratulations to Eliza and a goodbye, promising she'd check back sometime the next day.

Hannah, her mind in overdrive over the Zane Fox situation, was unable to sleep that night. She was still staring at the clock at two when Damien had come in. He'd been surprised to find her awake, and extra surprised when she'd pulled him to her and removed his shirt and pants. He was snoring gently within minutes of their lovemaking. He'd had a long day and a long week, so it wasn't surprising. What *was* surprising was that at four she was still awake.

It was only hearing a scream of delight from the yard below that made her realise she had fallen asleep at some stage. She forced an eye open to check the clock. Nine! She couldn't remember the last time she'd slept this late.

Her thoughts immediately shifted back to the night before and her conversation with Lia and Eliza. She still couldn't believe Eliza had been so lucky with her brother's investment. She smiled thinking about it. It sounded like Eliza needed a break and how lovely of her brother to provide it.

Her phone pinged with a text as she contemplated getting out of bed. She hesitated, praying it wasn't Zane Fox as she picked up her phone from the bedside table. She let out a deep breath. It was her father.

Would you be free to pop over at three for afternoon tea? There's something I want to discuss with you and Nat.

Hannah sent him a quick text back.

Let me check with Damien, and I'll get back to you.

It was unusual for her dad to have something he needed to discuss, although with the financial problems he and Sue were experiencing it wouldn't surprise her if he wanted to bring up the idea of selling the house.

She hauled herself out of bed and into the en-suite bathroom. She needed to get organised and face the day. Damien was the one who'd worked a late shift and yet he was up, and from the sounds coming from the yard, entertaining Amy and Bear. He must be wondering what was wrong with her.

After waving Amy and Damien off as they headed to the movies, at three o'clock she pulled into her father's driveway.

Hannah was shocked when she saw him; his face was pale and he had dark circles under his eyes.

'Are you alright?' The words slipped from her tongue before she could stop them. Heat flooded her face. 'Sorry, it's just that you look terrible. You're not sick, are you?'

Her father ushered her into the house and through to the kitchen. 'Sick with worry maybe, but no, not sick otherwise. We met with your fund manager this week. Things aren't looking good.'

Hannah's heart sank. Her poor father. This wasn't what someone about to retire needed. 'Where's Sue?'

'She's gone out for the afternoon. She thought it best that I have this discussion with you girls without her. She felt it wasn't her place to have an opinion, which I completely disagree with. She was also worried that you girls, well, Nat in particular, might feel awkward expressing how you really feel with her here.'

Hannah smiled. 'That's never usually a problem where Nat's concerned.'

There was a knock on the front door. 'That'll be Nat.' Worry lines deepened on his forehead. 'Expect fireworks.'

Hannah busied herself making tea while her father let Nat in. She was sure he was worrying about nothing. Nat would be the first to want to help him, she was sure of that.

Ten minutes later the three of them were sitting around the kitchen table, a plate of Nat's favourite homemade biscuits in front of them. Hannah had bitten the inside of her lip to keep from smiling when her father mentioned that Sue had spent the morning baking them. They really did think they needed to butter her up.

He explained the financial situation to Nat and what the fund manager had advised earlier in the week.

Nat's mouth dropped open. 'What about your savings? The money that's not tied up in your super? Surely you can live off that initially and hope the super fund performs better?'

'No, most of it's gone. I was talked into investing it in our super to help it grow quicker. I thought I was doing the right thing. We've only got a small amount left. Enough for a year or so, but not a lot more.' He took a deep breath and looked at Nat. 'One way that we could retire comfortably and still travel and do some of the things we planned is if we sold the house.'

Nat dropped her teacup back in its saucer with a loud clatter. 'This house? You're going to sell it?'

Her father shook his head. 'Not definitely. It was something I wanted to run by you. See how you felt.'

'And Sue wants to sell?' Nat's voice was shaky.

'She isn't attached to the house like we are, Nat,' her father said. 'Which is why she's not here this afternoon. She wanted this to be our decision. She knows we have our memories of your mother here.'

Tears filled Nat's eyes. 'That's exactly why it shouldn't be sold. Mum loved this house.'

Hannah was surprised at her reaction. Nat lived a fairly nomadic existence; she hadn't expected her to be attached to their childhood home at all. 'Mum's been gone for eighteen years. Don't you think she'd want whatever was best for Dad at this stage?'

'No, I think she'd want our memories of her preserved. There's something special about coming here. You can feel her when you're here.'

The pout on Nat's face took Hannah back twenty years. Even as a teenager it was her defiant look. The stance she took when she wanted her own way. Anger bubbled up inside Hannah. Why couldn't Nat think of someone other than herself? Couldn't she see their father needed help? 'And how often exactly do you come and visit? Other than the family events throughout the year, how often do you drop in to feel close to Mum?'

'That's not the point. I like knowing that I can.'

'It is *exactly* the point. Mum wasn't materialistic, and yes, she loved the house, but she would have moved in a flash if she'd needed to. Her home was where we were. She said that many times. It had nothing to do with bricks and mortar.'

'Okay,' their father interrupted, 'we don't need to argue about this. It was just an idea, and one that we appear to be divided on.'

'Nat,' Hannah said. 'It isn't your decision. Dad needs money, and with property values skyrocketing around here, this house could help him. He also doesn't need the maintenance of such a large yard. Think about him rather than yourself for once.'

Nat's eyes flashed with anger.

'Probably a good time to pay back any outstanding loans too,' Hannah added. 'Which I imagine you have plenty of.'

'Probably a good time for you to mind your own business. Any loans I have with Dad are our business, not yours. And for your information, most of them have been paid back.' She turned to her father. 'I'll pay you back what I owe you as soon as I can. I hadn't realised you were having problems.'

'Thanks, love. But there's no hurry. You don't owe me much and I hadn't ever really expected it to be paid back.' He ran a hand through his hair. 'To be honest, I'm beginning to wish I'd never mentioned the house or any of this. Sue and I can get by, it just won't be the retirement we'd been dreaming of.'

Nat frowned. 'I love this house, but of course I want you and Sue to be happy too. I just need some time to get my head around losing it. It will be like losing Mum again, I guess.'

It was on the tip of Hannah's tongue to tell Nat to stop being so melodramatic, but she stopped herself. Maybe she really did feel a connection when she was at the house. Instead she touched her arm. 'She's always in your heart, Nat. You don't have to say goodbye, just find her in different places, different situations. When I want to be close to her, I bake that ginger and pecan cake she used to make.'

Nat's eyes widened. 'But you hated that cake.'

Hannah laughed. 'I know, but I loved the smell of it when it was baking, and it reminds me of being loved and safe. The ginger and cinnamon are such a strong smell. When I need her close, I sit in the kitchen with it baking, enjoying a cup of tea. Luckily Damien loves the cake.'

All three of them were silent, caught up in their own memories. Eventually, Hannah stood.

'I think I'll get going, leave you and Nat to chat.' She hugged her father. 'You have my support one hundred percent. Let me know if there's anything I can do to help. When you and Sue find an area you're thinking of buying in let me know that too. I'll provide you with a full risk assessment.' She held up her hands, knowing he would probably object. 'You don't have to go by it, but it is interesting to know the facts and figures. You don't want to move into an area that's had prices skyrocket in the previous year or one with a high crime rate. All the risk assessment will do is ensure you're fully informed.'

'Do you ever do anything spontaneous?' Nat asked. 'Don't you get bored always analysing things, extracting the fun from them?'

Hannah hesitated. For just a few minutes she'd felt a closeness to Nat. A sharing of their love for their mother, and then, as usual, she had to spoil it. But she wasn't going to get riled by her sister. Instead, she smiled. 'You see, I'm lucky. I find analysing things fascinating. For me, it puts the fun into it. For instance, I would have weighed up the risks before deciding to ruin my niece's birthday. I would have realised that not only would I have unnecessarily upset a twelve-year-old, but I'd look petty and silly in front of my family. I would also have been concerned about the damage it would have done to my relationship with my sister. So, before I acted like a total bitch, I would have considered all of this and made a much better and more informed decision. Now, I'm going to head home and enjoy the rest of my weekend.' She flashed a smile at her father. 'No need to get up, I can see myself out.'

She turned and left the kitchen, the smile widening on her face as she pictured the daggers flying from Nat's eyes straight into her back.

Damien and Amy were still out at the movies when Hannah arrived home. Bear bounded down the stairs and sat at her feet, waiting to be showered with affection. She scratched his ears and was rewarded with the thumping of his tail. 'You're a good boy, Bear. A really good dog.' His tail thumped harder as she spoke.

She walked through to the kitchen with Bear at her heels. She really should think about preparing dinner. It was strange, after a confrontation with Nat she often felt disappointed or down, but not today. She was glad Nat had shown up. She'd been feeling angry towards her following Amy's birthday and hadn't had a chance to make that clear. She had now, and while her father probably hadn't enjoyed the tension between his daughters, they were things that needed to be said. What Nat had done was not okay. She felt lighter for having got her thoughts off her chest. She doubted her words would have any impact at all on her sister but they certainly helped her.

Hannah opened the fridge, planning to marinate some chicken for the evening's stir-fry when her phone pinged. It was Damien.

> Saw a double feature. The second movie's only halfway through. We'll be at least an hour and a half. Meet us in Box Hill for dumplings at seven?

Hannah grinned.

> Perfect. See you there.

She sent the text back and shut the fridge. They could have the stir-fry tomorrow night. She turned to Bear. 'Let's get your dinner sorted.' The dog shadowed her as she refilled his water bowl and filled another with his mix of chicken, rice and vegetables. She left him eating and went upstairs to her office and sat down. She wondered if Eliza or Lia were online.

She opened up her computer and logged on to the chat room. She could see the conversation between Eliza and Lia had continued after she'd left it the previous evening.

> PinkFish88
>
> So happy for you with the finances! Do you think there'll be other investment opportunities?
>
> LizaE

Not sure. Also, don't know if I'd risk any of this money. It feels like another sort of gambling. We were lucky this time, but like anything, there are no guarantees.

PinkFish88

You sound very sensible. The sort of person I need around me at the moment. If my sister had invested for me and made so much, I'd be chomping at the bit, wanting to do it again. That one transaction would have got me out of debt. Not that my sister would ever have done something like that.

LizaE

What's the deal with your sister? You've mentioned her a few times in a very negative way. Do you have any relationship with her?

PinkFish88

Not really. It's hard to be around someone who makes you feel inferior to them. Is always looking down their nose at you, suggesting you could do better. She's not very likeable.

LizaE

Has she always been like that?

PinkFish88

No. We were really close until my mum died when I was a teenager. It was never the same after that.

LizaE

That's a pretty hard situation for all of you. I guess your mother's death really affected her. Is she just like that with you or with everyone?

PinkFish88

She controls everyone but I think she's more on my case than anyone else's. There's rarely a time when I see her that she doesn't have something to criticise me about. I'm just not good enough in her eyes, and she's a fixer so she can't just let it go.

LizaE

What's her husband like? A doormat?

PinkFish88

He's a great guy. I can't imagine what he's doing with her. I've asked him a couple of times, and he's said that I choose to see one side only to my sister. That I can't see beyond her criticisms. He also doesn't think she's criticising me. He believes that she's trying to help and can't figure out why it gets my back up. I think he must have had a massive whack to the head at some stage if that's how he interprets the situation.

LizaE

Interesting. I can't imagine not getting along with my family. They are so important to me. I'd be devastated to have that kind of relationship. I always wanted a sister. Someone I could confide in and be best friends with. That's how I always imagined it would be.

PinkFish88

It was when we were younger. We were really close. Not only were we good friends but I admired her. She always had my back. But when our mother died things changed. She changed. She went from being easy-going to completely neurotic. On my back about everything. Nothing I did was good enough from that point on. If Mum had been really strict I would have thought she was trying to step in and take her place, but Mum was the most relaxed, carefree person you'd ever meet. I guess it was how she dealt with our mother's death, but knowing that doesn't make being around her any easier.

Hannah stared at the screen. She and Lia had more in common than she would ever have imagined. Both had sisters they didn't get along with and both had lost their mothers as teenagers. She thought back to when her mother died. It had changed her; she knew that. She could relate to Lia's sister. The accident that killed her mother had instilled a fear she'd not known before. It made her worry about everything. For months she'd worried her father wouldn't come home from work or that something would happen to Nat. She couldn't bear the thought of losing someone else. She wouldn't say she sucked the fun out of everything, although Nat thought she did. She just became overly cautious, weighing up the pros and cons of everything.

She thought back to Nat's comment earlier that day. 'Do you ever do anything spontaneous?' No, in all honesty, she didn't. But was that a bad thing? This is where she and her sister differed. Nat saw the way she lived her life to be negative, whereas being cautious and assessing risk brought great comfort to Hannah. If her mother had done this on her fortieth birthday, there was no way she would have been riding a horse without wearing a helmet. That one small change in what she did that day might have saved her life. When that was an example in your own family of the devastating effects being spontaneous could have, why wouldn't you be more cautious?

She could see from her status that Lia was away from the computer, but Eliza appeared to be online. She typed a message.

BrownDog40

How's your day been, Eliza? Still on cloud nine from your unexpected windfall?

LizaE

Sure am! It turns out Jacob has reinvested for us. I was in tears this afternoon when he dropped in. He wanted us to know that he was going to do everything possible to get us out of debt. Of course, now I'm worried that he's gambling to do it. He's assured me that this is what he does for work, that he'd be doing it for his clients, so adding in a little bit extra in a fund for us is no big deal. I honestly don't know what to say to him. I feel so loved right now.

BrownDog40

That's amazing. How does your husband feel about it all? Is he happy?

LizaE

The fact that you've thought to ask that question tells me you are a person with great empathy. Doug is doing his best to appear happy, but I know he's feeling like a failure deep down too. I'm trying to manage his feelings carefully. I'm sure he'd like to be the one bailing us out of the trouble he put us in, but right now he's not capable of doing that and Jacob is.

BrownDog40

I feel for him. It must be a horrible situation to find yourself in. But, on the flip side, I'm ecstatic for you. Your brother must be good at what he does.

LizaE

He is. He's done very well for himself and his family. He's married with two children, and they live in a beautiful house in Toorak. The kids are at private schools, and they take at least one four-week holiday every year to an exotic location. He has NO DEBT either! Can you believe that? A forty-five-year-old man living the dream off his hard work. I'm very proud of him. Enough talking about him though. How are you doing? Any more thoughts on what you're going to do about the blackmailer?

BrownDog40

I've done my best to put it out of my mind. I do agree with you though. Honesty is the best policy in the long run. I may have to trust that my relationship with my husband is strong enough to handle this. It's just whether I tell him now or whether I wait and see how it plays out. Who knows, the PI might only provide his biological mother with our details and leave it at that. I'm not sure if he'd go to the effort of telling my husband what I've done.

LizaE

I'm guessing he would. He'll be angry with you for not giving him the money. Suze, think about being the one to tell your husband. I've learned in the past that keeping secrets comes back to bite you. Just be careful. Now, I'd better go and rustle up some food for dinner. Chat soon. x

Hannah posted a smiley face into the chat box and stared at her screen. Eliza was right. She knew that. She just wasn't sure she could bring herself to do it. She'd like to think that Damien having the opportunity to meet his biological mother would outweigh the pain of learning about his father and about her deceit, but she wasn't sure that it would.

Over their dumpling dinner the previous evening, Damien had suggested they visit Phyllie the following morning. He'd driven past her house during the week and noticed the front lawn was getting long.

'I thought Aunty Nat was there to help out,' Amy said as they enjoyed a breakfast of pancakes with berries and yoghurt.

'She is.' Hannah pushed her pancake around her plate. Ever since Zane Fox had reappeared in her life her appetite had been lacking. 'I'm not sure that her help extends to lawn mowing. It will be a good chance to check on Phyllie. Nat says she's fine, but I don't know what to believe from her these days. She's been acting quite strangely.'

'Why don't we make a cake or some cookies to take with us?' Amy suggested. 'Phyllie loves those melting moments you make. You know, the ones with the oats and a cherry on top.'

'Great idea. Let's get them started straightaway. Then we can head off by nine. They won't take long.'

With the cookies cooled and packed in a tin, and Bear in the back seat with Amy, they drove the short distance to Phyllie's.

'I didn't tell her we were coming,' Hannah said. 'I thought we could surprise her. Hopefully, Nat won't be home.'

Damien raised an eyebrow. 'She might have something to say after your discussion yesterday.'

Hannah shrugged. 'I didn't say anything she didn't deserve.'

Damien didn't respond. He signalled and turned off the main road into Phyllie's quiet street. Amy and Bear were out of the car and running to the front door the second he stopped.

'Now, this is a lovely surprise.' Phyllie drew her great-grand-daughter into a hug. 'And to what do I owe this great pleasure?'

'Dad's going to mow your lawn and Mum and I made cookies.'

Phyllie laughed. 'That all sounds too good to refuse.' She held the door open, waiting for Hannah and Damien to catch up to Amy.

'You don't need to mow my lawn,' she said as they reached her.

'I certainly do,' Damien said. 'That's my job from now on. I'll check on it every few weeks, and if it needs mowing, I'll be round on the weekend. Of course, if you have a special occasion you need it mown for, you just let me know. I don't want to hear of you pushing that mower out of the shed again. Do you hear me?' He waggled his finger, causing Phyllie to laugh.

'I do, and I appreciate it. I'm sure Nat would have mown it if I'd asked.'

'Is she here?' Hannah hoped she wasn't.

Phyllie shook her head. 'No, she's starting a new job tomorrow and said she had a few things to prepare for it. I think she's gone to do a bit of shopping.' Phyllie searched Hannah's face. 'Everything alright between you and Nat? You looked relieved when I said she wasn't here.'

'Just the usual,' Hannah said. 'Now, let's make some tea and try these cookies. Amy says they're your favourite.'

The lawnmower was roaring in the background as they made tea and took it through to the living room.

'You've got a computer!' Amy sat on the computer chair and stared at the monitor. 'What do you use it for?'

'It's Nat's. I got her to move it down here so I could use it too. I'm a bit of a Facebook fanatic.'

'Really?' Hannah was surprised. 'How come you haven't friended me?'

'I keep it mainly to just my friends.' She winked. 'You can send me a request if you like and I'll consider it.'

'Can I turn it on? See what programs you've got?' Amy looked hopefully at Phyllie.

'Course you can. I doubt you'll find anything exciting though. Nat mainly uses it for the internet. I imagine she'll need it for her reports for work when she starts. It has Facebook though.'

'And Nat's been doing her online swimwear business from the living room? Hasn't that been intrusive?' Hannah asked.

Phyllie's eyes darted around the room. 'Not really. The workload has tapered off a bit with that, which is why she's gone and got the new job.'

'Really? I was under the impression she'd been working around the clock and hardly going out.'

Phyllie nodded. 'She was at one stage. We only moved the computer down here recently. I got sick of taking cups of tea up the stairs.'

'Hold on. You're not supposed to be going up the stairs at all. That was part of our deal.'

Phyllie shook her head. 'No, that was one of your instructions for me. But if it makes you feel better, other than when I need to go into the sewing room, which isn't very often these days, I won't go upstairs. As of tomorrow, Nat won't be here during the day anyway.'

Hannah suddenly thought of Lia. She was also starting a new job tomorrow. It made her realise she hadn't asked her what she did, and she would need to message her to wish her a good first day. She thought back to their conversations of the previous day. There certainly were a lot of parallels between their two lives.

'You're looking puzzled,' Phyllie said. 'Anything wrong?'

'I was just thinking of a friend,' Hannah said. 'Someone I've recently met. She's got a lot going on in her life at the moment and, like Nat, she's starting a new job tomorrow. She also lives with her grandmother and recently moved her computer into a shared area, like Nat has. I was thinking how strange the similarities are, that's all.'

Phyllie smiled. 'A small world, I guess. What does your friend do for work? Don't tell me she's a community support officer too?'

'Actually, I'm not sure. I'll ask her when we're next chatting.'

The lawnmower cut out suddenly and the room, other than Amy's tapping on the computer keys, filled with silence.

'He's finished the back,' Phyllie said. 'He'll be up the side any second, ready to do the front. Perhaps we should move out the back on to the veranda? It's a bit chilly, but the sun's out. What do you say?'

Amy looked up from the computer. 'Can I stay here? I need to do some research for my history assignment. I could use this time to read about the landing at Botany Bay.'

'What about Bear? You don't think he'd like a run around now Dad's finished out the back?'

They all looked down at Bear, who was lying under the desk, his head on Amy's feet, fast asleep.

'He's tired. How about I read the articles, and then I'll bring him out?'

'We can hardly say no to a girl wanting to do her homework.' Phyllie took Hannah by the elbow. 'Come on, you can help a poor old lady out to the back garden. In fact, I'm surprised you didn't bring a wheelchair with you.'

She broke into peals of laughter as they walked through to the garden, the scent of freshly mown grass filling the air.

Damien put the mower away in the shed and walked up the garden to join Hannah and Phyllie.

'Thanks, love, you're a good boy. So much like my Frederick,' Phyllie said. 'The lawn looks lovely.'

'I'll do the edges next time,' Damien said. 'They aren't too long at the moment, so they didn't need it. I'll also bring my whipper-snipper, as that one you've got in the shed is a bit archaic.'

Phyllie laughed. 'Frederick will be sending you evil looks from heaven for referring to his prized possession like that. He loved that thing. "Made to last, Phyllis", he'd always say. It did do a good job, but yes, I'm sure the newer, modern equipment is much easier.'

'Mum?' Amy stood at the back door, Bear next to her. 'The computer's doing something weird. Can you have a look?'

Hannah stood. 'I'll be right back.'

Bear ran past her into the garden. 'Let's get this fixed,' she said to Amy, 'then you can head out with Bear and throw him the ball or a stick or something.'

She followed Amy and sat down at the computer. A warning had come up saying the site she was trying to access had been blocked.

'That's weird. I wonder why Nat would have blocks on the computer. What were you trying to open?'

'Just a site that has lots of documentaries. They have a show on Arthur Phillip that might be worth watching.'

Hannah clicked through to the settings on the computer. 'Let's have a look and see if any sites are blocked. If they're not, it's probably just a glitch and you could try restarting it. I can't imagine Nat would need to block any sites.'

Hannah found the setting that showed what was blocked. She stared at the screen. There were a number of blocks in place. By the looks of them, they all blocked gambling sites. She sucked in a breath. Eliza and Lia had been talking about Gamblock and Poker Problems the other day.

'What are they, Mum? Anything that would be blocking the documentary site?'

Amy drew Hannah from her jumbled thoughts. 'Um, no, not that I can see. Let's just shut down everything and restart. It might clear whatever the glitch is.'

They spent a few minutes closing the open programs and restarting the computer. Amy tried the website again and this time it worked. She smiled. 'Thanks, you're smarter at this stuff than I thought you would be.'

Hannah wasn't sure whether she'd received a compliment or not but smiled regardless. 'Okay, have a look and then come out the back. We won't be staying much longer, and I'm sure Bear would love to have a proper play in the garden.'

She walked through to the kitchen and the sliding door that led out to Phyllie's patio area. All the comments Lia had made in the chat room were flooding her mind. It wasn't possible that Lia was

Nat, was it? She gave herself a mental shake. No, of course it wasn't. It had to be a coincidence, nothing more. But why were all those blocks in place on Nat's computer for online poker? It was only four or five weeks ago that she'd mentioned an interest in poker, after her big win at the poker night. Surely she couldn't have run up a huge debt and needed to ban herself in that short a timeframe? She took her seat back at the patio, her eyes fixing on Bear, who was sniffing around one of Phyllie's trees.

'Get it sorted?' Damien asked.

Hannah nodded, still deep in thought.

Phyllie frowned. 'You okay, love? You went into the house with rosy cheeks and have come out as white as a sheet.'

'Phyllie's right,' Damien said. 'You look awful.'

She turned her attention from Bear to her husband and grandmother. 'You two know, don't you?' It had just dawned on her that Damien's inability to look her in the eye when he'd mentioned a friend having gambling problems wasn't because it was him, but because it was Nat. And Phyllie, of course, had been the one to help Nat make changes. She was also the one who unwittingly gave Nat five thousand dollars, not realising it was being squandered on poker tables rather than invested.

'Know what?'

'About Nat's problem. Her addiction to poker.'

Damien's mouth dropped open. 'What makes you think that?'

'Don't lie to me. I can see right through you.' She turned to Phyllie. 'The computer's in the living room so you can monitor what she's doing, isn't it? And you encouraged her to put those blocks on it so she can't access the gambling sites.'

'I didn't exactly encourage her; in fact, I didn't even know about them. But when she mentioned them, I made sure she installed them. She wouldn't want you knowing anything about this, Hannah. She feels like a big enough failure as it is. She needs

254

help, and she needs compassion right now. She doesn't need a lecture or anyone pointing the finger at her and saying she's not good enough.'

Hannah sucked in a breath. 'I would never do any of that. I'd want to help her.'

'I know that,' Phyllie said, 'but she doesn't. She has a chip on her shoulder when it comes to you, so any attempts at help will be interpreted as you lording it over her. Just leave it alone, okay?'

'Leave what alone?'

They all turned as Nat came through the back door and out into the garden. She smiled at them. 'This is a surprise, perfectly timed too as I wanted to see Amy, which I've just done. But what do you need to leave alone?'

'Oh nothing, love,' Phyllie said. 'Damien's been kind enough to mow the lawns for us and offered to prune the liquidambar tree. I said to leave it alone. Probably just for another six months or so. It isn't out of control yet.'

'Oh.' Nat's eyes flicked around the garden. 'I'd planned to ask Leon to come and do those jobs for you.'

Phyllie laughed. 'I'm sure you can think up another reason to speak to Leon if you want to.'

Hannah watched with interest as Nat's face coloured. Was her sister interested in *goat boy*, as she'd previously referred to him? She sensed Nat's discomfort and changed the subject. 'Congratulations.' Hannah hoped her smile looked genuine and Nat wasn't going to read something else into it. 'Phyllie mentioned you're starting a new job tomorrow. The organisation sounds wonderful.'

Nat's eyes narrowed momentarily before she nodded. 'Thanks, yes, it certainly has a good feel to it.'

'And it's a community support officer role?'

'Yes, covering St Kilda, Elwood and some of the bayside area. There are a large number of support houses in that area.'

'I hope your first day and week go well. It sounds like a great opportunity.'

Nat didn't seem to know how to respond. They were interrupted by Amy, which saved her having to try.

Amy came out through the sliding door and flung her arms around Nat. 'Thank you, I love it.'

Nat laughed. 'You're welcome, and as I said, I'm sorry it was late and that I was in such a bad mood on your birthday. I promise to never be like that again. And I also thought that perhaps next weekend just the two of us could go out for lunch and a movie.' She looked across to Hannah. 'If that's okay with you, of course.'

Hannah nodded. What had just happened?

'Check this out, Mum.' Amy held out her arm, now sporting a black Fitbit. 'I've wanted one of these for ages. Skye and Brittney are always competing for how many steps they've done. Now I'll be able to join in. And I needed a watch too. It's perfect.'

'It's great, Ames, you're very lucky.' Hannah looked over to Nat. 'Thank you, that's very generous.' She wondered how on earth Nat had afforded it. Assuming she was Lia, then she had no money at all.

They stayed for another half an hour, making small talk before Hannah suggested they head home and leave Nat and Phyllie to their lunch and afternoon.

Hannah's head felt like it might explode by the time they arrived home. She waited until Amy and Bear had disappeared upstairs before turning to Damien. 'What did you know about Nat and the poker? Did you know she was in trouble?'

'Yes. She told me a few weeks ago. I told her to cancel her account and put blocks in place so she couldn't access the sites.'

'And did she?'

'As far as I'm aware, she did.'

'Did she tell you how much she was in debt?'

He nodded. 'Fifteen thousand, although I'm not sure if all her debt was due to gambling. God, I feel awful. If I hadn't invited her to poker night this probably wouldn't have happened.'

'It's not your fault, but I wish you'd told me. I would have helped her.'

He shook his head. 'You're not the right person to help her. She hates taking any advice from you. Any effort you made then, or make now, would be thrown back in your face. She specifically asked me not to say anything to you.'

Hannah swallowed a large lump that had formed in her throat. Tears glistened in her eyes.

Damien reached across and pulled her to him. 'Don't beat yourself up. It's just how it is.'

'I've let Mum down. From the moment she died I knew what she would have expected from me when it came to looking out for Nat. I've tried so hard to protect her from things and now look what's happened.'

'She's a grown woman. Your days of protecting her are long gone.'

'But the fact that we just don't get along, I'm sure that would upset Mum.'

'You can always change that. Be more tolerant and patient with her. Try and remain positive about everything she says and don't push her buttons by going on about real or imagined risks.'

Hannah nodded. 'Okay.'

He hugged her again. 'And I'm sorry. I hated keeping it from you, but I made a promise. I won't make that sort of promise again. Now, why don't you go and sit down, and I'll make us all some lunch?'

Hannah nodded again. She wanted to get back online and read through the previous conversations to see how many hints there were that Lia was Nat. Maybe she wasn't. It was possible it was just another coincidence.

It wasn't a coincidence. When Hannah read back through the messages, it was definitely Nat. The comments about her sister that Hannah had sympathised with were about her! Nat was discussing their relationship with total strangers. She took a deep breath. She couldn't be angry with her. She was doing exactly the same thing. Enjoying new friendships where she felt safe to say anything. After all, she never imagined meeting the other two women and certainly never imagined she would know one of them.

It was amazing to think that she'd not put two and two together earlier. But then again, why would she? Nat hadn't mentioned anyone's names or used her real name, and Hannah had no reason to suspect her sister had a gambling problem.

She leaned back in her chair and considered the situation they were in. In the short time she'd known Lia, she felt like she was developing a firm friendship with her. The same with Eliza. Part of her wished she didn't know that Lia was Nat. If she didn't know, it was possible they could have become great friends. If at some point the truth had been revealed, then perhaps they would have had a better relationship than they did now? The truth would have come out as they moved further along the track and discussed jobs and family.

Nat had no idea that Suze was her sister. Hannah shuddered at the thought. She definitely wouldn't want Nat knowing about the Zane Fox situation; she was likely to tell Phyllie, their father, or even Damien. Thank goodness she'd used a different name for herself. She hadn't told Lia or Eliza what she did for work or even where she lived. She knew that Eliza's brother lived in Toorak but had no idea where Eliza herself lived, other than it was in Melbourne.

Would staying in the online chat group be a way to have a relationship with her sister? It was certainly a way to find out more about what was going on in Nat's life and do her best to protect her where she could. There was no rush to do anything for now. She'd made two great friends, and if she could treat Lia as a friend, not as her sister, it might be a turning point in their relationship. What Nat didn't know regarding who Suze was wasn't going to hurt her.

Chapter Twenty

Nat couldn't believe how well she fitted in with the team at Endeavour Trust. She'd only been there four days yet felt like she'd been there for months. The staff were friendly and welcoming, and she could see that Col Fletcher's enthusiasm impacted on every staff member. They wanted to do their best for their clients and at the same time make their workplace a great place to be. Phyllie had been waiting for her each evening with a list of questions about her day, which she assumed had been carefully thought through to check that Nat was going to work and not lying about it.

'Drop in and see me one day like you said you would,' Nat suggested. 'I can tell you don't trust me.'

Phyllie's face had reddened, but she hadn't denied it. 'I believe *in* you and that is the main thing. And yes, I will pop in and see you at some stage. I wanted you to settle in first. We'll organise a time for next week.'

That had been a small victory in itself. That Phyllie hadn't suggested that she would drop in at a random time, as she had previously, meant she must believe Nat was telling the truth.

Nat smiled as she opened the dishwasher and put her dinner plate in. Verna had picked up Phyllie half an hour earlier for their monthly horticulture meeting, leaving Nat with an empty house for the evening. She switched the dishwasher on and went through to the living area and sat down at her computer. Sunday, when she'd last chatted with Suze and Eliza, seemed like an age ago. She wondered how they were going? She logged in and saw that BrownDog40 was online.

BrownDog40

Hey, Lia! Was about to log off thinking no one was here tonight.

PinkFish88

Phew, glad you didn't. It's such a relief having you guys to chat to. Each time I have the urge to log on to the poker rooms I check the chat room instead and one of you is often here. So, thank you! Never thought I'd make friends online that I rely on so much.

BrownDog40

Excellent that you're staying out of the poker rooms – well done! How's your new job going? You started this week, didn't you?

PinkFish88

Going well. The company has a great vibe to it, and my job is great. I'm a community support officer. I have to organise carers and help in some of the community houses we have in the St Kilda and Elwood areas. I go in and check on the clients and make sure both their needs and those of the carer are being met. I also have to find housing placements for new clients and make sure the dynamic in the houses is working.

LizaE

Wow, that sounds rewarding. Hi to you two by the way.

PinkFish88

Hey, Eliza! Yes, it is a rewarding job. I'm not sure what I was thinking getting caught up with the poker full-time. I think I was in some addicted haze. How are you going? Still celebrating your brother's investment? When do you find out if the second one was as successful?

LizaE

You won't believe it, but Jacob's just left. He turned up this afternoon with a bottle of champagne and a cheque for sixty thousand dollars. How crazy is that! He invested twenty thousand for us and increased it by three hundred percent. Can you believe it? We're not out of the woods, but eighty-seven thousand dollars is almost halfway there. I'm more shocked about this I think than I was at the debt Doug accumulated.

Nat stared at the screen. That was incredible. Eliza's situation was being turned around so quickly. Imagine having a brother who could do that.

LizaE

I should mention, Jacob doesn't always make such massive profits. What he's doing right now is high risk, but they see another three-week window of being able to make money quickly. He said it happens every two to three years. They refer to it as the 'salmon run'. They catch as much as they can before the river runs dry. Usually, they lose on their last investment, which is why they pace it out during the run. They expect a loss at some stage, so rather than investing millions at a time they minimise that final loss. Then once the loss comes, they go back to regular trading, hoping that the next salmon run won't be too many years away.

BrownDog40

It sounds like they know how to manage their risk, and to expect that loss is sensible. I'm so pleased for you Eliza. You deserve a fairy god-brother!

LizaE

What about you Suze? Aren't you due to see the private investigator this week?

BrownDog40

Yes, I've decided to tell him to get lost. I'm not going to pay him any more. I'm hoping to organise for my parents to have my daughter this weekend so I can sit my husband down and come clean. I have no idea how he's going to react but your comment about being honest resonated with me.

LizaE

Oh gosh, I'm no expert. I hope it's good advice. I think no matter what happens right now, at some point he was going to find out. Also, it does give him the chance to connect with his biological mother. That in itself might grant you forgiveness.

PinkFish88

If he's a decent guy, he's going to see exactly why you did what you did. It was for no other reason but to protect him. I think you're amazing.

Nat did think Suze was an amazingly strong woman. She could only imagine the guilt she must be carrying around for what she'd done and telling the truth was going to take a lot of courage.

BrownDog40

Thanks, Lia. You have no idea how much I appreciate your words. How are things on the family front for you? You mentioned you were a bit worried about your grandmother. How is she?

PinkFish88

Good, although forgetful at times. I am a bit worried, to be honest. She's starting to show signs of dementia. I may just have scared myself googling her symptoms though, so hopefully it's just old age.

BrownDog40

What sort of things is she doing?

PinkFish88

Forgetting things mainly, but also leaving the iron on and heading to social functions half-dressed.

BrownDog40

Half-dressed? What naked?

PinkFish88

God no! More that she's put a nice shirt on and some lipstick but then she's wearing her gardening trousers and boots. She's done that twice now, well twice that I've noticed.

LizaE

She sounds like she might need some help. Can you take her to her doctor's or get someone in your family to help?

PinkFish88

I thought I'd have a chat with my dad. She's his mother. He'll be discreet and not upset her, whereas my sister would have her committed if she got wind of this!

BrownDog40

Really? She'd move her straight out?

PinkFish88

She'd do everything in her power to try to. She's not leaving her house, but my sister can't see that keeping her there is the best thing for her. I do get it, she's not trying to be mean, she's genuinely worried for her, but she needs to understand that my grandmother would rather die tomorrow in her own home than be dependent on others. It's like my sister can't get her head around the fact that an old lady has her dignity. She's a very proud and independent woman and doesn't want to be pushed around.

LizaE

I never really understood people like that. Surely all of us want to make our own decisions and be in charge of our futures no matter how old we are. I get it if a person is ill and can't make these decisions for themselves, but it doesn't sound like your grandmother is like that.

BrownDog40

No, she sounds like an amazing lady. I would get her checked out though. You might find if there is something wrong it's as simple as giving her the right medication.

PinkFish88

Thanks, I'll have a chat with my dad and organise something. We'll have to do it in some way that she doesn't think we're worried about her.

BrownDog40

You could check if she's had immunisations for flu, shingles and pneumococcus. If she hasn't had them, then you could convince her that

that's what she's going in for. Have a chat with the doctor before the appointment to ensure he knows your real concerns. Just a suggestion.

PinkFish88

Great suggestion. Thanks, Suze. I'll suggest to Dad that that's what we do.

BrownDog40

And make sure he's sworn to secrecy. You don't want that interfering sister of yours involved!

PinkFish88

Will do. Now, I was thinking last night, Eliza. You said your brother lives in Toorak. Whereabouts do you guys live? You don't have to disclose that of course. But I'm in Blackburn and figured if we're nearby that it would be lovely to all meet for coffee or a drink after work one evening or perhaps even this weekend. My shout to say thanks for everything.

LizaE

I'm in Richmond, and yes, I'd love to catch up this weekend. I'd actually planned to suggest it myself. How about you, Suze, are you even in Melbourne?

BrownDog40

I am and would love to meet you guys. Can't
do the next few weeks but certainly down the
track. Don't let me stop you two meeting up
though. Now, I've got to run. Have a great
night and let me know if you do catch up, I'll
be so envious.

LizaE

Shame Suze isn't available, but great you are.
What do you say to this weekend? I'm having lunch with my brother on Saturday. Could
meet you after for a drink? We're having lunch
in Richmond at a new restaurant called The
Winery. They have some beautiful wines and
cheese. Hubby's taking the girls to his parents
for the weekend, and I've got out of it, so I
have the whole afternoon and evening free.

PinkFish88

Sounds great. Would love to. What time suits?
I'm good for any time.

LizaE

Let's say two. It doesn't matter if we haven't
finished lunch. It would be nice to introduce
you to Jacob. He'll have an expensive bottle

of wine on the go, so that will be the perfect
place for us to start.

PinkFish88

Fantastic, see you then.

Nat logged off the computer, a smile fixed firmly to her face. She was looking forward to meeting Eliza, and a restaurant was perfect. While her gut told her she'd made a genuine friend she knew that she still needed to be careful. At least in a public place she could call for help if Eliza turned out to be a crazy axe murderer. She loved that she didn't have to hide anything from her chat room friends. Her phone pinged with a text message. It was Pip.

Hear you're kicking goals already at Endeavour. Knew you
would. Proud of you, babe! P xx

Nat sent her friend a quick text back, thanking her again for the introduction to Col and the glowing recommendation. She thought back to Pip's reaction when she mentioned the online gambling. She'd been horrified. While she'd then done a wonderful thing and set Nat up with the job, the horror and disgust in her eyes that Nat had been gambling and lost was hard to forget. Neither Eliza nor Suze would be judging her. They both had their own problems to deal with.

Nat applied her coral lipstick and stood back from the full-length mirror, admiring the wispy, floral, long-sleeved shirt with its V-neck. She'd dressed her jeans up by adding a thick brown belt with a large silver buckle and knee-high boots. She had no idea what to expect of Eliza and wanted to find the perfect balance of casual chic. She snatched up her bag from her bed and hurried down the stairs. It was already one and she'd said she'd be in Richmond by two. Not that it probably mattered, as it sounded as if Eliza and her brother would be enjoying a long lunch. She was intrigued by the thought of meeting both of them. She felt so close to Eliza and had a feeling they would be lifelong friends. Jacob intrigued her, as she'd never met a self-made millionaire before. She wondered if the salmon were still running for him.

'Wow!' Phyllie clapped her hands together as Nat entered the living room. 'You look a million dollars. Where are you off to?'

'I'm meeting Eliza, from the online chat room, for a drink in Richmond. We've decided to meet in real life.'

Concern crossed Phyllie's features. 'Are you sure that's a good idea? So many people portray themselves to be someone they're not these days. Men posing as women, people befriending others to steal money from them. It's awful.'

Nat nodded. 'I'm meeting her at a restaurant, so it's a public place. If she turns out to be a guy, I'll run a mile, don't worry.'

'Do you know what she looks like?'

Nat shook her head. 'No, she uses a cartoon image on her chat room profile. No one uses real pictures as it's supposed to be anonymous. She's booked a table in her name, so it should be easy enough to find her.'

'You be careful, that's all.'

Nat leaned down and hugged Phyllie. 'Will do. And I doubt I'll be late. I'll cook us dinner when I get home.'

'Only if you're home in time. If you're not, I'm sure I can manage to boil myself an egg. Oh, and while I think of it, are you busy tomorrow? Hannah's asked your father and Sue to have Amy for the weekend as she and Damien have something on. I thought you might have time to take her out somewhere. She might be bored otherwise.'

Nat laughed. 'Sue is anything but boring. She'll have her doing something crazy, I can almost guarantee it. But yes, I'll give them a ring as I did promise Amy I'd take her to the movies this weekend as part of her birthday present. I wonder what Hannah and Damien are getting up to.' She winked. 'Dirty weekend?'

Phyllie shook her head. 'No, I'm not sure, to be honest, but from what your father said it sounded like they were having some problems and needed Amy out of the house so they could sort out a few things.'

'Really? Hannah and Damien having problems? I thought their life was perfect. I can't even imagine what sort of problems they could be having. Perhaps Damien put the dishes in the dishwasher the wrong way and Hannah's prepared a risk assessment.'

Phyllie tut-tutted. 'Don't be nasty. You should never make assumptions about another person's life. You have no idea what they might be going through. Hannah did mention to me that Damien had been a bit down lately, so it might be something to do with that.'

Nat would be down herself if she had to put up with Hannah any more than she currently did. Perhaps Damien had finally realised just what a pain her sister was.

Nat hurried out the front door and up Phyllie's path. She'd planned to catch the train into Richmond so she didn't need to worry about how much she drank.

A low wolf whistle stopped her in her tracks. She glanced up to see Leon grinning appreciatively at her.

'Sorry, couldn't help myself. You look fantastic. I assume you'll be dropping in for unsolicited advice and that glass of wine I promised?'

Nat laughed. 'Not today. I'm meeting a friend in Richmond. Just hurrying to get the train.'

Leon took his car keys from his pocket. 'Let me drop you at the station. It'll save you a ten-minute walk.'

'That would be great, thank you.' She followed him to a new-ish-looking Mazda 3 parked outside his house and climbed into the passenger seat. The car was clean and neat on the inside, not like her old bomb.

'He's a lucky guy, whoever you're dressing up for.' Leon gave her a sideways glance as he started the car. 'He'll probably fall off his chair when you walk in. He should anyway. Actually, if he doesn't, you let me know and I'll have a word with him.'

Nat laughed, her confidence growing with every word he said. 'That's very flattering, but *Eliza* probably won't be looking at me that way.'

He raised an eyebrow. 'More fool her then.'

They both laughed as Leon continued towards the station. It was only a couple of minutes' drive and they arrived far too quickly.

'If you need a lift home later just let me know,' he said, writing his number on a piece of paper. 'I have a hot date with Rainbow later on, but she'll forgive me if I cancel.'

Nat took the paper, opened the car door and stepped out. 'I wouldn't want to be the woman that comes between you and Rainbow.' She grinned. 'Particularly not between you and those horns she wears so well. Thanks for the lift, I really appreciate it.'

Leon returned her smile and she headed towards the station entrance. As she turned to walk up to the city-bound platform, she was conscious that his car hadn't moved. She stole a glance in his direction, her heart racing as he raised a hand and waved.

Nat's cheeks ached as a smile played on her lips from Blackburn to Richmond. Leon was a nice guy. There was definitely a spark between them. Not one, according to Phyllie, she would be allowed to do anything about though, but it was still lovely to feel desired and have a man like Leon flirting with her.

She was looking forward to meeting Eliza. A celebration seemed in order. Things in her life were improving. Her first week at Endeavour Trust had gone well, and she already felt part of the team. She was also on a weekly pay schedule and almost couldn't believe it when she'd checked her account balance that morning and there was actually money in it. She immediately transferred half of it on to the credit card, leaving her the rest to live on for the next week. She didn't have huge expenses but was still running a car and contributing to the food at Phyllie's. It left her enough to be able to go out for an afternoon without worrying.

She entered the bright foyer of The Winery, natural light pouring in through the floor-to-ceiling windows and large skylights. Her stomach suddenly fluttered. This was like a blind date. Except she did know the person on some level, and it was a woman, so definitely not a date.

She told the maître d' that she was joining Eliza Strawn and was quickly shown through to a table at the back of the restaurant. A woman, who she assumed must be Eliza, was laughing at something the blond-haired man with her had just said. She looked up, her smile reaching her eyes as she saw Nat. She leaped to her feet and threw her arms around her.

Nat laughed. Eliza was nothing like she'd imagined. It was ridiculous really, but from the conversations they'd had, she had a picture in her head of Eliza being a biggish woman with brown hair. She thought she'd have a friendly face and be one of those mumsy types that people gravitated towards. She wasn't expecting the petite, dark-haired woman who greeted her. Her make-up highlighted her blue eyes and high cheekbones. With Eliza wearing a tight black sheath dress, Nat felt underdressed in comparison.

'I'm so glad you came,' Eliza gushed. 'I was telling Jacob all about you and Suze and how we met in the most unusual of ways.' She elbowed Jacob. 'And he said you were probably some internet predator misrepresenting yourself and that you either wouldn't turn up today or you would – with some wonderful excuse for why you were a man and not a woman.'

Nat laughed and looked at Jacob. 'You must have been on the phone with my grandmother earlier. We had a very similar conversation before I left the house.'

Jacob held out his hand and shook Nat's. 'A pleasure to meet you, Lia, and I'm glad for both your sakes that you appear to be who you've presented yourselves as.'

'You're exactly like I imagined,' Eliza said as they sat down. 'Except you're taller than I thought and much thinner. Not that I thought you'd be fat, but I didn't picture you looking so athletic. I'd kill for your figure.'

'Really? I'd kill for yours!'

'And I'd kill for another glass of wine,' Jacob said. 'Shall I order a bottle?'

Eliza looked to Nat. 'Do you mind if Jacob stays for one more drink? He can get us a nice bottle, and after he's had one glass, he can leave us to get to know each other.'

Jacob stood. 'I'll go to the bar and order a bottle and settle the bill at the same time. I did say today was my shout.'

Eliza waited until her brother had moved out of hearing before turning conspiratorially towards Nat. 'I think he wants to make one hundred percent sure that you're not here to murder me. We'll get rid of him after that one glass.'

Nat laughed. 'Fine by me. I'm not a killer, by the way. God, I find it hard even to kill a spider.'

'It's so good to meet you. I've so loved getting to know you and Suze through our little group. I wonder how Suze is going? She was planning on telling her husband the truth today, wasn't she?'

'That's right, she was – poor thing. As much as I know she did it to support him, I'm not sure he'll see it quite like that.'

The waiter arrived with a 2015 bottle of Penfolds St Henri Shiraz. He held it out towards Eliza. 'Your companion asked me to bring this to the table. Would you like to taste it or are you happy if I pour?'

Eliza looked to Nat. 'Are you happy with red or would you prefer white?'

'Red's good with me. With this fire going it's perfect, in fact. I couldn't get over how cold it is outside.'

'Just pour please,' Eliza instructed the waiter.

They waited as he filled three large balloon glasses to the half-way mark, left the bottle on the table and retreated to the bar.

Eliza picked up her glass and raised it to Nat. 'To us. From online friends to real-life friends.'

Nat clinked her glass with Eliza's before sipping the wine. Soft, earthy, mocha-like flavours danced on her tongue.

Jacob rejoined them and picked up his glass. 'I love this vintage. It's gorgeous. Now, Lia, tell us about yourself. Eliza mentioned what a great job you have and how much you're giving back to the community. I'd love to know more about it.'

Nat found herself doing all the talking for the next twenty minutes as Jacob asked her questions about her job and the types of people that used the community housing.

'Sounds like they could use an injection of funds,' Jacob said.

'It's like anything, not enough budget to get things working to their optimum. But it's a wonderful service, so we can't complain.'

Jacob nodded.

'What are you thinking?' Eliza winked at Nat. 'I know that look. The cogs are turning.'

'The company will be looking to donate some of the money it made from the current salmon run, that's all. Something like the Endeavour Trust might be of interest. We're always looking at ways to assist the community.'

'That would be amazing. Eliza mentioned that you've had some success in the last few weeks with your investments.'

'We have. It's an unusual opportunity that occurs every two to three years.' He laughed. 'It's like the stars align or something, but it's never for long enough, of course.'

'Do you think your run is nearly over?'

He shook his head. 'I'm confident we have more time, possibly even a few weeks. We make investments daily that turn over very quickly. It is a good way to invest manageable amounts without the risk being too high.'

Eliza rolled her eyes. 'His idea of manageable is eight hundred thousand or even a million.'

Jacob smiled. 'It is, but keep in mind that's a tiny percentage of our overall portfolio.'

'Your clients must be delighted when this happens.'

'They are. It's why we retain our clients for many years. What they earn in this short-term period is more than any managed fund could ever return for them.'

'Would you allow Lia to invest?' Eliza suddenly asked.

Jacob leaned back in his chair, looking uncomfortable.

'Don't worry,' Nat assured him. 'I have nothing to invest. Today is the first day in weeks that I have a little money, and that's only because I received a week's pay. I have about five hundred dollars to my name. I'm not in a position to do anything.'

'We don't usually invest on behalf of friends, anyway.' He looked pointedly at Eliza. 'If things go wrong it's never good for the friendship.'

'Sorry,' Eliza said. 'Lia's just going through such a horrible time, that's all. I thought it would help a little.'

Jacob finished his wine and stood. 'I'd better leave you lovely ladies to it.' He leaned down and kissed Eliza. 'Good to see you, sis. I've left some money on the tab for you so you can order another bottle and have some dinner later if you want to.'

'Oh no,' Nat said. 'You don't need to do that. I've plenty to cover us.'

'Consider it my treat. That five hundred is better spent practically anywhere else.' He winked. 'Except the poker rooms of course.'

The next morning Nat opened one eye, then the other, her fingers crossed under the duvet. It was doubtful she'd get away with drinking the amount that she and Eliza had the previous afternoon and not be hungover. They'd stopped after the second bottle and ordered some finger food, but it was still close to a bottle each and a lot more than Nat usually drank. She was surprised to find she felt okay. No thumping headache and no churning stomach. She looked up at the ceiling and smiled in gratitude to Jacob. Eliza had said that drinking the expensive wine should mean they'd be fine, and it looked as if she was right.

'You alive up there?'

Phyllie's voice drifted up the stairs. Nat swung herself out of bed and went out on to the landing.

'It's after nine. I just wanted to remind you that you said you'd pick Amy up and take her to the movies today.'

Nat smiled. 'I haven't forgotten, just enjoying a luxurious sleep-in.'

'I've left you some money on the kitchen table. It's my treat today for you and Amy. There should be enough for the movies and some afternoon tea or something from the candy bar.'

Nat shook her head. 'No, don't be silly. I got paid yesterday, and I'm happy to take her out.'

Phyllie waggled a finger at her. 'You need to pay down that credit card, missy; no point splurging unnecessarily. The way you were giggling last night, I'd say your afternoon with Eliza probably cost you a pretty packet.'

'It didn't cost anything. Her brother, the millionaire, picked up the bill. That reminds me, I should get online and thank Eliza, or at least tell her to thank Jacob for me.'

Nat had arrived home just after eight the previous night. She and Eliza had chatted non-stop, finding out so many things about each other. It had been a lot of fun, and she felt even closer to her new friend. She'd been able to fill Phyllie in that Eliza hadn't misrepresented herself and was a lovely person. Phyllie looked like she still didn't believe her, for reasons Nat couldn't fathom. 'Not everyone in the world is out to cheat and steal,' she'd reminded her grandmother. 'There are plenty of real people in chat rooms. And anyway, who's going to misrepresent themselves in a gambling addicts' chat room? It's not as if anyone has anything of value you could prey on them for.'

Phyllie seemed to accept that point, and Nat enjoyed telling her more about Eliza's situation.

Now, she went back into her room and slipped on her white linen robe and Ugg boots before coming downstairs and switching on the computer.

Phyllie placed a cup of steaming coffee in front of her.

'There are perks to having the computer down here after all. Thanks, Granny!'

Phyllie slapped her on the arm. 'Don't you Granny me, girlie. It makes me feel like some frail old lady. I might be old, but I'm certainly not decrepit. Now, I'm going to visit Verna. I've left that money for you on the table, so make sure you take it.'

'Okay, thank you. I'll make sure Amy knows it's your treat.'

'No need to do that, I just want you to save your money for the moment.'

Phyllie collected her bag and let herself out of the front door while Nat logged on to the chat room. She smiled as the computer processed her details. For the first morning in weeks, she hadn't woken up wanting to play poker. The very thought of it repulsed her. Listening to Eliza's story last night of just how badly it had affected her husband, and also others she'd got to know in the chat room, made her cringe.

There was a message waiting.

LizaE

Hey, Lia, you there? Was great to catch up yesterday. Jacob has a message for you. Let me know when you're online, so we can chat. And Suze, if you're around, hope it went ok with your husband. We're here if you need us.

PinkFish88
Yes, I'm here. Thank you for a great afternoon too! Was so lovely to meet you (and hope we meet you also, Suze) and to find out you're not a seventy-year-old perverted male pretending to be someone you're not. You can be assured,

280

neither Eliza or I are weirdos, Suze. We both had reservations about meeting yesterday and were both relieved to find that not only are we normal, but we got along brilliantly. You'll, of course, have to prove you're not pretending to be someone you're not if we do meet! Although my gut feeling, which I can usually trust, tells me you're genuine too.

What's Jacob's message? I have a big thank you for him too. Can't believe we drank that much and I'm hangover free. If only I could afford top-shelf wines like that every day!

LizaE

Jacob wants you to know that he's decided to prove to you that he could find a better way to use your five hundred dollars than you could. He invested it overnight and turned it into three thousand! He's now taken that three thousand and reinvested it. He told me to tell you not to worry, you don't owe him a cent if he loses it all, but if it does increase it's all yours. Told you he was gold!

Nat stared at her screen. No way. Why would he do that? He hardly knew her. She couldn't accept it, that much she knew. This turning money into so much more overnight didn't ring true for her either. How could it be that easy?

PinkFish88

281

Wow! Blown away but I can't accept the money. Tell Jacob thanks but I never gave him any money so can't expect him to invest for me. Also, he's married, I assume he remembers that?

LizaE

Lol! He's not looking for anything more than to help you. He's very interested in our situation and has been looking into Gambler's Aid. Remember how he said the company were planning to invest in things that benefit the community? Well, he's thinking that helping addicts is a good starting place. He also said he might be in touch to find out who he should speak to at Endeavour Trust regarding the community houses. He's genuine, Lia, one hundred percent. Turning your money into a bit more is just because he can. If it turns into a larger amount it will help with your credit card.

Nat didn't know what to say. Could she accept money from a total stranger? No, she didn't think she could. Anyway, it was probably all just on paper. She doubted he'd actually invested anything in her name.

LizaE

See the screenshot attached. Jacob said he'd contact me at three and let me know if this

multiplied at all this morning. If it does, he
thought you might want to withdraw it and
decide whether to reinvest or use it for your
debt. Just think about it between now and
three. There's no pressure. As much as we both
expect everyone on the internet to be out to
rip us off, there are genuine people too. That's
what I recognised in you yesterday, and I hope
you did in me too. There's nothing to lose, and
that's the main thing. Have to run. The girls are
meeting friends at laser tag this afternoon – the
little princesses . . . not!

Nat smiled at the thought of Eliza's girls. She'd shown her some
photos of them the previous day. They were adorable but didn't
look much like Eliza. Two very tall blonde-haired girls. Apparently,
they took after their father. She could see that Suze wasn't online
but posted a final message before she logged out.

PinkFish88

Thinking of you and feeling for you. Ready to
chat whenever you need someone. Xx

Nat picked up her coffee cup and took it through to the kitchen.
She saw ten dollars sitting on the table with a note. *For you and
Amy, enjoy!*

She picked up the money and glanced down at the floor in case
Phyllie had dropped the rest. She hadn't. Was this a joke? The two
of them going to the movies and buying snacks would set them
back forty, if not fifty dollars. A memory flashed in Nat's mind from

many years earlier. She was about ten and Hannah thirteen and she remembered Phyllie calling to them.

'The money for the theatre's on the table. There's enough for two tickets and a small popcorn. No soft drinks, you hear me? It's all rubbish and will rot your teeth.'

Phyllie had always left them a ten-dollar note. They'd go to the matinee special, which gave you entry and a snack. Did Phyllie think it was still 1998? Back then the small local theatre they went to was cheaper than most of the mainstream cinema chains. You could get a ticket for under five dollars. You definitely couldn't do that today. An uncomfortable feeling settled over Nat as she walked back up the stairs to her bedroom, planning to have a shower and get ready. Hannah was right. There really was something wrong with Phyllie.

Chapter Twenty-One

Hannah slipped out of bed early on Sunday morning. She poked her head into Amy's room, where Bear lay curled up on the bed. He lifted his head when he saw her and then put it back down again. He looked miserable. They'd said no to Amy taking him for the sleepover at her grandfather's, but now she wondered if that had been such a good idea. Still, a break from each other meant they'd be even happier to see each other that afternoon. She went in and sat on the bed and rubbed the dog between the ears.

'She'll be back this afternoon, Bear.'

He moved closer to her and laid his head on her lap, his big brown eyes staring up at her. Hannah sighed. Wouldn't it be nice if her only problem right now was missing Amy. The house had been unusually quiet without her the previous night, and she and Damien had ended up going out for dinner. She'd been on edge all evening, trying to muster the courage to start the conversation about Zane Fox and Damien's mother, but she'd clammed up, and they'd come home and watched a movie on Netflix. She'd been so distracted she couldn't even remember what the story was about.

She'd met with Zane after work on Friday afternoon at Red Orchid, a small bar tucked away in an alley in Prahran, and her legs had trembled throughout the encounter. He was already there when she'd arrived, seated in a back corner, his trademark smirk on his face. He was sipping a glass of champagne, and another sat on the table for her.

He nodded at it. 'Thought we could have a drink to celebrate our last transaction together.'

Hannah had been tempted to knock back the glass in one gulp, but as it had been purchased by Zane, she chose to ignore it. 'Yes, this will be our last transaction. That much I guarantee.'

'Really? That's a bit presumptuous, isn't it?'

As soon as the words left his lips, she knew that she'd made the right decision. If she handed over more money now, he'd be back in a couple of months with some other threat.

He'd laughed. 'I'm just kidding. Yes, this will be the last time you ever have to see my beautiful face. Now, I assume you have a document you'd like me to sign?'

She stared at him, wondering how someone became so awful. What did he think when he got up each morning? *How will I rip someone off and make their life miserable today?*

'You look very serious, Hannah.' He glanced at his watch. 'We're both busy people. Let's just get this contract signed and the transaction completed.'

Hannah took a deep breath. 'There is no contract, Zane. I came here today to tell you I'm not going to allow you to blackmail me. If you decide to provide Damien's mother with information on how to contact him, that's your prerogative. I don't trust that you won't be back for more money if I pay you again.'

Zane shifted uncomfortably in his seat. It appeared he hadn't considered this scenario. 'I wouldn't come back for more. This is a one-time transaction. You have my word, and as I said, I'm happy to sign anything you need.'

Hannah pushed her chair back and stood. 'No. I came here in person to ensure there was no misunderstanding. You said when we last met that Janine had offered you the same amount to provide her with information. If you want money, that's where you'll need to go to get it.'

She turned on her heel and strode towards the door of the bar. She half expected Zane to already be on his phone calling Janine. She didn't dare turn and find out.

Now, as she continued to rub Bear between the ears, she wondered what Zane would do next. 'Regardless, we have to tell Damien before that prick does, don't we, Bear? That's not how we want this to play out.'

'Tell Damien what?'

Hannah's head snapped round. Damien was standing at the door, yawning and pushing a hand through his messy hair. He didn't wait for an answer. 'You're up early. I thought we'd be taking advantage of Amy being away for the night.' He grinned. 'Come back to bed. We can still make the most of our child-free morning.'

Hannah smiled at him. 'I think we did that pretty successfully last night.'

He moved into the room and sat down next to her. Bear lifted his head from Hannah's lap and moved it to Damien's.

'He's a great dog, isn't he?'

Hannah nodded. 'He is. He's missing Amy though. I probably should have let her take him to Dad's. I didn't think it was fair to ask them to have both of them.'

'It's good for them to be apart for a couple of days,' Damien said. 'Absence makes the heart grow fonder and all that.' He took her hand and squeezed it. 'Now, what were you talking to Bear about? What do you need to tell me before the *prick* does? And who is the prick, by the way?'

Hannah closed her eyes, a lump forming in her throat so large she imagined it might prevent her from talking.

'Han, you're scaring me. What's going on?'

She opened her eyes, her lip beginning to tremble. 'How about we go downstairs and make some coffee. I think I'll need it before I can even start.'

Damien pulled her to her feet, eyes filled with concern. 'Is this conversation we're about to have the reason you asked your father to have Amy this weekend?'

Hannah took a deep breath. 'Yes.'

Hannah was in no hurry as she used the coffee machine to prepare their morning drinks. She'd gone over what she was going to say a thousand times but no matter which way she spun it, she couldn't see the conversation going well. Damien was sitting at the island counter watching her as she moved around the kitchen. After five minutes of watching her fluff about, he stood.

'You go and sit down, and I'll finish making the coffee. I'm not sure what you're doing exactly, but by the time you give me a cup it's going to be cold.' He smiled. 'You don't have to be nervous, Han. I can't imagine anything you could tell me that I'd get angry about. Especially on a Sunday morning when we have the house to ourselves until at least four or five o'clock. It's only six a.m. now. That's hours and hours we'll need to fill, and I have many ideas on how we can do that.'

Hannah followed his orders to sit down but didn't respond to his innuendos. The likelihood of him still wanting to fill in those hours anywhere near her was unlikely.

Damien frothed the milk for their drinks and brought the mugs across to where Hannah was sitting. He placed hers in front of her and sat down.

'So?'

She drew in a deep breath and met his gaze. 'There's something I need to tell you, and I need you to let me finish before you ask any questions or get angry.'

He picked up his coffee. 'I can't imagine I'll get angry, but okay, go ahead.'

She hesitated before forcing the words out. 'Do you remember Zane Fox?'

'The guy who looked into my biological parents?'

Hannah nodded. 'He contacted me a few weeks ago to blackmail me.'

Damien sat his coffee back on the bench. 'What? Why?'

'He has information that he knows I would like kept private, and he intends to share that information.'

Damien was up off his seat. 'That bastard. I'll kill him, Han, I mean it.'

Tears filled Hannah's eyes. Her husband was on his feet ready to defend her without even asking what the information was. She reached out and took his hand. 'Sit down. When you hear what the information is you might not feel the same way.'

He sat back down on the stool, a vein in his forehead throbbing. Hannah imagined he was thinking about how he'd kill Zane Fox if given the opportunity.

'Twelve years ago, I did something that at the time I thought was the right thing to do. I weighed up the pros and cons of keeping some information to myself. It was more than keeping the information to myself. I lied about it. I changed the facts to protect the people I love. I honestly thought at the time it was in their best interests.' A tear trickled down her cheek.

Damien wiped it away, the anger on his face now replaced with concern. 'Han, anyone who knows you would realise that you'd have done a full risk assessment before making a decision like that. They'd know you wouldn't lie or do something to hurt them without very good reason.'

She drew in another deep breath. 'I hope you still feel like that when I tell you what I did.'

'You're really scaring me now.'

'Twelve years ago, Zane Fox told you that your biological parents were dead. That they'd been killed in an accident when bringing you home from the hospital.'

He nodded. 'I still have the newspaper article about their deaths.'

'The article wasn't about your parents, Damien, or you. It was another family. Their names weren't listed in the article, which was why he was able to use it.'

Damien froze. 'What? Why would he make something like that up?'

'To protect you from the truth.'

'The truth?'

She nodded. 'Your parents didn't die in a car accident. When Zane presented you with that story, they were still alive.'

'But they're not now?'

'Your mother is, but your father isn't.'

A flicker of hope sparked in Damien's eyes. 'My mother's still alive?'

She nodded.

He moved off the stool and began pacing up and down. 'My mother's alive. Okay, this is not the conversation I thought we'd be having this morning. Why did Zane Fox tell me they were dead?'

'Because I asked him to.'

Damien stopped pacing and spun round to face her. 'What? Why would you do that?'

'Zane found out a lot about your parents, and I thought the truth would be so damaging that you were better not knowing.'

'That wasn't your decision.'

Hannah nodded. 'I know, but please believe me, it was only because I love you so much. In addition to the truth being difficult to handle, Trish was going through chemo at the time, and I knew how scared she was about you finding your biological parents and not considering her your mum anymore.'

'I would never have done that. Mum's my mum. I would have liked to have met my biological parents, but it doesn't mean they would have become part of my life. I wanted to ask them questions, get a feel for who they were and where I'd come from. Also, to find out about my extended family, that's all.'

'Your mum was only one small component of my decision. It was really to protect you. I don't think finding out about your history will do anything to help you. I still don't.'

'Why tell me now then?'

Hannah took a deep breath. 'Because Zane Fox is blackmailing me. A few weeks ago, he demanded payment of ten thousand dollars. He signed a contract at the time which clearly stated he couldn't contact you to make you aware of any of this or disclose any new information about your parents.'

Damien's eyes were wide. 'You paid him ten grand?'

She nodded. 'And now he's after another ten. This time he's saying he'll provide your biological mother with information on how to contact you if I don't pay him.'

'What am I missing here? You said my biological father is dead and there's an opportunity to meet my mother. How can this be a bad thing? You need to explain what's going on, Hannah.'

She could see a mixture of uncertainty and anger rising in her husband. She needed to push through this and just tell him, then she could deal with the consequences.

'I've realised that Zane is going to continue to try and milk me for money, so I've refused to pay him any more. I now assume he'll contact you or your mother and explain the entire situation, including the reason I tried to protect you from all of this in the first place.'

'Which is?'

'Which is about the circumstances in which you were conceived.' Hannah wanted to reach out and hug him. This was going to tear him apart. She took another deep breath. 'Calvin Deeks, your biological father, brutally raped and attacked your mother when she was seventeen. Your mother, Janine, had a religious upbringing and abortion was not an option. Calvin was sentenced to twelve years jail time, and Janine went on to have you. It wasn't hushed up. Tallangetti is a small town, and the people rallied around her and supported her. The family organised for you to be adopted. With her age, and the circumstance, keeping you wasn't an option.'

The colour drained from Damien's face. He sat down on the kitchen chair nearest him and put his head in his hands.

Hannah slid off the stool and went over to him and rubbed his back. He shook her off.

'I'm sorry. I truly am. When Zane told me all this twelve years ago, I was horrified. I couldn't imagine how you'd cope knowing you came from the genes of a rapist.'

'You said he's now dead?'

Hannah nodded. 'According to Zane, he died about three months ago in jail. He'd been in and out of jail for years.'

'Why has Zane Fox appeared now? He's had twelve years to demand money.'

Heat flooded her face. 'He's an opportunist. The adoption people contacted him the week before he came to see me to say your biological mother was trying to make contact with you. I assume it reminded him that I had a secret I probably still wanted kept and he could profit from it.'

Damien looked stunned. 'She's trying to contact me?'

The hope in his eyes brought more tears to Hannah's. She nodded.

He stared at her for a moment before shaking his head. 'Jesus, I don't even know what to say.'

Tears spilled down Hannah's cheeks. 'Please know that I never did any of this to hurt you. I was trying to protect you.'

'That wasn't your call. You know how desperate I was to find out about my family. Regardless of anything, you've robbed me of twelve years of getting to know my mother. Even if she wouldn't have seen me back then, I would at least have known the circumstances and understood why she gave me up. I'm seeing a therapist to try and get over the death of my parents, for Christ's sake. You had no right to play God.' He pushed back the chair and stood. 'I'm going to get dressed and go out for the day. I've got no idea where I'll go or when I'll be back.'

Hannah closed her eyes as his footsteps retreated from the kitchen. To be the one to have caused that pain and hurt reflected in his eyes was almost too much to bear. A wet nose pushed into her hand as a warm head lay itself on her lap. She rubbed Bear's ears, grateful for the warmth and comfort of the dog.

The morning dragged horribly for Hannah. She kept wanting to ring Damien but knew she was best to leave him alone. He needed to process what he'd learned and figure out how he felt. It wasn't something he'd work out overnight. She tried to imagine if the situation was reversed how she would feel. She'd like to think that part of her would be grateful that he'd wanted to protect her, but she wasn't sure if gratitude would be an over-riding emotion.

At twelve she realised she was still in her pyjamas and had the afternoon to get through before collecting Amy from her father's. She should get out and do something. She could take Bear for a walk. She suddenly wished her mother was there to talk to. Other than her online friends, she hadn't spoken to anyone about this. Nat knew, although she didn't realise it was Hannah, of course, and there was only so much advice and support that people who didn't know you could give. She wondered if Phyllie was home. Her grandmother was the person she'd always gone to with problems before.

She picked up her phone and dialled. Phyllie answered on the third ring. 'Phyllie Jackson.'

Hannah hesitated. 'Phyllie, it's Hannah.'

'Oh, hello, love.'

'Don't you mean Williamson?'

'What do you mean? Are you going by your maiden name suddenly?'

'No, but it seems that you are.'

'Hannah, you're very confusing. What on earth are you talking about?'

'You answered the phone saying Phyllie Jackson.'

There was a silence at the end of the line.

'Phyllie?'

'I'm still here. Did I? How strange. I was thinking about my childhood when you rang, so perhaps that took me back and had me using my maiden name.' She laughed. 'Either that or, as I seem to constantly be telling Nat, my age is beginning to catch up. Now, what can I do for you, my favourite granddaughter who doesn't currently live with me?'

'I was hoping you might be free for a chat. Could I drop over and see you?'

'You can do better than that. Pick me up in half an hour, and we'll go out for lunch. I was hoping Verna would have lunch with me today, but she has a cold and isn't leaving the house.'

'Let's make it forty-five minutes. I'm still in my pyjamas.'

Phyllie laughed. 'Oh, that's right, a child-free night. How very decadent of you and Damien. Lucky you.'

If only that were why she was still in her pyjamas.

'I'll see you just before one.' Hannah hung up, glad she had a purpose for the afternoon and someone to confide in.

Phyllie was waiting by her letterbox when Hannah pulled up in front of her white weatherboard home. She hardly waited for the car to stop before pulling open the passenger door and climbing in. She beamed at Hannah.

'What a lovely surprise. I made reservations for us at Joey's. It's only about fifteen minutes from here. I hope that's okay?'

'Of course it is.' Hannah pulled back out into the street.

'Now, what's this unexpected visit in aid of?'

Hannah kept her eyes on the road. 'I'll tell you over lunch, if that's okay.'

'Sure. Now, I should fill you in on a few things while we drive. The goat situation is going exactly to plan.'

'The goat situation?'

'Yes, you know, Leon and his goat. He could be the one for Nat, I think.'

Hannah glanced at Phyllie. 'Really? She certainly seemed disappointed the other day that Damien had done the gardening and she had no reason to talk to Leon.'

'Exactly! I've made it very clear to her that she's not allowed to have a relationship with him. I'm hoping her natural instinct to do the complete opposite of what she's told will kick in.'

Hannah did her best to concentrate on Phyllie's story about using Leon's goat as an excuse to have Leon and Nat speaking to each other. Apparently Phyllie had earmarked him as a possible love interest for Nat years ago, when he'd first moved in, but had decided that Nat wasn't ready for a serious relationship. Until now she'd chosen to keep Leon's existence to herself, hoping he would still be available when she felt Nat was ready. Hannah did her best not to laugh as Phyllie talked about the 'goat boy'.

She pulled up outside Joey's. She hadn't been here for years. It was one of her grandmother's favourites, and she remembered a birthday lunch four years ago for Phyllie but couldn't recall if she'd been back since.

Phyllie was greeted like a long-lost friend when they walked through the arched doorway into the rustic dining room.

'It's been too long, dear Phyllie,' announced Reggie, the elderly maître d', before kissing her on both cheeks. 'We've reserved your favourite table overlooking the creek, and a complimentary bottle of Prosecco is chilling.'

Reggie gave Hannah a warm smile before leading them over to their table. He pulled out Phyllie's chair and laid the white napkin on her lap before doing the same for Hannah. 'Shall I pour the wine now or would you like to look at the menu first?'

'Wine please,' Phyllie said. 'I already know what I'll be ordering, but Hannah might need a few minutes with the menu.'

Reggie poured their drinks, replaced the bottle in the ice bucket and retreated to the kitchen.

Phyllie lifted her glass. 'Here's to a lovely Sunday surprise.'

Hannah chinked glassed with her grandmother, thinking that wine was the last thing she felt like right now. Still, it might help dull her constant need to cry.

'Now, look at the menu and choose something and then tell me what's going on. I'll be ordering the ploughman's platter, by the way. The goat's cheese is to die for.'

Hannah had a quick look through the menu, decided on the zucchini fritters, and closed it. She took a large gulp of her wine. 'This morning I confessed a secret to Damien I've been keeping for twelve years.'

Phyllie frowned. 'Twelve years? Not Amy?'

Hannah stared at her grandmother for a moment before registering what she was thinking. 'God no, it's not that. Amy is definitely Damien's. No, it has nothing to do with Amy. It's about Damien's biological parents.'

'I thought he was unable to find out anything about them?'

That was the story they'd spun their families twelve years earlier. Damien hadn't wanted to tell anyone he'd found out they'd died, so as far as the families were concerned it had been a closed adoption and there was nothing to report.

'The adoption agency was unable to help us, but we hired a private investigator. He found out exactly who Damien's parents were.'

Hannah went on to tell Phyllie what he'd found out and her arrangement with Zane not to tell anyone.

Phyllie nodded as she listened. 'I'm not saying you did the right thing, but I can certainly understand why you protected Damien. What I don't understand is why you've told him today?'

'That money you loaned me . . .'

'Gave,' Phyllie interjected.

'Okay, that money you *gave* me, which I used to pay off the private investigator. You were right when you said he'd probably come back for more.'

Phyllie put her champagne flute down, shaking her head. 'Nat's online friend Suze is going through the same thing. Two people I know, or know of, are being blackmailed.' She raised an eyebrow. 'What are the chances?'

Hannah felt her hand tremble.

'Please tell me you're not Suze?'

Hannah swallowed, realising just how bad this now looked. 'Let me assure you I had no idea it was Nat, to begin with. It was only a few things she said that were happening in her life that made me wonder.'

'But why were you on the gambling chat room at all?'

'Damien mentioned a friend was in a bad place with their gambling debts and I thought about his distant moods of late and was concerned he was covering for himself.'

'So, you went online?'

'Yes, I was hoping to get some advice from people who either had a problem, or were living with someone who did, about how to approach Damien. I wanted to be supportive, but I also wanted to find resources for getting him help.'

Phyllie shook her head. 'I can't believe we have two people in the family with gambling issues.'

Hannah smiled, realising she was leading Phyllie down the wrong track. 'We don't. Damien hasn't lost any money online. When he said a friend was in trouble, he was covering for Nat.'

Phyllie grinned. 'And you joined the chat room and happened to come across her?'

298

Hannah nodded. 'I only found out after I'd already joined and made friends with two women. One being Nat, although she calls herself Lia, and the other Eliza, whose husband has a gambling problem.'

'The one Nat went out for drinks with yesterday.'

'Yes. Please don't tell Nat, Phyllie. I know it's deceptive, but we've connected in the chat room. Probably for the first time since Mum died. I'm learning things about her that I never knew.'

'That's hardly fair though, is it? She thinks she's made a friend and she'll probably confide things she'd never tell her family – and certainly not you. I won't say anything, it's not my business, but I am making it clear that I don't think you should continue to misrepresent yourself.'

Hannah knew Phyllie was right. She sighed. After keeping a secret from Damien for so long, she shouldn't do the same with Nat. 'I don't think I should tell her,' Hannah said. 'I'd be better just to cancel my account with Gambler's Aid and not visit the chat rooms anymore.'

'You don't think Nat will put two and two together once she hears what Damien's going through?'

'There's no reason she would. We've never told anyone that Damien's parents died. If he does meet his mother, there's no reason to share the details. He's very private. He definitely won't make the circumstances of his adoption public information.'

They were interrupted as Reggie came back to take their order.

Phyllie frowned as he waited, pen poised. 'I'm not sure I've got any appetite left, Reggie. I've had a shock.'

Hannah's stomach churned. She should never have put this on Phyllie. What was she thinking? Could her heart even take these kinds of shock?

The old lady suddenly grinned. 'I'm only kidding, nothing could shock me these days, and my granddaughter's revelation is nothing compared to what I've seen and heard during my lifetime. We'll have a ploughman's and the zucchini fritters.'

Reggie refilled their drinks and took their order to the kitchen.

Phyllie raised her glass again. 'Here's to getting through difficult times. It might take a while, but Damien will come around.'

Hannah raised her glass to meet Phyllie's, hoping with ever fibre in her body that her grandmother was right.

Hannah dropped Phyllie home before making the drive to East Malvern to pick up Amy. She'd stopped after her second glass, which meant Phyllie finished the remainder of the bottle. She got out of the car when they reached Phyllie's house, took her arm and helped her along the driveway.

'I'm not drunk!'

'I would be if I drank two thirds of a bottle with lunch.'

'The cheese and bread absorbed the alcohol. I'm fine.'

Hannah gripped Phyllie's arm as she stumbled and laughed. 'You're not fine. You'll let me deposit you in front of the television with a cup of tea or coffee, and you'll stay there until Nat gets home. Do you hear me?'

Phyllie saluted. 'Yes, ma'am.'

'Can I give you a hand?' A deep voice called from the top of the driveway. Hannah turned to see a good-looking guy in his thirties walking towards them.

'Hey, Phyllie,' he said, smiling at the two of them. 'You look like you've been out partying.'

Phyllie laughed. 'Leon, meet my other granddaughter, Hannah. And no, I haven't been out partying, just enjoying being alive.'

'And a bottle of Prosecco,' Hannah murmured. So this was the 'goat boy' she'd heard so much about.

Leon laughed and took Phyllie's other arm and the two of them helped her into the house. She flapped them away as soon as she was settled in her armchair, insisting she was fine.

'Thanks for your help,' Hannah said as Leon walked her back to her car.

'No worries. Phyllie's amazing, I'd do anything for her.' He cleared his throat. 'You don't happen to know if Nat is about, do you? I was hoping to have a chat with her.'

'She's at our father's house, looking after my daughter. I'm about to go and collect Amy now. I'm not sure what Nat's plans are after that though. Sorry. Would you like me to tell her to get in touch with you?'

Leon thought about it for a moment then shook his head. 'No, that's okay. I'll catch up with her later.'

Twenty minutes later Hannah continued on her way to East Malvern. She wasn't sure what to tell Amy, if anything, about Damien's whereabouts. She wondered where he'd gone and whether he'd come home that night. As she pulled to a stop at a red traffic light her phone pinged; it was her mother-in-law.

Damien's with us this afternoon, and we've suggested he stay here tonight while he comes to terms with things. Just letting you know so you don't worry. His next shift is Tuesday, so he'll be home before then to collect his uniform. I know what you did was for us and I'm sorry you now have to deal with the fallout. Much love, T. xx

Tears filled Hannah's eyes as she read the message. Having Trish on her side meant so much. Hopefully she would be able to convince Damien that Hannah had only had the best intentions.

She pulled over and dried her eyes before reaching her father's driveway. She wasn't in the mood for any questions today. Nat's car was on the road. Her thoughts shifted from her own problems to her sister's. She wondered what had happened with the money Eliza's brother had invested. The returns sounded too good to be true, but as neither Eliza nor Nat had invested their own money in his scheme, she'd have to put her cynicism aside and believe there were good people in this world. Ironically, she'd have to log in to the chat room and ask Nat; she couldn't ask her in person.

Chapter Twenty-Two

Nat was laughing at an impersonation Amy was doing of her teacher. The high-pitched voice and flapping hands were not something Nat could imagine having to put up with all day, but then again, she was pretty sure it was massively exaggerated.

'I'm sure she doesn't sound like that.'

'She does. She's worse, in fact.'

Nat grinned. She'd had a lovely afternoon with her niece. Amy's love of old movies had seen them venture out to a vintage cinema in Elsternwick that was showing the 1946 classic *It's a Wonderful Life*. It was a fabulous movie, and she couldn't imagine she'd have seen it without Amy twisting her arm. After the movie, they'd had a look around the shops before coming back to her father's. He was now making them all hot chocolate.

The sudden shrill of the doorbell drew Amy's attention from the impersonations, and she hurtled down the hall.

Nat guessed it must be Hannah. No doubt her sister would be glowing from a child-free weekend and all the sex she and Damien would have had. She sat down at the kitchen table and accepted the hot chocolate her father placed in front of her.

'You spoil us, Dad.'

He laughed. 'A hot chocolate is hardly spoiling you. I'd better get back to it and make some more. I'm sure Hannah will want one.'

'I'll make them,' Sue offered, her cheeks flushed from the cool afternoon air. 'Let me just wash my hands as they're covered in dirt. I've planted a whole bed of Asian greens this afternoon. We'll be feasting on mizuna, tatsoi and bok choy before we know it. I just need Amy to help me feed them and we'll be done.'

Nat smiled. Sue was always planting vegetables she'd never heard of, although bok choy was at least familiar.

Amy's cry of 'Mum!' as the front door opened confirmed it was Hannah. Nat couldn't hear their conversation, but Hannah's boots clicked on the polished floorboards as they approached the kitchen.

Hannah entered the kitchen with Amy by her side, giving her a running commentary on the film.

'Hot chocolate?' Sue asked.

Hannah nodded. 'Lovely, thanks.' She smiled at Nat, her arm snaking around Amy's shoulders. Her face was pale. Actually, it was deathly white.

'Thanks so much for taking Amy to the movie today. It sounds like she had a fantastic time.'

Nat hesitated. It was a simple thank you, but that was unlike Hannah. Usually, she'd be quizzing them on the film's ratings, on what they had from the candy bar. Did they have Coke or any other soft drink? A lecture would then follow on the perils of sugar-filled food and drinks. Something was off. Hannah looked terrible.

'Are you okay? You look very pale.'

Hannah's white cheeks flushed at the question. 'I'm fine, thanks. Just a bit tired.'

Nat nodded. Phyllie had implied Hannah and Damien were experiencing problems, and by the look of Hannah, she'd been correct.

'I've had my hot chocolate,' Amy said, moving out of her mother's embrace. 'I said I'd help Sue in the garden before we leave. Do I have enough time?'

Hannah nodded and sat down at the table with Nat. 'Yes, of course. We'll get going when you're done. Let Sue enjoy her hot chocolate first.'

Sue picked up her cup. 'Why don't you go and play with Toby for five minutes and then I'll be out and we can finish off.'

Amy grinned and pushed her way through the bifold doors to the back garden.

'Are you sure you're alright?' Sue asked, turning to Hannah. 'I don't think I've ever seen you so pale or miserable-looking.'

Tears filled Hannah's eyes.

Alarm struck Nat. Her sister never cried; she was far too strong.

Sue came over and put a hand on Hannah's shoulder. 'I didn't mean to pry.'

'It's okay – just a difficult weekend. Damien and I have a few issues we need to sort out. It's why we asked you to have Amy.'

Sue squeezed her shoulder before sitting down beside her.

'Is there anything we can do to help, love?' Her father joined them at the table.

Hannah wrapped her hands around her mug. 'No, but thank you. Having Amy was a huge help.'

'And things are okay now?'

Hannah shook her head. 'No, but I don't want to talk about it. Damien's gone to stay with his parents tonight. He has a lot to process.'

He has a lot to process? Had Hannah had an affair? Nat couldn't think of anything else that might cause her brother-in-law to need to process things. Her sister, having an affair? If it was true, then it proved she didn't know Hannah at all. She'd almost be proud of her for breaking out of her rigid mould, but not at Damien's expense. Nat liked him too much.

'How's your new job going?' Hannah asked, breaking into her thoughts.

'Um, good, thanks.' Nat waited for the million questions that Hannah usually asked. But they didn't come.

'That's great.' Hannah sipped her hot chocolate. 'And I take it there's a new man on the scene?'

Nat frowned. 'Not that I'm aware of. Who?'

'Leon. I met him this afternoon when I dropped Phyllie back. He was asking after you.'

Nat's cheeks flushed bright red. 'Really? What did he say?'

Hannah smiled; her sister's reaction immediately told her she liked Leon. 'Nothing much. Just asked if I knew where you were, that he'd hoped to speak to you. He actually told me not to tell you he was asking after you. But it's too cute not to tell.'

'He's just a friend,' Nat said. 'Phyllie's claimed him as hers, and even if I was interested, I'm not allowed to date him.'

Hannah's lips curled into a small smile. 'That sounds a bit ridiculous.'

'You know what Phyllie's like.' Nat laughed. 'If I cross her, she'll throw me out.'

'Living with Phyllie's still going well?'

Nat nodded. 'Mostly. Although, as much as I don't want to admit it, I think you might be right about her having some difficulties.'

She cringed as the words came out of her mouth. She hadn't planned to talk to Hannah about Phyllie.

'What kind of difficulties?' Sue asked.

'Sometimes I wonder what year she's living in, and she's become a little forgetful.' Nat went on to tell them about the money for the movie, Phyllie wondering why Nat had come to visit one day, and then going out in her gardening clothes leaving the iron on. There were some other small examples that she mentioned too.

'Other than the iron, nothing else dangerous then?' her father said.

'No. But I am a bit worried about her. She corrects herself quickly, but there's a period of confusion when it happens. I thought perhaps we should take her for a check-up.'

Hannah nodded. 'I saw it for myself today. We had lunch, and at one stage she went and used the ladies' room. When she came out, she asked me where everyone was. For about thirty seconds she acted like it was four years ago when we were there for her birthday and she couldn't work out why everyone had gone. She suddenly came to and laughed it off, saying she was enjoying reminiscing and that was all. It wasn't a big deal, but there was a flash of fear that crossed her face. I think it frightened her not being in control of her thoughts for that short amount of time.'

'What do you think it is?' Nat asked.

'I'm not a doctor. How on earth would I know?'

Nat blushed. 'Sorry, I just thought you would have gone home and googled it and worked out what she needed.'

Hannah rolled her eyes. 'What, and ship her off to the aged care facility like she's so scared I was going to do?'

'Possibly.'

'No, I didn't go home and google it. I thought it was just a moment, one that a lot of older adults would experience. It certainly wasn't something that was putting her in danger, just unsettling her a little.'

'I'll organise a doctor's appointment,' their father said. 'She's my mother, and she'll go whether she likes it or not. Her father ended up with dementia, and as much as I'd hate that to happen to her, we should at least get her checked and know what we might be dealing with.'

'She's going to hate having to go,' Hannah said. 'I don't know how you'll convince her.'

Sue laughed. 'You'd be surprised what the lure of a high tea will do. I'll go with them and we'll make a quick stop at the doctor's on the way. There'll be no mention of dementia or you girls being worried. With the thought of scones and clotted cream on her mind, I'm sure it won't be an issue.'

'A friend of mine suggested we tell her she needs some immunisations, as they make a number available for the elderly these days.' Nat shrugged. 'Might be worth a shot.'

'Good idea,' Hannah said. 'Do you think you'll be able to continue to live with her? It's a huge relief knowing she has you in the house.'

Nat nodded. 'Of course. I don't have any plans to move out. The arrangement works well, and now that I'm a little concerned about her I feel better being there. She'd hate to have a stranger in her home, and as much as I hate to say this, I do agree with Hannah. She needs someone around.'

Nat waited for Hannah to start on the I told you so's, but they didn't come. Instead, she spoke with genuine love and concern for her grandmother.

'Poor Phyllie. She'd rather die than have dementia. She's such a strong and independent woman. I hope what she's experiencing is just old age and nothing more.'

Nat, Sue and her father nodded in agreement. They all loved Phyllie, and it would be devastating to watch her mind deteriorate.

Sue stood and placed her cup in the sink. 'I'd better go and finish off the gardening with Amy. Help yourselves to more hot chocolate.'

Nat's phone pinged with a text as they all sat in silence contemplating Phyllie's future. She took it from her pocket and checked the screen. It was from Eliza.

Check your account!

Jacob had sent her a link to an account he'd set up in her name which showed her deposits, investment gains and losses, and a balance. She clicked on it, her eyes widening. It couldn't be right. Twenty-seven thousand dollars? Her hand trembled as she opened up the transaction log. It showed the first five hundred dollars he'd deposited on her behalf with a subsequent transaction written as 'investment return' of two thousand five hundred dollars. It had then been reinvested, and a new 'investment return' transaction showed twenty-four thousand dollars, bringing the total to twenty-seven.

'Are you okay, love?' her father asked. 'It's not bad news, is it?'

She looked up to find her father and Hannah staring at her. She shook her head. 'No, it's amazing news. I'm just not sure whether to believe it.'

Hannah's eyes widened. 'Don't keep us in suspense then; we need some good news after all this depressing talk about Phyllie.'

Nat handed her phone to her father. 'A friend made an investment for me last night. It turns out it was a good one.'

She watched as her father's eyes grew larger before he handed the phone to Hannah. A strange look passed over Hannah's face as she digested the information. It wasn't surprise or jealousy, it was something else altogether. Concern?

'That's incredible,' her father said. 'Who is this friend and how on earth did he turn three thousand into twenty-seven thousand so quickly?'

Nat gave a slightly edited version of who Eliza and Jacob were, deciding it was best to say Eliza was someone from work, rather than someone she met in the gambling addicts' chat room.

'And he invested his own money on your behalf?' Her father shook his head. 'Why would he do that? He hardly knows you.'

'He's incredibly wealthy and successful, and from what Eliza's told me also very generous. What's happening with their business is something that only happens every few years. It can switch off as quickly as it switches on. He made that very clear when we met.'

'Are you able to withdraw this money?' Hannah asked. 'Or will he reinvest it again?'

'I assume I can. I'll contact him when I leave here.'

'Do it now,' her father said. 'Use my office if you want privacy. This is a large amount of money, and you don't want to lose it. I'd withdraw it.'

Nat stood. It was a sensible suggestion. She'd be able to pay off her credit card debt, pay Phyllie back, although she doubted her grandmother would take it, and still have money left over. How her luck had turned around . . . and literally overnight.

She hurried down the passageway to her father's office and shut the door. She rang the number Jacob had given her and waited for him to answer. He picked up almost immediately.

'Jacob Swain.'

'Jacob, it's Lia.'

His voice was rich and warm. 'Hey, Lia. Did you get Eliza's message? Your account is growing!'

'I know, I'm blown away. Are you sure this is okay though? This is your money.'

He laughed. 'It's totally fine. I'm just glad to have helped. From everything Eliza's told me, your conversations have helped her through an incredibly difficult time. I'd do anything to protect her and would pay much more than five hundred dollars for someone to do what you've done.'

'But it's twenty-seven thousand, not five hundred.'

'Yes, but five hundred is all I invested. The rest is pure profit.' She could hear his smile dancing on his words. 'Look, if it makes you feel better, when you withdraw your money you can take me out for a very swanky lunch, and you can pay me back the original five hundred dollars. This is not expected or necessary though, but if it makes you feel like it's your money then let's do it. Eliza already mentioned we should all get together again. I might even bring Jane, my wife. She likes swanky lunches.'

Nat smiled. He was a genuinely fantastic guy. 'I'll take you up on that.'

'Great. When do you want to do it? Next weekend? Oh, hold on, sorry, I just realised that I'm assuming you're planning to withdraw the money from your fund. You can, of course, leave it for reinvestment. We're confident we have at least another two weeks of solid returns before we'd start advising people to stop contributing, or at least minimise their risk with smaller investments.'

Nat hesitated. She'd planned to take the money now. There was no point in getting greedy and losing it all.

'It's a big decision,' Jacob said. 'Sleep on it. Go back into your account and select the "Pause Transactions" button. That will stop it being automatically reinvested until you give further instruction. Once you've made your mind up, you can click the "Recommence Transactions" button if you want it reinvested or the "Withdrawal" button and then link it to a bank account and it will be paid out. That usually takes two to three days to clear into your account.'

'I don't know what to say,' Nat said.

Jacob laughed again. 'Nothing to say. Just find a friend to celebrate with, stay away from those poker rooms, and consider this a fresh start. Now, I'd better go. Jane's folks are about to arrive for Sunday night roast. I need to open some wine and find my best behaviour. I'm sure it's lurking around here somewhere.'

Nat said goodbye and ended the call. She logged in to her account and paused the investments, as Jacob had recommended. She looked at the balance again and shook her head. Twenty-seven thousand dollars! This was real.

Hannah and her father were still sitting at the kitchen table when Nat returned from making the call to Jacob. She imagined Hannah had a thousand questions for her and would have all sorts of advice on what she needed to do.

'How did you go, love? Was it for real?'

Nat nodded, glad her father had spoken before Hannah. 'Yes, it is. I have the option to reinvest or withdraw the money. I've paused the account for now. I'll think about it tonight and most likely set up the withdrawal tomorrow. I need to link a bank account for the money to be deposited into, so won't be able to do that until I get home anyway.'

'That's amazing, Nat, really amazing.' Hannah smiled at her. 'I'm happy for you.' She stood. 'I might go and round up Amy so we can head home. Bear's probably wondering where his dinner is.'

'That's all you're going to say?'

Surprise filled Hannah's face. 'What did you want me to say? I'm truly happy for you. Sorry if it didn't come across like that. As I said, I'm a bit flat today.'

Nat shook her head. 'No, it came across as you being genuinely happy. I was expecting a lecture, that's all. About the risks of reinvesting.'

Hannah smiled. 'It's your call. There's not a lot of risk really when it wasn't your money to start with. You do what you want. I think you're sensible to consider withdrawing what's in the account now. I imagine it would be beneficial in paying off any debt or to have as a nest egg. If you're looking for me to have an opinion of some kind, then all I'd say is if you decide to reinvest perhaps don't do the full amount. Withdraw some, so if their river dries up, or whatever you said they call it, you don't lose it all.'

Nat stared after her as she crossed the kitchen and went out the back to find Amy. She saw her pull her jacket tight around her.

'Was that really Hannah?'

Her father looked concerned. 'Whatever happened between her and Damien must be serious. Like you, I would have expected more from her about this investment. That was not the Hannah we know.'

Nat's phone pinged again with a message from Eliza.

Amazing! Are you going to reinvest the money?

Nat sent back a quick text.

Not sure. Thinking about it.

Her phone went silent for close to a minute, then a long text arrived.

Jacob said you can add more of your own money to it too if you want to. Although knowing the financial position both you and I were in when we met, I guess that might not be an option! Limits your risk too. One of his friends invested the savings of five of his siblings, which really freaked Jacob out. It worked out okay and they all made money, but I think the more people involved the more personally responsible he feels. As he keeps reminding me, this isn't their normal trading cycle, so it does make him more concerned for everyone involved. But for now, I'm on cloud nine. Doug and I are almost out of debt! See you in the chat room tonight if you're going to be around?

Nat sent another quick text.

Will be online in about an hour. Just at my dad's now.

A smiley face emoticon blowing a kiss came back.
'Everything okay still?'

Nat looked up at her father. 'Yes, just Eliza. She and her husband were in a huge amount of debt, and she's just told me that it's almost been cleared. It's crazy! She also mentioned that I could add to my investment with my own funds or anyone else's, from what I can gather. I wouldn't want anyone to take that risk though, so I won't mention it.'

Her father nodded. 'Good idea.' He paused for a moment. 'Although, it is rather intriguing. Can you stick around for a drink or dinner even? I'd love to learn more.'

Her father ran his hand through his hair, frowning with concentration as he looked at the figures from Nat's investments. They'd brought Sue up to speed and now the three of them sat in his office, staring at his computer screen.

Sue squeezed Nat's hand. 'I'm so happy for you, hon. You deserve some good luck. It's the universe giving back to you after all you do for everyone else.'

'It's quite amazing. I've never seen anything like it,' her father said.

'I know,' Nat said. 'It would be interesting to find out what their total investments are each day. If Jacob can allow me this kind of return out of the kindness of his heart, how many millions are they making?'

'Many, I expect.' Her father frowned again. 'I have heard of this before you know, the salmon run, as you referred to it. A guy I used to play golf with mentioned that his company had it happen. He made a lot of money in only a few weeks and then retired. He wasn't greedy, just set himself up for a comfortable future. I remember thinking it was the perfect scenario.'

'Was that Stuart McCreedy?' Sue asked. 'He and his wife moved up to the Murray River to play golf and enjoy the water views.'

He nodded.

'Are you interested in investing in it, Dad?'

'I'm not sure.' He looked to Sue. 'Perhaps a small amount, just to dabble? I know Nat's not keen on us selling the house, which I understand, and something like this could at least buy us more time before having to go down that road. But I'd be too scared to risk a lot. If Jacob turned three thousand into twenty-seven thousand, I wonder what he could do with five?'

Sue nodded. 'We could risk a small amount, but nothing more. We do need to be extra careful at the moment.'

'If you want to do that,' Nat said, 'you can use some of the money that's in the account. It shows that we can split how much we invest. It doesn't have to be the full amount. I owe you just over five thousand from the money I've borrowed in the last few years.'

Sue and her father shook their heads in unison. 'We couldn't use your money,' Sue said.

'Yes, you could. How about this? We put five thousand back in, and that's me repaying Dad. If it turns into more, then you keep the five plus the interest it gains. If it loses, then I've paid you back.'

Her father hesitated. 'I'm not sure that's fair to you.'

Nat laughed. 'Of course it is. I'm getting an absolute bargain. I'm paying you back with money that wasn't even mine to start with!'

Her father and Sue exchanged a look.

'It's your call,' Sue said. 'I think it's an exciting opportunity, but I'd hate to lose any money.'

'It's a risk,' Nat agreed. 'But that's just the nature of life, isn't it? You take a risk to get a reward.'

Her father hesitated for only a second before his face broke into a wide smile. 'Okay, let's do it. I have a feeling our luck is about to change.'

Chapter Twenty-Three

Hannah leaned against the kitchen pantry, feeling Damien's absence more than she ever had before. If he was home, she'd probably be making them both a herbal tea right now. He often worked a night shift on Sundays, so it wasn't unusual for him to be away, but he'd never stayed overnight at his parents because of a disagreement between the two of them.

Amy was in bed, choosing to read for an hour before switching her light off. Bear was no doubt snuggled up with her. His dog bed had become a joke, having never been slept in. Still, it was an excellent place to store his toys.

Hannah poured herself a glass of water and took it upstairs to her office. She wondered if Eliza or Nat were online? The investment situation certainly sounded too good to be true, but so far even she, the risk expert, couldn't see a downside. Nat hadn't lost anything, and even if she lost every cent in the account, she still wouldn't have lost any of her own money. But Hannah couldn't see that being a problem. For a start, she didn't have any money, but also Eliza and Jacob had made it very clear that when the run stopped, it stopped instantly and his company went back to their regular day-to-day financial management.

Hannah opened her computer and typed 'Salmon Run Finances' into the search bar. It was something new to her. She changed the search term, trying to get something that wasn't related to the salmon industry, but didn't find what she was looking for. Perhaps it was an insider term, although the internet would usually still find something. She guessed if she trawled through hundreds of pages, she might get to something other than the catching of fish.

She gave up and clicked on the Gambler's Aid chat room instead. Nat and Eliza were already chatting. She skimmed through their conversation, seeing that they were both ecstatic about their recent financial gains. Hannah smiled as she read through Nat's description of her reaction that day.

PinkFish88

I'm worried about my sister. Her reaction was so calm, and she appeared genuinely happy for me. I couldn't believe it, to be honest. No suggestion at all that this was too good to be true and there were many risks I should take into consideration. I think she's struggling. She looked terrible. Problems with her husband, which still blows me away. I thought they had the perfect marriage. I'm assuming that's why I didn't get a lecture. I guess it will come in time.

LizaE

Hopefully, by then, you'll have a lot more money in the bank, the salmon run will be over, and there'll be nothing she can say, other than she wished she'd invested. Did you offer her the opportunity?

PinkFish88

No, your text came through as she was leaving so I didn't think to mention it. I guess I probably should. We'll see how this small investment goes, and if we're still doing well, I'll have a chat with her. I wouldn't want her to think I'd excluded her.

BrownDog40

Evening, ladies!

LizaE

Suze! How are you? We've been so worried about you. Did you talk to your husband?

BrownDog40

Yes, I told him everything. He left the house soon after we finished talking, which was at about six this morning. I hate to imagine what he's going through. He's got so much to deal with. I want to be with him to help him; coming to terms with what his father did is going to be incredibly difficult. But he won't accept my comfort now. He looked at me as if he hated me.

PinkFish88

Give him time, Suze. It's a lot to digest. He probably doesn't know what to think. Hopefully, he'll come around and realise that your only motivation was to protect him. That's got to win you some brownie points.

LizaE

Lia's right. He needs time and space. You seem like a decent and kind person. I'm sure he'll remember that at some point and come around. Just don't push him, let him do it in his own timeframe.

Hannah read their messages, nodding as she did. They were both right. Time was what it was going to take to get through this. Telling Damien she was sorry didn't cut it and wasn't the case anyway. She was sorry she was put in this position to start with, and she was sorry that she'd made a bad decision. But she reminded herself that she was pregnant with Amy at the time, Trish was undergoing chemo, and Damien was a big enough mess over the thought of possibly losing her. Adding this on top of everything else may very well have led him to a breakdown.

PinkFish88

We've been celebrating Jacob's investments while you've been having such a hard time. I'm sorry your weekend hasn't gone as well as ours.

LizaE

> The offer is still there from Jacob if you'd like
> to invest, Suze. Doesn't have to be a lot, but
> they are doing well at the moment. He thinks
> there's still a bit more left in the run, but it
> won't go on forever. Let me know if you're
> interested and I'll tell him to get in touch to
> answer any questions you've got and set up
> one of the accounts for you.

Hannah considered the offer. Each time Nat mentioned it, or she thought about it, as much as she couldn't come up with any good reason that Nat should stop, her gut still swirled uneasily. Things that sounded too good to be true usually were. Nat was right in that her usual style would be to voice all her negative opinions on the scheme, but this time she would do it differently. She typed back a message.

> BrownDog40
>
> Would love to hear from him, thanks!
>
> PinkFish88
>
> That's fantastic, Suze. I'd hate for you to miss
> out when we're all getting so much benefit
> from this.

When Hannah had left her father's, Nat was saying she planned to withdraw the money. It now sounded like this perhaps wasn't the case.

> BrownDog40

Are you investing more, Lia, or is it time to collect up your winnings and cash out?

PinkFish88

I was planning to stop, but Jacob seems so confident that there are still a couple of weeks left that I decided to try another investment. I owe my dad five grand, so he's asked me to reinvest that and if it gains anything then he'll take that money. His superannuation fund has let him down, and while he was planning to retire soon, he certainly won't be living the type of lifestyle he'd like to be.

LizaE

Oh, that's awful. Hopefully, the five grand will multiply for him. He could then reinvest it and make some more. Or even add some of his personal funds if he wants to get his future sorted.

PinkFish88

Not sure he'd want to take a risk like that and not sure I'd want to encourage it! If the five thousand works out for him, I'll be thrilled, as will he.

LizaE

Sounds perfect. You seem very close to your dad.

PinkFish88

Not overly close but I'm hoping that this investment might give us something special to share. Fingers crossed. Must say I'm having a strange kind of day. I took my niece out to the movies, which was lovely. She's a great kid, so much more mature than I remember being at twelve. Then I had a friendly conversation with my sister and Dad, which doesn't sound strange, but it is for us. My sister and I rarely agree on anything. Usually one of us says something to put the other offside. And then, after discovering that my money had multiplied nine hundred percent, I got home to find my grandmother passed out in her armchair. My sister took her out to lunch, and I think she must have drunk a bottle of bubbles by the looks of her! She's a classic. I'd better help her to bed.

LizaE

Night, Lia. Suze, let me know your email address and I'll get Jacob to contact you. I'm about to ring him about something else so will tell him you're expecting to hear from him. Chat tomorrow. x

Hannah sent Eliza the Gmail address she'd set up in order to join Gambler's Aid anonymously, then signed off and opened Gmail, a small smile playing on her lips. It had been nice having

322

a normal conversation with Nat at her father's earlier, and she was interested that Nat had acknowledged it too. Her thoughts went to Phyllie. They were lucky Nat was available to move in with her but that wasn't likely to last forever. She sighed. It was tricky getting older. At twelve, Amy was fighting for her independence. In their thirties, Nat and Hannah were having difficulty with a range of things, from finances to marriages. In his sixties, her father was facing issues as he neared retirement, and at nearly ninety, Phyllie was in the hardest place of all. A strong, independent and capable woman who was becoming a victim of old age. It had the potential to strip her of everything she loved, but mainly her freedom.

Hannah realised at that moment that she'd approached the Phyllie situation in entirely the wrong way by suggesting assisted living. What she should be doing was standing up for Phyllie's rights – being an advocate for her. If Nat was right, that she was struggling with her memory, and if anything as serious as dementia was on the cards, then they would have to do everything to ensure Phyllie lived out her years precisely as she wanted and deserved to.

Hannah sipped her water, thinking of her grandmother. At eighty-nine, they probably didn't have many years left with her. God, she would be missed. She'd filled their childhood with joy before and after their mother had passed. It was hard to imagine a world where she didn't exist.

An email notification popped up on Hannah's screen. She put her glass down and opened it. It was from Jacob. A very professional-looking email signed off at the bottom by Jacob Swain from BlueStar Financial Advisory. She clicked on their website link and started reading. She was intrigued to know more about this company and exactly who Jacob Swain was.

Hannah was on a mission the next morning when she arrived at work. She hadn't heard from Damien and needed something to distract her. BlueStar Financial Advisory was precisely that. She'd done further searches on BlueStar but had found nothing other than the website. That rang alarm bells. Surely successful financial advisors would have media coverage, or stories picked up by other sites that would come up in the search results. Searching on Jacob also only brought her back to the BlueStar website. She picked up the phone and dialled Julian Baker's number. He worked for Fraud Alert, a company that No Risk used regularly. Fraud Alert looked into companies that presented a risk and helped No Risk provide their clients with an even more substantial risk analysis than they could do on their own.

'Hannah Anderson! I haven't spoken to you in months.'

Julian was a lovely guy, tall and broad, with short clipped hair and always in dark suits. He presented himself how Hannah imagined an FBI agent would. They'd always got along. Julian had hassled Hannah to look after his wife when she was in the planning stages of setting up a new business. Hannah had done it as a favour, rather than billing Tracy, and Julian had been eternally grateful. He'd always said to get in touch if she ever needed a favour.

'I hope you're ringing to call in that favour?'

'I am. Although I'm happy to pay for your time.'

Julian laughed. 'After all you did for Tracy, no way would I be charging you. Now, tell me what you need.'

Ten minutes later Hannah hung up and forwarded him the information Jacob had sent her. It provided details on his company, the bank account to deposit funds into and a web link to view a sample online account to show what information was provided. Julian promised to get back to her within twenty-four hours, which was a comfort. She hoped for Nat's sake that Eliza's brother checked out, but the more she searched on the company the more doubts she was beginning to have. Mind you, what they were doing still didn't make any sense. She realised now she should have suggested to Nat that she withdraw at least some of the money to make sure it would actually be released. At the moment everything was purely on a computer register.

'Hannah?' Erica, No Risk's receptionist, stuck her head around Hannah's office door. 'There's a guy in reception who doesn't have a meeting scheduled with you but is very insistent on seeing you. Says it's a matter of life or death.'

Hannah scrunched up her face. 'Really? Who?'

'Zane Fox. Should I send him in?'

Hannah froze. What the hell was he doing here? She took a deep breath, reminding herself he had nothing over her now. Not only that, she'd planned to report him to the police. He shouldn't be allowed to operate as a private investigator if he was going to use his knowledge for blackmail.

Erica was waiting for her.

'Are any of the meeting rooms free?'

'You can use number three. I'll send him in. Do you want me to offer tea or coffee?'

Hannah shook her head. 'He won't be staying long.'

She made her way to meeting room number three and sat at the head of the long table. A minute later, Erica showed Zane into the room. Hannah didn't get up. She pointed at a seat to her left and waited for him to sit down.

'What do you want?'

'I thought I'd give you one more chance to buy my silence before I speak with Janine Markinson.'

Hannah shook her head. 'No. Now leave.'

Zane didn't move. 'I think you're making a big mistake.'

325

'No, I made that mistake twelve years ago when I decided to keep the truth from my husband. He now knows everything, so you have nothing to hold over me.'

Surprise registered on Zane's face. 'You told him?'

Hannah nodded. 'Yes. And as far as extorting money from Janine, I wouldn't waste your time. Damien contacted the adoption agency and told them exactly what was going on. They've probably already been in touch with Janine to ensure she's warned that paying you money is unnecessary.'

Zane stared at her, his eyes flashing with anger.

Hannah pointed at the door. 'You need to leave. You should also be aware that I'll be asking the police for a restraining order when I report your illegal conduct.'

'Report me?'

Hannah nodded. 'You shouldn't be allowed to keep your investigator's licence. Although that will be up to the police.'

Zane slammed his fists down on the table. 'You'd better be joking. I'll come after you if you speak to anyone.'

Hannah swallowed, doing her best not to flinch at his threat. 'Do I need to get security, or will you leave of your own accord?'

Zane pushed the chair back with enough force to knock it over and stormed out of the room. Hannah righted the chair and sank on to the one next to it. Her heart was racing. She reached for the phone. It was not an empty threat that she was going to report Zane. She couldn't have him blackmailing others on her conscience. But first, she needed to speak to Damien. She'd lied about him contacting the adoption agency and definitely couldn't risk Zane approaching Janine and finding this out. That would be her first call. The police her second.

Damien's phone went straight to voicemail when Hannah rang. Knowing Damien, it could be as simple as his phone not being charged, rather than him refusing her calls. She liked to think he would answer her regardless of the situation as it could be something to do with Amy. He wasn't on the roster until tomorrow, so he was most likely at his parents. She dialled their number.

'Hello, Han,' Trish said as soon as she heard Hannah's voice. 'How are you? I was going to ring you this afternoon and ask if you felt like a coffee. Thought it might be a good idea to chat about Damien.'

'I'd love that, Trish. Is he there by any chance? There's something quite urgent I need to speak to him about.'

'No, sorry. He went to the gym about half an hour ago. I also think he was going to drop by your house and collect his uniform and some other belongings. He's asked if he can stay another night or two. I said yes but did feel bad saying that. He should be back with you and Amy, trying to work this out.'

Hannah sighed. 'No, he needs some time and space. That's fine. Now, shall I come to you this afternoon or did you want to meet somewhere?'

'Why don't we meet, in case Damien comes home. How about Fredrico's by the park? I'm fine for any time, so whatever suits your schedule.'

'I'll take a very late lunch break. How about three o'clock?'

They agreed on the time and Hannah ended the call. She immediately opened her contacts list and scrolled through until she found the adoption agency. They needed to warn Damien's mother immediately. She just hoped they would believe her and pass the information on to Janine.

Hannah's morning had been taken up with phone calls to the adoption agency and the police. She hoped this would mean the end of Zane Fox's presence in her life forever. Now she sat across from Trish in the warmth of Fredrico's, feeling incredibly thankful for her mother-in-law's support.

'Both Edward and I feel that Damien owes you an apology,' she said. 'I'm sure he will too when he realises why you did what you did. I'm so grateful to you and I told Damien that. What I was going through at that time was horrendous. Adding in Damien trying to come to terms with his parents' situation would have done me in. You bought me another twelve years of mothering bliss, and for that I'll never be able to repay you.'

Tears sprang to Hannah's eyes. Yes, it had made sense to keep this from Trish while she was ill, but two years later she was in remission and five years after that declared cancer-free. Either of those milestones would have been an opportunity to tell Damien without Trish's health declining.

Trish met her eye. 'And we owe you an apology too. Damien told me that you'd noticed the money missing from the investment account. I'm very sorry we asked him to lie for us.' She looked away. 'Both Edward and I are very proud people and we hate having to ask anyone for help, especially financial help.'

Hannah took her mother-in-law's hand. 'I understand, but just know that we are always here if you do need help. I know you'd say the same to us.'

She nodded. 'You're a good person, Hannah. Damien's very lucky.'

'How's he coping, Trish?'

Tears filled Trish's eyes this time. 'Not very well. Edward suggested he book in with that psychologist he's been seeing, and he has an appointment scheduled for four o'clock this afternoon. Hopefully that will help put his thoughts in order. To be honest, the whole thing of you keeping it from him is secondary to what he really has to cope with – that he was the product of a violent act that traumatised his mother. Whether she's ever recovered I guess we might never know.'

'We will if he chooses to meet her.'

Trish nodded. 'I know. I need to get my head around that too. He's forty, for goodness' sake. I shouldn't be worried, should I?'

Hannah shook her head. 'Of course not. You're his mother. Janine might have given birth to him, but you and Edward are his parents. He knows that and loves you both unconditionally. I'm sure he'll be curious to meet Janine and find out more about her and any other relatives he might have, but nothing is going to change his feelings towards you.'

Trish sighed. 'I know you're right, it's just something I hoped we'd never face. I was so relieved when the adoption agency confirmed that it was a closed adoption and the biological parents were surrendering all rights to being contacted. The fact he went searching for them twelve years ago tells me that he has questions he needs answered.'

Hannah nodded. 'Unfortunately, one of the main ones about his father has been answered in a way he never imagined.'

Trish squeezed Hannah's hand. 'We both need to be strong and support what he wants. Edward and I will of course encourage him to come back to you as soon as possible. I don't imagine you want to be explaining anything to Amy about his whereabouts.'

'I can only say he's at work for a few days. She'll get suspicious after that.'

'Don't worry, love, I'll make sure he puts in an appearance over the next couple of days. Give him time to talk to the psychologist and let whatever she has to say sink in. Hopefully she'll be able to convince him that the actions of our parents can't be inherited, that we make our own choices and what his father did is no reflection on Damien. I think that's part of it; he's taken on a level of guilt that shouldn't be his. He was the outcome of the rape, not the reason for it.'

The two women finished their coffee deep in their own thoughts about the man they both loved. Hannah sympathised with Trish's position, but she also knew Damien well enough to know he'd do his very best not to hurt Trish. She just hoped he could forgive her and move forward without doing anything to hurt their small family.

Chapter Twenty-Four

Nat hurried down the stairs to the living room and powered up her computer. She could hear Phyllie bustling about in the kitchen and the kettle boiling. Good, she needed coffee. She'd hardly slept. There'd been no update in the investment account the previous night, and she was concerned that she was going to log in to find the five thousand dollars lost. Her body tightened in anticipation as the website opened. She almost didn't want to look. She so wanted this to have paid off for her dad. Even if it had only doubled, that would be a fantastic result.

The screen opened, and her balance immediately jumped out at her. Forty-two thousand dollars! She swallowed, hardly believing what she was seeing. She quickly opened another window and logged in to the chat room.

PinkFish88

Eliza, are you there?

LizaE

Sure am. Doug and I have just cracked open a bottle of champagne! I know it isn't even seven yet, but we can't help ourselves. We are not only out of debt, but we're ahead. We're in better shape than we were before he started gambling. I've just rung Jacob saying I need to plant a HUGE sloppy kiss on his cheek. I can't believe it! I assume your account is looking healthier too?

PinkFish88

Sure is, wish I'd reinvested the whole lot now! I'm about to ring my dad to give him the good news. He's made a fifteen-thousand-dollar profit!

LizaE

Why don't you come over and celebrate with us? I'd love you to meet Doug, and there's plenty of champagne!

PinkFish88

Would love to but have to go to work.

LizaE

I think if we keep getting results like this, it won't just be your dad retiring.

Nat stared at the screen. That comment suggested Eliza and Doug were going to reinvest. She just hoped they weren't silly enough to risk losing everything.

PinkFish88

You are saving some just in case it's the end of the run, aren't you?

LizaE

We are, although Jacob assures me we are okay for at least another ten days. Doug and I think we'll invest a few more times then stop. We don't want to risk losing anything. If you're worried, withdraw what you've made so far. It gets you out of debt and back on track. No point getting greedy (like us!) and potentially losing it all. Gotta run, champagne's flowing here! We must get together this weekend with Jacob too and celebrate. Are you keen?

PinkFish88

Definitely!

Nat closed the chat room window as Phyllie walked into the living room, coffee cup in hand.

'Oh, hello dear, I didn't realise you were up already.' Her gaze moved past Nat to the computer. 'You're not playing the tables, are you?'

Nat laughed. 'Of course not. I was checking the investment, and you won't believe this, it's increased again overnight. Dad's five thousand increased by fifteen thousand.'

'That's wonderful. He should be very pleased. That might go towards him taking Sue somewhere nice when he retires.'

'He doesn't know yet. I might pop upstairs and ring him.'

'Give him my love and tell him I'm delighted, won't you.'

Nat grinned and took the stairs two at a time. This investment lark beat online poker, that was for sure. She'd have to play and win for weeks on end to make a return like this. Her father picked up on the first ring.

'Nat, any news?'

'Yes, it's multiplied.'

His sigh of relief was audible. 'Thank God for that. I was worried after not hearing last night that we might have lost that money.'

'Nope, it made a fifteen-thousand-dollar profit.'

'Really? In such a short space of time?'

'Yes, it's incredible, isn't it? I checked the account this morning, and the balance is now forty-two thousand. I paused the activity once again to ensure we don't lose any of it. I wanted to check whether you were happy for me to withdraw it or whether you wanted to risk another round?'

'What are you thinking?'

'I'm not sure. Eliza told me that Jacob is confident they'll get another ten days' trading. She and her husband are going to risk another few investments between now and then. I think they're only using a percentage of what they've earned to minimise the damage if they were to lose it all.'

'Very sensible. I want to think about reinvesting. Can I call you at work a little later this morning and let you know how much I'd like to invest?'

'Do you mean you want to add some money to the fifteen thousand you already have?'

'I think it might be worth it. Just put in one lump sum and make one investment. Withdraw it as soon as we see the return. If Jacob says their safety net is ten days and we're only planning to invest over the next two to three then it's a low risk.'

'Kind of. Although both Jacob and Eliza have constantly reminded me what a high risk it could be, they've never suggested I invest anything beyond the money that's in the account.'

'But we could if we wanted to. That text he sent you on Sunday specifically said family or friends could invest.'

It had said that. Nat's gut was telling her something else though. 'I'm beginning to think we might have had our run of luck. I don't think I'll risk any of the money myself. I can invest some for you, if you like?'

'Actually, why don't you put me in touch with Jacob directly. I'd feel more confident speaking to him and having my own account. I'm a good judge of character, so it will help me decide whether he's a person to trust. He appears to be from what we know so far, but I should do my research.' A deep throaty chuckle came down the line. 'Imagine what Hannah would say if I didn't.'

'I'll forward you the information I have. Just don't do anything crazy. You can't afford to lose anything, by the sounds of it.'

Her father laughed. 'Usually, I'm the most conservative and least crazy person you'll meet when it comes to investment and risk. The superannuation situation was definitely outside my comfort zone. Don't you worry yourself about it. I'll speak to Sue and if she agrees we'll work out a small amount that it wouldn't be the end of the world if we did lose and see if we can invest it. But I'll wait to hear from your friend first, make sure he's okay with me getting involved. It sounds like he's gone above and beyond for you when he hardly knows you, so if he says no, then that's perfectly fine too.'

They ended the conversation and Nat went back downstairs to the computer and forwarded her father the information Jacob had sent her. She smiled to herself. Imagine if it was through her help that her father's retirement fund was topped up to where he'd expected it to be. It would be so nice to be the one helping for a change rather than the one asking for money.

As much as she tried to focus on work, it was a stressful morning for Nat knowing her father was considering investing some of his savings. As thrilled as she was at the prospect of helping him fix his financial difficulties, it concerned her, even though the past results suggested she need not worry. She surprised herself when, during her lunch break, she picked up her phone and dialled the last person she would dream of speaking to about this.

'Hannah Anderson.'

'Han, it's Nat.'

'Oh, hello!'

Nat held the phone away from her and stared at it. Hannah's tone was a mixture of surprise and delight. Maybe she had a friend called Nat and had mistaken her.

'Your sister, Nat,' she clarified.

Hannah laughed. 'How many Nats am I supposed to know? What's up?'

Nat took a deep breath. 'It's about the investments. I wanted your advice actually.'

'Really?'

'Don't sound so shocked.' Although she knew Hannah would be. 'It's just that Dad invested five thousand dollars, and it made some money.'

'That's fantastic.'

'Yes, it is, but now he's talking about making another investment with some of his savings. I'm a little concerned. Even though we've been lucky so far, it's a risk – one that Jacob's been very upfront about. He is predicting another ten days of trading before the salmon run dries up, but I'd hate Dad to find out the hard way that it's not the case.'

'I'd hate that too. What can I do to help?'

'Talk to him. He listens to you. I'm not against him investing, but I want to make sure he's being sensible and only puts in what he can afford to lose. He did say that's all he'd do, and he and Sue will work out what they can risk but I don't think they can afford to lose anything.'

'Fifteen thousand is all they can afford to lose,' Hannah said. 'That's the profit he's made. Perhaps we can convince him to only reinvest that.'

'Would you give him a call? Just to make sure that's all he does invest?'

'Of course. And what about you, are you reinvesting?'

'I'm not sure. I've paused my activity for the moment, so I do still have the option, but twenty-seven thousand is a lot of money. I'd like to keep it. My friend Eliza and her husband are continuing to invest, but I think there's a point where you can become greedy.'

'You sound like you've got it all under control.'

'Thanks. What about you? Dad said he forwarded you the information. Are you going to invest?'

'He did, and I'm not sure yet. Just weighing up a few things.'

Nat could hear the smile in her voice.

'You know me, pros and cons, risk versus reward and all that. By the time I've finished my process, the salmon run will probably be six months gone.'

Nat laughed at Hannah poking fun at herself. Whatever had happened with her and Damien she'd certainly mellowed. 'Okay, well, let me know if you do invest and also what happens with Dad.'

'Will do.'

Nat stared at her phone after she hung up. Something Hannah had said was bugging her. It was about the fifteen thousand dollars her dad had made. She was sure she hadn't mentioned an amount. She thought back over their conversation. She'd said something along the lines of *Dad invested five thousand dollars in it and it made some money.* Did she confirm the amount it had made? She didn't think so, but then again, she'd been so thrown by Hannah's enthusiastic response to her calling that anything was possible.

Chapter Twenty-Five

Hannah hung up after Nat's call, closed her office door and immediately rang Julian Baker. She left a message on his voicemail and crossed her fingers that he would get back to her quickly. The next call she made was to her father. He sounded less than pleased with what he termed her 'interference'.

'I'm not interfering. I'm just asking you to hold off investing any money for a few hours. I've got someone doing some investigations for me to check that this Jacob guy is legit. It all sounds a bit too easy. I'm hoping it is, but the fact that Nat never actually invested any money of her own and the amount she's supposedly made is only a line item on a website account concerns me. If she'd withdrawn some of the money, then we'd know it existed.'

Her father was silent for a few moments.

'Dad?'

'I'm here, and whatever you find is quite likely too late. Sue and I invested some money this morning.'

'If you did a transfer, it probably hasn't left your account yet. The batches are often run by the banks overnight.'

'I withdrew it from my bank this morning and paid it via bank cheque into Jacob's company account. We wanted the money to be invested today, so we'd see a quick turnaround. Jacob said if it got to him in time it would go with one of their twenty-four-hour investments and I'd be able to see how much it made by mid-afternoon tomorrow. It's incredible the amounts of money he's making, Han, really incredible.'

Hannah's gut churned. She thought back to Eliza and Jacob meeting with Nat. Had that all been for real or were they setting her up? Were they even brother and sister? She wished she could ask Nat more about that lunch, but Hannah didn't know about it – only Suze from the chat room knew. She couldn't ask her online either in case Eliza saw them messaging. She just had to hope for now that Julian would come back to her and confirm that BlueStar Financial Advisory was for real.

'I'm confident it will be fine, Hannah. Both Nat and her friend Eliza have benefited greatly from Jacob's generosity. He mentioned a large component of what they're investing today is combined money from a number of his relatives. He's hardly going to be popular if this one doesn't make money.'

'Can I ask you one thing, Dad? How much did you invest? I know you made fifteen thousand through Nat's account. Did you reinvest that?'

Her father cleared his throat. 'No, I used some money I was able to access. The amount doesn't concern you.'

'But it was more than fifteen thousand?'

'About five times that.'

Bile rose in Hannah's throat. 'You invested seventy-five thousand?'

'Even if it only doubles it'll recoup some of what we've lost in the super fund. If it does better than double, then Sue and I will be laughing all the way to retirement.'

'And if it does nothing and you lose it?'

'We'll still survive. Selling the house will have to become a priority, that's all. Now, how about I ring you tomorrow once the investment is complete? If it does what Jacob's predicting, we'll be over at your place tomorrow night with a bottle of Grange. I've always wanted to try it but baulked at the thought of spending upwards of five hundred dollars on a bottle of wine. Tomorrow, however, I might buy two.'

'Okay, Dad, let me know how you go. I'd better run. My other phone's ringing.'

Hannah hung up and picked up her mobile. It was Julian.

'You were right to be suspicious,' he said, without even saying hello. 'It's a set-up. It turns out they've just come to the Federal Police's attention yesterday and investigations are underway. It's a husband and wife team who are believed to be experts. They move from one job to another, changing their identities as they go. On this occasion, they've preyed on the families of gambling addicts. It seems they assume that these people are already in debt and have families that want to help. They set it up so they give you money up front and show it earning incredible amounts in periods sometimes as short as twenty-four hours. The gambler then enlists their friends and family to invest, and when this money is deposited into the account, it disappears. They've had close to six hundred thousand invested in the past two days, which our guys believe is about to disappear.'

'Seventy-five of it belongs to my dad and his wife.'

'I'm sorry to hear that, Hannah. You might want to go and visit them before they find out themselves. We believe that all traces of Jacob and Eliza, as they go by, will disappear in the next twelve to twenty-four hours, along with the money.'

'Surely if they're being watched then the money can be frozen somewhere?'

'I'd like to think that will be the case, but I can't guarantee it. If they're clever, that account your father invested into will have been instantly rerouted to a Swiss bank account or another offshore account that's difficult to trace. They've also made it very difficult to track them down. They are a very well-protected online presence. The police don't know who they are.'

'Really? But they met with my sister. Had drinks with her. If the police are monitoring the situation, wouldn't they know that? Surely they've read the chat room conversations?'

Julian was silent for a moment. 'I'll need to check, but yes, I would think the police are aware. As I said, they are monitoring the situation. But I'll pass it on anyway. Do you know the details of where and when?'

Hannah thought back to the chat room conversation about the meet-up. 'Yes, it was at The Winery in Richmond the Saturday before last. Nat met them at about two o'clock but, in theory, Jacob and Eliza had lunch there beforehand. They wanted me to go too, but I declined. That was all detailed in the chat room.'

'So, you don't know what Eliza looks like?'

'No, but Nat does. Do you want to speak to her?'

'I'll chat with my contact at the police. I imagine they have plans to contact Nat or will want to encourage another meet-up. That would be the easiest way to catch these two.'

'If you don't catch them, you're suggesting the money could be gone for good?'

'It's the most likely situation. For now, inform anyone in your family who was investing to stop immediately.'

Hannah was doing her best to digest all this information. Her father might have lost seventy-five thousand dollars, digging himself into an even bigger hole than he was already in. And she hated that she'd be the one who'd have to tell her sister. Nat was finally feeling like she was getting her life and finances together. Finding out that she was back at square one was going to be hard. But was it all lost? What if there was a way she could lead the Federal Police straight to Eliza?

Hannah couldn't sit at work any longer. She went and saw her manager and explained she had some unexpected family issues and would need to work from home for the afternoon. Martin was sympathetic and assured her it was no problem.

She phoned her father as she pulled out of No Risk's car park and organised for her and Nat to come and see him early that evening. She didn't go into any detail other than there was an issue with Jacob's company she needed to discuss, and her father needed to promise her he wouldn't invest any more in the interim.

Next, she called Nat. She knew her sister was going to hate her for this. She'd somehow decide what Jacob had done was Hannah's fault. Still, she needed to know, and there was no easy way around it.

'Why do I need to be at Dad's at six?'

'It's about the investments. I've found out a few things about Jacob's company and need to talk to you and Dad.'

'Why? What have you found out?'

'I'd rather talk to you in person. But Nat, don't invest any of your own money until we've met tonight.'

'I wasn't planning to. About an hour ago I withdrew the balance of my account. I decided I wasn't going to get greedy. Part of it is Dad's, so once it's cleared in my account, I'll be able to give that to him.'

Hannah could hear the pride in Nat's voice and hated knowing that there was not going to be any money for Nat to repay her father with. She didn't respond to the comment, merely confirming that Nat would be at their father's before she hung up.

She was home forty minutes later. She scratched Bear's ears as he greeted her at the front door and made her way straight up to her office. She wanted to read through the conversations they'd had with Eliza, to look for any hint that they were being played.

She opened her computer and logged in to the chat room. LizaE was online. She must have seen Hannah join the chat as a message popped straight up.

LizaE

Hey Suze! What are you doing here during the workday?

BrownDog40

Working from home so have a bit more flexibility today. Thought I'd drop by and say hi. How are you?

LizaE

Fabulous, still celebrating, to be honest. Wish we were sharing this amazing windfall with you though. Jacob's offer is still there to invest, but you'd probably want to do it in the next couple of days if you're going to. I have a feeling our run of luck is coming to an end. Doug and I decided to make today's investment our last one.

Hannah considered the message. It was like many others Eliza had posted. She created a sense of urgency to invest and at the same time looked sensible, worried that they might lose everything. She wondered how many people Eliza and Jacob, or whatever their real names were, had stolen from? They'd probably ruined many lives. Part of her desperately wanted to tell Eliza that she knew all about her and give her a lecture on why she was a terrible person, but the rational part of her knew she needed to play along. At this stage, she needed to keep her online as long as possible if there was any chance of catching them.

BrownDog40

I've decided I would like to invest, but my money is tied up. I checked with the bank, and it can be released by tomorrow lunchtime. Do you think that would be too late? It's quite a large amount, so I'm a bit worried about taking the risk.

LizaE

Let me check with Jacob and get back to you. He did say he thought we had another few days, but he'll have a better idea than I would as he's monitoring it by the hour (actually by the minute, or second, I think!).

BrownDog40

Okay. I'm at home, so message me when you hear from him or even ring me. If you let me know your number, I'll text you mine back.

Hannah doubted Nat would recognise her phone number, if she happened to join the chat, but she couldn't take the risk so asked for Eliza's instead.

LizaE

Perfect. Would be lovely to chat in real life!

Hannah leaned back in her chair as Eliza's number appeared on her computer screen, then she keyed the number into her phone. She was beginning to formulate a plan in her mind. She wasn't sure if it would work, but it was worth giving it a shot.

Hannah sent Eliza a text, and while waiting for her to speak to Jacob and get back in touch she used the time to make muffins for Amy's afternoon tea. Her daughter wasn't expecting her home, so it would be a nice surprise. They would take some with them when they went to visit her father and Sue. She wished she didn't have to take Amy with her, but with Damien still not in contact she had no choice.

Tears welled in her eyes as she thought of her husband. This was the longest they'd ever been out of communication. She missed him. She wished he was here now so she could share what was happening with the investments. But he had enough to worry about. Perhaps she was being selfish wanting to add this to his load.

Bear lay on the kitchen floor, one eye on her as she stirred the batter for the muffins. She was putting them in the oven when her phone rang. Her heart rate quickened. This was going to be the so-called real Eliza.

'Suze?' It was a male voice.

'Yes, this is Suze.'

'It's Jacob Swain, Eliza's brother. She was going to ring you, and will do later, but she wanted me to get in touch to talk through the risk associated with investing now.'

God, he was smooth.

'Thanks for the call, Jacob. As I mentioned to Eliza, I do have some money but obviously wanted to get a feel for how big the risk is at this stage.'

'To be honest, every day that passes increases the risk. Looking at the numbers, we believe we have a safe period of another six days. After that, it could drop off at any moment, and we'll be much more conservative with our investments from that point on. Anything you can invest in the next day or two should be safe. However, I obviously can't guarantee that.'

Again, just like Eliza, suggesting great things, putting urgency into it and then being the good guy and mentioning the risk. They were clever, very clever. No hard sell, just, 'Wow, look at this opportunity.'

'I could get the money to you tomorrow afternoon,' Hannah said. 'I've been told it will be released by lunchtime.'

'Can I ask you how much you're thinking of investing? If it comes under a certain amount, we can loan you the money to get your investment underway today. Of course, there is some paperwork to fill out guaranteeing repayment if it's required. We have a maximum amount we can do that with, so it depends on how much you're planning to invest.'

Hannah almost laughed. Again, he was making this sound so easy. Like their firm cared. Instead, she lowered her voice, hoping the seriousness of what she was doing would be conveyed. 'I'm having one hundred and sixty thousand dollars released. Does that exceed your cap for investing on my behalf?'

Hannah could almost imagine the happy dance Jacob was doing as he cleared his throat. 'I'm afraid it does. Twenty thousand is our limit. We'd be happy to get that first twenty rolling for you today. By the time you're ready to deposit the rest, you'll probably already be way ahead. Amounts are quadrupling at the moment.'

'You mean my one hundred and sixty thousand could get a four hundred percent return?'

'Honestly, my predictions are on the conservative side. I don't like to get clients' hopes up and then under-deliver. I think you'll be pleased with the result.'

'There's one other thing, Jacob. I know your time might be stretched at the moment, but is there any way we could meet up tomorrow morning before I transfer the money? I'd like to meet you in person. I hope that doesn't sound silly, but I'd feel a lot more comfortable having met you first. I can come to your offices, so it doesn't interrupt your day.' *Your offices that don't exist.*

'I'd love to meet you, Suze. Eliza has spoken so highly of you. Tell you what, don't come to my office, why don't we meet for a coffee around ten? I'm sure Eliza would love to come too. Is there somewhere that would suit you? Close to work perhaps?'

They arranged to meet at Cafe Reiki. Hannah hung up, butter-flies flitting in her stomach, and immediately dialled Julian Baker's number.

After speaking with Julian, Hannah was surprised to get a phone call from Amy just before four saying she'd be late home. She and Skye had decided to try out for basketball, and the training would go until after five thirty.

'Basketball? Do you even know how to play?'

Amy's response hadn't been convincing. 'We'll work it out as we go. Skye thought it would be good to have a sport we can play next year, and basketball seemed like a fun option. Anyway, I've got to go, Mum.'

'Hold on. I'm going to visit Granddad and Sue. I won't be home until at least seven thirty. Can you go to Skye's and I'll pick you up on my way home?'

'Yes, fine. See you then.' And with that, Amy was gone.

Hannah stared at the phone momentarily after she'd hung up. It was unlike Amy to try something new at the last minute, and basketball? What a strange choice.

She pushed it to the back of her mind. It would be easier to talk to her father, Sue and Nat without Amy there, so it had worked out well.

Hannah packed the muffins into a container and set about cleaning up the kitchen, her thoughts concentrated on how she was going to deliver her news. There was no good way to do it, and she could only expect them to be upset.

That was confirmed when just after six, sitting in her father's kitchen, she watched Nat's face pale as she delivered the findings about Jacob's company. 'I'm sorry, Nat, I hate telling you this, but my fraud guy was the one to provide this information.'

'What about the money I've withdrawn?'

'The money is only a figure on the computer screen. It doesn't exist.'

Nat turned to her father. 'You didn't invest yet, did you?'

He nodded, his face mirroring Sue's pale and shocked expression. 'Deposited a cash cheque into Jacob's account this morning. The money has gone from our account. I checked with the bank. It can't be retrieved.'

Nat put her head in her hands. 'I think I'm going to be sick. I'm so sorry.'

'You didn't make us invest the money. Don't be silly. It's not your fault.'

Nat raised her head. 'Of course it is. You wouldn't have even known about it if I hadn't mentioned it to you.'

Hannah rested a hand on Nat's shoulder, doing her best to convey as much sympathy as possible in her words. 'You were used, Nat. They're internet predators. It's believed they've done this before in a range of different circumstances. On this occasion, they preyed on people who had addictive personalities and were willing to take risks with money to get large returns. They counted on you getting money from friends or family. They probably never expected you to invest yourself as they knew you had no money.'

'But Eliza, the woman I met in the chat room. She's so lovely. I had drinks with her too, so it's not like she doesn't exist. I met Jacob as well. And what about Suze then? She's the other woman in the chat room group. I wonder if she was real like me or working with them?'

Hannah had to bite her tongue. The one thing she hoped not to reveal from all this was the identity of Suze. She knew Nat well enough to know that above and beyond everything else she'd have trouble forgiving her for this.

'Do you think I should warn her?'

Hannah shook her head. 'I think you need to stay out of the chat room for the next couple of days and just let all this play out. If you warn Suze and she's working with Eliza and Jacob, then it might alert them to the fact that they're being investigated. If they suddenly disappear, it will be tough for the authorities to take this any further.'

'Do you think there's a chance Dad and Sue will get their money back?'

Hannah thought back to her discussion with Jacob about keeping people's expectations low so that they weren't disappointed. That advice was relevant right now. 'I'm afraid I think it's unlikely. But it's not impossible, so let's keep our fingers crossed and see what happens over the next couple of days.'

Nat nodded, her face so stricken Hannah wanted to cry for her. Instead, she did something she hadn't done since they were teenagers. She took her in her arms and hugged her.

Nausea settled in Hannah's stomach as she drove away from her father's house. She hated that she was the one to deliver such devastating news.

Her phone rang as she turned left on to Warrigal Road and her stomach churned as the caller display showed it was Damien. She'd never felt so nervous about accepting a call from her husband before. She wasn't sure she could handle anything else tonight.

She cleared her throat. 'Hello.'

She wasn't sure what she expected, but it wasn't the frantic sound of her husband's voice.

'Han, meet me at Box Hill emergency department.'

'What?'

'The school called. Amy's had an accident, and they've taken her there.'

'Oh my God, is she alright?'

'Yes, she's had a fall and done something to her arm. She's in a lot of pain, but one of the teachers is with her. I have to go. I'm just walking in now and need to switch off my phone.'

Hannah accelerated through a light as it changed to amber. 'Okay, I'll be about ten minutes.' The call ended, and she did her best to clear everything from her mind and concentrate on the fastest route to the hospital.

Fifteen minutes later she hurried through the emergency room doors. She glanced around the crowded waiting room, but there was no sign of Amy or Damien. She went straight up to the desk.

'My daughter was brought in a little while ago. Amy Anderson.'

The receptionist checked her computer and looked up at Hannah. 'She's with a doctor. Just a moment and I'll have someone take you through to the consultation room.'

Hannah shifted from foot to foot, wishing they would hurry up.

'Mrs Anderson?'

She turned to find a male nurse standing behind her.

'If you'd like to come with me, I'll take you down to see your daughter. Your husband's with her already.'

A small flicker of relief registered for Hannah. She wasn't alone. She had Damien with her.

'Do you know what happened?' She asked the nurse as she followed him along the sterile corridor.

'I believe she fell. The arm needs to be X-rayed. Even without an X-ray, I'm afraid to say it's broken. Hopefully, it's a clean break and won't need surgery.'

A shiver ran up Hannah's back. *Surgery?* She hoped that wouldn't be necessary.

They turned into another corridor and the nurse directed her into a room. Damien was sitting in a chair next to a space where Hannah imagined a bed would usually be. He stood as soon as she entered the room and crossed the floor to her. He took her in his arms.

She could feel the tremble in his body.

'She's okay, isn't she?'

Damien nodded. 'They just took her to X-ray her arm. She's in quite a bit of pain, but the painkillers they gave her should work quickly.'

Hannah drew back from him. 'You're shaking.'

He gave a wobbly smile. 'It was a fright getting the phone call, that's all. Made me realise I should have been at home, not at Mum and Dad's.'

'She hurt herself at school. It wouldn't have made any difference.'

'I know, but it also makes me realise what's important. I'm sorry, Han.'

The nurse cleared his throat. 'I'll give you some privacy. You've probably got half an hour or so before Amy is brought back.'

They waited for him to leave, grateful that the other two beds in the room were empty.

'Did she tell you what happened?'

Damien nodded. 'She fell when she was mucking out the stables. Tripped over a piece of wood, apparently.'

Hannah froze. 'What? Hold on. She was at the stables?'

Damien nodded. 'It was her first afternoon working at the stables. She was lucky to get the opportunity. Although she won't be able to do it now, so they'll have to get someone else to replace her.'

'Let me get this straight. Amy was at the stables where she now has a part-time job?'

Damien nodded. 'Where did you think she was?'

'At basketball training. She lied to me. Why on earth would she do that?'

A small smile played on Damien's lips. 'You have to ask that question?'

'But, as much as I hate it, she's doing equestrian at school. I already know that. She didn't need to lie about this.'

'She probably didn't want to listen to another lecture.'

Anger welled inside Hannah. 'And now she's been hurt. You told me she'd be fine doing equestrian, that I had nothing to worry about.'

Damien placed his hands on either side of her shoulders. 'Han, she tripped over a piece of wood. She didn't fall off a horse or anything dramatic. She did something she could do in the back garden.'

353

'But she did it at the stables. If you'd gone along with me from the start, she wouldn't have been there, and she wouldn't have tripped.'

Damien shook his head and sighed. 'You need to let up, Han. She had an accident and she's going to be fine. These things happen.' He sat back down in the chair, his eyes locked on hers. 'You need to stop trying to protect everyone all the time.'

Hannah took a deep breath, reminding herself that Amy was fine and yes, this could have happened anywhere. She sat in a chair next to Damien.

'I can't believe she felt the need to lie to me. I need to change, don't I?'

'Just let go a little. Let us all deal with life and make our own mistakes.'

Hannah nodded. 'I know you're right, it's just hard when I love you both so much. I want to protect you from anything that could hurt you.'

Damien's face softened. 'And I love you for it. And, Han, I'm sorry.'

Tears instantly filled her eyes. 'You don't need to be sorry. I do.'

He shook his head. 'I'm sorry for the way I reacted; for taking off and not contacting you. I didn't handle it very well.' He reached for her hand and took it in his. 'I want you to promise me something.'

'Anything.'

'That from now on, you share everything with me. We never have any secrets, especially not secrets that are to protect me. I'm old enough to deal with anything that comes my way. I might need help, like I do right now, from you and the psychologist, but I'll get through it.'

Hannah nodded. 'I am sorry. I know I should have told you. I was worried about your mum as well as you, but I was thinking last night that there was no reason your mum would have had to know anything while she was sick. We could have left telling her until later.'

'Mum's the one who made me see sense. She's a smart woman.'

'Did she tell you we had coffee yesterday?'

He raised an eyebrow. 'No, she didn't mention it.'

'She wanted to talk, see how I was doing. She did admit to being scared of where it would leave her if you end up meeting your mother.'

He nodded. 'She told me the same. Hopefully I convinced her that she was my mum and that no one could ever take her place. I told her I was hoping to meet Janine. I contacted the adoption agency yesterday to make sure it's clear on my file that I would like contact to be made.'

'Did they tell you I'd been in touch with them?'

'Yes. I confirmed everything you'd already told them to ensure Janine knows about Zane Fox and doesn't give him any money.'

'I don't think we need to worry about that.' She went on to tell him about Zane showing up at the office and her contact with the police.

Amy was wheeled back into the room partway through their discussion.

Hannah jumped to her feet as soon as she saw her pale, scared face. 'Oh, hon, are you okay?'

'Am I in trouble?' Amy's voice was barely a whisper. 'I'm sorry I lied to you.'

Hannah's eyes filled again. She waited until the orderly moved the bed back into place before gripping Amy's good hand in her own. 'Of course you're not in trouble. I'm sorry that you felt you had to lie to me.'

'Will I ever be allowed near the horses again?'

Hannah gave a small laugh. 'As much as I'd like to say no, of course you will.' She glanced at Damien. 'I need to get over my fears and let you live your life.' A young female doctor entered the room, and Hannah's eyes blurred with more tears as colour returned to Amy's face and her mouth broke into a wide grin.

'Amy has a broken wrist. It's a clean break so no surgery will be required. We'll need to put a cast on it, but I'd like to wait a couple of days for the swelling to go down. She'll have a temporary splint in the interim. We're pretty busy tonight so there might be a bit of a wait for the splint, but once it's on you'll be able to take her home. We'll provide you with some painkillers and a report for your GP. They'll be able to put the cast on.' She looked over to Amy and winked. 'And no more tripping over sticks. At least fall off the horse next time and make it sound more dramatic.'

Hannah closed her eyes, willing herself to laugh at the doctor's joke. She wasn't able to do that, and probably never would be able to joke about accidents around horses, but at least she could let it go and say nothing at all. As the doctor retreated from the room, Hannah opened her eyes and looked at Damien.

He smiled at her, the understanding in his expression made it clear that he knew how difficult this was for her.

The painkillers had begun their magic, and the shock of the ordeal had Amy's eyes closing only moments later.

'She might as well sleep while we wait for the splint.' Damien moved his chair closer to Hannah's. He took her hand in his. 'I love you, Han. Promise me we'll be open and honest from this moment on.'

She nodded, the relief that he was beside her more significant than she could ever have dreamed. 'I promise.'

He leaned forward and kissed her, gently wiping the tears from her cheeks. 'With the Zane Fox situation, it sounds like you've had a lot going on while I've been gone.'

Hannah nodded. 'That's only part of it. Let me fill you in.'

Chapter Twenty-Six

Nat apologised to her father and Sue so many times that in the end they were the ones comforting her.

'Nat, it's not your fault,' Sue said. 'It was an amazing opportunity which we chose to take a risk on with the hope of some good luck. It wasn't to be.' She'd smiled, her eyes filled with love. 'It gives your father and me a challenge to work together to solve. We'll be absolutely fine. Look at this house for a start! It's not like we're roughing it.'

After hugging both of them, Nat left. She'd like to believe Sue's words, but she couldn't. It was her fault.

Now, as she pulled up in front of Phyllie's house, she wondered what she should do. Hannah had said to stay away from the chat room, but she knew she had to log in. She didn't plan to chat with Eliza or Suze, but she wanted to read through their previous conversations to see what she'd missed. Surely there must have been something said at some point that should have alerted her to the fact that it was a set-up?

'Hey, Nat.'

Nat turned as she climbed out of the car and saw Leon approaching her.

'I'm nearly bursting with all the unsolicited advice I've been storing up for when you visit. Every day Rainbow looks out hopefully, but you never appear. Should I tell her it's never going to happen?'

Nat's stomach flipped as she looked at Leon. He was smiling but there was something else in his face. She wasn't sure if it was hope or desire or a combination of the two. Part of her would love to say yes right now and go and join him for a glass of wine, but after the day she'd had she needed to get on to the chat room and see what was happening. What if Suze was lured into their trap too?

'I've had a difficult day and have something I really need to attend to right now,' she said.

Leon immediately looked concerned. 'Can I help?'

Nat stared at him for a moment. She would love to confide in him, tell him everything that was happening. Have his strong arms comfort her . . . She gave herself a mental shake. This wasn't helping. 'Thank you, but probably not at this stage. I'm hoping it will be sorted out in the next few days.'

'Well, if you do need any help, just let me know.'

'Thanks. And please tell Rainbow I'm not standing her up. In fact, tell her I'll come over on the weekend with a bottle of my favourite red, a carrot, an apple and whatever other suitable goat food I can find along the way.' She grinned. 'I guess I can just pick flowers from your garden before I arrive.'

Leon's eyes twinkled. 'Speaking on behalf of Rainbow, she's looking forward to it already.'

Nat was still smiling as she pushed open the front door. She stopped, her smile slipping. Phyllie, hands on hips, was standing on the other side of the door as if she'd been waiting there all afternoon.

'What have you been up to, missy?'

There was not a trace of humour in Phyllie's words and her face was contorted with anger as she waited for Nat to respond.

Surely she wouldn't be this angry about Nat agreeing to spend an evening with Leon? 'He's just a friend, Phyllie. I promise I won't ruin anything you have with him.'

'I'm not talking about Leon. I'm talking about something else.'

'Then you'll have to be a little more precise with your questioning. What specifically did you want to know?' Nat closed the front door and moved into the house.

'I would like to know why your father and Sue are coming to collect me on Friday morning to take me to the doctor's for' – she raised her fingers into air quotes – 'a check-up. What exactly have you been saying to them?'

'What reason did they give you?'

Phyllie shook her head. 'That's not answering my question. In my entire adult life, your father has never suggested he take me to the doctor. Yet, a short time after my granddaughter moves in, suddenly I need a check-up. I'm not stupid, Nat.'

Nat sighed and held up her hands. 'Okay, fine. Dad, Sue, Hannah and I were talking, and we decided that as much as you hate us interfering in your business, we did at least want you to have a check-up every six months to make sure you're kept in optimum health. There are some vaccinations you should have every ten years too, like whooping cough. We wanted to make sure you were up to date.'

Phyllie narrowed her eyes. 'That's all it is? Just general health and some vaccinations?'

Nat nodded. 'As far as I know. Unless you've got other issues you need to discuss with the doctor?'

Phyllie shook her head. 'No, I don't, and I don't know why your father couldn't have just said that when I asked him. His cock-and-bull story about receiving a letter from the government saying as next of kin it was his responsibility was just ridiculous. Did he think I'd be too scared to have an injection?'

Nat couldn't help but smile. Her father had never been very good at making things up on the spot. She guessed they should have come up with a better story when they decided to make the appointment at the doctor's.

Phyllie sank into her armchair. 'I've been worried all day for nothing. Now, you'd better go and fix me a whisky. That blasted computer of yours has been playing chimes all day too. Next time, could you turn it off before you go out?'

Nat had a quick look at the computer. She'd been in a rush that morning and hadn't switched it off like she usually did. The only program that was set up to chime with new messages was the online chat room. She opened it quickly and saw twelve alerts. Scrolling through them she saw they were Eliza checking if she was available. Interesting. She stepped away from the computer and went through to the kitchen to get Phyllie's drink. She filled a tumbler with ice before pouring a decent measure of whisky into it and carried it through to the living room. She placed it on the small side table next to Phyllie's chair.

'Not joining me?'

'No, I need to have a look at some of these messages. I'll make us some dinner a little later, if that's okay?'

'I already ate,' Phyllie said. 'Shepherd's pie – it was delicious.'

Nat stared at her grandmother. 'The one with the grated cheese on the potato?'

'Mm, yes, my favourite. I highly recommend it. There's none left though. The baking dish is soaking.'

Nat went back to the kitchen. She'd made the shepherd's pie when she'd arrived home from work the previous day, and they'd eaten it for dinner. So what had Phyllie eaten tonight? There was no baking dish in the sink. She opened the dishwasher. It was full of breakfast dishes, and a small plate that she assumed was from

360

Phyllie's lunch. There was nothing else – certainly no baking dish or a plate with remnants of shepherd's pie.

She walked back to the living room, choosing not to say anything, and plonked herself down in front of the computer screen. Thank God she'd spoken up about Phyllie to her father and Hannah and something was being done. She was feeling guilty enough about her father's money. She didn't want to add guilt about Phyllie to her load.

Another alert chimed on her screen. It was Eliza.

LizaE

You there, Lia? Have some news. Dying to share it with you. Can see you're online so hopefully you'll see this message.

Nat clicked on the 'Hide Me' icon so she could appear offline as she navigated the chat room. She scrolled to the top of the conversation with Eliza and Suze and read through every entry. Reading this, it was hard to believe anything was wrong; it all seemed so genuine, so much like they were making friends. It was crazy to think that Eliza had organised them meeting up too. Who would do something like that? Wouldn't you want to remain anonymous? But then again, it certainly made it all the more believable. And Doug, she guessed he didn't even exist. So she'd been receiving advice on her gambling issues from a woman who had probably never experienced or knew anyone with similar problems.

'Found what you were looking for, love?'

Nat continued to scan the messages, just grunting a yes to Phyllie's question.

She got down to the bottom and saw a brief exchange between Eliza and Suze that made her draw breath.

BrownDog40

Spoke to Jacob and excited about investing. We're meeting tomorrow morning at a cafe near where I work. Wondered if you were free to join us? I would love to meet you.

LizaE

I'm free! Send me the details, and I'll meet you and Jacob. Should we see if Lia's free too?

BrownDog40

Let's keep this between us this time (sorry Lia if you are reading this!). I don't want to share too much about the details of my investment. I imagine she'll be working anyway.

LizaE

No worries. Sure, she'll understand. Great to hear you are planning to invest. Perhaps we'll organise a celebration on the weekend once your investment is returned. Would be great for all three of us to meet.

BrownDog40

Sounds perfect! I'll look forward to that. Champagne all round.

The real stuff too, not just sparkling wine. I've always wanted to try Cristal but could never justify it before.

Nat watched as their conversation petered out and they said their goodbyes and how much they looked forward to meeting the next morning. Suze had sent through the details of the cafe they were meeting at. The address was very close to Hannah's office. She'd never had a reason to visit Hannah at work but did know she was based somewhere around 300 St Kilda Road, which was where the cafe was. She wondered what she should do. It appeared Suze was genuine and knew nothing about the set-up. It also seemed she was about to hand over an amount of money for investment.

'You okay, love?' Phyllie broke into her thoughts. 'The frown on your face is likely to stay there permanently, looking at how deep those lines are etched.'

Nat relaxed her face, realising just how tight her entire body was. She was wound up with fury and concern.

'You chatting with those poker girls again?'

Nat shook her head. 'No, just reading their conversation. The whole investment thing went a bit pear-shaped.'

'Oh no, you didn't lose any money, did you?'

'No, I never put any of my own money into it. Others have though, and they stand to lose a lot.'

'There are never any shortcuts to making money,' Phyllie said. 'It comes down to hard work and being smart. Sure, you can invest and increase your nest egg, but it doesn't happen overnight. You ride the highs and lows of the market like anyone else.'

'Some people make a lot of money.'

'And they lose a lot too. If it was easy to make millions overnight everyone would be doing it. You keep that in mind, won't you?'

Nat nodded. Phyllie was right. She should have woken up earlier to how unrealistic the entire idea was. She guessed she wanted to believe badly enough that there were kind people out there, like Eliza and Jacob had presented themselves to be, and that it was possible to turn her finances around.

'I know you said you'd had dinner, but I'm going to make myself something. Did you have enough earlier, or would you like a little snack?'

'Funnily enough, I am hungry. Ridiculous considering I ate the shepherd's pie.'

Not ridiculous at all considering you ate the pie over twenty-four hours ago. Nat hoped that the doctor wasn't going to find anything too wrong with Phyllie, but she was concerned that he might. The mix-ups and forgetfulness seemed to be happening more frequently. Was it happening before but none of them were aware because they weren't with her full-time? 'I'll put some cheese and crackers together with some fruit and nuts.'

Phyllie held up her empty tumbler. 'Add a top-up of whisky and it sounds divine.'

Nat called in sick at work, and arrived at nine thirty the next morning at the address Suze had given Eliza. She'd left Phyllie nursing a headache, which was not surprising after drinking whisky on an empty stomach. She'd made Phyllie laugh when she'd handed her a strong cup of coffee and declared a hangover at eighty-nine to be something to strive for. Now she wasn't smiling, instead she was a bundle of nerves. She hoped Suze would be early and she'd be able to talk to her first. The problem was she had no idea what Suze looked like. At this point, however, she was happy to approach any woman on her own and ask her. It was too important not to. She'd know who she was the minute Eliza and Jacob turned up to meet with her, but that wouldn't be the right time for the conversation.

She swung open the door of Cafe Reiki and stepped inside. The smell of ground coffee beans instantly made her mouth water. A coffee would go down nicely right now. Two women were sitting together at a table and a couple of solitary men at others, but that was all. She walked over to the women, on the off-chance Suze had come with a friend.

'Excuse me, would either of you be Suze?'

They shook their heads, looking at her strangely. She retreated to the counter and ordered a long black. She'd get that and then wait outside out of sight in case Eliza or Jacob turned up early. The coffee took a few minutes, and only one other man entered the cafe in that time. She'd tried to contact Suze first thing that morning with a private message providing her phone number and asking her to ring her urgently. She hadn't heard back. Logging in to the chat room, she saw Suze was still offline and there was no guarantee she would read the message from Nat before she had her meeting.

She thanked the barista and paid for her coffee before taking it out to the street. The traffic was heavy, and the dinging of trams as they zoomed along the median strip made Nat realise that Suze, Jacob and Eliza could appear from any direction, using a range of transport modes.

'Lia!'

Nat froze. Jacob's deep, rich voice was unmistakable. How was she going to explain what she was doing here? She turned, and he enveloped her in a bear hug.

'It's so great to see you again.'

Nat nodded, forcing a smile to her lips. She was staring at the bastard who'd robbed her father. 'You too.'

'Eliza didn't mention you were joining us.'

'She doesn't know. I noticed her message with Suze about meeting up and thought I'd at least stop and say hi. My sister works nearby, and I had to drop something off to her. I don't think Suze wants me hearing the details of her investment, so I'll say hello and be on my way.'

'Don't be silly. Suze can write the figure down if she wants to keep it private. Eliza was talking about celebrating on the weekend with all of us, so this can be the preliminary one.' He rubbed his hands together. 'Let's grab a table inside, shall we. It's chilly this morning.'

Nat followed Jacob into the cafe and sat opposite him, her back to the door.

'Your funds should clear tonight.' He grinned. 'I hope it's helped you out. And I'll have the return information for your dad later this afternoon. It's looking good at this stage.'

God, how she'd love to pick up the napkin dispenser and smash it into his face. But she couldn't. Instead, she tried to look as excited and grateful as possible. As Hannah had said, she couldn't let on that she knew anything. Not if it had the potential to affect the investigation. 'The money would make a huge difference to my life.'

'Will, not would! Hey, there's Eliza, and I assume that's Suze she's got with her.' He stood and waved.

Nat swivelled round in her chair. *What the hell? That definitely wasn't Suze. Why on earth was Hannah walking in with Eliza?*

Hannah hesitated when she met Nat's gaze. Her face paled, and she gave her head a slight shake, her eyes boring into Nat's as if she was trying to communicate something. She needn't worry,

Nat wasn't going to say anything. She honestly had no idea what was going on.

'Lia!' Eliza hurried to the table and hugged Nat. 'I didn't realise you were coming. It's so good to see you.'

'She wasn't,' Jacob said. 'Her sister works nearby, so she thought she'd stop off and say hi before dropping in to see her. She wasn't planning on staying, but I've convinced her otherwise.' He reached out his hand. 'You must be Suze.'

Nat watched as Hannah shook his hand and smiled. 'Nice to meet you, Jacob.' She turned to Nat. 'I'm so glad you did decide to stop by, Lia. I feel like I already know you.' She leaned closer to Nat and hugged her. 'Play along,' she whispered in her ear.

'Shall I organise coffee?' Eliza suggested.

Jacob shook his head. 'You three ladies chat and I'll place the order. Lia, did you want another?'

Nat shook her head.

'Suze, what's your poison?'

Hannah's response blurred as realisation hit Nat. Hannah was Suze! She'd been communicating with her own sister in the chat room and Hannah had never said anything. Even when she'd delivered the news to both Nat and their father, she hadn't told her. She closed her eyes momentarily. How was this even possible?

'You okay, Lia?' Jacob asked.

Her eyes flicked open and she did her best to smile. 'Yes, sorry. I've got a lot on my mind, that's all.'

Jacob smiled back. 'Let me get the coffee while you ladies make yourselves comfortable. Hopefully we can help Lia relax too.'

'How exciting is this?' Eliza said as he disappeared towards the counter. 'I can't believe how our lives have been turned around in such a short space of time. And I feel like I've gained two new best friends in the process. To be honest, I was only looking for friendship; the financial side of it is just a massive bonus.' She laughed.

'And to think we met in a gambling addicts' chat room. You never know what life is going to bring.'

Hannah and Nat both laughed along with her. She was good, Nat had to admit. In one way it was a relief to see how easily this woman could fool you. Part of her was still questioning whether Hannah's fraud guy had got it right or not. At least one thing was guaranteed, Suze wasn't there to invest money.

Jacob returned to the table. 'Coffee will be a few minutes. Now, Suze, we're here to talk about your investment. Feel free to write down any figures if you'd like to keep them discreet.'

Hannah shook her head. 'No, that's okay.' She smiled at Nat. 'Lia's been very open with the financial side of her investments, and I'm happy to do the same.'

Not quite what her message had said the previous night in the chat room, but Nat now understood why. She didn't want Nat to know she was Suze. It raised a million other questions. Why was Hannah in the chat room to start with, and why hadn't she told Nat that she was Suze when she'd worked out who Nat was? Had Phyllie set her up? Told Hannah to spy on her in the chat room? Phyllie was the only person who knew about it. That didn't seem likely though, especially as Hannah was in the chat room the first day she'd gone there herself. She suddenly sucked in a breath. Had Hannah shared real information? So the story about her husband and his biological father being a rapist was actually about Damien? She looked across at Hannah, who frowned at her. She was glad of the distraction of Jacob talking.

'Suze, ask me any questions you need to about the investment. I can answer most of them and provide you with supporting documentation. The firm does take four percent of any gains during the salmon run. It's about double our usual fee, but this is an offer we only make to select clients. You pay a premium for this.'

Hannah asked questions that she'd obviously thought through before coming. They sounded like reasonable questions anyone would ask before investing. The final one she asked related to the term of the investment.

'Is it true my money will only be invested for twenty-four hours?'

Jacob nodded. 'If it goes into our account today it will be invested immediately. We have a portfolio opening at four p.m., which will provide its return by four p.m. tomorrow.'

'Perfect timing to celebrate on Sunday,' Eliza said. 'I thought we could meet for a picnic in the botanical gardens. It will be chilly, but the forecast is for sunshine, and I'm happy to bring the food and the Cristal, as discussed.' She winked at Nat. 'What do you all say?'

'As long as I'm in a position to celebrate then, yes, I'll be there,' Hannah said.

'You didn't mention how much you were going to invest, Suze?'

'One hundred and sixty thousand.'

Eliza gasped. 'Really? You're going to risk that much?'

Jacob frowned. 'She's right, Suze. That is a lot. I'm more than happy to accept it, but only if you guarantee you could survive if the investment didn't work out.'

'Perhaps she should split it across a couple of different portfolios?' Eliza suggested.

'It doesn't make any difference with the salmon run,' Jacob said. 'When one portfolio collapses, the whole lot will too.'

Nat watched the supposed brother and sister team working them. You would think this was a genuine conversation, not a complete set-up.

'I'll keep it as one,' Hannah confirmed. Her phone pinged with a text message. She checked it, frowned and placed her phone back in her bag. 'Sorry, I'm going to have to go. Emergency at

369

work.' She looked at Nat, her eyes trying to convey a message. Did she want Nat to stay with them or leave? She couldn't tell. Jacob decided for her.

'I'll get our coffee to go, in that case.' He stood and embraced Hannah. 'You've got the details for the transfer but feel free to call me if there are any problems or you have any concerns.' He turned to Nat. 'And it sounds like we'll meet again for a proper celebration on Sunday.'

Nat did her best not to cringe as he kissed her on both cheeks, and then Eliza did the same. 'I'll message you both with a time and meeting place for our celebration,' Eliza said.

'I'll walk out with you,' Nat said to Hannah. 'I need to go and drop something to my sister anyway.'

They waved goodbye and walked out on to the street.

'Keep walking,' Hannah said. 'Don't ask any questions at all. Just stay beside me.'

Her tone was serious and commanding. Nat didn't question her, just did exactly what she said. Hannah walked to the next building and turned into an entrance way. She hurried up a flight of stairs to a small balcony that overlooked the street below. They had a clear view of the front of Cafe Reiki. She gripped Nat's arm tight. 'Just wait.'

Nat did as she was told. She had no idea what she was waiting for, but her heart was pounding and a trickle of sweat ran down her back. Considering how cold it was that made no sense at all.

A small group of men approached the cafe as the doors opened and Jacob and Eliza stepped out. Coffee cups in hand, they were smiling and laughing together.

'Dogs,' Hannah hissed.

They stopped as the men approached them, their smiles fading quickly. Jacob glanced around, dropped his coffee and ran. He wasn't fast enough. One of the men chased him and tackled him to the ground. Within seconds he had his hands cuffed behind him.

Eliza didn't run. She retained her coffee in her hand and allowed one of the men to guide her by the elbow to the street, where two black four-wheel drive vehicles waited. Jacob was helped into the back of one and Eliza the other. The doors shut and the vehicles pulled out into the traffic.

'Holy shit!' Nat turned to her sister. 'You knew that was going to happen, didn't you?'

Hannah nodded. 'The police came and spoke to me last night and talked me through what to expect. The text was from them, telling me to leave the cafe. They'll be in touch with both of us later this morning to get statements. Now come on, let's go back to the cafe and have a coffee, or something stronger if they'll serve it this early.'

They walked in silence, and once inside Nat sank into a seat while Hannah ordered. She came back to the table with two shot glasses and passed one to Nat. 'I don't know about you, but my legs are shaking so hard right now. I'm probably going to need a few of these.'

Nat took the shot and threw it back, the whisky burning the back of her throat.

'Coffee's coming, but do you want another?'

Nat shook her head. 'No, I want an explanation. What the hell has been going on, Hannah? Or should I say Suze?'

Hannah sighed. 'I'm sorry, okay? I had no idea you were Lia to start with. We'd been chatting for quite a while before I realised. When I did, I thought how nice it was to be getting to know you again. I felt like we were becoming friends and I enjoyed it. Of course, I had no idea that Eliza was setting us up.'

'So the information you shared with us, about your husband and marriage problems, that was all true?'

'Everything I said in the chat room was true, other than my name and relationship to you.'

Nat reached across the table and laid her hand over Hannah's. 'Oh Han, I'm devastated for Damien. How's he handling everything?'

Tears spilled down Hannah's cheeks. She extracted her hand from Nat's and wiped her eyes. 'Sorry, the last few days have just been too much.' Her phone rang as she pulled a tissue from her bag. 'It's Julian, my friend from the fraud company. I'd better take it.'

Nat waited, still trying to piece together precisely what had happened as Hannah took the phone call. She was mainly answering yes and no, so it was impossible to know what was going on. She hung up and looked at Nat.

'They've been taken into custody, as we just saw, and their company and accounts have been frozen. Julian's confident that Dad and Sue might see their money. The account hadn't been emptied. It might be tied up for some time while they're prosecuted, but there's a strong chance it will be returned.'

A broad smile broke out on Nat's face. 'Thank God for that. Do you want to ring them now and tell them?'

Hannah smiled. 'Kind of, but another part of me thinks we should make them sweat it out a bit longer. Can you believe they were willing to take that sort of risk?'

'They're more desperate for money than I realised.'

'They need to sell the house. Real estate in East Malvern is worth a fortune.'

Nat nodded. 'I'll talk to Dad. See if he needs a hand getting a real estate company involved. You were right when you said there are other ways to feel close to Mum.'

The coffee arrived, and Nat wrapped her hands around the steaming mug, still feeling shaky from the excitement and shock of the morning.

'Was Julian working with the police on this?'

Hannah nodded. 'Sort of. Just from the information I passed him. He has a contact on the force who's kept him in the loop. After he passed on my information, they contacted me, as I mentioned, and met with me last night. Until now the police haven't been able to track Jacob or Eliza down. In the last two days they've had agents posing as investigators in the chat room. It appears we weren't the only ones that Eliza was having private conversations with. The police weren't able to engage her, even though one of their agents was talking to her and discussing investing. They asked to meet with her, and she declined.'

'Really? So why did they organise the meet-up with you today? It makes no sense.'

'No, it doesn't. Although she had built a relationship with us, whereas her relationship with the undercover cop is very new. Both Jacob and Eliza were clever. They might have decided it was too risky at this late stage.'

'I'm surprised they risked having lunch with me that day. What if they'd been caught on camera or something?'

'Apparently they were. The restaurant had some CCTV footage, but as their images didn't match up with any databases they couldn't be identified. Jacob also paid the tab with cash, leaving no credit card trail. I guess they must have known they'd be hard to track down. We can ask the police more when we speak to them. Julian said to expect contact this morning.'

Nat shook her head. 'One thing's for sure, I'll never be visiting another chat room. You can't trust anyone. I trusted both you and Eliza and look at what I got. Eliza scamming my family out of money and you enjoying a phoney relationship with your sister and thinking it meant something.'

Hannah's face crumbled. 'Believe me, Nat, it meant something to me. Based on our conversations in the chat room I think we can be friends. I know I need to be less bossy and more interested in what you're doing. I listened to everything you said, and I'm sorry for the way I've acted up until now. As stupid as it might sound, I think when Mum died, I lived in a permanent state of panic that something would happen to you or Phyllie or Dad.' Hannah's cheeks flamed red as she raised her eyes to meet Nat's. 'It's no excuse, but me trying to control things was to prevent another tragedy. After the accident, and even now, I think of the worst-case scenario and do everything I can to try and prevent that from happening.'

More tears welled in Hannah's eyes. 'I'll never forget that day, Nat. If I hadn't insisted on that saddle, we might not have gone riding. The accident could have been avoided.'

Nat stared at her sister. 'It wasn't your fault.'

'But Dad wanted to take Mum to the theatre and out for dinner. If only I'd gone along with that and not pushed her to go riding.'

Nat drew in a breath. Hannah actually believed it was her fault? That was ridiculous. She reached across and squeezed her hand. 'You didn't have to *push* Mum to go riding. It would have been exactly what she wanted to do that day. Dad might have suggested the theatre but Mum would have only gone along to please him. Remember she fell asleep through *Cats* and *Phantom of the Opera*, so it was hardly her thing. And, don't forget, Mum rode without a helmet all the time. It could have happened on any of those days.'

Hannah sighed. 'You're probably right; she didn't love the theatre, but I'll still always wish I'd thought of something different for her present that year. I've always thought that if I'd changed just one little thing she'd be with us. I guess I do that with everything now too. I try and look at ways to make sure there's a safe and secure outcome, which of course has come across as controlling. I'm sorry, Nat, I really am. Your life is yours to live and I should be completely supportive of your choices. After the accident I did everything I could to protect us, and that seems to have become a huge part of my personality. Avoiding risk, wrapping Amy in cotton wool and having far too many opinions. I am trying to change my behaviour.'

'I always thought you resented me after the accident and that's why you became so overbearing – to punish me.'

Hannah frowned. 'Why would I resent you?'

'Because I'd lied to Mum, said I was working when I was really with Callum. It was her birthday and I should have put her first, not myself.'

Hannah shook her head. 'I never resented you. If anything I was incredibly sad for you that you didn't get a chance to say goodbye. We both did things behind Mum and Dad's backs all the time. It was just really bad luck. I know I changed that day, but it wasn't because of anything you did. It was because I was devastated and wanted to make sure we never had to go through something like that again.'

Nat stared at her sister, who was gripping their mother's heart-shaped pendant. This was probably the most honest and raw Nat had ever seen her. They'd both suffered with guilt since the day of the accident and taken it out on each other in different ways. If only they'd spoken about it back then. Regardless of their confessions now, Nat wasn't sure she'd be able to trust Hannah again. Presenting herself as a stranger in the chat room was a form of betrayal. Nat couldn't come to terms with how she felt about it right now. She sipped her coffee, then stood. 'I'm going to go. I've got so much to think about, and I want to check up on Phyllie.'

'She's alright, isn't she?'

Nat nodded. 'Yes, although she was a bit weird again last night. It'll be good when the doctor has a chance to look her over on Friday.'

'I'd better go too. Damien's at home with Amy, but I'm taking the rest of the day off.' She went on to tell Nat about Amy's accident.

'Oh, the poor thing. Is there anything I can do to help?'

'Maybe drop in and see her in the next couple of days. She'll be getting a cast on Friday, and I'm hoping she might be a bit more comfortable once the swelling has gone down.'

Nat nodded. 'Will you ring Dad, or shall I? We should let him know what's happened.'

'I'll ring him on my drive home.'

They walked out of the coffee shop and on to the footpath. Hannah gave a little laugh. 'As glad as I am that those two have been arrested, I was expecting something more dramatic, like you'd see on TV.'

Nat raised an eyebrow.

'You know, a van screeching to a halt and ten guys dressed in black with semi-automatics jumping out and storming the cafe.'

Nat laughed. 'In that case, what happened was very underplayed. I didn't even see a gun.'

'I think you'll find they had them.' Hannah smiled. 'I am sorry, Nat. Please believe me, and I hope you'll forgive me. It was an incredibly selfish thing to do, but I loved getting to know you for who you are rather than the version you allow me to see.'

Nat nodded. 'I need some time to think everything through. As you said, it's been a big few days. Now I'll go home and check on Phyllie. Let me know how you go with Dad. And, Hannah, I'm sorry about what you're going through with Damien. It couldn't have been an easy time making that decision all those years ago. I hope you two will be okay?'

'Thank you. I think we will be.'

The two sisters parted company, both deep in thought.

Nat frowned as she pulled to a stop in front of Phyllie's. Leon was walking down the footpath with Rainbow ahead of him on a long lead. Had the goat escaped again? It had better not have caused any more issues for Phyllie.

She climbed out of the car as they reached her.

He grinned and held his hands up before Nat had a chance to speak. 'Just taking her for a walk. She hasn't been out on her own. Thought we could both use some exercise.'

Nat smiled. 'Okay, good to know. Not every day you see a man walking his goat.'

Leon laughed.

'I wouldn't stop for long though.' She nodded at Rainbow, who was now chomping on Phyllie's magnificent display of yellow marigolds.

'Shit!' Leon pulled the goat away and waved to Nat as they continued on in the direction of his house and garden.

'Tell Phyllie I'll be down with a box of chocolates tomorrow.' He winked. 'Gives me an excuse to visit both of you.'

Nat smiled. He was cute, charming and flirtatious. She was looking forward to their date, if it was a date, on the weekend. Her stomach fluttered at the thought. It was nice to smile after the stress of the day. She was still blown away to think that Suze was Hannah. What were the chances of them meeting like that? Knowing she'd kept the secret of Damien's parentage for twelve years, she might never have revealed her online identity if the Eliza situation hadn't imploded. Nat was beginning to wonder if she knew her at all. She did have to admit, she preferred her friend Suze to her sister.

The front door was locked, so Nat used her key and pushed it open. She had stopped at the shops on the way home and bought a bottle of Phyllie's favourite Prosecco. She thought they could spend the afternoon on the small patio in the back garden that caught the winter sun and she would fill Phyllie in on all that had happened.

Her grandmother had been very interested in the whole Eliza and Suze friendship, so she imagined her eyes bulging when she told her the story.

When Nat walked in, Phyllie was asleep in her armchair, a lopsided smile on her face. She didn't wake her, instead she went through to the kitchen and put the bottle in the fridge. She'd chill some glasses and have them ready for when Phyllie woke up, although she was probably going to want a coffee before she moved on to wine. She switched on the kettle and sat down at the kitchen table. A photo album was lying open with a blank page. She turned to the next page and found a photo of a young Phyllie and her husband, Nat's grandfather, staring back at her. Their arms around each other and laughing at the camera. They looked so young and happy. It was hard to believe she'd never met her grandfather. That Phyllie had been widowed when she was forty and lived the next forty-nine years alone. Nat continued to turn the pages of the album. She hadn't seen these photos before. She wondered if Hannah had. She bet she'd love to see them.

She glanced at the clock in the kitchen. Phyllie would probably be mad at her if she let her sleep for too long, as she'd be up all night. Nat stood and walked through to the living room. The lopsided smile was still on Phyllie's lips, and the missing photo from the album was gripped in her left hand. Nat smiled as she slid it carefully from her hand and looked at it. It was of her grandfather, in his air force uniform, proudly standing next to a plane, his captain's cap under one arm. He looked like a model. She could only imagine how much Phyllie must miss him. She hoped one day she'd love someone with the same intensity as her grandmother had loved Frederick.

Phyllie's hand had dropped to her side after Nat removed the photo, making her look incredibly uncomfortable. It was time to wake her.

'Phyllie?' Nat kept her voice low, not wanting to scare her.

She repeated her name a few times and then took her hand, planning to give it a gentle squeeze. Nat froze. Phyllie's hand was cold. Not cool, but cold.

'Phyllie?' She spoke louder and gave her a shake. There was no response. Nat put her fingers on her grandmother's neck, praying she would find a pulse, but all she felt was cold, taut skin. She dropped her hand and sank to her knees.

Chapter Twenty-Seven

The tightness in Hannah's chest seemed to be worsening as each day passed. Phyllie was eighty-nine, they'd all known she was coming to the end of her life, but nothing had prepared Hannah for the shock and grief she would feel at losing the woman who'd filled the role of mother and grandmother for most of her life. Everyone said that time would help heal the loss, but right now she felt like she was suffocating. She'd taken time off from work, and if it wasn't for Amy, she doubted she'd have the energy to get out of bed each morning. How could they go on without Phyllie's wisdom and humour in their lives? It was unfathomable. She wasn't the only one struggling. It was an enormous loss for the entire family. The coroner confirmed the cause of death was a massive stroke, and when Nat had spoken about Phyllie's drooping cheek and her headache earlier that morning, it all added up. Further discussions also suggested that their concerns about Phyllie showing signs of dementia were wrong. Her headaches, dizziness and memory problems indicated she might have suffered one or possibly several silent strokes.

'What time's Nat coming over?' Damien asked as Hannah stared blankly into her coffee cup.

She looked up, conscious of the worry in his eyes. 'In about an hour.'

He nodded then came around the island bench and put his arms around her. 'Why don't I make you an omelette or some toast and then you go and have a shower before Nat gets here?'

Hannah shook her head. 'I don't feel like food.'

Damien sighed. 'Babe, you have to eat. It's been a week and you're fading away. I know how much you're hurting, and I'd do anything to bring Phyllie back, but I can't watch you slide into a depression.'

Tears filled Hannah's eyes. 'I'm grieving. It's normal.'

He stroked her hair. 'I know that, but I also know that if Phyllie were here right now she would give you a swift kick up the backside.'

A gurgled noise, something between a sob and a laugh, escaped Hannah's mouth. Damien pulled her closer. He was right, of course. Phyllie would be furious if she could see how Hannah, someone she would normally count on to be the strong one in the family, had fallen to pieces.

'You know, I'm pretty sure that not getting out of your pyjamas three days in a row presents a seventy-four percent increased risk of suffering from depression in the future.'

Hannah pulled back from Damien and looked at him, seeing the humour in his eyes. 'You made that up.'

He nodded. 'I did. But that's the sort of stuff you should be spouting at Nat and your dad. Look at what a great job you've done with helping Amy cope.'

Hannah nodded. When she was with Amy, she made a huge effort to comfort her, talking about what Phyllie would want her to remember about her and emulate in the way she lived her own life. But the moment her daughter left the room, Hannah sank back into her own thoughts and sadness. Phyllie had been the backbone of their family. The person you could go to for advice, knowing you would not be judged and always be helped. While Hannah was a strong woman and capable of making her own decisions, knowing she had Phyllie's strength to fall back on had always been comforting. Now she had no one.

'You have me and Nat, your dad and Sue, you know,' Damien said, as if reading her thoughts. 'I know it's not the same, but all of us are there for you anytime you need us.'

Hannah leaned forward and kissed her husband. 'Thank you. And you're right. I need to get myself out of this funk. I'll go and have a shower and eat something once Nat gets here.'

Damien smiled, his eyes still filled with worry.

An hour later, Hannah returned downstairs feeling more human. She'd washed and dried her hair and put on jeans and a t-shirt rather than the pyjamas she'd been living in. She could hear Nat and Damien chatting in the kitchen.

She stopped at the kitchen door when she saw Nat. Her eyes were red-rimmed, her face pale and drawn. Her heart immediately ached. Nat had been living with Phyllie. She'd be feeling her absence even more than Hannah.

She went straight over and hugged her, tears rolling down her cheeks as Nat began to cry.

Damien cleared his throat. 'I'll be out in the back garden if you need anything.' He left the sisters in their joint grief.

Eventually they pulled apart and Hannah passed her the tissue box.

Nat gave a weak smile as she wiped her tears. 'I've been through a lot of these this week.'

'Me too.'

'She'd kill us if she could see us,' Nat said. 'You know that, don't you?'

Hannah smiled. 'That's pretty much what Damien said to me earlier this morning. But how can we not be sad?'

'It doesn't help that we have to wait a month after her death to have any kind of goodbye for her. Why on earth did she make that a stipulation in her will?'

Hannah shrugged. 'Phyllie had a reason for everything she did. I'm not sure if we'll ever find out why she did that, but I'm sure she thought it was a good idea. At least it's given us plenty of time to plan the celebration she wanted and let everyone know.'

'Let them all know they can't come, you mean.'

Hannah smiled. 'We have to follow her wishes. Immediate family, Verna and Leon only. Verna said her friends are organising their own celebration of her life just to spite her.'

Nat laughed at this. 'Good for them.'

'Do you want to move in with us?' Hannah suddenly asked. 'Living at Phyllie's must be really hard.'

'No, it keeps her feeling close.' She blushed. 'And Leon's been checking in on me every day, which has been rather nice. But it's the house I wanted to talk to you about. She left the house to both of us. I'd like to keep living there but I can't afford to buy you out. I'll understand if you want to sell and split the money, but ideally I'd like to save and eventually buy you out.'

Tears filled Hannah's eyes again. 'I'd love you to stay there. Phyllie is such a part of that house, I'll be able to visit her and you at the same time.' She stared at Nat as the words left her lips. 'This is how you feel about Dad's house, isn't it? Oh Nat, I'm so sorry. Losing Phyllie's home would be like losing another part of her. I didn't feel like that about Mum with Dad's house. Maybe it's because Mum's been gone for so long. I don't know. I'm sorry I didn't get it until now. And I think it's probably too late.'

Nat nodded. 'Yes, they are planning to sell. It makes sense. It's a big house and a big garden. Regardless of finances, it was probably going to be sold at some point. I'm okay with that now, and I'll be okay with selling Phyllie's house at some stage too. Just not now.'

Hannah nodded. 'For once we're in total agreement.' She reached up around her neck and unclasped the necklace holding her mother's heart-shaped pendant. She held it out to Nat. 'I want you to have this. It's brought me closer to Mum every day. You won't have the house anymore, but this might help.'

Nat's eyes widened in surprise. 'Really? Are you sure?'

Hannah nodded and pushed the necklace into Nat's hand. 'Completely sure. I've had its comfort for the last eighteen years and now it's your turn. Put it on, it will look great on you.'

Nat did as she suggested, then met Hannah's gaze. 'Thank you. This means a lot.' Her fingers stroked the pendant.

'You mean a lot, Nat. I hope you know that.'

'You do too.' Nat laughed. 'Geez, Phyllie would fall out of her chair if she could hear us being so nice to each other. She'd probably think we were up to something.'

Hannah gave a wry smile. 'I'm sure she'd have something to say about it.'

The two women sat in silence for a moment, lost in their own thoughts. Nat was the first to speak. 'Damien mentioned you've been struggling to get out of bed most days, and you haven't been back to work.'

Hannah sighed. 'I just need time, that's all.'

Nat nodded. 'I've been the same. I took this week off, but have spent most of my time at Shared. Digging is therapeutic, I've discovered.'

'She'd be proud of you, Nat. You're setting a good example, one I need to follow. I know I have to get my head together, it's just so scrambled. How are you even getting up in the mornings?'

'Honestly, I've just decided to adopt the Phyllie policy.'

Hannah raised an eyebrow.

'From now on, in every situation, I think to myself, what would Phyllie do? And then I do it. She was so kind, supportive, fun, tough and wise. We learned so much from her, Han, we now need to carry it through.'

Nat was right, it was exactly what she needed to do. She squeezed Nat's hand before standing and moving towards the fridge. 'I know exactly what Phyllie would say we need to do right now.' She opened the door, took out a bottle of Prosecco and held it up.

Nat grinned and pushed off her stool. 'Yep, you've got the hang of the Phyllie policy already. I'll get the glasses.'

Following her morning of drinking Prosecco with Nat and crying, laughing and reminiscing about Phyllie, Hannah felt her strength returning as each day passed. She brought Nat's Phyllie policy into action every day, finding it comforting to have her grandmother's voice playing in her head when she was making decisions. It had been especially helpful when Damien tentatively told her that his biological mother wanted to meet him, and would she prefer he postpone it until she was feeling up to it. Phyllie would have thrown her arms around Damien and supported him every step of the way as his own doubts and worries plagued him about meeting his mother. And this is exactly what Hannah had done for the last five days since Damien had told her.

Now, she slipped her arms around her husband as he stared at his reflection in their bedroom mirror.

'Do you think I look okay?'

Hannah smiled. 'Aren't I the one who's supposed to ask that question?'

He turned and faced her. 'No, really. Is this appropriate?'

She kissed him softly on the lips. 'You look gorgeous. The shirt brings out the grey in your eyes, and your haircut is incredible. Did they cut every piece of hair individually?'

Damien blushed. 'I know I'm being overly sensitive, but this is a big deal.'

'I know it is. It's not every day you get to meet your mother.'

'Are you sure the timing is right? With everything that's happened? I can still postpone seeing Janine.'

'Phyllie would be the first to say go and meet her, you know that.'

Damien smiled. 'I know, I just thought I should double-check. I think Amy's a bit put out that she can't come today.'

'If all goes well and Janine wants to, then I'm sure you can introduce Amy to her next time. Don't forget, as nervous as you are, Janine is equally nervous right now, if not more so.'

'Do you think so?'

'Definitely. Imagine going through what she did, then carrying a baby for nine months and having to give it up as soon as it was born. It's something that would live with you forever. Her age makes no difference to that. I bet she's thought of you every day since.'

Damien pulled down his shirtsleeves. 'Do you think I should wear my cufflinks? You know, the ones I wore when we got married.'

Hannah leaned forward again and kissed him on the nose. 'No, I don't. We're only meeting at a cafe, not a fine-dining restaurant. You don't want her to think you're some rich, vain guy who wears fancy accessories the whole time. Particularly when you don't. You've googled her enough times and the photos we've found always show her in very casual clothes. I can't imagine she'll be turning up in a ball gown!'

Damien smiled. 'Point taken.' He inhaled a lungful of air. 'Okay, let's go. If we leave now, we should be there a little early.

That way she won't be waiting for us. I want to get a good table where we can watch the door and wait until she comes in.'

Hannah bit her tongue to stop herself from saying anything. He was nervous. So was she. Her thoughts drifted to Trish. She wondered how Damien's adoptive mother was. She was probably a mess wondering how this was going to play out.

'I sent Mum some flowers this morning.' It was as if he could read her mind. 'Hope you don't mind me splashing out, but I know she'll be in a funny mood today. Wanted her to know that I was thinking of her and that I love her.'

Hannah blinked back tears. This was precisely why she loved her husband. He was going through something difficult but still had the empathy to think of others.

Unable to speak, she took his hand and squeezed it before leading him down the stairs, through the internal access to the garage.

She hoped that after the last two overwhelming weeks things would settle down again soon. Plans being put in place to meet Damien's biological mother had been a pleasant distraction from the situation with Eliza and Jacob and then the shock of Phyllie's death. At least they'd had confirmation the previous day that their father and Sue would be receiving their full investment back. The Federal Police had managed to trace all the funds Eliza and Jacob had stolen and were working to retrieve them. Hannah shuddered when she thought of how different the circumstances could have been for her father and Sue if those two con artists hadn't been stopped. She wondered briefly what their fate would be. Prison for many years she hoped.

The scenery along the Eastern Freeway sped past in a blur, and thirty minutes later Hannah and Damien sat across from each other at Thirst, a small cafe on Collins Street in the heart of the city. Hannah pushed all thoughts of Eliza and Jacob from her mind and imagined how Damien must be feeling right now. Janine had come down from Tallangetti by train the previous evening, and they'd arranged to meet for morning tea.

Damien drummed his fingers on the table and kept checking the door. 'What if she doesn't come?'

'She'll come. Just be patient. We're ten minutes early.'

An excruciatingly slow ten minutes passed, and there was still no sign of Janine.

'She's not coming.' Disappointment flooded Damien's face 'I should have known she wouldn't. It was too much to expect. I don't blame her.'

Hannah reached across the table and took his hand as a movement outside the window caught her eye. She drew in a breath. The woman who'd just walked past was without doubt Damien's mother. Tall, with long black hair, high cheekbones and a fine jawline, there was no question who she was. Hannah squeezed his hand and nodded towards the cafe door as it opened.

Damien stood up, his nerves visible by his shaking hands. Tears welled in Hannah's eyes as she watched his reaction. He walked towards Janine, who immediately froze when she saw him. A shaky smile appeared on her lips, and she took a tissue from her pocket and dabbed at her eyes.

'Damien?'

He nodded and tears instantly cascaded down her cheeks. He put an arm protectively around her shoulder and led her to the table.

'I'm so sorry,' she managed. 'This is incredibly overwhelming.'

Hannah smiled warmly and extended her hand. 'I'm Hannah, Damien's wife, and yes, this is overwhelming for everyone. Damien's been a mess all morning, if it's any consolation.'

Janine smiled at him through her tears. 'Really? I've been so worried about what you might think of me. I know you've been told the reason I put you up for adoption, but I've been concerned at what you've thought all these years since you were old enough to learn that you were adopted. I didn't want you to think I didn't want you or love you. I didn't hate you either, which someone recently suggested you might think.'

'I only found out in the last few weeks the real reason you gave me up for adoption. Up until then, I'd been led to believe that you'd died in a car accident taking me back from the hospital. When I learned the truth, I didn't hate you. I felt awful for what you'd gone through.'

Janine nodded. 'That's hardly your fault, and from what I can see you certainly have more Markinson genes in you than Deeks.'

'I was thirteen when my parents told me. At that time we'd been told it was a closed adoption, so there was no way to find out anything about either of you.'

'I don't think there was a day that went by that I didn't think of changing that on my file, just in case you ever wanted to get in touch. But I didn't know if finding out the truth would be good for you. From what I know about Calvin Deeks's family, there's not a lot to be proud of.'

A flash of anger crossed Damien's face. 'There's nothing to be proud of at all about him. He's not who I'm interested in getting to know.' His face softened. 'But you are.'

Janine hesitated for a moment before clearing her throat. 'There's only one question I need an answer to from you, Damien, and then I'm happy to answer anything you might like to know.'

Hannah wondered what on earth it could be. Wouldn't she have a million questions? She knew that she would.

'It's the one thing that has haunted me since the day I handed you to the nurses and honestly believed I would never see you again.' She hesitated. 'Have you had a happy life?'

Damien's face broke into a wide smile.

Janine dabbed at her tears again. 'I think that answers the question for me. I always hoped you would be placed with a nice family, but I could never be sure. And then to torture myself I'd search for stories about adoption cases on the internet and discover children had been abused or mistreated. I prayed every night that you were happy and safe.'

'I was. My parents are the nicest people you could ever meet. They couldn't have children, and they treated me like a gift. I couldn't have asked for a better upbringing. I wasn't spoilt, but I was given many opportunities and always knew I was loved with absolute devotion.'

'Were your parents supportive of you coming here today?'

Damien frowned. 'They are supportive, but Mum's a bit worried, I guess. She said it took her years to relax after the adoption went through. She couldn't believe that she and Dad had been blessed with a newborn. There was a part of her that always worried that something would happen, that someone would turn up one day and tell her it was all a mistake. So even though I'm forty now, and she knows that I can't be taken away from her like I could have been as a child, I guess she's worried that someone else might take her place.'

Janine nodded. 'I'd like to meet her at some stage.' She blushed. 'Assuming you want to see me again after today, that is. I'd like to thank her, and your father, for everything they've done. I'd also like to reassure her that she is your mother. I'm not here to get in the way of that. I want to get to know you, if you'll let me, and I thought you might enjoy getting to know me and my extended family.'

Hannah lifted a photo album from her bag and pushed it across the table. 'Trish, Damien's mother, put this together for you. She thought you might like to see some photos of him growing up.'

This time it was Damien's eyes that welled with tears. Hannah knew that he'd be thinking how selfless Trish was, and how thoughtful and generous.

Janine ran her finger over the cover of the album before meeting Hannah's eyes. 'What an amazing lady to do something like this.'

Hannah nodded. 'She is. Now, why don't I order us some drinks and cake while you and Damien have a look through the album? I'm sure there are plenty of embarrassing photos in there he'd like to cover up.'

They laughed, and it was as if the pressure lifted from all of them. Hannah took their coffee orders and went over to the counter and chose some cakes and slices to share. She looked back at Damien, who was covering his face in mock embarrassment as they looked through the album. There was an undeniable connection between the two; anyone could see it. They might have just met, but they had a shared history that linked them in some unexplainable way.

It was two hours later that they stood and said their goodbyes.

'I really would love to meet Amy, if you allow me,' Janine said as they walked to the front door of the cafe. 'And I'd love you all to make a trip to Tallangetti at some stage so you can meet my family.'

Hannah nodded. 'I'm sure Amy would love to meet you.' They'd discovered that Janine had four brothers, all married with children. Amy had many cousins, as it turned out. How strange; Hannah hadn't thought beyond what having Janine in his life might mean for Damien. Amy also had blood ties to a huge extended family. It would be nice for her to get to know them. With Damien an only child and Nat yet to have a family, Amy often complained that she didn't have any cousins or lots of aunts and uncles.

'We'll organise something soon,' Damien said. 'I'd like you to meet Mum and Dad too. I think it would help Mum to feel more comfortable about everything.' He leaned in and hugged Janine. 'Thank you for coming today. It means so much to me.'

'Me too.' Janine reached into her bag and took out a large thick envelope. 'This is something my mother asked me to give you.' Her voice cracked as she spoke. 'She wanted you to know that you were loved as a grandson from the day you were born. I didn't know about this until two days ago, when she handed it to me. I only had a little look and then packed it away.' She drew in a deep breath. 'I found it too painful to think about all that we lost by not having you with us.'

The ache at the back of Hannah's throat confirmed she was going to need a tissue at any moment. What a burden to live with.

They said their goodbyes, with Janine and Damien promising to be in touch later in the week.

'We'll probably both need some time to digest all of this,' Janine said.

Hannah was sure she was right. Damien sat in silence in the car as she drove them out of the city centre and back towards Donvale.

'She was lovely,' Hannah said. 'So much like you.'

Damien looked at her. 'Do you think?'

She nodded. 'In appearance, mannerisms but also in her kind heart. We obviously won't ever know anything about Calvin Deeks, but I think you can safely bet that you inherited a large percentage of your mother's genes. That plus the incredible influence of Trish and Edward have made you who you are today.'

Damien reached across and laid his hand on her leg. 'Thank you for coming with me. I don't think I could have done that alone.'

'But you're glad that you did?'

He nodded. 'It's only the start of learning about my background, but already it's put a lot of questions to rest. It's crazy to think I have this whole other family out there. I hope Mum's going to be okay with it.'

'She's a strong woman. She beat cancer, and I can guarantee she'll find a way to make this work for her. As long as we're sensitive in what we say, and warn Amy to be too, I think she'll work out a way to accept that this is how it is.'

They travelled in silence for a few minutes, then Damien pulled out the envelope Janine had given him. He peeled it open and peered inside.

'What is it?' Hannah was dying to know what his biological grandmother had done for him.

He pulled out a handful of envelopes. Each was marked with a number. 'There's a heap of them in there, all with different numbers on them.' He opened the top one with a twelve on it and pulled out a card. He turned it over and discovered a birthday card with the number twelve embossed on it and a picture of a boy catching a fish. His hands trembled as he opened it. He cleared his throat.

> My dearest boy. Happy twelfth birthday. I trust you are growing into a fine young man and enjoying every day that comes your way. Every morning I imagine what you might be doing that day. School, of course, on some but on other days, I imagine you skateboarding and fishing and hopefully loving life with a wonderful family and plenty of friends. Dearest boy, you are forever in my heart. With all my love on your birthday, Grandma.

Tears rolled freely down Hannah's cheeks as he finished reading. She looked across to him, and his cheeks were as wet as hers.

'You're a lucky man, Damien Anderson. Not only were you loved by the parents who raised you, but you've been loved by people who for forty years you've only been a memory for, and now I love you with a ferocity I never knew possible.'

Damien didn't speak, he just let the tears that had been accumulating for so many years run down his face.

Chapter Twenty-Eight

A CELEBRATION OF LIFE

Hannah polished her favourite knee-length boots, doing her best to contain the tears that once again rolled down her cheeks. It wasn't possible that they were farewelling their beloved Phyllie, was it? Her grandmother's will had been very specific.

> No funeral, no flowers, just a gathering of the family and a few close friends to say nice things about me. You are to serve Prosecco, strawberries, brie and crackers and those chocolate brownies Hannah makes that are to die for. Nothing else. No beer, no catering for dietary requirements. You may include a soft drink for Amy only. Everyone else will drink Prosecco.

Hannah had covered her mouth to stop an unexpected bubble of laughter from escaping when the lawyer read this out. He'd had them all gather at her father's the day after Phyllie's death, which was part of her instructions. She didn't want them wasting time planning a funeral and putting notices in the papers – she strictly forbade them to do any of that. As a result the arrangements were straightforward. Exactly one month after her death they were to take her ashes to Blackburn Lake Sanctuary for an elaborate picnic celebration. Each person was to say something about her, preferably favourable, and they were to drink as much Prosecco in her honour as they could manage. She'd made a list of who she was allowing to attend the celebration. Other than the family, she'd included her friend Verna, and Leon – 'the goat boy', as she'd named him in the instructions. That was it. No one else was permitted to come.

Phyllie had left instructions that her ashes were to be added to the urn that had sat on her mantlepiece for the past forty-nine years.

> Add me to Frederick's ashes and give us a good
> shake, so we're mixed together for eternity. Then,
> at my festival of life, scatter our ashes through
> the garden beds after you've had your picnic and
> made your toasts in my honour. And remember
> how much pleasure you've all given me and how
> much I love you.

With her boots now gleaming, Hannah hurried upstairs to get dressed. Damien was in the bedroom, looking incredibly handsome in a black suit with an aquamarine tie. He pulled her to him as she entered the room and gently wiped her tears before kissing her on the forehead.

They didn't need to exchange any words; the love in his gesture warmed Hannah's heart.

'Is Amy ready?' she asked.

He nodded. 'I'll just go and make sure she's left Bear clean water and some food.' He glanced at his watch. 'We should leave in ten minutes to stop at the florist on our way.'

Hannah smiled. Damien wasn't budging on the flower situation. Phyllie's instructions had said no flowers, but Damien was insisting. He'd ordered a bouquet of Phyllie's favourite pink roses and was planning to have them as the centrepiece, next to the urn with her and Frederick's ashes.

The sky was blue, a gentle breeze blowing as they reached Blackburn Lake a little before twelve. A noon celebration had been instructed, and that was what they were doing. Nat and Leon were already there, setting up two tables side by side for the food. Hannah watched them from a distance, chatting and laughing together. She smiled. Even in death Phyllie was doing her best to bring them together.

She helped Damien retrieve the cooler boxes with the Prosecco, finger food and glasses from the boot.

Her father and Sue drove up in Sue's Toyota. They were planning to sell both their cars and buy a four-wheel drive and do a 'lap of Oz', as her dad was calling their proposed journey around Australia.

Verna arrived, wearing a pretty lace dress with a pink flower fascinator. She blushed when Hannah remarked on the fascinator. It seemed an unusual item to wear, other than to a wedding or the races. Verna explained that she'd been given instructions to wear it.

'Instructions? What do you mean?'

'I received a letter from Phyllie's lawyer two days after she died. It had specific instructions on what I was to do following her death and exactly what I was to wear to her life celebration. She always loved this fascinator. Her note specifically referred to an incident when I wore it at the Melbourne Cup back in the fifties. I drank too much champagne and slipped over in a gigantic pile of horse poo.'

Hannah stifled a laugh.

'Oh, laugh all you want. It turned out to be the most romantic thing that ever happened to me. A gentleman in a pinstriped suit and top hat held out his hand and pulled me up. Six months later he put a ring on that same hand. As Phyllie used to say to me,

"Never underestimate what shit might bring." She was right. Over sixty years of marriage, that's what it brought. If Byron hadn't died last year, we'd be celebrating our sixty-fifth in a couple of weeks.'

Nat joined them, coming over to hug Verna. 'I bet you're missing Phyllie.'

Verna squeezed Nat's arm as she pulled out of the embrace. 'More than you'll ever know. Although I expect you're finding living in the house on your own very difficult.'

'No, actually, I love being there. I can feel Phyllie in every room. I can imagine what she'd be saying to me over certain things and how she'd be yelling about others. She would have been yelling today, that's for sure. Leon's goat got out again, and I found it in the backyard. But the funny thing was it didn't eat any of Phyllie's plants. It stood next to one of her favourites – her prized black prince dahlias, which are in flower – and did nothing. It was almost like it knew she was gone and was mourning her. Leon says I'm crazy, but I think it was.'

Her father clapped his hands together to get everybody's attention. 'Come and grab a glass of Prosecco and some food and we'll begin. As per Phyllie's instructions we are all to say something about her. If you've written it down, you can read it out. The person talking needs to stand at the edge of the lake, so that it's the backdrop for us to all to look at. She's left a list of the order she'd like us to talk in.' He rolled his eyes. 'Not that I'm first on the list, but I will say this about her, she knew her own mind in life, and it appears even more so in death.'

They laughed at his comment, a feeling of joy and celebration in the air, rather than sadness.

Amy spoke first, her arm sporting a purple cast because it was one of Phyllie's favourite colours. She brought tears to their eyes as she spoke of her great-grandmother and all the wonderful things she had learned from her. She finished with a list of Phyllie's best advice, the final being, 'You can only be truly mad at someone you really love.'

'That's so true.' Nat grinned as she looked over to Hannah. 'Our history confirms we *really* love each other. Phyllie was a very wise woman.'

'Phyllie didn't make that up,' Amy said. 'She was quoting Christian Grey's mum. I think it was her way of telling me I'm ready to watch the *Fifty Shades* movie.'

Hannah covered her mouth to stop from laughing. She hated to imagine what other conversations Phyllie had had with Amy if this was the type of quote she'd been using. There was no way Amy would be watching *Fifty Shades*, regardless of anything she wanted to read into Phyllie's wisdom and advice.

Her father spoke next of what a strong, independent and dedicated woman his mother was. Of how she'd not only stepped in and cared for Hannah and Nat when Carmel died, but she'd been the one thing that saved him from slipping deep into depression. 'She wouldn't let me, that was the reality. Said I had a duty to Carmel and the girls to get out of bed each day.' He smiled. 'She said I was allowed to wallow in my grief and self-pity only on a Sunday. She came over every Sunday and cleaned the house and made meals for the week, insisting I went out on my own for the day. If Hannah and Nat were home, the three of you often went out for lunch or to the movies together.'

Hannah did remember that. She'd had no idea it was to give her father a break from them and time to grieve.

Verna regaled them with many hilarious stories of mad things Phyllie got up to on holidays, and at the various clubs and associations they belonged to. None of it surprised Hannah, if anything she was just so pleased to hear that Phyllie had had such joy and happiness in her life.

There didn't seem to be any rationale for the order of their speaking, and Leon spoke briefly after Verna, saying how touched he'd been to be included in today's celebration and what an inspiring woman Phyllie was. Sue spoke next, praising Phyllie for her acceptance of her into their family and the friendship she'd offered her. Then it was Damien's turn, and they were all surprised when he revealed something no one knew. He talked about the many phone calls he'd received from Phyllie over the years asking for advice on all sorts of matters. 'She seemed to think that being a paramedic meant I was qualified for many things that I knew nothing about. I'd get questions about anything from the weather forecast to how to bottle stone fruit to which horse was going to win the fourth race at Caulfield on the weekend.' He blushed. 'One day, when I asked her why she rang me with such random questions, she said that on the phone my voice sounded like Frederick's. She was asking me the questions she'd have asked him, just to hear her husband's voice.'

Tears ran down Hannah's cheeks as she listened to Damien. She looked across to Nat, who was also wiping her eyes. There wasn't a dry eye in the group.

'When Phyllie told me this was why she rang me, I made sure I always had answers for her. I made some up, or when I was near a computer, I'd quickly google her question to try and sound more informative. Or I'd ask her something that I hoped Frederick might have asked her about her garden or what her plans were for the weekend. We had some very unusual conversations.' He wiped his eyes. 'Conversations that I will always treasure and will miss.'

Hannah hadn't been aware of how much Phyllie still missed her husband. She'd not given much thought to her being a wife and a mother. She was always just Phyllie.

'That leaves Hannah and me,' Nat said. 'Which of us speaks first?'

'Neither,' her father said.

Hannah's head shot up. 'What, why?' She'd spent hours poring over the words she hoped would sum up how she felt about her grandmother.

Nat looked as distraught as she felt.

'She's left a letter that she would like you to read out before we scatter her ashes.' He took an envelope from his pocket and held it out to Hannah. It was addressed to her.

Hannah's fingers trembled as she slid open the seal. She shook out the pages of neatly typed pages and began to read.

> My dearest girl,
>
> I'm sorry that you are having to read this letter, especially as you probably spent hours working on the brilliant words you planned to share about what a wonderful grandmother I was. I wish I knew how to use those smiley face things, emojis or something like that Nat calls them, as a laughing one would be very appropriate right now. I shouldn't make fun, should I? I know that you love to have things in order and planned to the finest detail, and I've taken part of that away from you today so that I can talk to you instead. And Nat, don't think you're getting away with anything, the second page is for you to read.

Hannah glanced up at Nat, her heart aching as she saw the tears rolling down her face.

> I decided a few months ago to write a new letter every month and send it to my lawyer, so that whatever you are reading today is recent and not

written years before my death. Funnily enough, while circumstances have changed each month, my underlying message to you hasn't. You are a wonderful mother, wife, daughter and grand-daughter. Don't ever change, Hannah.

Hannah had to stop reading for a moment. She closed her eyes and willed her voice to cooperate.

I know we tease you about being so caught up with assessing each situation for risks and choosing safer paths than some of us might like to travel, but that's who you are. Your mother's death shaped who you are today. You had no con-trol over what happened to her, but you've spent your life since trying to control the things you can. That's not a bad thing, but make sure you listen to those around you if you are trying to control how they live their lives. I should also add that I see your mother's kindness, her loyalty and passion in you every day. I treasure those qualities and know those who love you do too.

No matter what happened for me to die and you to be reading this, never think that I was seri-ously upset about you suggesting assisted living and other ways to help me. I know that everything you suggested you did out of love for me. Without your badgering I might not have thought to invite Nat to move in with me, and for that I am eter-nally grateful. Not only did it keep me in my own home, but it made my days interesting. Your sister is the other half of your mother. Impulsive, crazy and a joy to be around. She's also a wonderful friend if you let her be and I am instructing you to make sure you do. Strange things bring people together, and your friendship formed in the chat room is what you need to keep close to your heart and treasure. You were real with each other.

Keep being you, Hannah, you truly are an amazing woman.

Now, hand the next page to Nat, please.

Hannah could hardly see through the blur of tears as she handed Nat the page. She accepted a hanky from Damien and wiped her eyes as Nat began to speak, a tremor evident in her voice.

Nat, my gorgeous, fun-loving and at times crazy granddaughter. Thank you. While I may have led you to believe otherwise, you've made my last months the most enjoyable since you girls grew into young women and no longer needed me as often. I have adored sharing my house with you and hope that you and Hannah will come to an arrangement where you will continue to live there. As I've also said to Hannah, don't change, Nat, you are indeed one of a kind. Your generosity for helping people is something rare. I admire your work ethic and the way you view fairness for all in the world. One thing I would like to say to you is to embrace Suze. She was a true friend to you and can continue to be if you'll let her. As annoying as you sometimes find her . . .

Nat looked up at Hannah and smiled through her tears.

. . . she only ever has your best interest at heart. She's always looked out for you, before and after your mother died. And like you do with others, she's always put you first.

Heat flooded Nat's face as she continued reading.

And don't ignore the kindness of strangers, in particular those who keep goats as pets. I think if you give him half a chance, you'll find that you and Leon have much more in common than you would ever expect. As part of the conditions of my will, I am adding a clause which I expect Leon and your family to uphold.

Nat cleared her throat, her eyes fixed firmly on the letter.

Hannah felt a twinge of sympathy for her. Phyllie would have known how embarrassing this would be. But she was used to getting her way. Even now, after she was gone, she was going to make sure a few things happened.

Nat continued.

Tomorrow night, you and Leon will cancel any plans you may have. There is a bottle of Penfolds Cab Sav in the bottom of the pantry. I bought two of these bottles on the fourteenth of March 2015, as I knew that day something special was going to happen to you. Ask Leon what was special about this day.

All eyes turned to Leon, who looked confused. 'It was the day I moved into Phyllie's street,' he said. 'The minute the moving truck left she came over with a lasagne straight from the oven and a bottle of Penfolds. She introduced herself, told me about her wonderful granddaughter and said if I was still single in a few years, she hoped to introduce us.'

'Why a few years?' Hannah asked. 'That's weird.'

Leon was now blushing, seemingly unable to look at Nat. 'She said Nat wasn't ready yet. That she was still in her "wild phase", as Phyllie called it.'

'And you waited all this time to meet her?' Sue's mouth dropped open at the thought.

Leon laughed. 'I'm sorry to say, but no. That first day I just assumed Phyllie had a few screws loose. I played along as her lasagne was to die for and there was something about her that I liked. Over the next couple of years, I got to know her better, but she never mentioned Nat again, so I thought perhaps she'd changed her mind or Nat didn't exist. And then, of course, Nat moved in.'

'Keep reading the letter,' her father instructed. 'I have a note from Phyllie here saying any interruptions to the reading must be kept to ten seconds maximum.'

Damien laughed out loud at this. 'She's a classic.'

So yes, that was the day I met Leon and told him about you. It has only been recently that I believe you are finally ready for him, although I have a sneaking suspicion you and Leon might have come to this conclusion yourselves already. You are to take the Penfolds and two glasses to the bottom of my back garden at exactly eight p.m. Lie back on the picnic rug and count the satellites and shooting stars. You will be amazed. I'll be watching you two, so make sure you do this. And while you're with Leon, make sure that bloody goat of his stays away from my garden.

Love you, Nat, stay true to who you are and remember that you made an old lady's last few months some of the happiest in her life.

Nat folded the letter and handed it to her father, tears streaming down her face. Hannah caught the 'Sorry,' she mouthed to Leon.

He shook his head and reached over, took her hand and squeezed it. 'We have strict instructions for tomorrow night, and there's no way I would go against Phyllie's wishes. She'd probably send lightning bolts at us from heaven if we did. And more importantly, I can't wait.'

Hannah smiled watching the exchange between Leon and Nat. The attraction between them was obvious.

'The last thing we've been instructed to do is to scatter Phyllie and Frederick's ashes.' Her father held up the urn.

Hannah wondered how he was doing. She hoped that his worries had eased, now that they'd had confirmation the money would be returned within the next month. They'd put the house on the market, and it was looking like they would sell for a very healthy price. Sorting out their financial future seemed to have taken ten years off her father. Even dealing with the grief of Phyllie's passing, he looked less weighed down.

They all moved to the area Phyllie always said housed her favourite garden beds, and he took off the lid. 'Thank you, Mum.' He held the urn up high and allowed the wind to scatter the ashes. 'You've taught us all so much, but the main thing you've taught us is how to love and how to be loved. For that, we'll be eternally grateful.'

Damien pulled Hannah to him, and she reached out for Amy and drew her close as Phyllie and Frederick's ashes danced in the wind and scattered, precisely as had been instructed. Tears glistened in Hannah's eyes as she looked across to Nat, whose hand was still entwined with Leon's.

'It sounds like we have some instructions to follow, Nat. I'm game if you are,' Hannah said.

Nat smiled. 'I don't need a protector or an advisor, I need a sister and I need a friend. And, through an unlikely friendship with a woman called Suze, I've discovered I'm lucky enough to have both already.'

ACKNOWLEDGMENTS

Thank you to all the people in my life who continue to support and encourage my writing journey. I truly treasure our friendships.

A big thank you to Judy, Maggie, Ray and Tracy for providing feedback on early versions of the story – your insights were invaluable.

Robyn, thank you for our daily chats and laughs. You definitely help me to remain sane when things get crazy!

To the Lake Union Publishing team, in particular Sammia Hamer; thank you for all the hard work you contribute in order to bring a book from concept through to publication.

An extra special thank you to Celine Kelly. Your input to this manuscript has elevated the story and characters to a new level. I feel incredibly lucky to have had the opportunity to work with you and look forward to future projects.

To Gillian Holmes and Anna Swan, thank you for your insights and input; it has been a pleasure working with you.

And lastly, to the wonderful readers who continue to comment, review and message me – thank you.

ABOUT THE AUTHOR

Louise has enjoyed working in marketing, recruitment and film production, all of which have helped steer her towards her current, and most loved, role – writer.

Originally from Melbourne, a trip around Australia led Louise and her husband to Queensland's stunning Sunshine Coast, where they now live with their two sons, gorgeous fluffball of a cat and an abundance of visiting wildlife – the kangaroos and wallabies the most welcome, the snakes the least!

Awed by her beautiful surroundings, Louise loves to take advantage of the opportunities the coast provides for swimming, hiking, mountain biking and kayaking. When she's not writing or out adventuring, Louise loves any available opportunity to curl up with a glass of red wine, switch on her Kindle and indulge in a new release from a favourite author.

To get in touch with Louise, or to join her mailing list, visit: www.LouiseGuy.com